MURDER BY APPOINTMENT

NEAR the dead body was a drawing of the snarling face
of a jungle cat—the Panther's mark! But the Panther,
famous for his murders in a dozen cities, was known to be
dead. Was this murder his doing, or the work of a new
genius of crime? The Panther's claws reach out again. A
friend of the rich and respected Georges Raynel is the victim. Raynel offers a huge reward for the capture of the
Panther. What do the famous detectives Dupree and
Croyant discover when they investigate? How do they
save charming Helen Avery from a life of disappointed love and bring to Jeribzoff, the
fugitive, a future of glorious happiness?
There are thrills galore in this
superb mystery thriller.

MURDER BY APPOINTMENT

ELEANORE BROWNE

WILDSIDE PRESS

MURDER BY APPOINTMENT

ELEANORE BROWN

WILDSIDE PRESS

CHAPTER I

DIAMONDS AND PEARLS

THE limousine that drew up to the door of the jewelry establishment of Henri Cutot was impressive. Its shield identified it as one of the most expensive, if not the very most expensive car of American make. Its chauffeur, who wore a trim whipcord uniform, appeared to be French, though his huge goggles prohibited certainty. The tall slightly round-shouldered young man who had sat with the driver in the front seat and now stepped to the pavement, was unquestionably as American as the car itself. The tortoise-rims of his eyeglasses would have testified to his nationality anywhere on the Continent. Of the young woman who relaxed in the luxurious depths of the car, one could not be so sure. Idlers on the sidewalk who paused to inspect the imposing turn-out had the impression of a dark young loveliness agreeably accentuated by the caressing effect of rich furs. She had round, dark eyes set in a face radiantly beautiful and might have been French, Russian, Spanish or even from one of the Southern States.

The young man spoke to the passenger briefly, as if he assured her that he would not be long, she nodded quietly, then he went into the shop.

Monsieur Henri Cutot was seated at his heavily carved table in the enclosed office at the rear of the shop when his chief clerk entered to inform him that a gentleman wished to interview him about an especial order.

"An American gentleman," added the clerk significantly. "I have the feeling it is to be a profitable matter."

Monsieur Cutot hastily cleared his table of letters he had
begun to sign and the clerk would have gone out to produce the caller, but his employer motioned him to be not
unduly prompt. It was better that prospective customer
who was American and, therefore, undoubtedly a Crœsus,
should not find the proprietor of the House of Cutot too
completely disengaged. The House of Cutot was a distinguished establishment. There were not many in Paris itself that could boast a greater elegance and there, in the
city of Bordeaux, the hallmark of Cutot was as the hallmark of Tiffany to New York. The visitor should be kept
waiting. But not too long. Monsieur Cutot compromised
nicely between no delay at all and a wait that would have
been too long, and motioned to his clerk that the caller
would be received.

The American explained, when he faced Monsieur
Cutot across the carved table, that he was the private
secretary of Mr. Andrew Banton of New York and Palm
Beach. Perhaps Monsieur Cutot was aware that Mr.
Banton had recently arrived in Bordeaux to take possession of the old Chateau Brissac which had been vacant
for so many years.

"My employer, as you probably have read in the press,"
the American mentioned, "is enjoying his honeymoon."

He hesitated over the word. He spoke French meticu-
lously, his American accent very decided. He could not
manage "honeymoon" without stammering so he said it
in English. The jeweler, a short, portly and pompous man
with a moon-like face, stared at him blankly.

The secretary frowned and tried again. *"Lune de miel,*
moon of honey," he translated at last.

"Ah, *lune de miel?* But yes, yes!" The jeweler beamed.

His mind raced ahead. He anticipated with considerable accuracy just what was coming. He had never heard of Mr. Andrew Banton but he reasoned at once that if he had leased or purchased the house and grounds of the late Duc de Brissac, he would indeed be wealthy. And what man is not generous on his *"lune de miel"?*

He was immediately assured that he was right.

"Mr. Banton," said the secretary, "desires to make a present of jewelry to his young wife. They left New York immediately after the wedding and the present was postponed until they were settled over here."

Monsieur Cutot was to understand, the secretary made it clear, that anything in the line of diamonds and pearls probably would be most attractive to Madame. Also that his employer would be irritated by anything not of the very best. Being confronted with what pleased Madame Banton and was, at the same time, of the first quality, he would not be likely to think of economy.

The jeweler announced his happiness to place all of his wares, which, being Cutot wares, would be only of the very best quality, at the disposal of the American new-comer to Bordeaux. He was then instructed to appear at the Chateau Brissac with whatever he thought might suit. The secretary's ideas on jewelry were rather vague. "A few rings and bangles and things, diamonds; and a few ropes of pearls," he suggested. "Unfortunately, Madame, who is waiting in the car, is fatigued from shopping. Otherwise she might have come in and given more definite instructions.

Monsieur Cutot understood that perhaps Madame would rather not. A woman is not always too eager to see her wedding presents in advance. He inquired as to Mr. Banton's convenience and was told that he should be at the Chateau, or send a representative, punctually at three o'clock tomorrow. Mr. Banton, being an American financier, was very busy and chary of his time.

Monsieur Cutot beamed as his visitor rose. He attended him through the shop, assuring him that Monsieur Banton's requirements would have his best personal care. A colossal door-commissionaire bowed when the American stepped onto the pavement. Monsieur Cutot was enthused by the sight of the long, costly car, its liveried chauffeur who sat at the wheel in a sort of military rigidity, and the oval, beautiful face nested in its aura of furs within the car.

When the jeweler retreated from the street doors he was elated. It was an exceptional stroke of fortune that one of those over-rich Americans should have taken the long abandoned Chateau. One did not know what he might require from time to time in the way of ornaments for that exquisite creature with whom he enjoyed the honey of the moon. Perhaps, Monsieur Cutot mused, he had not on hand a sufficiently wide choice of first water diamonds and pearls. He instructed his clerk to telephone Paris at once, the telephone conversations to be confirmed by telegram, ordering some especially choice samples to arrive by mid-day tomorrow.

The jeweler was a proper business man. He proceeded to make discreet inquiries about Mr. Andrew Banton. He discovered that the least of the Chateau had been handled by a real estate agency whose chief official he knew very well. His friend spoke to him over the phone.

"My dear Henri," said the agent, "your man Monsieur Banton has more money than he knows what to do with. He ran across the old Chateau when he was motoring nearby two years ago. When he was already returned to New York we advertised the place for lease to such a fool as would comply. We did not mention the word 'fool.' He wrote to us and concluded arrangements by cablegram. He was not due to take possession until later in the month but a cablegram from New York changed his plans. His secretary assumed custody of the keys last week. At any day I am to be summoned to present myself to the Monsieur Banton at the Chateau itself."

One more question lingered on the jeweler's tongue.

"He will pay in cash for my wares, would you say? For such of them as are designed to ornament his joy of the moon? These millionaires, they sometimes have the long patience with the short needs of tradespeople."

His agent friend was amused.

"Sleep on your back, my good Henri, and do not have trouble. He is one to dismiss his dollars curtly. We were prepared to halve our asking price. Lo, there came the draft without bickering. But you say 'joy of the moon?' Are you slightly bewildered, Henri?"

"Eh? I said 'joy'? I meant to say 'honey of the moon.' It is the same. And it is of no matter. To one man a woman; to me, my dollars."

Until he paused to supervise the putting up of his shutters that evening, Monsieur Cutot engaged himself at the task of assembling the finest of his diamond baubles and clusters and bangles and his pearls with the most iridescent sheens, checking over his lists and arranging the prices. He did not "sleep on his back" that night, for he tossed with considerable worry about the shipments from Paris. Would they arrive in time to be taken to the Chateau at three o'clock?

They did, but they might as well have come later. Just before noon on the following day a telephone message came through from the Chateau. The private secretary spoke to Monsieur Cutot. Mr. and Mrs. Banton unfortunately had been called to Montauban to meet some American friends who were passing through on their way to Toulouse. They had motored and would not return before the evening. Monsieur Cutot would therefore oblige Mr. Banton if he would send his representative at nine o'clock in the evening, neither earlier nor later. No other time could be appointed since Mr. and Mrs. Banton were leaving for Paris in the morning to be gone several days.

The rotund jeweler was undisturbed. He had already arranged adequate protection for his trip to and from the Chateau. There was, indeed, less risk in carrying jewels at night than in the daytime. Thieves might notice the movements of a jeweler with hand bags moving about in the daytime, but would not expect him to be abroad at night with a huge fortune in diamonds and pearls. There was a bright moon to light the way. He had but to step into his car at his door and leave it at the porte-cochère of the Chateau.

And, as he had foreseen, the drive to the house and grounds of the late duc was without incident. Monsieur Cutot had arranged with the local branch of his insurance company for a chauffeur who was an ex-poilu and knew well how to handle the automatic pistol resting on the seat beside him. He had arranged with the police for an armed detective to sit in the back seat at his side. The bags containing his own most precious wares and the added supply from Paris were snugly between himself and the detective.

When the car swung into the motor path of the Brissac grounds the headlights revealed the sad state into which the long neglected park had fallen. Weeds grew where there had been beautiful gardens, and the trees along the drive were gauntly naked. Their twigs, meeting overhead, formed a mesh through which the moonlight filtered in a ghostly mist. Observing the state of dilapidation Mon-

sieur Cutot smiled to himself. The good hard dollars of
Monsieur Banton would change all this in a few months.
That young woman he had seen in the back seat of the
limousine—she would be one to want flowers and running fountains and the scent of dew on newly mown
grass.

The Chateau itself was a gloomy pile. But tonight the
house was ablaze with light from ground floor to dormers
and the tall French windows shed a bright radiance across
the stone flagging of the terrace.

It was just nine o'clock and servants apparently had
observed the approach of the jeweler and his guards. The
doors opened before Monsieur Cutot could descend. The
chauffeur and detective saw a stiff, liveried footman and,
coming down a deep hall, emerging from far shadows
into the orange light from a great pendant lamp, was an
elderly gentleman who could be none other than the
American millionaire himself.

Monsieur Cutot was a little astonished that his customer should be of so many years. The bride in the
limousine was a springtime bud. While this reflection was
flashing across his thoughts, she appeared in the flesh,
far down the hall. She was coming down a stairway
and carried a great white fan. The white fan was a gleaming splash against a velvet sheath of a rich burgundy hue.
Her shoulders were like old ivory. Monsieur Cutot would
have liked to see her closer, but he was not to be gratified.
At the foot of the stairs she paused but an instant, apparently to inquire about the arrivals. Her husband sent
her a brief word across his shoulder and she disappeared
into a room that flanked the hall. The jeweler sighed
while he crossed the terrace. The husband to the breath
of spring that descended the staircase could not be so far
into his own winter. It was his white hair that was decep-

tive. Monsieur Cutot saw him with new eyes now, and saw that his physique and carriage belied the hair. He was tall, straight, and carried himself with the alert flex of an Olympian athlete. About him there was only one marring detail. The tortoise glasses that hid his eyes. These, however, increased Monsieur Cutot's confidence. They were the authentic stamp of the American.

The jeweler stepped inside the hall and bowed to his client. Before the door closed the watching chauffeur and detective heard Monsieur Banton's greeting, in a clipped French that sounded much like the bark of a huge mastiff.

"You are on time, sir. Good! Don't like to wait. Come, now, let's get down to business. What've you got?"

The butler closed the door and the detective and chauffeur had nothing to do but wait until the transaction was concluded and the jeweler ready to be driven back to Bordeaux.

They talked to each other of nothing in particular. From their position they could see along the left wing of the house. Lights were turned off in a distant room as if Madame Banton had entered that room and was now leaving it. The nearer room, beyond the French windows, remained brilliantly lighted. They could see the shadow of the footman moving about setting furniture in order. Presently the servant's shadow was seen no more, but now and then some other shadow crossed the windows.

An hour passed. The house was quite still, as a well conducted house should be at that time of the evening when there were no guests save a jeweler displaying his goods. Some thirty minutes later the detective remarked without much concern that nobody was moving about now. It was as if he just missed the shadows on the windows which, for all he knew, might have ceased a long time ago.

The chauffeur pointed out that these old houses had an "office," or general-purpose chamber, usually well back on the first floor. "They've probably gone in there and the servants have gone to their own roosts."

Another thirty minutes went by. Each man, governed by a common instinct, had begun to listen. On the nearby river, the Gironde, a motor-boat sputtered. The sharp staccato died away, emphasizing the silence of the night. The detective's nerves became jumpy. At eleven o'clock he crossed the terrace and was followed by the chauffeur.

"Strange," grunted the officer, "that M'sieu' Cutot is so long about this business. There wasn't much dilly-dally in that American monsieur's bark."

"Maybe we'd better ring the bell."

They were discussing this step when their uneasiness was dispelled by the sound of music from behind the French windows.

"Somebody's turned on the radio," the detective said.

"M'sieu' will be coming along now," the chauffeur predicted. "Madame is having a little music to go to bed by."

The chauffeur picked up the tune and whistled it. He knew it very well. It was recent and only last night he had danced to it with Zinette, the plump-breasted daughter of his landlady. He'd tell Zinette that he'd caught a glimpse of the new lady of the Chateau, that no less than four ostriches had been turned into her fan, and that she liked the same tunes common folk dance by.

A different tune came out to make the night more cheerful. The chauffeur whistled this one also. Then another.

"That's not a radio," the detective said. "That's a phonograph."

Both men listened attentively, a shade of their uneasiness creeping back. There was something eerie in the monotonous precision of changing tunes, the interval between each so exactly timed that it might have been with a stop watch.

"One of the new-fangled automatics," the chaffeur pointed out. "Changes the records itself. One after the other."

Suddenly the detective moved. He quickly crossed the terrace to the door and pressed the bell push. He heard the responsive ring inside the house but there was no other sound. No one came to the door. He rang again, sharply. The bell carried the unmistakable impression of emptiness. The chauffeur joined him and together they hammered on the door. The music kept on playing with inhuman insistence.

"Through the windows. Quick!" the detective cried.

He smashed in a French window with the butt of his pistol, opened the catch and plunged into the brilliantly illuminated room. The chauffeur ran to the phonograph. He held up a small clock to which wires had been attached. The wires broke and the music stopped.

"A timer, set to start the music at a certain minute," the detective said. "It fooled us and gave them more time."

"What do you think has—?" the chauffeur began, but stopped abruptly. What to think was only too plain. Monsieur Banton, Madame Banton and her white fan, and the liveried butler would be gone.

"Where's M'sieu' Cutot?" he demanded fatuously.

With their pistols drawn they searched, and found him when they came to the back room the chauffeur had described. He was lying on the floor as if he had dropped down to take a nap. His amiable, moon-like face was turned to the ceiling and he was smiling. On the floor, just beyond his feet, lay the great white fan, folded until it seemed to be one huge feather. Monsieur Cutot's smile had been directed to Madame, who must have appeared suddenly and folded her fan in a woman's coquettish gesture. Then the jeweler had fallen and the fan had been tossed aside. It had served its purpose, to engage his attention while the slender bladed dagger had been driven into his heart by someone who moved up beside him. The hilt still protruded. On a divan, dark with the red of old brocade, were Monsieur Cutot's leather bags. Where there had been a city's ransom was now only emptiness.

The detective knelt briefly over the man on the floor. His fingers touched a pulse that was quiet, his ears listened for a heart-beat that was still. He got up cursing and shouted to the chauffeur to "Come on! We'll see what we find—which'll be exactly nothing."

The chauffeur had picked up the fan. He was dully reconstructing his intention to describe it to the plump-breasted Zinette. He dropped it to the floor on the detective's summons and followed the officer on their fruitless search of the house. Of the American secretary, the man with the white hair, the young woman and the butler, there was no trace.

The detective searched in the hall and in the front room for a telephone. The chauffeur returned to the death room. He was still fascinated by the white fan. He was young and had an admiring eye for a pretty woman. A vision of the young woman who came down the stairs kept returning to his mind. He tried to recapture details of her face, her hair and bare shoulders, telling himself that his Zinette would ply him with a thousand questions about the look of a woman who could use her fan to lure a man into eternity. But the more he strove to augment his memory of that one fleeting glimpse, the more hazily the figure on the stairs dissolved into the white splash of her fan.

He recovered it from the floor where he had replaced it and was spreading its feathers and staring at it when the officer reappeared.

"Wires cut! Expected that," the detective announced succinctly. "I'll leave you here while I drive to the nearest phone. They've had a good start but the department will cross the roads with a cordon in a hundred mile circle while we comb Bordeaux."

He observed the fan in the chauffeur's fingers.

"Here, give me that. You shouldn't have touched it. It's got to be on the floor, as it was, when the chiefs arrive from the Sûreté."

He moved to take it from the other's hand. When he saw what the man was staring at he stopped, rigid as stone. Deftly drawn by a delicate brush on the full-spread inner expanse of flaky white feathers was the sleek head of a great, snarling cat, its nostrils aflare, its ears pointed.

"Mon Dieu!" the detective gasped. *"La Panthère!* And I saw him—with my own eyes—within arm's reach!"

Within ten minutes the sensitive police machine of France had been vitalized into eager life by the sputter of its radio code from Bordeaux and two hundred men on noisy motorcycles were converging onto the periphery of a hundred mile circle laid across roads and lanes and fields with Bordeaux as its center, a circle broken only where it touched the sea. In the city itself the police had begun to comb. The wheels thus started, Monsieur Granard, Chef de la Sûreté, who was at home and asleep, was awakened from whatever are the dreams that flit through the slumbers of a superintendent of police.

His assistant, chief of the Bureau du Soir, the night squad, excitedly reported the cat's head, symbol of "The Panther." Monsieur Granard swore roundly.

"But you are a clown! The Panther and his *carte-de-visite?* Bah! He has been dead this full year. Does your man who babbles of a white fan recall the remains of a man in a burned house in Leningrad? The Panther's corpse? It is a witless one, your diamond thief, who plays a threadbare game and thinks to delude you with a joke. Find him in some thieves' den in rue Mirable. I return to sleep."

But Monsieur Granard did not return to sleep. With repeated remarks upon the imbecility of the Chef du Soir he agreed to see for himself at the scene of the crime. He arrived in a big Lancia half an hour later at the Chateau Brissac. The chief clerk had been brought, in pajamas under a top coat. The chauffeur waited. The Medical Examiner was ready to remove the body when Monsieur Granard should consent. A half dozen detectives from the Bureau du Soir saluted their irascible chief and reported that they had examined the grounds and every cranny of the old house. Footprints, leading from a rear door, had been traced across the dead grass, not toward a highway where a car might have been waiting, but towards the banks of the river.

That was all. In the house itself there were no clues of any sort, from cellar to roof.

"The photographers?" demanded Monsieur Granard.

"They have finished with this room, even to the knife hilt and the lady's fan. They have examined their plates under a red globe in a closet. When they are developed they will reveal nothing."

"The fan!" said Monsieur Granard, and it was handed him. He opened it, clumsily as a man does, but it was spread before him and the outline of the cat's head confronted him. His subordinates watched his white moustachios. They were a barometer to their chief's reflections. When he drew in his lips, tightened to his teeth, the white wings flattened and bristled, as they did now.

He snapped the fan shut and put it on a table, and wheeled upon Monsieur Cutot's clerk. The clerk could give only a meager description of the American who visited the shop, but could say a great deal about the young woman who sat in the car. She had large dark eyes. She had rich furs. She had an oval face. Her lips were full and——

Monsieur Granard grunted with distaste. "You'll be telling me in a minute about the contours of her knees! One decides you have the fibre of a gigolo."

The young man, who with his rumpled hair and rumpled pajamas certainly had none of the ear-marks of a gigolo, protested. "But my chief, sir, the poor M'sieu', he also observed the young lady. He spoke of her repeatedly. 'Hot-house bloom,' he called her, 'appropriate to the soil of a very rich and doting gardener.'"

Monsieur Granard turned to the chauffeur. "And you! What do you remember?"

"She came down the stairs, sir. She wore a red dress and held the fan against it, wide open."

Monsieur Granard swore a round oath, swung on his heel and went into the yard. From every window of the house a light was blazing now. Monsieur Granard spoke to the detective who had accompanied the jeweler. "How was it when you arrived?"

"As it is now, sir. Alight. Warm looking, and hospitable."

Monsieur Granard murmured, "You heard a motor boat?" and re-entered the house without waiting for comment from the detective. When he faced his Chef du Soir he was rubbing his hands gently and speaking as if he mused aloud for his own benefit.

"But it is charming. 'Enchanting' would be a better word. The killer we have thought to be dead returns and sets his stage as a dramatist might. The limousine and its lady outside the jewelry shop. A glimpse of round eyes and oval face to whet the taste of clerks and even Monsieur Cutot himself. A fleeting vision of beauty that justifies the most expensive diamonds and pearls. The chateau ablaze with lights, shadows on the blinds. But what is remembered by the dolts who see? A lady in a car and on the stair with her pretty fan! Escape down the river while the music plays to a ship at sea or a plane at the river mouth."

The Chef du Soir was not slow to remind his superintendent that he had been sworn at for suggesting that the affair had been the work of an arch criminal whom the police of the Continent had been pleased to think had anticipated his arrival in Hell by burning in his own fire trap in Leningrad a year before.

"I am glad you have changed your mind, sir," he began, but his superior shut him up tartly.

"Imbecile! Is it not apparent? And would you permit the night to pass while you gape? Notify Europe."

CHAPTER II

NEWS FROM MONTE CARLO

MAJOR SELWYN CROYANT arrived in Bordeaux by train from London the night after the affair at the Chateau Brissac. The famous Englishman, who persistently denied that he was any kind of policeman but only a blood-hound for the companies that insure jewels, was expected at Monsieur Granard's offices at the Police Administration.

Dupree, the best man of the Paris Sûreté, had waited his arrival. Weinrath, *Ober-Kapitän* of the German Police Intelligence, who had flown over from Berlin, also waited. Herr Weinrath had been stiff to a Scotland Yard deputy commissioner who hurried down as soon as the official station atop Eiffel Tower radioed Europe that the killer known as The Panther and his organization were again functioning, but the great German man-hunter grunted satisfaction when informed that Major Croyant would be along later. He was mildly astonished that the Englishman should potter with a train.

"Regard his avoirdupois," murmured Dupree. "A fat man has a certain distaste for wings."

Every few minutes a messenger tapped at the door of the Chef de la Sûreté, opened it and laid upon Monsieur Granàrd's desk a fresh sheaf of telegrams and radio messages, the former on pink forms, the latter on lavender. As one who was nominally Dupree's superior, Monsieur Granard read the messages first and then passed them to the detective who had been chosen as the one man in France best equipped to match cunning with the Unknown whose bombastic trick was to leave behind him his *carte-de-visite*.

From a new batch of tinted reports that recorded the pulse beats of the aroused police body of France and Western Europe, Monsieur Granard held aloft one pink and one lavender, and tapped them with his pince-nez. He nodded to Dupree and Weinrath.

"Ah! We proceed, messieurs, from the empty speed boat that was found abandoned in the estuary of the Gironde."

Dupree jumped from his chair. He crouched a little, like a hunting dog ready for the horn.

"We proceed, Monsieur le Chef? Do we arrive at a destination?"

Monsieur Granard glanced at the typed forms, drew in his lips and flattened his moustachios. Dupree shrugged his shoulders and sank back into his chair.

"We may take a step," said Monsieur Granard. "Only a step. It is not sufficient but it is a start."

"Let's have it," Weinrath grunted.

"A tug captain arrived in the harbor night before last. He came down the coast from Lisbon. Somewhat earlier than the twilight—*Sacre!* why can they not look at their watches and point the hour itself?—but it was earlier than the dusk. Above him he sees a seaplane. An observant chap, this tug captain, says the Agent of Marine at the harbor. A seaplane is as common as a gull. But this one, the captain notes, shows no identifying insignia. It is not numbered and lettered, as is required. He enters the matter in his log."

"He should have telegraphed the Air Bureau," said Dupree with elaborate irony.

"Wait, Monsieur Dupree," the Chef de la Sûreté commanded sternly. "He crossed the harbor—I refer to the tug captain—and well after dark entered the estuary of the Gironde. He makes a fresh entry in his log. When he has chosen an untraveled finger of the estuary, where he expects to idle while he makes some repairs to his hulk, he steams so close to the unidentified seaplane, resting on the water, that there is almost a collision. The plane showed no lights. The propeller was turning slowly. It was ready to rise. It was in this finger of the estuary that we found the abandoned motor boat."

"He has adopted the air!" Weinrath exclaimed. "Your step leaves us hanging in the clouds."

Monsieur Granard referred to the second of his reports.

"The Gendarmerie of the Medoc country—" he paused to explain to Herr Weinrath that the Medoc country lies between Bordeaux and Spain—"say that an airplane which can not be traced flew over the country sometime after midnight. It was seen by watchmen at a number of isolated posts. It was headed on a diagonal course for the Riviera. One post was favored by the moonlight and observed that the plane was amphibian with unmarked wings."

Monsieur Granard put down his slips, shoving them along the polished shelf of his table to Dupree. "He will alight on the Mediterranean. That much is clear. Our first step is to Nice, Monte Carlo and Cannes. We will find him enjoying himself with his little lady along the Côte d'Azure."

"Yah!" grumbled Weinrath. "We will go to the Riviera. We will promenade from Marseilles to Ventimiglia. We will meet pleasant gentlemen and many pretty ladies. We will dine with them and talk with them and perhaps one of the gentlemen will be more charming than the rest. That one may be La Panthère, but how shall we know?"

"It is by her mistakes that we come at last to know a woman," said Dupree, now pacing the floor, frowning. "The rule for the butterfly is good for the wasp. He will make a mistake. Sometimes there will be a little clue, a tiny clue. He has been at rest for a year and is overbold. When before did he parade for us the open faces of his aides? When before did he give us a woman for the crowds in the street to stare at?"

"And remember of her only bright eyes and an ornamental face!" Monsieur Granard snorted. "There's a pack of them wherever there are men to look and strut. When he seems to be bold he but draws a herring across the trail."

"There is a smell to a herring," snapped Dupree. "Soon there will be another drawing of the cat's head. I prepare to follow the scent backwards instead of forward. Back from the motor boat and not after the plane."

Monsieur Granard bethought himself of the non-appearing Englishman. "It would be as well," he said testily, "to have competent noses smelling in both directions." He telephoned to the hotel Major Croyant was known to favor and was told that he had risen early and gone at once about his business."

"Ask him," interposed Dupree, "if he was whistling."

Monsieur Granard frowned. "You are of a mood to be facetious?"

"But *non, non!* I am eager to know the state of my friend's stomach. When it is of pleasant disposition he whistles."

Herr Weinrath made a fatuous exclamation. "He is not there. He is not here. Where?"

"One reasons a matter out," murmured Dupree. "We are concerned that Monsieur Cutot lost his breath. It is the loss of the loot that distresses Selwyn. His people insured it. He is at this moment bent over the table of the late Monsieur lugubriously listing the baubles that are missing from the safes. I shall descend upon him. If he whistles, I shall present him here."

Major Croyant was, indeed, bent over the table of the late Monsieur Cutot in the back of the shop. He was not whistling. The chief clerk stood near with a harried expression. When the Englishman saw Dupree he tapped a document, one of many spread across the table, with a puffy finger and addressed the visitor as if he had stood there all along instead of stepping in from a separation of many months.

"Consider this, Dupree! A choker of diamonds. A hundred carats on a single string. Eight hundred thousand francs. Monsieur Cutot would not be content to receive his assassin here in his own shop, but must carry this string of diamonds to a rendezvous more convenient for the rogue!"

The chief clerk did not neglect what, apparently, was an oft-repeated loyalty to his departed master. "But I assure you, sir, the car and the lady were most impressive."

The Major regarded the clerk with a heavy scowl and then appeared to realize that it had been six months since he had seen the celebrated French detective. He rose and reached out his hand. He bulked massive behind the table yet moved with an easy agility. A florid man, with heavy features, his face still impressed as being finely chiseled and was singularly alert.

"Dupree!" he exclaimed. "And in Bordeaux! I am curious at once. If you assign yourself to find the fellow

who has Monsieur Cutot's diamonds and pearls I shall
return to London with an easy mind."

"Diamonds! Pearls! *Ma foi*, my friend! Is it an occasion to compute pounds and sixpence? *Regardez vous!*"

Dupree was ever emotional—when he thought his audience would be appreciative. France loved him as it loved
its actors who could turn in a trice from comedy to the
grimness of the executioner who loves his task. Now he
brought out the slender package that had protruded from
his coat pocket. He removed its wrappings with a flourish
and, with a Delsartian gesture, spread the feathers of the
fan that had been carried down the stairway at Chateau
Brissac. He pointed an articulate finger at the brushed-in
design of a cat's head.

"Regard!" he repeated. "Your pretty ornaments are
vanished. This time you will not find them in your Mile
End dives of London, on the water front at Danzig or
in the secret pockets of crooked lapidaries at Amsterdam.
These have escaped you but *this* remains to snarl again
and again carry off in its jaws more little diamonds and
pellets of pearl. Attend the fastidiousness of my soul,
friend Selwyn, and permit me to think that we shall join
hands to trap the monster for the saving of other lives.
If you reserve the thought that we but remove a future
risk to diamonds and pearls, it shall be secret with you.
I shall prefer to credit you a nobler purpose."

The Englishman dropped back into his chair. He looked
at the drawing on the fan with a curious interest the
Frenchman seemed to distrust. He looked up with a sigh.

"You disturb me, Ariste. Surely you don't believe the
things your Eiffel Tower is sputtering into the air?"

"Do not believe, my friend?"

"That Monsieur Cutot's assassin was your old friend
of beloved memory? This rogue of Bordeaux has not

actually imposed upon you with his forgery? He's converting the notoriety of The Panther to his own uses."

Dupree laid the fan, still outspread, onto the table. He shook his head violently.

"I will not take you seriously. You do not mean that you believe it a forgery. You have some purpose in that pretense. The stage setting, the effrontery, the color—a woman who comes down a stair in a red dress, her fan an implement of coquetry, not a bit of paper mind you, or an ivory disc from a roulette table, but a fan that carries the signature. It is left at the victim's feet. While we open it we think of beauty, lo! we see the warning of more death to come. Are we not terrified, Selwyn? Another *carte-de-visite*, still another and then will not all who have wealth with which to buy their safety be also terrified? The *cartouche* of The Panther will arrive in advance of death. The millionaire will reach for his gold cigarette case and discover that during the night it has been engraved with the cat's head. Madame will toy with her vanity and recoil from the fangs of the cat under her powder puff."

While he drew the scene of his imagery Dupree strode the confines of Monsieur Cutot's elegant little room. Now he paused to make his effect. He stood at the table and looked down into the placid face of the Englishman.

"What will occur, Monsieur le Major? The millionaire will divide his millions in great haste with The Panther. Madame will pawn her jewels and collect theft insurance that she may make up the sum demanded. You see, my friend, always there is a risk to jewels as an incident of The Panther's freedom."

Major Croyant brushed a hand over his wide forehead. He seemed to settle within his own ponderous frame.

"Splendid, Ariste! Splendid! Monsieur Cutot's office becomes a theater. Almost you convince me."

The actor in the Frenchman retreated before another personality. He seated himself and selected a cigarette from a converted snuff box. "I will reason the matter out with you. I would spare you the futility of searching in the underworld, the ordinary underworld, for a trace of your baubles and your thief."

The Major gathered the documents on the table, made them into a neat sheaf which he gave to the chief clerk, instructing him to put them into his bag and deliver them to his hotel. Dupree watched him covertly. Once the Major's generous lips pursed as if to whistle a theme, but relaxed silently. Dupree thought his friend a little tired. His mind ran back over half a dozen engagements in which the Englishman had opposed the sharpest criminal minds in Europe, and had come home with his prisoner —and usually the jewels that had been involved. It would be distressing if he were tired at this important moment. To Dupree's mind the Englishman was stolid, unimaginative and unemotional. No actor at all. But tenacious, and possessed of resources denied the average detective.

The chief clerk closed the door behind him. Major Croyant settled back in the stout chair the clerk had thoughtfully provided. He appeared to forget for the moment that the Frenchman proposed to reason against him.

"I suppose," he said, "there is a real Andrew Banton? The American who leased the Chateau?"

"Monsieur Granard assembled the information. There is. Bona fide. Very rich. But instead of coming on a honeymoon, his wife, who has been of his bosom some forty anniversaries, entertains the rheumatism. They are in mid-ocean on the *Aquitania*. The real Madame Banton commands that the room in which the event occurred be sealed."

"And the American car? If it did not arrive by boat?"

"It was purchased from a dealer in Toulouse. He received an order for one of its make some weeks ago from an American whom we identify as the secretary."

"I grant an intelligent organization that extends to New York where it learns the movements of the bona fide Bantons," Croyant conceded. "That's interesting. A new alliance between the two worlds. But why purchase the car in Toulouse? Was it not a blunder, since it must have a meaning? The dealer would have to bring one from Paris. Why not Paris in the first place? Have you thought of that?"

The Frenchman shrugged his shoulders. "It is unimportant. Toulouse or Paris. There is no clue at Toulouse. The Panther himself did not appear. There will never be a clue except where he has paused to bite." He leaned forward. His face became almost cherubic. "I ask you, my friend, to alter your method of hunting first for the booty. Let us link arms and march together upon La Panthère. You will be, as I have declared, re-insuring your wares against the future."

Now Major Croyant whistled. His expression was ludicrous when he puckered his heavy lips. He was too big a man, far too monumentally imposing to be whistling gay snatches of Fra Diavolo, the lament of Mimi, or the fantasy of Humoresque. But Dupree was delighted. He spread his elbows and pointed his fingertips together and reminded of a stump speaker about to have his picture taken.

The whistle broke off on a dissonance and the Frenchman straightened, *en defenser*. Croyant had waved a thick hand between them as if he interrupted the weaving of a mutual bond.

"I repeat, Ariste, you are letting your imagination run away. You want a prodigious sensation you can be glum about. You want a Mephistopheles to whom you can become a Faustus. I admire your delightful versatilities but you mustn't divert me from my undramatic quest of Monsieur Cutot's lost gems among the usual fences where the commonplace crook will sooner or later dispose of his thievings. Could I swallow The Panther I should be alarmed. I am a heavy man to take on the extra weight of an alarm. I'd find myself doing something about it. I'll swallow The Panther only when you have explained the body found in the burned house to which he had been traced in Leningrad."

"Let us reason away the matter of Leningrad. Attend! I proceed."

It was ordered that he should not proceed. There was a startling interruption ushered in by the insistent clatter of the bell which commanded attention to the telephone on the table. Dupree stared at the instrument as if to rebuke it for impoliteness. Croyant regarded it dubiously and fished for a push button to summon the chief clerk. He was relieved when that individual appeared, from no farther away, the Englishman was convinced, than the keyhole.

There was a brief interval after the clerk's "Allo!" He shivered perceptibly and handed the instrument to Dupree with jerky alacrity. "It is for M'sieu' l'Agent. The Police Administration."

At the first words that came over the wire unheard by Croyant the Frenchman stiffened. His face darkened and his eyes shone through the cloud like cold beacons. "*Incroyable*—incredible!" he ejaculated again and again.

"Oui oui, Monsieur le Chef. My friend is at hand. I shall transmit. You will be so good—a plane at the airport! I lose little time."

He put the instrument down sharply. Excitement was in every fibre of his face but he could not deny himself a pose of mysterious triumph. Croyant refused him a sign of expectancy, his face remaining inscrutable as if he guarded against concessions.

"Attend, my friend!" Dupree cried. "Monsieur Granard has a lavender slip from Monte Carlo. It concerns a Señor Alphonse Veragua. Perhaps you know him?"

Croyant evinced a shade of lazy interest. "The cattle king from Buenos Aires?"

"That one. Incredibly wealthy."

The Major brushed a hand across his mouth and was thoughtful. "At Deauville. Yes. I met him. There was a lady with a good-looking throat. He improved it with Ceylon sapphires. I had my people discontinue the insurance. It was regrettable."

"Regrettable?"

"The lady's throat was not a good risk. She took it about too freely, here and there. Too many suspicious fingers had access to it. But it didn't matter to the Señor. His friend, Georges Raynel, whom I know much better, assured me he was provoked."

"Ah, yes! Georges Raynel. Also a magician in money, not so?"

"Also. An engaging chap. Young enough to brave the dangers of romance." The Major sighed heavily. "I envy him."

Dupree permitted himself to be shocked out of his pose by the suggestion that Croyant could envy any speculation in romance. He recovered himself quickly. "Monsieur Granard's radio from Monte Carlo informs us that the Señor returned to his hotel, the fashionable Bristol, from a Cap Martin party at three o'clock this morning. Some three hours ago his valet found him dead in his bed, his heart pierced through by a stiletto. It is a detail that a young woman who has been identified as one of the Casino's *mascottes* was also quite dead in an antechamber, having been attended to in advance of her lover."

Croyant blinked but gave no other sign of inward emotion. "Thus a brilliant dash through our European society comes to a close. With a *mascotte* in the other room. A woman, Ariste, is a dangerous thing." He looked up at the detective, who was regarding him fiercely. "Come, Ariste. There was more to Monsieur Granard's radio. It hovers on your lips."

"A million francs was taken."

"A million?" The Major was incredulous. "A million in his rooms? And a *mascotte?*"

"Also a quantity of emeralds. They, too, are to be explained. They hold your attention, eh? Perhaps they are insured! Dismiss them for a moment. An additional detail. The woman's handkerchief had been borrowed. It wrapped the hilt of the stiletto."

The Frenchman's pause was dramatic. He pointed the tip of his impeccably manicured finger at the white fan still spread on the table. The cat's head trembled in each stir of air that ruffled the feather tendrils. Croyant glanced at the design and scowled.

"Out with it, Ariste."

"Drawn on the handkerchief! Did I not say that he would bite again, and swiftly? It is sooner than I dared think. He could not have put his seaplane down until dawn yesterday morning. One day passes, we hear from him again. I stop at the Sûreté, then I'm off."

Croyant got up from the table and recovered his hat and stick. Dupree made for the street and a taxi with a great show of haste. The monumental Major seemed to move leisurely but kept pace with his slighter friend.

"I'll go as far as Monsieur Granard's," he said. "I'm interested in the emeralds."

CHAPTER III

THE MAJOR LIES BLANDLY

AT the Sûreté more details had come through from Monte Carlo. Paris had ordered that a full account of the double murder be relayed to Dupree as fast as assembled. Through the despatches and radio messages ran an undercurrent that dramatized the consternation already spreading along the Mediterranean's play-shore. Señor Veragua was more than a rich man, of whom the Riviera knew many. He was a meteor come out of South America to flash across the world of casino and drawing-room. He and his constant associate, Georges Raynel, as rich as he and even more dashing, were a colossal pair.

The affair at Bordeaux, of which the newspapers had made much, had failed to impress a large section of the public with the significance of that design painted on the feathers of a white fan. People were inclined to ridicule the anxieties of the police. They created a fantastic figure out of keeping with the times. But as word spread along the Côte d'Azure that the cat's head had been found snarling over the heart of the gallant Señor, the new danger began to be understood.

Señor Veragua's secretary was the main source of information as to the Señor's movements during the hours immediately preceding his last appearance alive. He had waited for his employer's return in the lobbies of the Bristol. There were important cablegrams from South America requiring prompt attention that the answers might be despatched to Buenos Aires with regard to the difference in trans-Atlantic time. Ordinarily he would have waited in his employer's suite but on this occasion he displayed the discretion which had made him invaluable to his master.

A lady had been admitted to the suite earlier in the evening in accordance with orders given in advance to the valet. The secretary had not seen her, did not know her, but in a short conversation with the valet in the foyer he had gathered a certain impression. It was not that the valet had spoken at length of his master's guest, the secretary explained, but there had been a flutter of the servant's eyelid.

While he waited below, the secretary enjoyed the stream of people coming in from parties at Nice and Cannes and from the gambling rooms of the Sporting Club. When the Señor arrived he was not in a good humor. Perhaps the celebration at the Cap Martin villa had been dull. He waved aside the cablegrams and instructed the secretary that they be brought him at midmorning. The secretary did not see him again until he stood beside the Medical Examiner and shuddered as the slender bladed stiletto was withdrawn.

Monsieur Granard had assembled all the information covering the young woman. It appeared that she was one of that transient bevy of butterflies who support themselves and pay for their clothes by bringing good luck to gamblers. A *mascotte* is engaged for the evening of play. Her prettily pointed finger tips touch each chip before it is risked. Her patron's winnings increase her fees. They are very ornamental, these *mascottes,* and as a rule are complaisant. There are occasions when their patrons are not content to part with them when the Casino's gambling rooms are closed.

Monsieur Granard read his epitome aloud.

"Mademoiselle Essant had been popular at Biarritz, Dinard and Monte Carlo. She was not easily, that is to say, not inexpensively, accessible. There is nothing against her in the police dossiers. She obtained the favor of Señor Veragua and, apparently, felt obliged to render him her favors in return. She was in extreme dishabille when found on the floor of his ante-chamber. It does not seem that she could have been a party to the tragedy beyond being one of its victims. It was her great misfortune that the Señor could not have chosen some earlier night to receive her."

Monsieur Granard handed his condensation to Dupree. "I dismiss Mademoiselle Essant from consideration. She had no suspicious affiliations who might have broken faith and removed her rather than leave her alive. You, however, will do as you think best. I retain my regret that she could not have lived to enjoy the magnificent emeralds which had been delivered the Señor the day before and which I assume were purposed for her charming throat in the morning.

"It will be a point for my friend," said Dupree maliciously, "whether the gems were conclusively paid for. It would have a bearing upon the extension of the dealer's insurance."

"It will be a point," Croyant admitted gravely.

The despatches explained that the secretary was not astonished that his employer should have had a million francs in his rooms. His taste was for high gambling. He may have expected high stakes in some impromptu game at Cap Martin. He was ready to play at all times and it was his whim to pay his obligations on the spot. A million, the secretary insisted, was but a flea-bite.

"There was not even a little clue for Monsieur Dupree?" Croyant inquired, no suggestion in his tone that he returned Dupree's malice.

"None," Monsieur Granard returned. "The valet is an old man long in the service of the family. He was asleep in his room at the far end of the suite. The night latch was set. The lock had been installed by the Señor himself and only he and the valet had keys. The clerks noted no strangers entering the lifts."

Dupree prepared for a dash across the city to the plane waiting at the airfield. Herr Weinrath announced that he would accompany him. He wanted to see the handkerchief and its cat's head. The Monte Carlo police found the tiny square of lace to have been Mademoiselle Essant's unquestionably. Its fabric and tints were matched in the gown on its hanger in a closet. The killer had impuaently delayed his flight while he drew his signature on the bit of lace and then used it to erase fingerprints from the stiletto hilt.

Dupree and the German paused to plead with Croyant to follow them to Monte Carlo by train. Monsieur Granard added his persuasions.

The Englishman slumped in his chair and shook his head. "Perhaps the emeralds were not insured," he said. "I do not like the Riviera at this time of year. To visit it I need a motive."

Dupree loosed an exclamation of fury upon his phlegmatic friend. "Motive? *Nom de Dieu!* The Panther leaves his mark and you speak of motive!"

His emotion overcame him. Before he could rush from the room a fresh batch of messages arrived from the south-east. Monsieur Granard read them with a start and handed them silently to Dupree. The detective made a hissing sound through his teeth and wheeled upon the Englishman.

"*Attendez vous!* It is the friend who takes a hand. Perhaps you will be stirred, Monsieur le Major. He is magnificent, he whom you admit is also of your own acquaintance."

Croyant protested with a gesture. "We are linked only by the romance I spoke of. A little lady of whom I'm fond agrees with you that he is magnificent. That is all."

"I compliment the lady. He is a great person, this Monsieur Georges Raynel." He tapped the lavender slip impressively. "I salute the man who will revere the memory of his companion at the cost of five million francs!"

"Eh?"

"It amazes you? Monsieur Raynel is summoned from his yacht in the harbor. He looks upon the body of his friend and holds the handkerchief in his fingers. *Voila!* It is here in the radiogram. Monsieur Raynel's reward of five million francs to the man who captures The Panther! A pretty little bonus, Monsieur le Major."

And as if no more were to be said to bring Croyant into the great hunt, Dupree hurried out with a flighty salute to Monsieur Granard, and with Herr Weinrath following in more dignified haste.

Croyant spent an hour with Monsieur Granard. He begged use of a telephone connection to London, explaining that he must inquire if his companies were concerned by the disappearance of the emeralds delivered to Señor Veragua. While they waited an answering call, Monsieur Granard produced the dossier of The Panther, a bulky file distributed by the Sûreté at Paris to important provincial jurisdictions. He assembled certain sheets headed "Leningrad" and while he did so did not neglect a reference to the stupendous reward of five million francs offered by Señor Veragua's friend.

"You spoke of a romance of mutual interest to you and Monsieur Raynel," the Chef observed.

"We all like to see a romance turn out well. For both sides. I knew the young lady's father. An American. We were together during the war."

"I remember the announcements in the press. A Miss Avery. It will be an important match. One who has five million francs to spare is a catch, and one who spares it in token of a friendship is a great man."

"My little friend won't miss it," Croyant said, tonelessly. "He's plenty more for her. I'm thinking perhaps there was a bit of funk in the gesture. May be getting a bit nervous on his own account."

"It would be a nice reward to earn, Monsieur le Major."

Suspicion of a twinkle came into the Englishman's eyes. "Ariste will find his little clue. He will go backward until he comes to where an identity was left lying about. It is an admirable method. He will become a rich man with five million francs."

"You do not believe in the method?" Monsieur Granard's tone made it clear that he did not believe in it, either.

"I should be afraid of coming back to the Nevsky Prospekt," Croyant admitted softly. Monsieur Granard gave his attention to the sheets marked "Leningrad."

"Ah! Here we have it. Let us approach the Nevsky Prospekt. Let us start some two years beyond. America was having its first taste of organized crime but we, in Europe, were faced by an organization that so appalled us for a time we wondered if it were not a figment of our own disordered imaginations. The drawing of the cat's head, a panther's head, appeared and re-appeared. Occasionally it was the signature to a brilliantly executed robbery—emphasized with death. At other times a warning delivered to some rich man of what the consequences would be if he did not pay over some exorbitant sum in cash or jewelry. Of these warnings we heard of those only which had been disregarded. And as the months passed into years, and the cat's head when it was found was invariably symbol of a murder so boldly and skilfully done that we, of the police, could do nothing about it, we ceased altogether hearing of the advance warnings. People who received the drawing, on a card, on a metal plaque slipped under their pillows, or in a florist's box, paid the demand and remained silent. Raids upon gangs of known criminals produced no result. Indeed, the ordinary criminals were as puzzled as were we, and immeasurably envious. The Panther became bolder."

Monsieur Granard looked up from his papers. Croyant was composed easily in his chair, gazing out the window onto the bright shawled women who haggled over their vegetables in the markets across the way.

"You people lost the insurance on many gems in those years, Monsieur le Major," the Chef remarked.

Croyant did not look away from the vegetable women. "I've never forgiven Ariste," he grumbled, "for not bringing me up to him. The fellow might have told me what he did with his loot."

Monsieur Granard returned to his documents.

"Dupree arrived in Nevsky Prospekt, sad to say, too late. You will remember the circumstance of the Russian refugee at Warsaw?"

"I credit Ariste for that," Croyant acknowledged. "He was even then working backward to where The Panther had at some time permitted himself to be unguarded."

"Yes, Monsieur. Dupree had traced his man to Poland. He scooped in a net full of prisoners, gained nothing, but remained convinced. A woman's voice reached him at his hotel, if you remember the details. An hysterical voice that has never been traced. The woman screamed that a man was being tortured at an address she gave. She repeated an incoherent protest, 'But I told him nothing—I told him nothing!'"

Croyant was silent for a time while Monsieur Granard paused. His attention was still devoted to the markets. "I should like to meet the owner of that voice," he murmured at last more as if he spoke to one of the vegetable women across the street. Monsieur Granard started, affected by some quality in the Englishman's tone. He took up the reminiscence of Warsaw quickly.

"Dupree surrounded the house and broke in. They found a young Russian bound to a wall. On his bare chest the point of knife had traced the outline of a cat's head. To a portion of the spreading wound an acid already had been applied as if it were being administered slowly. The container was on the floor where it had dropped when the torturing fiend fled from the interruption by the police. The Russian collapsed. In his delirium at the hospital he mumbled again and again, 'The Panther.' At other times he groaned, 'She didn't tell me. I spied upon her but she didn't know.' After a week of agony, the acid burning deeper and deeper despite medical efforts to conquer it, he sprang up in his cot and shouted 'Follow him to Sixteen Nevsky Prospekt.' He sank back into delirium and died calling upon some unnamed girl to dance for him."

Croyant moved. Monsieur Granard watched him. The Frenchman knew the other was familiar with each detail of the history he had recited, yet he had not interrupted while it was being repeated. "Yes," Croyant said, still talking out the window, "a girl danced for him. Perhaps she's dancing somewhere now."

He turned into the room suddenly. His hands spread as if they emphasized an ending of some sort.

"Pretty plain," he said, "that the Russian knew The Panther was due at the Leningrad address, and there was ample reason for a visit. It was the house of Count Jeribzoff, one of the few aristocrats permitted by the Soviet to keep their mansions. He had done something at some time for Lenin. He owned one of the world's fine collections of pigeon rubies. Ariste arrived in the street at a dramatic moment not of his own staging. The house was a smoldering ruin. The burned body of the Count was identifiable. He had been stabbed before the fire was set. Attached to the knife hilt was a metal disc on which the cat's head had been traced. The house had been searched apparently, even to a concealed safe found open. A second body was found in the street foyer, burned beyond recognition, but it was clear this man had been fleeing the flames and had been trapped. His foot had caught and twisted in an iron grille and the blaze reached him before he could extricate himself. Dupree and the Leningrad police had no doubt that the unknown was The Panther."

With the privilege of an older man, Monsieur Granard pointed an accusing finger. "You know better now. You know better, and if you are stubborn it is for a reason you do not share with us. We were too easily deluded, the wish being father to our thoughts. The Jeribzoff rubies— have they ever turned up?"

Croyant shook his head.

"They were not among effects kept at a bank. They could not have burned in the fire. The second body was not The Panther's. He was in the house that night, search-

ing for the rubies, for such a thorough search scarcely
would have been for anything else. But he escaped after
killing the Count. Sooner or later we will know why he
has been inactive for a year. He knows that Weinrath is
after him, and Dupree. I should like him also to know
that you are after him. He knows the methods of Weinrath and Dupree. He will not know yours. And—there
are Monsieur Raynel's five million francs."

Croyant blinked against the persistency of the accusing
finger. Slowly a sheepish grin took shape about his mouth.
"He might serve me with his cat's head. We'll wait for
word from London."

The word came within a few minutes. While London
talked Croyant's expression was blank, yet the information he was receiving was alarming.

The emeralds ordered by Señor Veragua were still covered by insurance taken out in London. They had been
delivered for the Señor's approval. Their value was enormous. The directors of the Major's companies were in a
panic, facing a loss of such magnitude so soon after Monsieur Cutot's diamonds and pearls. The directors suggested that he join the Continental police in the effort to
meet the revived menace of The Panther.

When he put down the instrument Croyant whistled a
snatch from the aria of Il Trovatore. Monsieur Granard
lost patience and grimaced.

"They were not insured," the Major lied blandly. "I'll
have to leave the fellow to Dupree. And the five million
francs."

He whistled as he went out of Monsieur Granard's office, but outside the building of the Police Administration he stopped whistling, and his mouth took on a grim
cast.

CHAPTER IV

ROUND EYES, OVAL FACE

THERE was a night train for Dieppe and the Channel which Croyant might have taken and traveled comfortably, since he appeared to be determined to return to London instead of going on to Monte Carlo to consider the matter of the emeralds delivered to Señor Veragua. But he disliked night trains. He liked to watch the scenery rolling by, though he was pretty familiar with all the outstanding trees, the picturesque hillsides and the daffodil fields that flowed past the Continental expresses. He engaged a seat on the morning train and amused himself through the early evening in thoughtful idleness.

Thoughtful he surely was, because he didn't whistle.

He should have been, by all custom, reaching across Europe to touch the springs of a personal organization that was ever ready to come alive when there were stolen jewels and jewel thieves to round up. Rumors of illicit diamonds thrown onto the market eventually would converge upon Amsterdam. Pearls slipping from crooked fence to furtive dealer would roll inevitably into Brussels, and it was ordained that emeralds would come at last to the emerald market at Prague. But, it seemed, Croyant acknowledged the futility of stirring his organization to a hunt for booty gathered in by The Panther. Instead he took a stroll in the Avenue Pryan, stopping occasionally for a glass of red wine at the bower-hung sidewalk cafés where the waiters look Spanish and talk their French with a strong Portuguese accent. He turned into Boulevard Marechal Foch where a long, slowly parading line of little painted ladies regard each pedestrian with a certain hopefulness. Such of these as won from him a casual glance turned quickly away. A man who is very glum, with a play of hard glints in his gray eyes, is not a fit companion for even the most commercial play at transient love making.

The pretty *filles de joi* would have shivered indeed had they known that the massive man who walked with such an incredibly youthful stride was thinking of murder, of an assassin so terrifying as La Panthère, and with an intensity of thought oddly at variance with his intent as professed to Monsieur Granard to keep his hands washed of that formidable antagonist.

He walked on until the ornate lights of the boulevard were succeeded by the quavering gas flares that descend a hill into the sinister zone of the Apaches beyond the line of the old fortifications implanted by the sixteenth Louis as a warning to the Spaniards. Girls in cotton waists opened low on impudent bosoms, with short black skirts and black stockings, slipped out of the shadows, red-lipped wraiths of the night, to peer insolently into his face and then slink back to receive the blows and curses of their men for passing up such a promising customer. The Apache girls would not have allowed a man who whistled to elude their charms so easily. But a man who talked to himself in a growl was not one to whom kisses might be lightly sold.

When he made the astonishing discovery that he had passed so far beyond the old fortifications that he was approaching the Medoc country, he returned to his hotel where he composed a curious telegram to his principal agent at Warsaw. It did not direct that representative onto the train of diamonds or pearls or emeralds, or to the lair of a jewel thief, but into the wake of a dancer's heels.

Not a single dancer, but many dancers. Any and all who might have been amusing the public of the Polish capital with her quicksilver toes during the season of twelve to fifteen months ago.

Of each of these, whether she danced at the theater, the Opera or in a wine garden, he required photographs, with much personal history attached. Police dossiers if any, past engagements and subsequent movements. Her friends and companions if of these a record could be traced. Her love affairs particularly. And if among them all there should be one dancer who had been mistress to a young Russian emigré who died in a hospital, of that one all possible information even to the size of her boot. He ended his telegram with a puzzling sentence. "It is a clue I want. It may even be found in a dancer's feet."

While his day train wound northward through the sunniest fields of France he read the morning papers out of Paris. They blazoned the sensational tragedy at Monte Carlo with considerably more excitement than they had felt over the affair at Bordeaux.

"Dupree is right," Croyant reflected. "That is what the fellow wants. Cumulation of shivers until he has produced an ague."

The press predicted a veritable reign of terror unless The Panther were promptly unmasked, and expressed the hope that he would be by the aroused police. But there was a pessimistic note.

There was much commiseration for poor, pretty Mademoiselle Essant. To have accomplished by her charm a rendezvous with a lover of such enormous wealth as the South American, only to have her couch of Venus become also her bier! The first impression that the magnificent emeralds were destined to add the touch of green to the alabaster tint of Mademoiselle Essant's throat was corrected, however. The Señor's friend, Georges Raynel, guarded well the memory of the man whose joy of life he had shared. For Mademoiselle Essant a generous portion of the million francs in the Señor's rooms might have been intended. A woman, Monsieur Raynel declared, attained freedom from all financial distresses when she experienced the arms of Señor Veragua. But the emeralds had been intended as a wedding gift for Mademoiselle Avery, Monsieur Raynel's fianceé, the charming American girl. The Señor had asked his friend to suggest what would please Miss Avery.

Reading thus far, Croyant dropped his paper while he looked out at the scenery. He thought for a while of Helen Avery, but his musing came suddenly to a frown. He shook his head as if to drive an unpleasant thought away and returned to his reading. There were many paragraphs, he discovered, devoted to compliments for the girl destined to such a brave husband as one who would flaunt five million francs reward in The Panther's teeth. Croyant smiled. The French still think that it's the woman who's lucky at the marriage ceremony rather than the man.

He turned from Helen Avery to Dupree's theory that a criminal so resourceful as The Panther, who applied the psychology of an Aristotle to the stage technique of a Bernard Shaw, would never leave a clue to his exits, but would some day stumble at his entrance upon a crime. There would be that "little mistake" on the scene, something in the execution or the preparation, but no need to follow him. Go backward. Dupree reasoned that at any given moment The Panther's wits and his organization would be concerned with the job of going on, going on safely. From what was behind them they had successfully emerged. The trail behind had been passed; it would be forgotten. Along the trail he had successfully passed Dupree would catch up with his identity.

'Croyant granted the excellence of the theory and that Dupree, if any man alive, would be the one to work it out. With this credit to his emotional colleague, he shrugged his shoulders with the inference that Dupree might have his theory if he liked it.

The train rolled down the verdant Brittany slopes into the busy town of Dieppe. The cross Channel boat for Newhaven would leave in three hours, an hour behind schedule. A Brittany train was coming in from Dinard and stations along the north coast in between. Dusk had long since become full night. There is little travel out of Brittany at night, and from this arriving train only one passenger descended from the first class coaches. A woman, apparently a young woman judging from the contours of her figure. She walked quickly and gracefully across the *trottoir* toward the railway ticket offices. Perhaps Croyant would not have been conscious of her at all, a single figure among a score of others emerging from the Brittany train, if she had not parted from her traveling companions on the *trottoir* to walk, sharply defined under the pier and station lights, to the railway office. The majority of travelers arriving by train at Dieppe flock at once to the windows where Channel tickets are passed out.

Having his own boat ticket in his pocket, as well as the red pasteboard that granted him a cabin for even so short a trip, Croyant turned back, across Square St. Vincent, into the town. He would have a wine omelet and a liqueur at Café Danton, under the birch trees of rue Sept.

Few travelers to Dieppe know of the Café Danton. It is a sharp walk from the docks. It does not cater to the tourist who demands a quick bite while porters are carrying luggage to the customs benches. Its tables are for town folk who like to sip their wines leisurely and enjoy the twinkling of the far harbor lights through the web of birch boughs. Those who know the excellence of an omelet flavored with a good claret under a respectable Burgundy sauce.

Croyant regarded his omelet with the satisfaction of an epicure and returned to his "littlest clue."

"Dupree will never find it on the spot," he mused. "Perhaps in London, on the pavement under his feet and obscured by the fog, or in the reticence of a prisoner in Bucharest who will not reveal his reasons for killing another man, or in a night dive in Rome. Never——"

He broke off his musing with an effort and was aware, for the first time, of the young woman from the Brittany train who apparently had not come into Dieppe for the Channel boat but for transfer to the south. She, too, evidently, enjoyed the wines of the Café Danton. She sat at a table only a yard or two away, her back almost fully turned. That she was the same young woman there was no doubt. An expensive fur draped jauntily across her shoulders. In her posture, though she merely sat upon a Café Danton chair—a not very comfortable chair— there was a definitely graceful poise. She knew how to compose her body, or else it fell into its relaxations with a rare inherent naturalness.

She had ordered a bottle of white wine. A waiter who hovered near was horrified when she siphoned into her glass a spray of carbonated water. No one, woman or man or imbecile, who was a patriot of France would thus insult a good white wine. An Italian might, but Croyant decided after a fleeting glimpse of her profile that she would not be Italian. Nor English nor German. His attention remained more upon the shocked waiter than upon the girl. She poured more of the wine into her glass and reached for the siphon. While she held the bottle of carbonated fluid over her glass the back of her hand was visible to Croyant. He was toying with the impression that it was very shapely when his gaze focused suddenly on a great red splash on her middle finger. The pigeon blood pool of an enormous ruby.

Croyant's mind instantly leapt across the catalogue of the world's outstanding rubies and searched the blue book of their owners. One far less acquainted than he with the waters of gems would have known at once that here was no costume piece or reconstruction done with powdered amethyst, but a fortune, as many estimate a fortune, comprised within the area of a man's thumbnail. The girl put down her siphon and her hand lingered for a moment at the rim of the table. Her ring released a shower of fire that might well have been tears from the bursting heart of an old claret. Croyant estimated it to weigh not far from sixty carats. There are not many such rubies in the world: the famed Rajah, of the British Crown jewels; the eight great stones in the Toledo crown in the Spanish royal collection; the betrothal gem of Elizabeth, of Austria; and——!

Croyant started suddenly. He leaned forward in his chair and put down his liqueur glass. Fingers that could have crushed a metal goblet toyed gently with the fragile glass stem. In his different aspect he might have been Ariste Dupree crouching and waiting for the first note of the hunting horn.

The young woman pushed away her siphon and prepared to leave. There was another flash of red as her hand described an arc while she gathered an end of her fur and fixed its clasp. She arose while she fumbled in her purse and the waiter hurried close.

Croyant arose with her and edged past the waiter, behind him. The girl did not look up and the Englishman glanced down, over the waiter's shoulder. Her hand was silhouetted against the black of her bag while she fished out francs and centimes.

The ruby, as Croyant had thought from the distance of his table, was perfectly round and of the unmistakable ninety-facet cut designed for a ruby by the Russian artisans of Alexander the Second. Croyant's lips pursed in a silent whistle. He retreated to the Café Danton's bar and fortified his liqueur with a stiff brandy highball.

He found her easily on the train walk. She chose to avoid the mustiness of the badly ventilated waiting rooms and strolled along the tracks. The singular grace of her carriage impressed him anew. All about her was the busy flux of a port of entry and departure yet she seemed to detach herself completely from the scene. Croyant kept a good distance from her, catching brief glimpses of her face when she made her turns. A Russian, unquestionably. Once she stood for a moment under the flare of a platform arc and looked about her idly. Before she resumed her pacing she touched the back of her hat and her ring splattered a sharp brilliance like a red star over a sea.

A runner for the telegraph office caught Croyant's signal and handed him a tissue pad of forms. Watching the young woman out of the corner of his eye he scribbled a message to Dupree, addressed in custody of the Police Jurisdiction. It was a cryptic message that seemed to have in it a nuance of the elusive ballet theme Croyant whistled while he scribbled.

"Would it not be splendid, my friend, if you could add to the round eyes and oval face of the Stair lady the body of a Warsaw dancer and in place of the fan she lost ornament her with a Jeribzoff ruby?"

While the runner hurried to send his telegram on its way a train for Paris and beyond prepared fussily to depart upon the arrival of the boat. There would be a good sized crowd coming across the Channel, Croyant decided, since a switching engine was shunting into place a string of first class coaches and *waggons lit*. The young woman summoned her porter and demanded her bags. She would have entered a *waggon lit* but the porter shook his head, pointing out that the train would not be opened until the boat slid past the dock heads.

She kept the man in attendance until the boat was roped to the pier. He settled her in her compartment and his face was alight when he emerged onto the platform, which would indicate, in a Dieppe porter, not less than a five franc tip.

The man hurried to meet the influx from the arriving boat but Croyant intercepted him with a twenty franc note between his thumb and forefinger. The porter understood at once that a man of taste could very well be curious as to the destination of a personable young lady who traveled alone and, accordingly, unprotected.

"*Oui, oui, M'sieu'!* I observe the *carte-de-passage*. Mademoiselle travels to Toulouse."

Croyant reached the ticket windows before the rush from the boat. He accepted the prospect of a night trip to Toulouse with unwonted complacency.

CHAPTER V

EVENING IN TOULOUSE

IT was well toward noon before the train slid into the station at Toulouse. Croyant remained in his compartment to avoid attracting the girl's attention. Once observed he was a man not to be passed another time without recognition. He had the impression that she also remained in seclusion. She did not, at least, pass his corridor door on the way to the café car behind. A tray carried forward by a train porter would be, he thought, her breakfast.

At Toulouse the train platform was quickly crowded, but the movement was to and from the third class coaches, with a sprinkling of second class travelers. There was but one passenger who descended from the *waggons lit* beside himself. She had changed her costume to a tweed suit that caressed the lines of her lissome figure provocatively. Her cloche hat of Dieppe had given way to a jaunty beret. She was familiar with the platform, making her way directly from the train, carrying her own bags, to an exit gate that opened at once onto a brick-laid esplanade across which stood the waiting line of horse-drawn Victorias that in so many provincial towns have stubbornly resisted the invasion of the taxi.

Croyant cut through the station building and was just in time to point out her vehicle, already clattering down the street, to the nearest cabby. The driver shook his reins and his ancient steed started off at a slow trot.

Croyant was afraid he would lose all trace of the Victoria
ahead in the twistings of Toulouse streets. Repeatedly it
passed from view and when recovered was each time
farther toward its next turning.

"*Allez plus vite!*" he urged the driver but it made no
difference.

"*Beaucoup de temps, M'sieu*." Plenty of time! The
driver shrugged his gaunt shoulders as if to say, "What
if we lose her, M'sieu'? She is nothing but a *fille*. My
horse and I know where to find you another just as good."

The Victoria ahead seemed hopelessly lost when a street
it turned into was empty by the time Croyant's driver
reached it. He settled back in his seat telling his jehu
to take him across Place du Forum to a hotel in Rue des
Arenes. He would trust to his luck at identifying the
other's cab at the station. But his own driver refused to
be swerved from his purpose. It seemed as if he had
instructed his horse to follow the other and had left the
matter to the animal. With no guidance from the reins
the nag finally jogged into Place Lamartine and there,
before the portico of an ambitious pension that had taken
to itself the dignity of a hotel, the young woman in the
tweed suit was paying her fare.

It was only after a threat that amounted to a promise
of mayhem that Croyant persuaded his driver to go on
past. The man shrugged his shoulders again and mumbled through his beard a supplication to his saints to
forgive him a passenger who follows a woman and is
afraid to do what a man does when he catches up with
her.

Croyant smiled at the cabby's indignation, lined in the
tilt of his back. He repeated the name of his hotel in Rue
des Arenes and fell to whistling while the cab rattled
along the pavements. As a rule he whistled vagrant

snatches from the melodic moments of familiar opera or operetta, his whims running a catholic gamut from Gilbert and Sullivan to Beethoven. What he chose to whistle now was not the measures of a popular aria or ballet theme but a strange, sense-stirring crescendo that rose on a minor in an Oriental rhythm to a tonal poem, finishing in a triumphant largo.

Twice he whistled the phrase and then stopped, suddenly frowning. He tried it again and floundered hopelessly. The tune became a phantom that eluded him and try as he might to recapture the notes he had just whistled so blithely, he couldn't. His brain groped for a key, for a memory. A vague wraith stirred in his mind, as of a familiar trying to make itself known, then it was gone and with it every note of the voluptuous tune he had whistled.

His hotel loomed and his driver drew up. He made a pretense of extending five metal francs, the precise amount of his fare. The driver's glum expression didn't change. He would expect anything from a passenger who taxed his horse with double the weight of an average fare, followed and fled from a pretty girl in the bargain, and whistled.

Nor was there a change when the Englishman wrapped the metal pieces in a ten franc note and handed up the lot. *"Bien, M'seiu'. It is good."* The cabby whipped up his horse in great dignity.

While he unpacked his bags Croyant debated the wisdom of calling upon the local police for an advance inspection of the registration forms at the hotel in Place Lamartine. These forms would be delivered at the local Sûreté in the morning. They would bear the new arrival's name, or whatever name she had chosen for the moment, and other information of dubious credibility. It would

not be unusual for a gendarme to look over the cards at
once. He decided against this procedure. He summoned
the porter of his own hotel, examined him critically and
concluded that he could be trusted up to a reasonable
point.

"The hotel in Place Lamartine, M'sieu'?" said the
porter. "It is the Hotel du Monde. The Hotel of the
World. A very big name for such a very little hotel."

"And you have a brother, or a cousin, or at least a
brother-in-law on its staff of servants?"

The porter nodded vigorously. "But yes, M'seiu'! One
who is closer than any of those. My fiancée attends the
beds. She is very intelligent, my Yvonne. She was a cocotte at Marseilles until I offered her marriage if she
would earn a dower degree of virtue."

Croyant murmured the hope that Yvonne would not
find a return to virtue too irksome and described the new
arrival in Place Lamartine. He mentioned also fifty francs
as a possible addition to Yvonne's dower. Little more
than an hour had passed when the porter confronted him
on the pavement in Rue des Arenes in front of the hotel.
He was just returning from Place Lamartine. Yvonne
had made notes on a piece of paper in a great childish
hand from which her fiancé read proudly.

The new guest was one Mademoiselle Tanya Amon.
As such she had signed the police registration forms.
She was not unknown at the Hotel du Monde, having
been a visitor of two, three former occasions. She was
Russian, as her name indicated, and possessed a refugee's *carte-d'identité* in lieu of a regular passport. On
former occasions she remained at the hotel three, four
days. It was not remembered where she went on her
departures. She seemed to have no friends or affairs in

Toulouse, yet she quite surely had a purpose in her visits.

"Yvonne suggests, M'sieu'," the porter volunteered, "that she is the mistress of a very rich man, even in Paris perhaps, but has a husband in Toulouse to whom she is still loyal and must now and then visit."

Yvonne's virtue might have become that of a bed attendant's, but her imagination was still a cocotte's.

"Why does your fiancée specify that her lover would be a rich man?" Croyant wondered.

"My Yvonne has made a list, for M'sieu', of the contents of her baggage. She remarks that Mademoiselle's under apparels are not cotton, or batiste, or even linen, but an expensive silk, M'sieu'. With the very best lace of Valenciennes."

The porter would have read the contents of Mademoiselle Amon's bags but Croyant stopped him. An arrangement was entered into which guaranteed his instant notification if Mademoiselle Amon prepared to depart from Toulouse or, indeed, if she prepared for an excursion into the town.

Croyant set out for a visit to the motor car dealer who had provided the American car that had so impressed Monsieur Cutot and his chief clerk. While he crossed the town Mademoiselle Amon and her ruby occupied his mind. An empress, a great lady of fashion, or a demimondaine who has found a lover of great wealth, might possess a ruby of value enough to ransom a city. The demimondaine perhaps might even wear such a jewel in public. But that demimondaine's name would be as well known in circles where the world's rare jewels are objects of professional interest as would be the identity of the empress or lady of fashion. What runner, for example, for a jewel house in Rue de la Paix or Bond Street could not recite at once the names and estates of the last five owners of the "Heart of Kasmir," the forty carat beauty found on the finger of the dead Countess Vetsera at Meyerling? Only forty carats, that deep blood-hued stone of tragedy, yet a jeweler's messenger would know that the Baroness Stromberg was its present owner. Croyant himself had told the Baroness Stromberg that there were only twenty other rubies more beautiful and rare, the Jeribzoff string, each stone approximating twenty carats more.

Mademoiselle Amon flaunted to the world a Jeribzoff ruby, lost to sight after The Panther's visit to the house of Count Jeribzoff in Leningrad—and no one who kept an account of famous jewels ever had suspected the existence of the slim and graceful Mademoiselle Amon!

Croyant had come to the turning into Rue Fontan, the street of the motor car agency. Suddenly he stopped, dead still. He realized he had been whistling the strange measures that had come to him unbidden earlier in the day. The tune had slipped out of the back of his mind again, but now that he was aware of it he couldn't get it back. It was there, lurking in his store of scores of familiar tunes, an alien yet a familiar, an elusive ghost of some past hour that his conscious mind had forgotten.

The thing puzzled him. His was an orderly mind. Out of almost every day's events he habitually sorted what should be kept for future reference or enjoyment, and these things he put away in a memory cell from which they could be instantly summoned. What was of no interest he promptly forgot. And what he forgot never came back. Yet unquestionably he had forgotten this tune and now it was trying to creep back into his whistling repertoire.

The motor car agency appeared at hand and he could

give no more puzzling to the elusive tune. He had carefully invented an excuse for the visit and discovered at once that he needed none. Bordeaux newspapers as well as the local sheets had called the motor car merchant to the attention of his neighbors as one who had unwittingly come within The Panther's orbit. Then the Paris papers, recounting the affair of Monte Carlo, mentioned him again in their recollections of Bordeaux.

The dealer enjoyed the sunlight of publicity and was eager to illumine the stranger.

"Never before, M'sieu'," he assured Croyant, "did opportunity come to me for the making of such a handsome profit. Out of the very skies he dropped, this young man of the dark glasses who dispensed his order for a hundred-and-fifty-thousand-franc automobile with the air of one who buys a cravat. Already in his hand was an order on the post office for one half the amount."

"It must have seemed like a fête day," Croyant admitted. "But why did he come to you? And why did he purchase here in Toulouse at all?"

"Ah, M'seiu' speaks as do the inspectors from the sûretés of Bordeaux and Paris. But what shall I say? Only that he seemed to know my agency. Even my name, which is not included in the street sign. He was familiar with Toulouse, that one."

"Was there a woman?"

"But no. He came alone each time, one time to leave his order and again to inspect his car and drive it away. The police have found no track of him in Toulouse yet I have reason to believe he remained within the city. When he came the second time he spoke of having seen me with my family, my wife and two little boys, M'sieu', upon both occasions of my attendance at the theater during the interval between his two visits. He was a very pleasant one to talk with, which I understand to be a quality of Americans."

Mademoiselle Yvonne devoted herself diligently to the earning of additional francs for her dower, earnings which laid no strain upon her resurrected virtue. Upon Croyant's return to his hotel the porter emerged from his box at the entrance door with an expression of great relief.

"It would have been a misfortune had M'sieu' not returned. Perhaps it will be of a consequence that the lady of Place Lamartine goes into the Place du Forum?"

` "To the old Roman arena? Do not all visitors to Toulouse go into the Place du Forum to see the ruins?"

"Some go to keep a rendezvous, M'sieu'."

Croyant gave the man a more interested attention. "Your Yvonne is proving that her ears are sharp, eh?"

The porter nodded with high pride in Yvonne. "One's wits are sharpened by the business of being a cocotte. There is a summons to the telephone at the Hotel du Monde. It is a voice that requires the Mademoiselle Yvonne is certain the summons was expected, for she came quickly and was not in negligée. What was said to her Yvonne could not hear but what she returned, that my fiancée noted for M'sieu'. Mademoiselle said, 'Very well. When it is dusk. At the dark column in the Place du Forum.' She said no more."

Already it was approaching dusk. Croyant turned back into Rue des Arenes and followed the curving street until it brought him onto the rail-guarded platform that provides a vantage walk from which one may look down into the ruin of what once was a great monument of Rome. In the amphitheater there are only broken, weed-grown tiers of seats, and a few worn stones and blocks of marble that suggest the lines of the stage. Of the proud colonnade that was once part of the stage wall only two columns remain, one of pure Carrara and the other, some distance off, of an almost black marble. These columns had been raised perhaps when Augustus ruled. They were there when Constantine stopped in Toulouse.

Croyant swept the scene with a searching glance. The arena appeared to be empty. Here and there were shadows cast by large stone blocks but they veiled no visitors. At the broad base of the dark marble column there was no movement. Croyant had viewed the ruin before but never in the twilight. For a moment The Panther, the Jeribzoff ruby, the round eyes and oval face of a girl who walked with a dancer's grace, retreated from his brain. He dwelt upon the simple loveliness of the two remaining shafts of stone crowned with their ornate capitals and supporting the last remnant of an architrave. In the growing dusk they had an airy, magic grace alien to a world that harbored murder.

He dismissed his reflections and moved to descend from the platform to the keeper's lodge on the lower level where, with the payment of a fee, the visitor may pass through an arch into the arena itself. But he was held against the platform rail.

Two figures emerged from behind the pedestal-like masonry on which the darker marble column stood, a man and woman who had been completely hidden from his view. The light was rapidly dimming but there was no mistaking the woman. Every line of her figure identified the girl of the station platform at Dieppe. She came around the column and stood with her back to the masonry while the man continued to talk to her. A faint light, cast from the garret window of a house on the street that passed the far end of the ruin, fell upon her and Croyant saw that she had fallen into a pose that was almost in rhythm with the classical simplicity of the setting.

The figure of the man was totally unfamiliar to Croyant. There was a provincial suggestion in his attire which made it possible for him to be a resident of Toulouse. He was a sharp contrast to the smart, Parisian grooming of the girl. She stood facing him, so that his back was turned to the platform. Croyant decided that the man was arguing with her, gesticulating animatedly, emphasizing every word with a movement of hands and shoulders.

Croyant could not see the girl's face distinctly but her head was lowered and he thought her whole body expressed a tragic tensity of resistance to the other's pleadings. When she looked up she shook her head quickly, angrily. Croyant thought she stamped a foot. Once she threw up her hand quickly in a protest of some sort. Croyant was sure that the thin light from the nearby window picked up the blood-red fires of her ruby.

He studied the man, though only his back was visible. But often the back of a man who talks with gestures will stand out in one's memory sharper than his face. The girl Croyant could pick out in any future crowd. He had the feeling that the time might come when he would want to find, and know him when he found him, anyone who might be near enough to her affairs to argue and plead with her as this man was doing.

Abruptly, the man appeared to end the scene in anger. He turned on his heel without warning and started toward the archway to the stone steps and the street. Croyant moved to cut him off, but the man turned back as abruptly as he had turned away. The girl had not moved. She still leaned against the masonry, her head high, as if she rested it against the column in line with her body.

A few short words were spoken, words without anger now. The man bent and touched his lips to the girl's. She laid her hand on his shoulder for a moment, then dropped it. He came across the arena, now, walking fast. Croyant had the impression that he examined every shadow as he passed it. This furtiveness kept the Englishman from confronting the man on the stone steps. He would like to have a closer view of his features, but it would be just as well not to have his own face scanned and remembered, perhaps instantly identified. A great many furtive men knew him by sight, men in all parts of Europe.

He waited until he heard the man's feet on the platform behind him. Quick, light treading feet, that would be running away from something no matter where they walked or how slowly. Croyant knew the sound of a foot-tread like that. When he was certain the fellow was out of sight down the curving street he went below, gave five francs to the woman who attended the lodge gate, and passed through the arch. The girl was not at the column. He thought, for a moment, she might have hurried across the arena and followed the man. But when he looked down a ruined aisle he saw her.

She had crossed to the Carrara column and seated herself on a flat cut stone at its base. Croyant stood for a moment in uncertainty. His presence among the ruins could not be considered strange. They were a public place and, as soon as the moon arose, they would be a rendezvous for a score of lovers and magnet to such tourists as were about. He wished there were a crowd around now, then he would not stand out to hold her attention. But he wanted, if possible, to get a close and leisurely look at her.

When he moved down the aisle he saw that she was completely unconscious of any intrusion upon her privacy.

She had fallen into an attitude of utter dejection, or despair. In the shadow of the column she seemed oblivious to any movement around her, and sat staring directly in front of her. Croyant saw her face for a moment clearly. He started before its Cassandra-like tragedy. While he was studying her she suddenly hid her face in her hands and fell to weeping. The Jeribzoff ruby shone clearly on her hand now.

Croyant cut across an open space of wiry grass and found a stone for himself against a square of crumbling masonry that once had been the base of a statue. When she uncovered her face and looked up he would be in a direct line with her and could, for the first time, photograph in his mind every feature. His body, however, would be virtually lost to her, so deep was the shadow he had chosen. His face would hardly be distinct. She might, he knew, be so astonished to see him there that she would speak to him. He would like it if she did. He had a remark prepared about the splendor of her unique ring. He would watch her face. Something might come into it that would lead him on to——?

Almost any scene might develop.

She continued to weep. Her sobs were deep, for her shoulders shook, but she wept silently. Curiously, Croyant began to be as impressed by her manner of weeping as he had been by the poise of her carriage. He thought of a young priestess weeping before an altar, too accustomed to the control of her body to lose it in her moment of misery.

All at once he realized that he had been so intent upon the girl and the mystery in the significance of her ring that he had forgotten himself and fallen to whistling. The elusive, unknown tune again. The girl dropped her hands and stared through the dusk at him. Her eyes were large and round, inordinately large and round, just as he had thought when he glimpsed them first at Dieppe. And in them now whatever there had been of her despair had fled and in its place was stark terror. Croyant sat dead still, fascinated. The girl's face, turned full upon him, was radiantly beautiful and strikingly expressive. In that moment, Croyant's lips but just stopped their whistling, her face was a mirror for every emotion.

Deliberately, Croyant began to whistle again, softly, and to his astonishment the strangely persistent tune came to his unconscious bidding. He was whistling it before he knew what he had chosen, and this time it was fixed in his mind. He would never forget it again.

The girl's expression changed. The terror subsided. She stared straight at Croyant, who feigned abstraction but watched her out of the corner of his eye. She seemed to listen for the cadence of his tune, and know when he approached the last of his few measures. A look of submission came into her face. Even relief, as if she came to a decision to throw off a restraint, or take an easier course.

She arose, drawing herself straight in a splendid pose. Croyant had the feeling that she commanded him by that momentary pose to disregard her recent weeping.

She moved quickly, coming across the 'patch of wiry grass to pass directly in front of him. She said no word but gave him a brief, unmistakable inclination of her head. He remained in his shadow watching her go down the aisle between the crumbling tiers of seats. She disappeared under the archway.

While he walked back along the Rue des Arenes to his hotel and his dinner he speculated upon the curious circumstance of a vagrant tune having such an effect upon the young woman. And he groped furiously through the sea of faces of which his mind had stored away impressions bridging years. He was certain he had seen the girl before Dieppe. Someplace, somewhere.

And he was equally certain that Mademoiselle Amon purposed that he see her again, and soon. Her nod was not to be misunderstood. It would have a consequence.

CHAPTER VI

A TOAST TO THE LITTLEST CLUE

AT the hotel were telegrams from London, from his directors. Their panic was not quieting down. The messages were a paraphrase of, "The Lord knows where he'll strike next." Scotland Yard had meaningly inquired if Major Croyant were co-operating with the Continental police and there was a suggestion from the Paris Sûreté that he call upon the Bureau for its full facilities.

The directors would like some assurance from the Major that he considered the advisability of moving directly against the source of the newly arisen risk to all the important jewels scattered across Europe. There was a personal message from his friend, Sir Philip Gregg, who was also an important director. It read, briefly, "What about it?"

Croyant scribbled a reply to his friend and had it despatched while he changed for dinner. "The losses have staggered me also. Don't begrudge me a pleasant vacation."

When he went down to dinner he discovered unwonted activity in the hotel lobbies. The evening train had brought a number of English and American tourists. Two large open cars were driving away from the main entrance when he stopped at the porter's box to leave an installment for Yvonne's dower.

When he entered the dining-room he found it crowded, a mixed scene of cosmopolitan fashion and "trippers" who stared at everybody and ordered the cheapest wines. He was brought up sharp, however, by an agreeable surprise. From one table where an impressive party was gathered, a girl arose and came to meet him with her face alight. Helen Avery, blithely American in every spontaneous movement. And from the table she left her mother's face smiled a greeting.

"Imagine running into you here in Toulouse!" the girl cried while she extended both of her hands. "We've been motoring—to Cannes tomorrow—a jolly time. Only Georges——"

Croyant had become aware, while she chattered on, of her fiancé, Georges Raynel, seated at the table with Mrs. Avery. The handsome face of the millionaire was turned to him with a look of recognition. Even at that distance Croyant thought the man's manner was somewhat subdued.

"Poor Georges," Helen Avery was saying. "He feels so deeply the death of his friend. It was horrible, wasn't it, Major?"

She, too, Croyant observed, had been deeply affected by the murder of Señor Veragua—who would have endowed her throat on her wedding morning with a priceless circlet of emeralds. He realized anew how close The Panther's bite had come to her by reason of her engagement to Raynel.

They went over to her party's table where Georges Raynel was host. Croyant had not seen him since that time at Deauville when Croyant had been instrumental in withdrawing the protection of insurance from the sapphires bestowed by Señor Veragua upon a young woman whose throat, he had decided, would come under the caressing touch of too many unknown fingers. Raynel had commented at that time, with a hearty laugh,

upon the widely different appraisal two men can make
of the same woman. And he had been sincerely pleased
when Croyant returned, "But you and I, Monsieur, see
Miss Avery with the same eyes."

There were strangers at the table and Raynel made the
introductions. An English pair, Mr. and Mrs. Ransom,
of whom Croyant knew vaguely as being of high standing in London's Mayfair. He had the impression that
they had entertained Mrs. Avery and Helen at their
house in the country. Also there was an Armand Duval,
a Frenchman, a colorless but rather self important young
man.

Mrs. Avery explained to her friends that Major Croyant had been her husband's closest friend, that they
earned medals together during the war, one always match-
ing the other's newest medal with a fresh decoration from
his own country. The Major took his attention from the
girl long enough to insist that all they did was to sit
on committees together. There was immediate protest
from Mrs. Avery but the girl re-engaged him.

"We've really been having a delightful trip. We
wanted to get Georges away from himself. We drove up
to Tarascon, circled around to Toulouse, and now back
to Cannes. We've two cars and there's room in one of
them beside me. Can't you look for somebody or hunt
something on the Riviera and go to Cannes with us in
the morning?"

Raynel had been talking to Mrs. Avery. He broke off
and turned to Croyant. "I'd like to support that suggestion, Major," he said, earnestly. "I'd give a great deal
if you'd come to Cannes with us. I'd like to talk with
you at length. An important decision would be involved."

The girl added more persuasion. "You really haven't
been keeping as careful track of me lately as you prom-

ised Father you would," she pointed out. "You should know what I've been doing."

His amused glance at Georges Raynel told her mutely that it was quite apparent that she had been doing a great deal. She kicked him under the table, maliciously.

"Any plans I make tonight," he said to her fiancé, "are bound to be upset tomorrow."

Raynel repeated, "I should like to see you at Cannes." He added, after a pause, "Otherwise, perhaps there will be an opportunity before we leave in the morning."

Croyant knew he was thinking of Veragua and The Panther. There was a momentary change in the man's expressive dark eyes. Fleetingly they revealed a hardness. of purpose. Helen Avery saw and touched his hand affectionately. Instantly his eyes were soft again.

Croyant was deeply interested in Raynel. His was one of those fortunes said to have been swiftly built on bold and brilliant speculations in America—in both the Americas, for his friendship with Veragua dated back to South America. In his face, sharply but handsomely chiseled, any one could read determination and inflexibility and, also, something of the romantic nature that appealed to the American girl he had chosen to share his millions. Croyant decided the man would spend much of his fortune, perhaps all of it, to get his own way, to accomplish a desire.

Georges Raynel might very well be The Panther's worst enemy, more dangerous to him than Dupree, or Weinrath. His five million franc reward would be only a drop in the bucket to what he would spend if necessary to bring about the success of the hunt for the slayer of his friend.

Helen Avery chattered of Deauville, of a recent leisurely sail along the Mediterranean in Georges Raynel's splendid yacht, of the bazaars at Scutari and an excursion to the desert's edge at Biskra where she had witnessed with Georges, as guests of the military commandment, a special performance of Ouled Nail dancers. Mr. and Mrs. Ransom claimed her attention and Croyant found a moment for a quiet study of the girl whose father he had promised to "look after her" when, even before her husband's death, Mrs. Avery began to prolong her visits to England and France. Mrs. Avery had always been ambitious for Helen and thought her prospects better in Europe than at home. She had brought a great deal of money to John Avery and he'd felt like letting her have her way. He'd wanted Helen, however, to be in love with the man she married—whatever his nationality. Croyant recalled, vaguely, that for a time Helen threatened to take matters into her own hands. There had been a young man at home, a young American who was partly Russian—strange, he thought, that the Russian background loomed so frequently during the last few days; The Panther and a burned house in Leningrad, the girl of Dieppe and the Place du Forum, and the Jeribzoff ruby turned up! Now he remembered, while he watched the animated play in Helen Avery's face, that she had been in love with a young man who was partly Russian. Russian mother, he remembered, who had come out of—Leningrad! He remembered distinctly, that the young man had followed Helen to Europe when her mother brought her away from him, and that Helen, on her part, had defied her mother and in turn had followed him to Leningrad. Something had happened, as so often does in these first love affairs. Mrs. Avery had appealed to him to "reason" with Helen, but the thing blew over. Here she was, bride-to-be of a man reputed to be one of Europe's most eligible and richest bachelors. Odd, how some young girls can get along!

Helen turned to him for a moment when Raynel was engaged with her mother and the English pair. "I do hope I have a chance to talk with you," she said, in an undertone, "about Georges and his friend, and the terrible murder. But I don't bring it up when Georges is around. He suffers so. Tell me, do you really believe there is such a person as The Panther? And if there is, won't they get him? Stop him?"

Before he could reply the girl was drawn back to the conversation going on about her, conversation in which all the others joined save the young man, Duval, who was carrying on a flirtation with an English woman at a nearby table.

Croyant returned to his own reflections. He was dubious about this match between Helen and Raynel. Obviously, Raynel was much older than the girl, well along in this thirties, although a fine physical specimen. His mouth was a symbol of arrogant self-confidence, but pleasantly shaped and always ready for an affable smile. Undoubtedly a man of breeding with a mixture of Latin and Nordic blood, by instinct a great gambler. There were tales of ten-million-franc stakes at the Gould Casino at Nice, of stakes lost with as little emotion as earned by stakes won.

He wondered if Helen had not been merely dazzled by this glamorous figure. If she knew her own mind, and really loved him—all well and good. Certainly her mother had laid no pressure upon her. The story of Raynel's ardent wooing was too well known. But try as he might Croyant couldn't drive from his mind a clairvoyant vision of The Panther striking at his five-million-franc foe through the daughter of his trench-friend, John Avery.

The young man, Duval, spoke at last. A comment on the wine. Croyant agreed with whatever the comment was. He didn't hear it clearly for at that moment he glanced up the dining-room toward the few steps that descended to the dining-room floor from the higher level of the tea lounge that opened off from the lobbies.

There, at the head of the steps, scanning the crowd seated at the tables, was Mademoiselle Amon.

She had changed to a simple frock of clinging lines, high necked and full sleeved. Not a dinner gown, but quite in keeping with the mixed crowd in the dining-room. As she stood there, calmly surveying the scene as if she hunted a face more than a table, she was more radiant in her dark beauty than many women in the room who had donned elaborate evening gowns.

A waiter hurried forward and stood, expectant, at the bottom of the steps. She ignored him for another moment. Then Croyant had the impression that her glance found him. She seemed to examine the rest of the party at the table. The young man, Duval, saw her and stared quite openly. Georges Raynel glanced up the room, seemed to take her in from head to foot, and then returned his attention to Mrs. Avery.

The girl moved and came down the steps with the casual air a woman adopts when she knows that a room full of people are staring at her. She shook her head when the waiter proposed a table deep in the room, and indicated one not far from the steps to the tea lounge. When she sat down she was hidden from Croyant's view.

At the Avery table the meal drew towards coffee. Helen reminded Georges Raynel that they had planned to see the old Roman arena in the moonlight. It was agreed that the party should walk the short distance along Rue des Arenes to Place du Forum and have coffee when they returned. Helen and her mother pleaded with Croyant to go along, but he demurred. He had seen the forum once under the mystic spell of the moon, he explained, and declared it to be one of the experiences that should never be repeated.

"Why!" Helen cried. "You are almost romantic. Who'd ever have thought it of you?"

"No one," he assured her solemnly, and walked with her to the tea lounge where, he said, he would probably be waiting when they returned.

He ordered coffee and brandy to be served him in the lounge. He seated himself in a cane chair before a wicker table. He could look down, over a rail, and see the back of Mademoiselle Amon's neck. But, he looked away quickly when he saw that she had brought out her vanity and was covertly watching his every movement reflected in its tiny enlarging mirror!

Presently he was aware that a waiter had answered her summons and that she was paying her *addition*. She got up and came around to the steps and mounted them slowly. On the tea lounge level she paused a moment to adjust her hat and seemed to be dubious of its tilt. She looked around and chose a mirror that hung on the wall directly behind Croyant. There were other mirrors which she could have approached without disturbing any of the loiterers in the lounge but she deliberately moved toward Croyant's and he had to rise hastily and hold back his chair to allow her to pass.

She made a little gesture of apology and murmured, "Pardon, M'seiu'."

She looked into the mirror and pulled her hat closer over her dark hair. Her ruby flashed when she lifted a hand to adjust the collar of her frock at the back of her neck. And in this action she dropped her hand-bag.

Croyant, with instant understanding, bent to recover it. Her own movement toward it seemed instinctive yet her hand deliberately sought his when they touched the fallen bag and she thrust a tightly folded bit of paper into his fingers.

Then, with a murmur of thanks, she was gone.

He returned to his table and quickly spread the paper. It was a sheet which bore the masthead of the Hotel du Monde. On it was written in a meticulous hand, "Michael Ballou is in Cannes. I have failed. He has shown me the rubies and given me one of them but of what you want there is no sign. Perhaps they are close. He does not suspect me but it is useless for me to go on. And I can not."

Croyant regarded the sheet of paper quizzically. "Now who," he murmured to himself, "can Michael Ballou be?"

He chanced to glance across his coffee cup toward the entrance doors of the lobby. There was a narrow view of the street through the doors and he was just in time to see Mademoiselle Amon's unmistakable figure stepping into one of the few taxis of which Toulouse boasts. He saw the chauffeur settle her in her seat and reach inside his car to fumble about her feet as if he rearranged luggage.

He came to a quick decision. Thrusting the paper into his pocket he strode across the lobby and reached the porter's box just as the taxi drew away with a noisy squeak of its high pitched horn.

The porter emerged from his box with excitement. "But this minute, M'sieu', was my Yvonne able to make use of a telephone in Place Lamartine. But it is not too late. The Mademoiselle is departing. With her baggage.

A sudden change in her plans to remain. She went directly to the station but——"

"To the station?" Croyant repeated. "Your Yvonne for once mislaid her wits. That was the Mademoiselle who just went out. She dined here."

The porter was crestfallen. "Yvonne could not have been mistaken. Again the Mademoiselle altered her plans. She instructed her driver to take her to the station. But there is time for M'sieu'. There is no train for yet a full hour. The Paris train."

With an hour to spare Croyant was content with one of the horsedrawn vehicles that waited in Rue des Arenes. But at the station there was no sign of Mademoiselle Amon. Her faster taxi should have dropped her ten minutes before. A Victoria driver assured him there had been no taxi with any sort of passenger, and who indeed would come to wait an hour for the train?

Croyant had a premonition that Mademoiselle Amon would not arrive at any time. He waited across the street, from where he could command a good view of the station approaches. While he waited he reconstructed the scene in the Forum. Mademoiselle Amon's apparent recognition of the strange tune he unconsciously whistled. The change that came over her. The terror that replaced her dejection, and the submission that came into her large eyes.

The tune affected her, but not as a mere memory attached to some episode of the past. It had a distinct meaning to her. It brought that inclination of her head when she left the ruins. It brought her to the hotel in Rue des Arenes—and how did she know he would be dining there?

When she came close to him in the arena, and passed him in the tea lounge, there was no sign that she knew him for what he was. Rather, acceptance of him as an agent. Agent for whom?

He visualized the note that was tucked in his pocket. "Michael Ballou is in Cannes." To whom was it important that Michael Ballou was in Cannes? Not to him. Inevitably his thoughts came to the last line in the note. It had engaged his attention apart from the rest when he read it spread on his table in the tea lounge. "And I can not." Could not "go on," she meant. He thought that when he examined the note again he would discover that that last line had been written in some sort of agitation. As if it were an afterthought, a welling up. Whoever Michael Ballou was, Mademoiselle Amon not only found it useless to spy on him any longer, but had discovered that the woman in her refused to do him that disservice.

A disservice for whose benefit?

A taxi drew up at the platform across the street. He watched while a passenger descended. A man with numerous bags. The chauffeur carried the bags to the waiting room and Croyant recognized him with a start. A while before he had seen him arranging her bags about the feet of Mademoiselle Amon in front of the hotel in the Rue des Arenes.

He hurried across the street, got into the empty cab and gave the name of his hotel. A block from the station he ordered the driver to draw up to the pavement, invited him to regard a handful of francs, and asked him what he had done with his recent passenger.

The man's information was interesting.

He had been summoned to the Hotel du Monde. The lady had ordered him openly to take her to the station. It was not his business, M'sieu', to warn the lady that more than an hour must elapse before a train's departure. Women have whims no one can understand. "But what is it that occurs, M'sieu', when we turn out of Place Lamartine? 'I have changed my mind, driver. You will stop in Rue des Arenes and wait while I dine.' But that is not all, M'sieu'. As if it is a good trick, this change of the mind, she does it again. When she has dined it is 'Now, to the station.' But when we would pass the Place du Forum she taps on my window. 'Go around the ruins to the back. Stop where a car waits.' A car waited, M'sieu'. A big car with a long nose. At the wheel was a man who wore dark glasses. My fare paid me and entered the big car and was driven away."

Mrs. Avery and Helen were in the tea lounge when he reentered the hotel. The Ransoms and young Duval were not in sight. Georges Raynel, Mrs. Avery explained, had gone to his apartment to attend to some letter-writing.

"Helen and I thought you would be coming back. The attendant told us you had left your coffee untouched."

He would have liked to give his thoughts to Mademoiselle Amon and re-examine her note, but there was no dodging Mrs. Avery, and Helen had a hundred things to say to him. And he liked to be near the fair young American girl. He liked to think of her as something virginal in a world full of betrayals. She took him back into his own youth.

He remembered, suddenly, that Mrs. Avery was a musician. In her New York home, before Helen's father died, she had been surrounded by musicians and in Europe she took an interest in all their works.

To Helen he said, with a grimace at her readiness to poke fun at him, "I've been taking my whistling rather seriously, of late." To her mother he explained, "I've caught myself whistling a thing I can't place. Perhaps you'll recognize it." And disregarding Helen's wrinkled nose he came out with it, whistling it softly, its notes coming now with the ease of an old familiar.

Mrs. Avery listened intently. She nodded once, as if to announce that she identified it, then frowned. Whatever recognition came close had escaped her.

Helen listened, and reached a hand to touch Croyant's wrist, but withdrew it. When Croyant glanced at her she was looking down, her face hidden. Her hand, dropped to the table, quivered.

"I know it," she said in a small, tremulous voice. "Don't you remember, Mother? In Warsaw—at the opera —Michael——"

Her voice quavered out. She got up suddenly and without giving Croyant a look at her face hurried across the lounge and disappeared through the door to a chamber reserved for women who would repair their make-up. Croyant, that "Michael" ringing in his ears, stared at her mother.

Mrs. Avery made no attempt to hide a worried expression. "You didn't know, of course," she said, "but I'm sorry you had to touch an old wound with your melody. I remember it now. The temple girl's dance from Silberta's *Dancer of Kashmir*. We saw it produced in Warsaw a year or so ago. The dancer and her music never could be completely forgotten."

Croyant jerked upright so suddenly that Mrs. Avery started. A veil was lifting in his brain to uncover a secret recess of memory. He saw the stage of a theater in Berlin. A temple scene, the Kumbarti fires of sacrifice burning on an altar. The wild, pagan dance of the god's wives and the première ballerina who danced out from among them to the strains of the music he had whistled to throw herself into the altar fires. A dancer whose name rang across Europe and then was lost in oblivion.

"You are remembering too?" Mrs. Avery said.

"She was Darya Vaskaya," he replied. "A Russian who had her season and has disappeared."

He might have added, but he didn't, that Darya Vaskaya had just disappeared a second time, in a car from behind Place du Forum, in the guise of Mademoiselle Amon.

Mrs. Avery nodded in her turn. "She came to Warsaw from Berlin. A young man was with us the night of her debut. Helen was in love with him, but I didn't think it wise. It was her last evening with him, for I brought her to Paris the next day. You know of him, that there was such a one. An American whose mother was Russian. You will remember that she met him at home and he followed her over here."

"And his name was 'Michael'?"

"At home he was Michael Ballou, but over here there was some reason why he called himself Michael Jeribzoff. I'm afraid, very much, that Helen has never got over him."

The mother went to find her daughter and Croyant went into the hotel bar to find a table where he could be alone, safe from interruption.

He spread before him Mademoiselle Amon's—Darya Vaskaya's—note. He tried to study it but discovered that when he looked at it the final sentence overshadowed the rest of it. "And I can not!"—go on.

There was a break between what had been written before and the last sentence. She had finished her note. Her pen had begun to go aside. She brought it back and wrote the last four words. Wrote them quickly, defiantly. Almost in a different handwriting. The old, old story of the spy who had fallen in love with her victim.

He thought of the dancer in Warsaw—a year ago!—

who had fallen in love. That time she was being spied upon. She must have known, for she telephoned to Dupree to tell him that her lover was being tortured close to his death by The Panther.

Darya Vaskaya danced in Warsaw to the tune he had whistled in Place du Forum. Darya Vaskaya's lover in Warsaw sent Dupree to the house in Leningrad where the cat's head was found. The safe was open, the Jeribzoff rubies gone.

Croyant fingered his glass of Chartreuse, twisting it so that its honey-gold fluid was a miniature whirlpool. He looked into it and saw a dark shape in a burgundy gown coming down a stairway behind a white fan. He shook this vision out of his mind and glanced at the note held on the table top by his other hand.

"Michael Ballou is in Cannes.—He has shown me the rubies—Of what you want there is no sign."

Mrs. Avery's voice came to him quite clearly. "At home he is Michael Ballou. Over here—Michael Jeribzoff."

Little Helen was in love, not with the rich and gallant Georges Raynel, but Michael Ballou—Jeribzoff.

That thought, Croyant put away quickly. Helen mustn't be brought into anything concerning The Panther and Darya Vaskaya.

But why was Michael Ballou, who was in Cannes, also a Jeribzoff—with whom Darya Vaskaya couldn't "go on"? Who had shown her the Jeribzoff rubies and given her the priceless gem that shone on her finger?

What was it "somebody" wanted of which Darya had found no sign? "Somebody" who wasn't concerned about the rubies themselves? And who was the "somebody" for whom the note was intended?

He folded the note with a sudden sweep of his fingers

and put it into his pocket. He lifted his glass and held it poised in the air for an instant before he drained it. In the instant he murmured, half aloud, "Monsieur la Panthère, let us drink to Dupree's littlest clue!"

He was awakened in the morning by the insistent clamor of the bell at the head of his bed. Helen Avery's voice came over the line, as cheerful and bright as the morning sun that had begun to stream through the windows.

"I'll be glad," he grumbled, "when you're married. You'll learn that a man likes to sleep mornings."

"You mean that I'll teach my husband that the world is at its best when it faces the new day. But are you coming to Cannes?"

"At least I'll come down to see you off."

"Please hurry. Georges is terrible when he's made up his mind. He's determined to leave at nine. And he wants to talk to you. Also I've got to have your ear. It's something I ought to sit in your lap and talk about but I could never get into a lap in the morning. I'll talk standing up."

There were telegrams under his door but he thrust them into his pocket unopened. Mrs. Avery, Helen and Raynel, the Ransoms and Duval were grouped in the lobby. Their two open cars waited in Rue des Arenes. Helen came up first to Croyant but Georges Raynel was close behind her. He insisted gently that she wait for her session with the Englishman and she drew back with a moue.

Raynel came to his point with sharp directness. "I am sorry you can't come to Cannes, but I understand, of course, that circumstances dictate your movements."

"Just now," Croyant returned, "I am making my own circumstances. A vacation. We don't search for stolen jewelry in Russia, nowadays, so I may go there. Any place where there'll be no business for me to attend to. Possibly the Riviera, where any diamond may be a stolen gem and I'd feel more at home."

Raynel smiled. "I fancy you'd find it harder to play than to work. However, I'd like to spoil your plans for a vacation." His face sobered. His mouth set into hard lines. "I should like you to think of me as a friend, Major, particularly because of Miss Avery. Then you will understand my feeling about Alphonse Veragua. The man who killed him must be caught and punished. I am not concerned that he is one whom the police seem to think of with shudders. The Panther or a common crook, it would be the same. I have offered a large reward but I have no intention of stopping there. I know your reputation. I feel that you, if any man, could give me the murderer's execution as a wedding present. If you will undertake the job I shall put at your disposal every penny I have. Don't give me your answer now. We are all staying at Cannes. I shall hope to see you there and know that you've decided to help me."

The man's appeal had become an intensity of emotion. Croyant felt his magnetism. He would be a hard man to swerve from a course he had decided upon.

Helen came at once when Raynel rejoined his party. She took Croyant into a corner of the lounge. Wistfulness had crept into her mobile mouth.

"I don't want you to misunderstand—about last night," she said, her brown eyes pleading up to him. "I do love Georges."

She said it with all of a woman's will to make her words sound like a vow but Croyant, who cared little for what people said, man or woman, but a great deal for what was in their eyes while they spoke, knew in that moment that she did not love Georges Raynel, for all of his glamor and devotion to her. He knew that her heart had stopped beating back in Warsaw where she left a mysterious young man whose name one place was Ballou, at another, Jeribzoff.

"Your father," he said, "had a single thought. He wanted you to love and be loved. If you've managed that you've done fine."

She nodded. "Yes. I've done fine. I love and I am loved. And I shall have gobs of money. That's enough for any girl, isn't it?"

She was smiling brightly. Croyant thought the smile a deed of bravery.

"That's what I wanted you to know. That he *is* out of my mind. I am not unfair, even a little bit, to Georges. Last night, just for a moment, you brought Michael back. He's gone again, now. Back in Warsaw, where I left him. He went to Leningrad, where his Russian people are. I'm sure he's married a Russian girl. And I'm to marry Georges. You see, everything is all right with me."

While he watched the party drive off, watched them until they disappeared toward the Place du Forum and the open highway beyond, he wondered if everything was all right with her. He felt a premonition. She was going to Cannes. Her Michael was in Cannes. Darya Vaskaya had been spying upon him. Her Georges Raynel was defying The Panther, and the young man who would never be out of her mind, and who might claim her at any time he wished, Croyant was afraid, had been spied upon by Darya Vaskaya in the interests of——!

He was conscious of a cab drawing up to the hotel curb and of a figure that descended. He turned about. The man who had descended to the pavement regarded him glumly. Croyant showed no surprise or said no greet-

ing. He spoke to the other as if he but a moment ago had
turned away from him.

"Here's going backward for you, Dupree. Find out if
Michael Ballou who is also Michael Jeribzoff was in
Leningrad when The Panther visited the house in Nevsky
Prospekt."

"Meanwhile, your telegram from Dieppe?"

"A lot of water has passed over the dam since then,
my friend."

CHAPTER VII

THE YOUNG MAN AT CANNES

IT is a full two weeks since Dupree came in answer to Croyant's cryptic telegram from the station platform at Dieppe to confront him before the hotel in Rue des Arenes at Toulouse. The sun is shining in Cannes. Close to the gardens of the Casino a military band is playing the Valse Triste. The audience assembled about the band rotunda wears tinted glasses and furs. The glaring sun is doing its best to heat the day, but an inconsiderate wind is stealing down from the Alpes Maritimes.

It is warmer along the shop fronts in the Croisette, the Fifth Avenue and Rue de la Paix and Bond Street of Cannes. Here there is a brilliant stream of shoppers, real and window, examining the display of precious things, curious bits of jade, enameled boxes, jewels, damask stuffs and glistening dresses. In and out of the throng a news vendor weaves under his red hat. Many buy his papers, French, English, and American editions from Paris, who would not ordinarily be interested in the day's news. But there has been a tragedy on the lower road from Monte Carlo to Mentone. An American millionaire who has lived - on the Riviera since his own country went dry, was killed last night when his car, returning from up the coast, swerved from the road at a turn and rolled down the hill which, at that point, descended steeply into a stone floored canyon.

There were other passengers in the American's car,

including, mysteriously, an inspector of police attached to the Administration at Nice. He was so badly torn that he died after a few hours. The chauffeur was in a critical condition. The other passenger, the American's secretary, a young man, was also in a bad way.

The American, a Mr. Albert Whelan, was celebrated for his parties and his freedom with his American dollars. Accordingly he was widely liked along the playshore. His untimely death was something of a shock to many who would not permit themselves easily to be shocked. And it was thought strange that his car should have left the road at that particular spot. The road was broad, for the turn, and the turn itself was gentle and graded. Drivers returning from up the coast in a hurry were accustomed to take the turn at any speed, from fifty miles an hour down. There had never been a serious accident at that point before.

People are buying the news vendors' papers and reading about Mr. Whelan with the sad realization that they couldn't flock out to his villa any more and enjoy his excellent fare of wines and whiskeys. While they read they are wondering if any or all of the little ladies Mr. Whelan favored had been thoughtful enough to well feather their nests. Probably so.

Beyond the Croisette, the Esplanade is spread with cane chairs and anyone may sit here, for one franc for the morning, and look out over the sea. There are not many vacant chairs, today, for the season is in full swing. Parasols gleam in a hundred colors. There are silk frocks and mink wraps. There are people of all shapes and sizes from a little Japanese to a bulky Moor from Morocco in turban and white robes.

A rug pedler slips along the inner rim of the Esplanade. A fellow who might be fairly tall if he should stand up straight. But his back is bent under his roll of rugs. He wears a curious hat, part fez, part cap with a long peak that hides much of his dirty face. Someone else had worn out his shoes long before he adapted them to his own feet. A furtive, unpleasant figure who hurried as fast as he could to get past the dawdling assemblage scattered among the franc-a-morning chairs.

Beyond the Esplanade is a less fashionable stretch where there are free benches for any who may want to use them. From here one may look over a sweep of the bay where the white yachts ride at anchor. One of the white yachts, one of the longest and most graceful, will someday be Helen Avery's. It is Georges Raynel's now, but it is generally understood he will make it one of his gifts to his bride. People hope she will entertain aboard as lavishly as Georges Raynel did before the death of his friend and probably will again. A party in white is coming down a ladder, two or three men and two or three women. They get into a gig and start for the shore. One of them may be Helen herself, but from the benches one would need a glass to make sure.

On one of the benches a young man sits under a shivering palm. He is a good-looking young man, not yet in his thirties surely, with clear eyes and an extremely well shaped mouth. A rather delicate mouth, as if it were very sensitive. He wears clothes of a faultless make, either American or English. He really should be sitting in one of the chairs on the gay Esplanade, but for some reason he has chosen the free benches which mostly are occupied by people down in their luck.

The young man is gazing across the bay a little mockingly, a little grimly. He is looking directly at the white yacht of Georges Raynel. His glance follows the party getting into the gig. When the gig disappears landward his gaze swings in a circle that takes in the spires of the old church, "Notre Dame d'Espérance," where Helen Avery will be married, and comes back to the walk in front of him to meet the sharp, piercing glance of the rug pedler.

There is something in the pedler's face that causes him to start, and frown with impatience.

"You again?" he grumbles. "Haven't you learned yet that I have no use for a rug?"

"Good luck rugs, M'sieu'," the pedler wheedles in a curious pitch that is like a falsetto laid upon a hoarse basso. "You stand on my rugs while you make a wish— roulette, chemin de fer, baccarat, whatever good luck M'sieu' desires. Good luck comes. See, I have a pretty new one."

He would unroll his pack but the young man waves him off angrily.

The pedler goes on, past the Cercle Nautique, until he comes to the splendid terraces of the Hotel Crillon. He starts across the marble terrace past the potted palms and fuchsia and when an attendant liveried in bright blue rushes up to brush him off as vermin he does not turn tail. He shakes his head and gesticulates and another attendant, in a higher livery comes, and still another who is in no livery at all and is, therefore, an officer of the hotel staff.

While the rug pedler argues on the terrace below, Major Croyant, in a comfortable suite on the fifth floor, is having trouble with two Sealyham dogs who want to taste his shoe polish. The dogs belong to a gay young woman who has dropped in upon Croyant to have a drink. He is the only man in Cannes or anywhere else before whom Clare Fraser will take a drink in the morning. "Even my husband," she has a way of saying, "was shocked until the very day of his death whenever I took a highball in the morning. Unlady-like, he called it."

Clare Fraser is a china-doll kind of woman, with flaxen hair and blue eyes. She seems not to take her widowhood seriously, though it could not be long since she was bereaved. She can't be much more than thirty if, indeed, she is that old. She seems to have a great deal of money, is an American and a recent addition to the Riviera crowd, and already has begun to cut quite a splurge. She has shown a great fondness for Major Croyant, who seems to have been in earnest when he wired his friend, Sir Philip Gregg, that no matter how panicky the directors were, he was going to take a vacation. He chose the Riviera, after all, and Clare Fraser picked him up at once, as soon as she arrived. She says he reminds her of her late lamented "Bill" who was also a big man.

"Now that I've had my drink," says Mrs. Fraser, "I'll stop only long enough to say how terrible it was for poor Albert Whelan to be killed last night. And what was the policeman, a detective inspector, doing in his car?"

"It would have been just as terrible for anyone," Croyant replies, "and you are not the only one wondering, so it seems, about the inspector. A little too high in rank to have been a body guard."

"Albert had been acting queerly of late. Always looking around corners, I thought."

Mrs. Fraser gathered the dog leashes. "I'll be glad," she says at the door, "when I find some nice young man to take Pete and Betsy for their walks."

She tosses the Major a radiant smile from his door. She stops to listen while he answers a telephone call from a hotel staff captain. It is something about a rug pedler and Croyant is saying, "Some mistake. What the devil would I do with a rug?"

Mrs. Fraser laughs. "They call them 'good luck' rugs, Major."

The staff captain below is saying over the wire, "The fellow is quite insistent, Monsieur. He says he has a rug he is to deliver into your hands. He says he was sent by someone of the name of Michael."

Mrs. Fraser frowns a little when she hears Croyant say, "Send him to my rooms."

"What on earth," she exclaims, "do you do that for? If you let him unroll his pack he'll sell you the lot. I'll wait and watch."

"Peter and Betsy are impatient," the Major returns. "And they might bite a rug pedler."

So Mrs. Fraser understands she's not wanted and goes, and from the service lift used by the servants, the pedler is spewn into the corridor and shown to Croyant's door.

He bows and scrapes before the attendant who had escorted him. Croyant waves him into the room and shuts the corridor door. The pedler sweeps off his curious hat and bobs his head repeatedly before the big man who is regarding him with a quizzical glumness.

"Well," Croyant growls. "What's the meaning of 'Michael'? I don't remember anyone of that name."

There is a chuckle from under the rug seller's matted beard. He suddenly stands straight and a sweep of his hand pulls off a coal black wig. Croyant grunts and for an instant looks a bit sheepish.

"Sacrebleu!" swears Dupree. "The rug business is not a joke!"

"A man wouldn't go into it," Croyant agrees, "without a reason."

"Not a sane man. No more than would a sane man take a vacation when there is work to be done." The Frenchman's eyes suddenly were alive with glints. He dropped his voice. "Work to be done, and quickly, my friend. Last night, under our very noses, he swoops down upon the American. On the very day he named when he served Albert Whelan with the cat's head."

Croyant's mouth sets grimly.

"I took it for granted that it was no accident that sent the American's car hurtling down the hill from the Lower Road."

"You knew that M'sieu' Whelan had received the drawing, scratched on an ivory card counter? But I have not seen you meanwhile. I could not have told you."

Croyant smiles. "Others have not neglected me as you have, Ariste. Whelan hurried to the Police Jurisdiction as soon as he received the decorated card counter. A cool million and a half was demanded. To be carried with him and turned over when he should find himself suddenly and unexpectedly called upon."

"When he came to the police he sentenced himself to death. That I knew. 'Within one week,' read the warning. Always a guard was with him. Even while he slept. He was a stubborn man. He would not be intimidated and robbed. Alas! While an Inspector of Police, an armed chauffeur and armed secretary watch the road for the smallest movement of a shadow, a block of wood, cleverly turned to divert the wheels, is thrust from a bush in the path of Monsieur's car. Monsieur may not die. People survive motor accidents of the utmost gravity. But The Panther makes certain. Leisurely he selects the groaning form of the millionaire and fires a bullet into it, thus insuring death."

"A bullet?" Croyant exclaims. "The papers say nothing of that."

"Nor will they. Nor of the cat's head. We will keep that a secret from the public if we can."

Croyant looks out his window. He follows the curving shore of the Gulf of Napoule and rests his eyes for a moment on the ancient tower that was built by the Saracens and still stands. He is thinking, but of what his face doesn't tell.

Dupree grumbles into his false beard which he does not remove because of the gluing required to affix it. He drains a goblet of wine from a bottle on Croyant's table. Croyant turns from the window.

"You found the young man?"

Dupree makes a grimace of distaste. "I peddle my rugs in the *boits de nuit* of Marseilles and the bistros of Nice. I wheedle coppers from the fish wives of the Condamime and I go wherever the hard-lucks gather. But where do I find him? Sunning himself and his exquisite tailorings at the very edge of the Croisette where all the world gathers. He comes every day to look into the water."

Croyant waits while the other helps himself to more of the wine. Dupree's humor is improving. In a moment he will come to the real object of the visit he was so careful to hide under his masquerade. He will tell Croyant that through Moscow the Paris Sûreté has learned that Michael Ballou, otherwise Michael Jeribzoff, was in Leningrad on the night The Panther was in Nevsky Prospekt. And he will tell him, also, that the chauffeur and detective and chief clerk at Bordeaux have examined photographs of Darya Vaskaya, which Croyant received some ten days ago from his agents in Warsaw, and that there is no longer any doubt that it was she who came down the stairs behind the great white fan. They will talk quite a while, Croyant and Dupree.

The news vendor in the Croisette came along the Esplanade. He still had papers to sell so he went on into the less fashionable extension of the boulevarde. As a matter of fact it was here that he sold the most of his local Cannes papers. People who sat on the free benches were often interested in the local want-ad columns.

The young man in the well-cut suit who had been bothered every day for the last few days by a rug pedler bought a paper, *Les Affaires* of Cannes. Before he opened it he looked out into the bay. The gig was returning to the long white yacht. He could tell that it was empty save of its helmsman and one other who would be a sailor. He stirred on his bench and looked at the paper in his hands. The mocking light in his darkish eyes was more pronounced. His sensitive mouth curled a little, as if he felt a great scorn. He made a motion with the hand that held the paper, then he opened the sheets.

He opened directly to the page devoted to small advertisements. They were not separated into classifications, these small announcements, as in an American paper, but all run together. A young woman, twenty-two and *très joli*, wished to know a young man who was in business. Soldiers and sailors and other transients not welcome. Underneath this, a "very pretty brunette, 30, affectionate, desires arrangement with gentleman, 40."

The young man skipped all of these however and found at once the announcement he sought.

> WANTED. Personal secretary, male, young, of pleasing personality, good linguist. Must know Russian, English, French. Write fully to the Villa Amette, La Grasse.

When he found the announcement that the owner of Villa Amette, whoever he or she was, desired a personal secretary, he frowned. For a moment his shoulders slumped a little, as if he were disappointed. Then he took courage. Two days ago he had answered that advertisement. His application would not have been delivered, perhaps, until yesterday. Or it might not have received consideration until yesterday. If he were to be given a personal inspection at Villa Amette, he would hardly receive a summons until tomorrow. It was very likely the advertisement would be continued until a satisfactory applicant had been chosen.

He turned a leaf of the newspaper. There was a glaring headline describing the misfortune that had come upon the millionaire American, Albert Whelan, and his companions in his car. A Greek tourist had thrown six sixes in the dice room at the Casino and won twenty thousand francs. There was other important news, but the young man turned at once to the columns devoted to personalities.

"M. Georges Raynel was host last night to the first party given on board his yacht, the *Ariadne,* since the unhappy tragedy which ended the life of his friend, Señor Alphonse Veragua, some three weeks ago. Monsieur Raynel's guests of honor were Mrs. John Avery and her lovely daughter, Miss Helen Avery, who is M. Raynel's fiancée. Miss Avery was enchanting in a simple frock of ivory point. She wore no jewels save the huge pearl which was her fiancé's engagement gift. While the party was at its merriest there was a touching interruption when M. Raynel suddenly called upon his guests to drink, in silence, a toast to his friend, Señor Veragua. Miss Avery is becoming very popular along the Riviera. It is understood that she will spend her honeymoon in her native America, whither she and her husband will travel in the *Ariadne*."

The young man read the social item a second time. He glanced onto the bay. The gig had been drawn up the *Ariadne's* side, and hung from its davits.

He dropped the paper about his feet, as people do who sit on the free benches, and brought out a gold case from which he chose a cheap cigarette. He took a deep inhalation, his eyes almost closed.

A drably dressed man in a broad-brimmed hat approached the bench. The young man saw only his bulk at first and may have thought it was the rug pedler coming back, for he moved angrily. But the man was not the pedler. He passed the bench, but he turned after a step or two and came back. He sat down carefully and with some exertion, as if his body were not in the best of condition. He spoke in Russian, with a gentle intonation.

"So much of each day's news is tragic."

The young man drew sharply on his cigarette. A white shadow seemed to cross his mouth. He stared at the stranger with a queer look in his eyes, of both fear and suspicion.

Yet there was something familiar about the squat, bulky person in the broad-brimmed hat. The look in his eyes deepened and he seemed to draw away, to shrink. Yet the other's glance was warmly soft.

"M'sieu' will pardon," the stranger said, again in Russian. "I took you to be Russian, like myself. And in a foreign land one's own are good to see. But now that I see you closely, I am not so sure. Yet I see that you understand me."

"I—I assure you that you are mistaken," the young man said with an obvious effort to be coldly aloof which

failed because of a too earnest wish to be convincing. "I
am an American." Suddenly he realized how oddly it
must sound to hear a man say he is an American in perfect Russian.

The stranger smiled. He seemed to be compellingly
gentle. Like an actor who plays a role which calls for
mildness.

"I am a Khamov," he said. "Makar Ivanovitch Khamov. I think we are neighbors. Did I not see you last
night, and other nights? I have a room in rue des Pomegranates."

The young man seemed to know why, now, the stranger
had been familiar.

"Yes," he answered. "I am also living in rue des Pomegranates." He paused to smile a little wryly. Few men
live in rue des Pomegranates. It is a street given over to
young women and women who pretend to be young, with
very red mouths. Pomegranate mouths. With a voluptuous taste if you are not overly particular about the
freshness of your fruit and like it to be inexpensive. But
lodgings are cheap and it is the one street in Cannes
where your neighbor minds her own business and mixes
not at all in yours. "My name," the young man finished
in common courtesy, "is Michael Ballou. You see I am
an American as I said."

"But there is Russian blood," the other insisted. "We
will not speak of it, because I understand, but it is in
your features and in your tongue."

The young man picked out a phrase. "What is it you
understand?" He spoke sharply.

Khamov seemed not to hear.

"I have seen an actor, or a great actress, try to hide
the touch of the steppes that is in his being, her being,
while on a stage. I remember a great dancer who ab-

sorbed the soul and the very breath of a Hindu temple girl which she danced before an altar fire—but never could she hide, while she danced with a temple girl's khol on her eyelids, that under the lids were Russian eyes. I wonder——" He stopped and seemed lost in thought for a moment. The young man had stiffened, and was eyeing him closely. He demanded again,

"What was it that you understood when I told you my name?"

The stranger took up where he had left off.

"I wonder what has become of her? It was in Warsaw I saw her. A year ago. It was her opening night and there was a very brilliant audience. Sometime after, not very long, I left Poland, for Leningrad. I wanted to go into Nevsky Prospekt. I have not heard of the dancer since. Her name——" He turned full upon his young companion. "Wasn't it Vaskaya? Yes, yes. It was. Darya Vaskaya."

"She does not—!" The young man broke off abruptly, with a stammer, as if he suddenly realized that he was speaking. He put on a tone of irony. "She does not keep you acquainted with her movements, then?"

The stranger was not offended. He took no notice of the irony. He got up, again showing difficulty in his movement, and announced that he would go to the Casino. "Every day I risk a few francs," he explained. "Sooner or later I shall win a great deal. It is the way. If you set out with an objective, never give up." He lifted his hat in the Russian manner. "Since we are neighbors perhaps you will do me the honor to dine with me tonight," he said. "You will not say no, my dear Michael Ballou. I will stop at your address."

He hurried off. Once on his feet he appeared able to move with great agility.

The young man got up and turned from the Croisette into rue d'Antibes where he stopped for a drink at an American bar. Then he went to his room in rue des Pomegranates. He thought the mail man on his afternoon round might bring him a letter from Villa Amette, but none came. He went out again, to a film theater, and sat through a screen drama he had seen in New York two years before. He couldn't remember the circumstances under which he'd seen it, and thought that at the time it must not have made much impression, for while it was all familiar its episodes were unexpected. But when a short subject, a comedy, came on the screen, he remembered. He remembered who had sat with him in the dark corner of the New York theater one afternoon while it rained outside. They'd run in from the shower and chosen the dark corner in the back of the house like any two young lovers stealing their sweets out of the day where they find them. They'd been so busy with each other they scarcely glanced at the screen until a comedy came on. Then they'd watched and laughed. Strange, that here in Cannes, two years later, the same comedy should follow the same dramatic film.

He got up and left the theater, walking as if he were partly blind. He went back to his room, decided that he would not have dinner with the curious stranger. But when Khamov came to his door he went with him. They went to a small place in Boulevarde d'Italia where the meals were five francs a head, wine included. The young man was uneasy. He showed it plainly. The stranger did nearly all of the talking. He rambled over a wide field. Nevsky Prospekt in the moonlight. That dancer—Darya Vaskaya—strange how he'd never thought of her until today. And he asked questions, innumerable questions which the young man answered briefly. They seemed natural questions coming from a man with a curious disposition but the young man started once or twice, with suspicion in his glance. Some of the questions seemed as if they might have been calculated, rehearsed and carefully introduced. The man spoke of the sensational descent upon the Riviera of the arch murderer, the one called The Panther. That was a sad affair—this Georges Raynel would be the undoing of The Panther, would he not, with his huge reward. What do you think, Michael Ballou?

"They will never catch him. He will kill and rob as long as he likes. When he is tired he will retire."

The stranger regarded his guest with a penetrating glance. He appeared to be somewhat astonished by the other's conviction expressed so sharply.

When coffee was in order, Khamov suggested that they go to his house and have coffee royale prepared with a special and very old brandy of which he had a part bottle. The young man demurred, but only half heartedly. After all, the other had been the evening's host. The man's room was like himself, untidy. He pitched his broad-brimmed hat onto a bed littered with newspapers and brought out his bottle of brandy from under the papers. Then he hunted for loaf sugar in a drawer stuffed with odds and ends.

The young man watched him. Time and again his lids narrowed while he watched and his mouth set grimly—for a mouth so mobile. The other's short, bulky body was repellent, with a suggestion of dirtiness, yet his voice and eyes at times were exceedingly gentle. While he rummaged for his loaf sugar the young man happened to glance into the drawer. He started and drew back from sight of an automatic pistol of the largest, and most deadly pattern. The stranger saw the expression in his face and laughed loud and heartily. He pointed a finger at the weapon.

"Who knows," he said, in great good humor, a bovine merriment, "but that La Panthère will descend upon me? He will mistake me for a rich man and descend upon me. La! I am ready for him. Is it not good, Michael Ballou?"

"Let us have the coffee royale," the young man said. "It is late and I must go."

The last thing Khamov called out to him when he turned down the stair toward the street was, "Remember my little joke, Michael Ballou. I am ready for La Panthère. Ha ha! But we are friends, you and I. Yes, yes. We are good friends. You joke me about Darya Vaskaya but we are good friends still."

If he had not been a Russian and subject naturally to quick changes of mood and childish manifestations, one might have thought him a little crazy.

The young man hurried down rue des Pomegranates as if he were in a fever of anxiety. Once within his room he shut the door and locked it, drawing its additional bolt. He went over to his fireplace, the provincial French fireplace enclosed by thin brass shutters that slide upward and disappear when a fire is laid. He slid the shutters up and, kneeling, reached his arm into the box-like aperture that was nothing more than the bottom of a chimney. His fingers brushed over the burned bricks until they fastened on a space that other fingers would not have separated from the area around it. They brought out a thin but heavy case that was deftly carved out of two small slabs of marble and bound in brass.

Still on his knees he laid the case on the hearth and opened it. There was an instant constellation of pigeon red fires. Nineteen great round rubies lying on a cushion of white velvet plush. The stones were rimmed with gold and held together by a braided gold chain; the chain had been broken at the end where the twentieth ruby had been.

The young man stared at the gems for many minutes. At last he touched them, lifted out the chain and dripped it through his fingers. Once his hand tried to bunch the priceless things in his palm and he half arose, as if he would leave the marble box where it lay while he hurried off with its precious contents. But the impulse passed as quickly as it came. He put the great gems back on their white cushion, closed the box and fixed its brass clasps, and reinserted it in the crevice between two bricks. He rolled a newspaper then, set it alight, and held the smoking flame over the burnt-brick area he had disturbed. Then he closed down the shutters and went to bed.

In the morning a letter came about the advertisement. It was written on Hotel Crillon stationery, in a fluttery, rambling hand, and it read,

"I shall be glad to receive you at Villa Amette, La Grasse, at four this afternoon."

It was signed, "Clare Fraser."

In the fifth floor suite at the Crillon, Dupree, a grotesque figure in his rug pedler's clothes, stringy beard and green stained features, paced the floor with quick steps. Croyant sat in a easy chair facing the window, his back to the room. He had the air of one who refused to take to himself any shade of the other's suppressed excitements.

He had just said, "The records at Leningrad are credible, Ariste?"

"Completely. The Russians are the masters of records. They combed the house while it still smoldered for a clue, a footprint in the debris, a finger print on a burning wall. Even I, who watched, presented them my compliments. But we were certain, when we found the cat's head, that the man whose foot had caught in the grille was the Unknown. They filed the only fingerprints discovered. These were strewn about the safe hidden in the wall. They were put away as mementoes of the dishonorable dead. But now, when they look in the records of transient visitors who cross the border and discover that Michael Jeribzoff arrived in Leningrad that day to visit his uncle in Nevsky Prospekt, they compare his passport prints with the prints found on the safe—found there and nowhere else. They are the same."

"And you find him every day," Croyant murmured, "sunning himself beyond the Esplanade!"

Dupree frowned to the other's tone. There was a trace of irony in it.

"But what then, my friend? Arrest him?"

"I should like to watch while you say, 'Michael Jeribzoff Ballou, you robbed the house of your mother's brother in Nevsky Prospekt. You, who alone knew of the existence of your uncle's safe, opened it and robbed it and fled from the flames behind you.' "

"Wait, wait! You think it was he who set the flames?"

Croyant moved a shoulder. "Perhaps. Who knows? Or might he not have found them brewing? Arrest him and beg him to set you right."

Dupree glowered for a moment, then broke into a hearty laugh. "One forgets that you are enjoying a rest. One may joke when he plays."

Croyant sighed deeply. He got up and examined the wine bottle on the table. It was quite empty. He found another in his closet and the two men, each in his fashion held to be the greatest detective in Europe, made a great to-do over the correct holding of a bottle of 1911 Burgundy while the cork is being drawn.

"Never on the slant, my friend," Dupree cried.

"But my face is in range if I hold it vertical," Croyant pointed out.

"There is a trick. When the cork eases you hold it from you, your arms level. You must be quick, while the cork is sliding. Here. I will perform. *Attendez vous!*"

He splashed himself shamefully and Croyant taxed him the cost of one of his rugs as fee for the chambermaid who would have to rub salt in the carpet. Then they drank.

Croyant put down his glass thoughtfully.

"If The Panther wanted the rubies," he said, "he'd get them. The young man went so far as to display them to Darya Vaskaya. He is afraid of them, yet he is careless. He made her a gift of one of them."

"There are moments," Dupree said dryly, "when the most careful man is careless. When a woman grants him the first kiss and when he has collected the rest."

Croyant filled his glass again, an unusual thing for he guarded his already generous girth. He drank slowly.

"There was something else in the safe, Ariste," he said at last. "Did Darya Vaskaya fail, or was she on the right track?"

CHAPTER VIII

VASKAYA WATCHES THE AVERY GIRL

DUPREE prepared to go. He reaffixed his black wig and made his stringy beard into a greater tangle, if that were possible.

"But I shall not lose sight of our Michael Ballou," he declared. "He is watched. If I am troubled it is because The Panther has not already replaced the dancer. If it is not the rubies he wants, it is strange he permits him to be unattended by Vaskaya's successor."

"The message she wrote in Toulouse," Croyant returned, "miscarried. He may not know the young man is in Cannes."

"It may be. It may be. I am going out of the rug business. I shall try furs. One sells a fur to one like Vaskaya but not a rug."

"You are determined to find her?"

"You told of tears in the Place du Forum at Toulouse. There were tears in Warsaw when her lover of that season was being so prettily scratched on the breast. An exquisite woman who weeps over her lovers. A woman who sobs may be played upon."

He was going out into the corridor, bent, his roll on his back, his face hidden by his long-peaked hat, but turned back.

"I almost forgot. I brought the sheet from Paris that gives us what history of Monsieur Ballou Jeribzoff the dossiers contain. I have memorized it. It is of little value and you máy destroy it."

He brought from an inner pocket a folded form from the Paris Cabinet des Dossiers where there is a history of many thousands of men and women who would never suspect that their goings and comings are so carefully recorded. From the first time the Bureau d'Etrangers discovered that a young American of the name of Michael Ballou, with an American passport under that name, also carried a *carte d'identité* as Michael Jeribzoff, he had been subject to police reports.

The sheet handed over, Dupree departed. He went to the servants' elevators and bowed and scraped in humility before the contemptuous attendant who dropped him to the hotel basement and rear exits. He was warned not to cross the shining marble terraces.

Croyant was familiar with the dossiers. Dupree had reported them on his last preceding contact with the Englishman, a week before. But he read them over again now and made brief notes on a sheet of paper with his fountain pen, as if he epitomized the dossier for his own memoranda or for another's perusal.

He ignored everything beyond Warsaw.

The French police had noted the young man's departure to the Polish capital from Paris. He crossed Germany by plane, as if he were in a great hurry. Croyant remembered that Helen Avery was then in Warsaw. That was thirteen months or so ago. Some two months later he reentered France by way of Cherbourg from Stockholm. Previously he had been in the habit of frequenting the more fashionable hotels, enjoyed gay activities and spent money rather freely. Now, however, the police reported a change. He frequented economic lodgings and less pretentious cafés. He did not resume old friendships. He had gone into Switzerland and was lost for a time to the French police but was observed again when he recrossed the border.

"And enter now, Mademoiselle Amon," Croyant murmured aloud.

The border guards duly noted his re-entry and, because has name was on their "Police Report Demanded" list, it was recorded that he entered in company with Mademoiselle Tanya Amon, a Russian, and the quaint French explanation was added, *"En alliance."*

When Croyant copied onto his sheet of paper this notation he underscored it.

In Switzerland Darya Vaskaya had found Ballou unhappy and lonely, Croyant supposed. However such things happen, she had succeeded in attaching herself to him. He must have experienced a definite thrill in engaging the affections of one who had been among the foremost of Europe's dancers. How she explained her absence from the stage and change of name, there was no hint, of course, in the methodical dossier. Croyant thought it impossible that the young man should not have known her real identity, having seen her on the stage in Warsaw.

After Switzerland the record stopped. There was added a copy of an application for employment made to a steamship company at Havre, in which Michael Ballou had described himself as American, of a Russian mother who had been the sister of a Count Jeribzoff in Leningrad. He mentioned that both of his parents were deceased. The application had been passed through the police at Havre, a custom on the part of the shipping companies who contemplate engaging non citizens. Whether or not the young man landed that job was not noted. Croyant did not copy a reference to this paragraph.

When he was finished with the dossier, Croyant tore it

into bits and carefully burned them on an ash tray. Then, from a drawer in his desk, he brought out a little sheaf of photographs of various sizes, a young woman and a man. Of the girl's face there could be no mistake, though it was photographed in various stage make-ups. Darya Vaskaya, caught by the camera during her season at Warsaw. Of the man there were police photographs only, mounted on record cards abstracted from the Warsaw police files. A thin, furtive face, with sensuous lips and heavily lidded eyes. Sullen, before the police camera, yet the face once would have been handsome, with a certain dashing quality. It was evil now, but once had been gently appealing.

"Dope," Croyant muttered. "Needle and pill and hasheesh."

Accompanying the photographs was a bulky envelope briefly labeled, "re: Vaskaya" in the handwriting of Croyant's principal agent at Warsaw. This, the pictures themselves and his own notes made from the dossier, he wrapped into a tight package which he fitted into an inner pocket of his coat. He was careful that it did not bulge.

He went downstairs then, whistling to himself. Since Toulouse he had been careful never to whistle the Dancer of Kashmir music.

It was the dead part of the afternoon, four o'clock. There were few loungers about the hotel lobbies and few on the Esplanade. At four o'clock in the afternoon all Cannes seems deserted. Luncheons are finished and it is not yet the cocktail hour. The shops and the Croisette are quiet. People are resting for the furious round that begins after five and goes on until the first break of dawn from over Corsica.

Croyant turned into the Casino and strolled about aimlessly. It seemed that for one to whom a "vacation" came so rarely, any hour of the idle day was not an hour to miss. Thanks to the effervescent Mrs. Fraser, he had met quite a number of people at Cannes though, to tell the truth, hardly any of them appealed to him. He knew how too many of the women came by their jewels and how many of the men had secretly substituted paste pearls for the necklaces their wives still thought genuine.

These play-folk weren't the kind he liked. Still, he was enjoying himself, for he whistled almost constantly when there was no one close to be amused at him and show it.

He played for a few moments in the boule room. There was only one other player at the table, the man in the broad-brimmed hat who had just left Michael Ballou among the free benches, and who would dine that night with the young man. The bulky fellow played some curious system, risking five francs at a time. Croyant saw that he was consistently winning, but much too slowly. Croyant tossed a hundred francs onto the table, saw that the rubber ball wouldn't jump his way, and gave up.

On the balcony overlooking the harbor and the yachts he caught sight of Clare Fraser at a table against the balcony rail and canopied by the weaving fronds of a banana palm. He would have turned back into the boule room but Mrs. Fraser saw him and sent him a typically American "Heigh, there!" He looked glum for a moment but went down the balcony to the young widow's table.

She was very charming in a wide hat, a foulard gown and fur jacket. Across from her was a tall, broad-shouldered and russet bearded individual whom the Riviera had come to know as the Count Alexi Tanaroff. Mrs. Fraser would explain that one really should slip the patronymic "Vladimirovitch" between the Alexi and the Tanaroff, "but what's the use of the vitch part?"

The American widow had been literally swept off her bird-like feet by the towering, pompous Count on whose hero's breast it was said the Czar himself had once pinned the St. George medal. She admitted that he'd swept her off her feet. She was enthusiastic in the confession. The way she waved one gloved hand toward him now, while she extended the other to Croyant, was as much as to say "See! Is he not splendid?"

He was, in truth, a splendid specimen, physically at least. A fire-eater in his army days, no doubt.

"You know the Count?" Mrs. Fraser said.

Croyant bowed, none too genially. Mrs. Fraser insisted that he occupy the third chair at the table. He glanced at a thin, ascetic looking young man with a pale face who stood behind the Count.

"He's interpreting," Mrs. Fraser explained. "He won't sit down in the presence of the Count. He adores him."

"I remember," Croyant murmured, brushing a grin from his heavy mouth. "The Count doesn't speak anything but Russian and you stop at English and French."

"Oh, he can say an occasional word in French. But not well enough for conversation."

"Still, you get along?"

"Splendidly. He has converted me to all of his political views. My heart is just bleeding for his poor countrymen. Especially the refugees along the Riviera. I'm going to do something for them. One thing, I've agreed to have all Russian servants at the Villa."

"Oh," grunted Croyant. "And when are you moving?"

"Day after tomorrow. Tomorrow I shall employ my staff. At two o'clock I am interviewing the kitchen prospects. At three o'clock, the gardeners and chauffeurs and a butler's staff. And at four I shall see a young man who can take the Sealyhams for their walks. He'll be a secretary and interpreter too."

"You've found one, then?"

Mrs. Fraser pursed her lips. She was not yet certain. "I think so. I liked his letter. It came in answer to my advertisement. If he is good-looking, and likes the Count, I suppose I shall engage him. When once I've sent for some one I hate to turn him down."

Through all of this conversation the Count sat stiffly erect, fingering his bushy beard and glaring at Croyant out of watery but fierce gray eyes. He spoke now, in a gruff voice. The young man interpreted.

"Monsieur le Major is an acquaintance of Monsieur Raynel. Monsieur Raynel is a fool. He has five million francs to spare for the capture of some dandified Apache who will hang himself in his own noose one of these fine days at no cost at all. Monsieur le Major can use his offices with Monsieur Raynel to have the five million transferred to a treasury for the restoration of old Russia."

When the interpreter had finished his translation Mrs. Fraser shivered prettily. "Don't let us talk of murderers. And I am reminded, Major Croyant, Mr. Raynel passed along the balcony only a little while ago. He had called upon you at the Crillon, he said, but you had gone. He left a card but should I see you, he asked, I should make his message verbal. He hopes you will dine aboard the *Ariadne* tonight. His fiancée also insists. They're taking a sail along the Spanish coast tomorrow and will be gone three or four days."

"Shall I see you aboard?"

"No. I'm taking the Count out to the Villa. He's promised to make many suggestions for my Russian room. I'm to have one big room done with only Russian decoration, you know."

"I didn't know," Croyant murmured. "I shall like to see it finished."

At the Casino steps Croyant was undecided which way to turn. The Esplanade was beginning to come alive with the promenaders who come out with the glorious Mediterranean dusk, when the scents of mimosa and clematis float through the clear air. The newsvendor of the morning was abroad with evening editions. A headline devoted to The Panther caught Croyant's eye and he purchased a paper.

Only that the police of Berlin, acting on instructions from Ober-kapitän Weinrath, who was said to be on the Riviera, had raided a criminal nest in the Selmstrasse and were convinced that at least two of their captives were members of The Panther's band. Under police "persuasion" they had as much as admitted that they obeyed his orders but so far the "persuasion" had evinced nothing more. The news item concluded with the hope that the killer had deserted the Côte d'Azure for Germany although, said the writer, there persisted an alarming rumor that the police of Nice and Monte Carlo were concealing the truth about the unfortunate death of Albert Whelan, the American millionaire.

Croyant tossed the paper aside and was still undetermined which way to walk. Berlin, Rome, Paris, Milan and Vienna might be keyed to a tremendous fury of activity in the grim determination to do or die in one mighty effort to run The Panther to earth, but he didn't know whether to stroll this way or that.

His course was unexpectedly decided for him. Down the Esplanade hovered the unmistakable figure of the rug pedler. Apparently Dupree had not yet gone into the "fur business." And he had seen Croyant, for his antics, rushing back and forth across the Esplanade, accosting whoever came into his path, were to attract the Major's attention. Croyant turned in his direction, walking briskly.

"Buy a rug please, *s'il vous plaît,* milord. *Très bon et bon marché,*" the falsetto-over-basso voice wheedled. Croyant touched the roll of rugs. With a great show of enthusiasm Dupree brought the roll around and began to fumble with it.

"Vaskaya," he snapped, when Croyant bent close to examine his wares. "She's here. I saw her not half an hour ago—I knew her—the face in your photographs." He held out a rug. A pedestrian came close. His voice wheedled promptly. *"Très bon,* good stuff, milord, *M'sieu' le duc.* I sell him cheap."

"You can find her?" Croyant said, sharply.

"No such luck. I went onto the Guy de Maupassant pier. I debated pitching my rugs into the water. I looked around and she stood there. I knew her as quickly as I'd know an old friend. Stood straight and bold. She was watching that Avery girl."

Croyant's face darkened, but he spoke softly.

"You are sure, Ariste?"

"The Avery girl and her mother were going down the pier steps. Getting into the *Ariadne's* gig. She watched. She looked out to the yacht, then back. She watched till the gig shoved off.—*Bon marché,* fine stuff, your highness. Pretty Persian—buy him, nice rug.—I thought I'd follow her. But she crossed the Croisette and went into a shop. She didn't come out. She used a rear door into the Arcade of the Jewelers. A slick one, that."

"I don't like her interest in the Avery girl. I'd like to have seen her face while she watched her."

"Coming close to home, eh, my friend? What does it

mean? She's back under orders again. The Panther's orders. She's scouting. She'll know the Avery girl next time, any time she sees her. How did she look? Like a stone goddess. Her face was blank but you knew what was there. Contempt. Pretty butterfly in the pretty white gig. Happy with her rich man. Vaskaya contemptuous of one who doesn't know what the morrow holds. I'm afraid. First time Dupree has ever been afraid. He'll strike at Raynel with the same contempt that was in Vaskaya's face. He'll remove his pretty butterfly."

While he talked in sharp, jerky sentences, Dupree scanned the Esplanade crowd, guarding against being overheard. But the corner of his eye kept track of the cloud that crossed Croyant's eyes. The Frenchman knew that if Helen Avery were seriously threatened The Panther would indeed be coming close to his friend.

"Three hours ago," Croyant reminded him, "you chattered of a woman who wept. She could be played upon. You paint her now with a different brush, Ariste."

"But I've seen her. I saw her eyes. I might have thought she hated the Avery one. But why should she hate? So it is that she but despises. One who laughs today and may not laugh again."

"While she's on the yacht, she's safe. We must see that she's guarded ashore. Are you giving up the rug business soon enough to show up at the local Sûreté? I'd rather you'd ask for men and not I."

"Oh, I'll not trouble you to go back to work," Dupree scoffed prodigiously. "I'll set the guard. I'll use my own men."

By now the crowd was too thick on the Esplanade for a rug pedler who talked so long to a big, well groomed man, not to attract too much attention. Dupree shuffled off, whining his wares. Croyant walked leisurely toward

his hotel. He looked about him with the interested gaze
of one who enjoys the panorama of life flowing past him
but his mind was filled with Darya Vaskaya.

Was Dupree right? Was The Panther planning to use
the dancer in a horrible gesture of his contempt for Raynel's five million franc reward? Use her to strike at
Helen Avery, the thing Raynel loved most in the world?

Or was there another meaning to that scene on Guy
de Maupassant pier? Michael Ballou once had loved Helen
Avery. Probably loved her still. Did Vaskaya know that?
The last four words of her note at Toulouse—they were
eloquent of Vaskaya's woman's feelings for the man
she'd spied upon. "She couldn't go on."

Had Michael Ballou told her of Helen Avery? Had she
come to the pier only to study the girl who held a love
she, herself, couldn't arouse?

There was a great deal of relief in the latter thought.
It fitted the scene at Toulouse, when the dancer sat on the
stone slab lost in dejection and despair. He would like to
have relief on this thought but he would not predict on
his own authority which way a woman would turn.

Vaskaya might think to pay a score of her own while
she did The Panther's bidding. He didn't think so, but
the chance was there.

At the Crillon he found his friend Sir Philip Gregg, a
thin, angular man with a monocle, baggy clothes and an
Oxford accent. Sir Philip had come down from London
with the vitriolic comments of the Lords' directors upon
the stubbornness with which the Major refused to be
concerned about the risk to the profits of the various
companies insuring the gems The Panther might take a
notion to collect.

"I came myself," he explained, "to save you a delega-
tion. We've been appointing committees to put you on

the carpet. Those emeralds of Veragua's will set us back sixty thousand pounds. You're not expected to recover them until, some time in the future, they come into the market of their own accord. But you should be helping check The Panther's progress."

"Because of the jewelry alone, or with a thought for human life?"

"Now, now," Sir Philip protested. "There isn't a director among the companies who wouldn't congratulate you with more happiness for the saving of one life than all the risks in the filing cabinets." Sir Philip was silent a moment, looking at Croyant queerly. "Well, I've done my duty. I've told you how my associates feel. If I haven't made it strong enough, add your own imagination. And now, old boy!"

Croyant had been lighting a cigarette. He looked across his flare with a start. Sir Philip had fixed his monocle and was grinning broadly.

"Eh?" the Major grunted. His cigarette remained forgotten in the air.

"Just so! What are you up to?"

"It's inconceivable, I suppose, that I should want to knock off for a few weeks?"

"It is," Sir Philip agreed heartily.

Croyant gave his attention to the cigarette. When its glow satisfied him he looked at Sir Philip blankly. For a moment neither spoke, their glance holding. Then Sir Philip:

"I ran into Stanhope, the Yard commissioner, the other day. Two weeks ago he was begging us to see that you cooperated with Dupree and the other Continental chaps. Of late he hasn't peeped. I asked him why. He stared at me."

"Stanhope's a dull fellow. Nearly all of the Yard's big bugs are."

Sir Philip grinned. "He told me you've almost the whole of your organization assembled on the Riviera. Said you had Ballato of Rome, and the big bear, Chenkin, the Soviet's star at Moscow, under cover down here running errands for you. The Yard wondered, he said, why Dupree didn't know what you were doing. He thought we were in a conspiracy of secrecy with you."

"Good God, man! You didn't let him get away with it?"

Sir Philip nodded vigorously. "Of course. But I told him to help us keep it dark. And, equally of course, I left my own associates uncomforted. So, again, what are you up to?"

Now Croyant grinned, sheepishly. "I'll have to confess," he said, "that I've been hoping to arrange a little rendezvous of my own with The Panther."

CHAPTER IX

TWO NUMBERS IN RUE DES POMEGRANATES

THE dinner party aboard the *Ariadne* was a small affair. There were the same people at the table in the oak-paneled dining cabin of the sumptuous yacht as had assembled in the café of the hotel at Toulouse, with only three additions. Besides Mrs. Avery and Helen, Mr. and Mrs. Ransom and the young man, Duval, there were a Lord and Lady Severn, a young pair, acquaintances of the Ransoms who had found a kindred spirit in Georges Raynel. Croyant had taken it upon himself to bring Sir Philip and both Helen and her fiancé made him feel he would not have been forgiven if he had not done so. Sir Philip knew the Ransoms. He and Arthur Ransom had been at Oxford together. The Severns had not long been returned from Abyssinia where young Severn had filled a semi-diplomatic post. They had an inexhaustible store of anecdotes including Lady Severn's account of her visit to a slave market where a bevy of "fresh goods," girls from the Galla country, were chained to their stone benches awaiting purchasers. She told how she had bought one for the thrill and didn't know what to do with her. "Bertram," she declared with a moue at her husband, "wanted me to give her to him, but I thought of a better thing. I gave her to the Emperor. The Empress, you know, manages to marry off all of his young slaves quickly and an Empress-fostered wife usually has a fair time."

Sir Philip took an instant liking to Georges Raynel.
Both had traveled extensively and Sir Philip held important interests in South America with which Raynel was
familiar as a result of his stay there with his friend
Veragua. At the first opportunity Raynel took Sir Philip
into an interior lounge cabin while the others went onto
the after deck. Croyant was amused. He knew that Raynel
would appeal to Sir Philip to use his influence with him.
On each occasion of their meeting Raynel had brought
up the matter of The Panther. Instead of his bitterness
over the fate of his friend subsiding it seemed to be deep-
ening and The Panther becoming an obsession. Even
Helen, on one occasion, had begged him to do something
to comfort her fiancé. He had always returned the same
reply in its varied phrasings. The police were aroused.
Every capital was co-operating. For once he would let
them do the work, confident that they would succeed.

Helen, that one time of her intercession, had said unhappily, "I believe Georges would feel better, actually, if
he should receive the dreadful thing they talk about—the
cat's head. I think he would be easier if anything should
happen, even if such a challenge was thrown at him."

He stood with her now against the yacht's rail looking
out over the water toward the long line of shadowed
shore with myriad lights and firefly train of motor lamps
skimming the Corniche Road.

"You're sailing tomorrow for Spain?" he asked.

"Georges has some business at one of the little towns
this side of Barcelona. It's a meeting of some sort, with
people coming from Toledo. We sail early in the morning,
all of us except the Ransoms. They're not overly fond of
the water."

"Are you going ashore tonight?"

She looked up quickly, her eyes questioning. "Mother

and I are not, but how queerly you sound! Almost as if you hoped I wouldn't go ashore."

He pointed out that she was being preposterous. "If you were coming aboard from land in the morning I'd have to get up and see that you kept your feet dry. And you'll remember I warned you at Toulouse that you'll learn a man likes to sleep mornings."

She laughed and was satisfied. Her fiancé came out after a while to stand at the rail with them. Croyant saw that her hand sought his instantly and snuggled into it. Raynel looked across her brown head at Croyant with the quick pride of a man who has won from the world the gift of one of its precious things. A faint moon laid a mist across his dark eyes but they shone through the veil. Yes, Croyant mused, Helen might be right. The man might be happier if The Panther should challenge him. He would be quite capable of waiting patiently for The Panther to strike, superbly confident of outwitting—even overwhelming him. But for Helen's sake he hoped the situation would never arrive.

The next afternoon at four o'clock Michael Ballou presented himself at Villa Amette. He was a little surprised by its location. It occupied the narrowest part of La Grasse, the stretch of land that separates the railroad and the sea. All trains between Cannes and Nice rumbled past the back of the house and just behind the railroad was the Boulevard d'Alsace with its constant stream of traffic from towns and villas up and down the coast.

The house itself was of nondescript architecture, set well back in grounds that had been woefully neglected. Michael gathered while he approached the house that they would soon be a different sight. A half dozen men who seemed to have just been engaged and ordered to go to work at once were handling gardeners' tools with the uncertainty of workmen who don't know just where to begin.

Mrs. Fraser received him in a sun parlor. The interior of the house was in a turmoil but the sun parlor was cheerful. He had wondered what kind of woman "Clare Fraser" would be. He had made no such picture of her as she turned out. He was glad she was an American. She was very business-like and direct, despite her air of fluttering fragility.

He could hardly believe his ears when he heard her saying, without asking for more details about himself than he had included in his letter of application, "You will go on duty at once and stay through the evening unless you have an unbreakable appointment for dinner. I shall call you my personal secretary, but I'm afraid you'll be a little bit of everything. I hope you play tennis."

He got his breath and admitted that he played fairly well.

"Splendid! You'll attend to the business of the house of course. Paying the servants and looking after them, things like that. And you must think a great deal of Count Tanaroff. You'll have to interpret him for me and me for him. And the Sealyhams. I'll put them in your care. And now that it's all settled, I'm dying for a game of tennis. We'll find you shoes and you can play as you are. I'm worn out from engaging people."

He played tennis with his new employer for half an hour and outplayed her roundly. He was a little afraid he had made a mistake but she complimented him with gusty sincerity. She led him, then, to what was to be his work room, his "office," and left him to make what order he could out of scribblings on odd bits of paper, which when turned into head and tail, were a list of the servants and gardeners and chauffeurs she had engaged, their wages, individual duties, and various other household items.

He was a little worried about his neighbor, Khamov. Last night, when they parted, he had spoken of their dining together again on this evening, when Michael should be host. Mrs. Fraser showed signs of keeping him late. She was arranging to have a food service brought out from Cannes in a caterer's wagon. There was nothing he could do about his neighbor save let him stand at his door and think as he pleased. He would stop at his room later in the evening and make his explanations. Meanwhile Khamov would have to put him down as a thoughtless fellow who invites a friend to dine and then saves his five francs by leaving him to cool his heels.

Khamov, however, did not stop at his door that night.

At about the time Michael was entering the Villa Amette, wondering what sort of woman Clare Fraser would be and if he were to have this job he wanted so badly, a thickly built sailor lumbered along the Cannebiere in Marseilles with a leering eye for the flower girls and a watchful one for the policemen who guard the Cannebiere from their little wooden boxes at the street intersections. The sailor, not a young man yet with the appearance of being physically prime, was an officer of some sort, a third mate, perhaps, on a middle-rate freighter plying in from the African coast. He was clean shaven, black hair glistening under a coat of some pungent pomade, and looked as if he were all set up for a holiday.

The flower girls, one after the other, tried to sell him a boutonniere. He grinned good naturedly, the glance of his eyes complimenting their charms, but he bought no flowers. To one who was more persistent than the rest and would have affixed a blossom to the lapel of his shiny blue jacket whether or no/ he said, in execrable French, "*Non, non, Ma'mselle!* I find a better flower. Wild flower."

The girl thought he would be a Levantine. Faces from Morocco were darker and Egyptians were pastier. This fellow's face was warm-hued, but all sorts come out of the Levant. She was particularly struck by his nose: It was hawk-like, she thought.

Sailors and water front people as a rule do not promenade along the Cannebiere, which is a street of middle class but quiet cafés and modest shops. The street itself is mainly given over to trams that spread out onto the fan-like track-fingers of the city's transportation system after going the full length of the Cannebiere. Buses, too, make the boulevard a kind of elongated depot.

The sailor chose a bus and settled down into the back seat as if he were in for a long ride. The bus turned off the Cannebiere, descended into a humbler street closer to the water front and threaded its way through an industrial quarter, where tall factory chimneys were sending up smoke. It emerged from this district with a startling abruptness into a cobblestoned road flanked on either side by rough tenements. At the corners of the streets were grim looking cafés out of which came frowsy women and coarse featured men in all manner of garb.

About the quarter was a distinct foreign air. The green, olive skins of North Africa were in preponderance. Occasionally a young woman with aloe eyes who walked, wrapped in a bright shawl, as if she carried a burden balanced on her head, came out of a tenement or café or bar and went around a corner on flat treading feet. Arab women, these, from the desert's edge. Smuggled in by *maquereaux* or other agents who deal in flesh.

Sailors know of the quarter, the "Old Port."

The man on the bus got off, walked past the front stoops of a string of tenements and turned into a narrow roadway that meandered down to the water. He paused before a den identified by a black curve of letters on the pinkish wash of a wide and unspeakably dirty window. *"Auberge des Cochons,"* House of Pigs.

The sailor's glance showed satisfaction when he read the curious sign. Inside he found a typical bistro, a bar room, doors leading to mysterious chambers, and beyond a dance room with a platform at the end for musicians and with tables lined about the walls. There were no musicians at this hour of the day, nor drinkers at the tables. In the bar room was the usual company of loungers, French, African, Apache and nondescript men who seemed to be of no classification at all, evil and furtive and glum humored at sight of a stranger.

The sailor went up to the bar. If he shot keen glances over the company and about the room, taking note of doors and passageways, his manner might have been put down to nothing more than a wary man's curiosity over strange surroundings. Sailors are wont to have a good look around when they are in a strange port.

He gave his order to the bartender in Russian. The barman frowned darkly and became truculent. He was suspicious of a foreign tongue not familiar in the quarter. Most tongues were. Spanish or Italian or even English would have done nicely. But Russians are few among bistro frequenters.

But if the bartender showed signs of being truculent, the newcomer was as quick to bridle when he saw that he wasn't understood and wasn't welcome. His eyes, that had been two soft pools of gentle friendliness, hardened. His hands gripped the bar rail and his face shot forward toward the other's. He poured out a stream of staccato Russian.

A slight, wiry chap, little higher than the stranger's arm pit, detached himself from the others.

"You Russki, eh?" he said.

"Da, da! Ya Russki!"

"I talk Russki very well. I learn from my woman in Constantinople. She was a princess once. I taught her how to get down on her own knees and she taught me how to talk her lingo. What you want here?"

The stranger was very pleased to meet a man who not only could speak his language but had taught a princess to get down on her knees to him. He put both his hands on the little fellow's shoulders in what was almost an embrace.

"Da, da! That's the way. Take the kink out of their necks, eh?" He laughed in great good humor. The little fellow swelled up perceptibly. If this stranger would only buy a drink now, he'd tell him about the princess in Constantinople. He said,

"Buy a *pinard* while you tell what you want this place. I get you anything you want."

The Russian shook his head. His whole face was smiling. The nose that had been hawk-like seemed to assume a gentler shape.

"Na," he said with a great appearance of slyness. "I got what I want. What you mean. The flower girls on the Cannebiere, they try to sell me pretty blossom. I say *non, non*, Ma'mselle, I go now to a wild flower."

The little man understood. One of the Moorish women from Tangiers, or an Algerian, who abounded in the quarter.

"That's all right. But they're around the corner or on the water. What you do here? And you buy?"

The stranger ordered red wine instead of a pinard of cheap beer. He showed a moderate amount of change. He explained with a grotesque smirk that he was a regular fellow. Always give a lady a treat. He wanted to buy a half bottle of eau de vie of a first class quality. Strong, but good.

The little man interpreted to the bartender who immediately dropped his truculence. The sailor grinned at him amiably and when the man turned his back, studied a door that opened through the wall at the end of the bar and behind it. A woman had come out of this door, taken a bottle of wine from the back bar and returned. None of the patrons of the place, however, used it. The little man told of the princess in Constantinople. She'd come over to him in a cabaret on the Scutari side across the Bosphorus Bridge, and sat in his lap. He'd pushed her onto the floor with a bump. The sailor laughed loudly at the spectacle of a princess falling to the floor with a bump. The little man finished his wine and the sailor bought more.

"I made her sit on the floor beside my chair," the little man explained. "When she tried to get up I smacked her. I made her drink out of my glass until she was drunk then I picked her up and carried her off. She was a princess all right. Bolsheviki business."

When the stranger went out he was still laughing over the story. He turned back at the door to bow and touch his cap to the little fellow, the bartender and the others. "You will tell me more," he called out. "If my wild flower doesn't find my money—" and he tapped his middle in the region of his belt— "I'll come back and buy for everybody."

He went down the cobbled road toward the water, his bottle of eau de vie under his arm. Around the corner of a warehouse he threw the bottle away. The section was deserted, with no activities in the warehouses and dockhouses that occupied it. The man found a doorway from which he could watch the entrance to the *Auberge des Cochons* and remained watching until the dusk shadows darkened into night. The green light that hung over the bistro door was not radiant enough to reveal the figures that passed inside to any degree of distinctness, so with the night the watcher slipped out of his doorway and found a miserable café open to the street, where the tea was terrible. He managed to do with a bare bite of the greasy food set before him. He passed the time, however, until it was well toward ten o'clock. Then, with a shrug of his shoulders as if, mentally, he cast a die, he paid his bill and turned back toward the *Auberge des Cochons*. Before he pushed in the door he felt of his pocket and the bulge of a pistol.

He appeared to be a little drunk when he leaned against the bar. Drunk, with a satisfied smirk in his face. The bartender gave him a quick inspection, nodded to an unspoken greeting, and grunted reassurance in the argot of the district for the benefit of the crowd that hadn't seen the stranger in the afternoon.

The little man came from a table in the back room where there were three or four couples dancing to the music of an accordion.

"Have a pleasant evening?" he asked. "Did she find your money?"

For a moment the stranger, getting drunker every minute, seemed not to know the little fellow. His face darkened unpleasantly.

"You remember me?" the other said quickly. "Remember the princess—on the floor—bump?"

The thick fellow remembered and laughed uproariously. He called for pinards for the house, everybody, in the dance room, too. For himself and his little friend he would have red wine. Or white—"I've got my money!" He showed a handful of small notes. Not enough to slit a man's throat for, but enough to buy several rounds of pinards with two wines on the side. Three wines on the side, since the bar man took wine without being asked.

In an hour the stranger had heard many more details about the princess and had bought many more pinards. He could hardly navigate now. He rolled along the bar until he came to the end of it. He had called for another round of drinks and was counting out his change when he staggered against the door in the back wall. It gave with him and he floundered through it, into a dark passage that led deep into the building.

The bar man came after him, cursing him for a fool. The door slammed behind him and the barrel of a pistol prodded his ribs. If Michael Ballou had been there he might have recognized the big, business-like automatic he had seen in the drawer of his neighbor, Makar Khamov. He would have found no gentleness in his neighbor's eyes now, however, and would not have recognized his clipped but excellent French.

"Make a sound and I'll drill you. If you rouse your gang I'll wipe them out. Alexander Amon is in this house. Take me to him."

The bar man, a burly ruffian, tensed his muscle and, for a moment, appeared ready to put up a fight. The other waited motionlessly, his pistol still prodding. The bartender surrendered and led the way to a room at the end of the dark corridor. There were sounds of voices in undertones in other rooms that opened into the passage, but no one interfered.

In the back room a slender man in good clothes that were a sharp contrast to the garments of the loungers at the bar swung his feet over the edge of a ragged sofa and sprang up in alarm. He let fall to the floor an illustrated Paris weekly he had been reading. His face, which once had been handsome, was peaked and sullen. His lips were loose, his lids drooping as if their nerve muscles were weakened. He stared at the "sailor," then to the bar man and back to the other.

"What the devil is this, Bibi?" he demanded of the bar man.

"Good evening, Alexander Vaskaya," said the stranger, in purring, liquid Russian. "It's good to see you looking so well."

The bartender made a furtive move toward the door behind him. The stranger stopped him with a gesture of his weapon. "Wait a moment, my friend. Then you may go."

He waved the man across the room, so that he stood within range while he took a step toward the younger man. To this one, who now stared at him with a look of terror gradually filling his weak-looking eyes, he said, "Tell him it will be better if he decides not to raise a row. If he keeps his mouth shut."

The younger man thrust forward his face, until it was close to the stranger's. Then he swayed back, his own face a sickly pallor, his loose mouth quivering.

"My God! It's you! It's——!"

"Stop! Keep your tongue for our bar friend. Tell him to go back, and no funny business. It will be better for you."

The one whom the other called Alexander Vaskaya turned, trembling in every limb, to the bar man. "For God's sake, Bibi, do as he says. Don't interfere. Don't tell anyone that—that I have a visitor."

The stranger stepped back for the bartender to pass. The man made a quick exit, relieved to get out of the mess. As soon as the door closed behind him the slender man turned to the stranger cringing.

"How did you know I lived here? What do you want? I've done nothing—nothing—that you should hurt me."

"Perhaps not," retorted the other softly. "But we are not always spared because we don't deserve to be harmed." He put the automatic back into its holster in his pocket. "We won't argue the point of what you deserve, Alexander, and what you'll get. Where's your sister?"

The man's face showed relief, perhaps because of the retreat of the pistol, perhaps because of the question. He answered in a sullen tone.

"I don't know. Why should I? I have nothing to do with her."

"Where is she?" The stranger's voice remained quietly gentle.

"I say to you I do not know. She goes her way. I go mine."

The thick man moved toward him. Alexander Vaskaya fell back. His calves struck the frame of the sofa and he collapsed, sitting down as though his feet had been struck from under him.

"Keep your hands off me," he cried. "You don't dare kill me here. You were seen."

The other stood over him chuckling silently.

"Would you like me to drop a card to the Police Palace in Warsaw, Alexander, and tell them the name of the

betrayer of the young man who was found bound to a
cellar wall with acid burning into his breast? The Warsaw police would like to pay that young man's betrayer.
Or would you like me to tell Darya when I find her that
it was her beloved brother who caused her sweetheart to
be taken to his torture?"

Alexander shrank back against the sofa. Perspiration
beaded his forehead. "You wouldn't do that—not to
Dolly!"

"Where is she?"

The younger man shivered from head to foot. His eyes
were bleak with terror but he clung stubbornly to his protest. "I tell you I don't know. I saw her last in Toulouse.
I swear it."

The stranger reached into his jacket pocket and brought
out a small vial and a pocket knife with a thin, pointed
blade. While the other stared, fascinated, color draining
from his features, he opened the knife and held a thumb
to flip the rubber stopper of the vial. His free hand
reached for the slender man's throat.

"You know how the acid burns, Alexander," he said.
"Perhaps this is the better way."

"No, no!" screamed Alexander. "I'll tell you. Let me
go. Put that damnable stuff away."

"I'll not wait long, Alexander."

"She has an apartment. In Marseilles—here. In Rue
Duane. It is not far from the Cannebiere. *Numéro
quatre.*"

"If you are lying you will not escape me. It was not
difficult to find you."

"It is the truth. I swear it. Not a soul knows but I.
She wants no one to know until she is ready to go away
again. She has been looking for someone."

"Who?"

"That I do not know. But why do you ask me that?"

"Never mind. What name does she live under?"

"Belot, Mademoiselle Belot."

The stranger flung the man back onto the sofa and released his throat. He asked if there was a way to the street that was not through the bar and was told there was a door in the corridor that led to a hall and an alley. He found this door and emerged without meeting anyone. In the main road he boarded a bus, from which he changed to a cruising taxi when they drew near the Cannebiere.

Rue Duane was a quiet street and Number Four once had been a pretentious residence. It was now divided, two apartments to the floor and kept by a motherly old woman who came to the street door in answer to the bell, with a blue kimona over her night dress. She had expected a tenant who had forgotten his key and would have quickly closed her door when she saw an ill kempt man in sailor's clothes. The caller held open the door and spoke. The gentle, liquid quality of his voice and his cultured accent eased her alarm.

"But it is a friend of Mademoiselle Belot," the stranger explained. "She will expect me at any time of the night."

The woman pointed out that it was almost midnight. "She will be asleep. She has not gone out all evening, so she will have been long in bed."

The visitor was insistent—and persuasive. She agreed to knock at Mademoiselle's door, which was on the second floor. She would not permit the stranger to go up alone.

There was no response to her knock and she would have turned away determinedly, "She sleeps sound. I will not waken her."

But the caller reached past her and rapped loudly.

"Darya Vaskaya!" he called, loudly. When there was no sound he tried the handle of the door, against the woman's alarmed protest. The door gave and disclosed darkness. The visitor snapped a pocket flare. The woman pushed past him and entered the room, throwing a light switch.

"But she is gone!" she cried. "Mademoiselle has departed."

Signs of a hurried flight were all too apparent. The room was in disorder, as was the small bedroom behind it. An abandoned dress, a dropped stocking before the chest of drawers, a pair of hats on the shelf in the closet. On tables there were ash trays that quite surely did not go with the furnishings, and must have been the girl's personal property.

The woman looked for her tenant's bags. She said Mademoiselle had come with three large bags. She kept them under the high bed. They were gone.

"It is most strange," the woman exclaimed, wholly at a loss to understand this flight. "And she was paid up," she said, "for the full week to come."

"You saw her today?"

"But of a certainty, M'sieu. As late as five o'clock. She came in from the street. I met her in the hall. She spoke pleasantly. I am sure she did not plan then to disappear."

On the dressing table were several toilette articles that had been forgotten in a hasty packing. And on the floor a handkerchief which, evidently, had dropped from a purse closed at the last moment before its owner turned from her mirror to go. The stranger stooped to pick up the handkerchief. He thought he had seen a small square of paper protruding from its folds, and discovered he had been right. The woman, still loyal to her furtive tenant, didn't know about his examining into her private affairs, but the stranger gave her no heed. He unfolded the paper, which proved to have been torn from the head of a newspaper page. On it had been written, in pencil,

> *"Rue des Pomegranates, Numero Trente. HE is*
> *at Numero Cinquante et un."*

Michael Ballou's number in Rue des Pomegranates— Number thirty, and the number, fifty-one, of his own house!

He put the bit of paper, carefully refolded, into his waistcoat pocket. The woman said, "I hope you find her, M'sieu', if you are truly a friend."

"Somebody will find her," he returned. "One or another, friend or foe. It will not be long."

CHAPTER X

DEATH IN RUE DES POMEGRANATES

THREE nights after the visit of the Russian, Khamov, in the garb of a sailor, to the *Auberge des Cochons*, there was a murder at the entrance to Rue des Pomegranates, where the street leads off from Boulevard d'Italia. It was not late, scarcely eleven o'clock, but the streets were virtually deserted.

Three men had come out of a bar on the Boulevard and were standing under the trees talking and singing. There was music from a mechanical piano coming out through the open bar door. Three shots fired in quick succession sound from a point a few yards up the Boulevard across the mouth of Rue des Pomegranates. The three men ran at once into Rue des Pomegranates to investigate. Others came running out of doorways and all gathered over a body that lay at the juncture of the Boulevard and the side street.

One of the men thought he saw a shadow slip into an area way between two buildings. If the shadow was a man, he ran between the buildings into Avenue du Prado, a short street with only one entrance. The sergeant of police stationed at this entrance on fixed post because the Avenue du Prado is an evil street, saw no one leave the neighborhood. He must have had a retreat in the Avenue.

The crowd augmented rapidly but everyone was afraid to touch the body. The man was a slender fellow, neatly dressed, with pallid features. Presently a heavy man under

a broad-brimmed hat came out of Rue des Pomegranates.
A little later some members of the crowd remembered
that he came up quite spryly, but that when he walked
away he moved slowly, as if walking bothered him.

This one had an air of authority, sharp, decisive. He
knelt down and felt for the man's heart. When he took
his hand away it was wet and warm. He turned the man's
shoulders so that his face was fully revealed, and brought
out a pocket light which he played full onto the dead face
of Alexander Vaskaya. The crowd shivered and murmured.

The one who seemed to know just what to do in a
matter of this kind bent his head close to the other's chest,
so that the broad brim of his hat almost covered one part
of the body. If his hands groped among pockets, in the
coat, the vest, and trousers, those who watched saw only
that he did the mysterious things a medical man does, felt
for the flow of blood in the pulse or for additional
wounds, or sign of a twitching muscle. It is well known
that it is not sufficient just to look at a man if he has
been shot at or stabbed.

The thick man raised his head. Now the crowd understood that there was no life and raised a clamor of indignation. The noise attracted a policeman who hadn't
even heard the shots. He came running up, followed by
another, and another.

"What's happened? What's this? What's wrong with
this fellow?"

The man who had knelt over the body got up, with a
painful effort, and brushed the dust of the road from his
trousers.

"He is dead, M'sieu'. Stone dead."

"How do you know?"

"I have examined him. I thought it might not be too

late and I might assist. He has been shot through the
heart by a very good marksman, and died at once."

"You felt him? You touched him? Don't you know it
is unlawful to do that before the Medical Examiner
arrives?"

"But what would you, M'sieu'? One first must know
that the Medical Examiner is required."

The policeman looked at his companions doubtfully.
There was truth in what this queer chap under such a
broad brim had to say.

"Who are you?" the agent asked. "What is your
name?"

"Khamov, M'sieu'. I live in Rue des Pomegranates.
Number fifty-one."

The officer took copious notes. The names and estates
of all who had come upon the body but had seen nothing.
The man who thought he had seen a shadow was very
important. There was so much shouting and excited interchange among the crowd that the policeman became very
stern and ordered everybody to be quiet, strictly silent,
until he had completed his notes.

Because the crowd was obeying the officers at that moment, and was fidgeting in silence, Michael Ballou,
coming home from the Villa Amette in a taxi, did not
pay any attention to the knot of people when his cab
swung into Rue des Pomegranates from Boulevard
d'Italia. He got out at his door, paid his driver, and went
up to his room.

When, just within his door, he had switched on the
electric lamp, he stood immovable, rigid with consternation which quickly developed into fear. His room had
been entered and his belongings thoroughly searched. His
two suitcases had been lifted onto his bed and opened.
Their contents were thrown onto the floor in confusion.

Every corner of the room had been gone into. Drawers had been pulled out and emptied and still lay on the floor, overturned. His papers and letters had been dumped from the desk drawer.

The disorder of the room and its meaning held his attention only for an instant. He locked his door, ran to the fireplace and felt the surface of the bricks in the chimney. The marble jewel case was there. He brought it out and opened it, and was satisfied with one flash of red fires. He swiftly replaced it.

He dropped onto the edge of his bed and faced the unmistakable evidence that he was being watched, followed, tracked. Unseen forces were mobilized around him. Long hands were reaching. As far back as Switzerland, at Basle. Not long after he had met Tanya Amon and recognized in her the great Darya Vaskaya, the dancer. It mattered not that she chose to be known under the new name. He was keeping away from Helen Avery, then, and Tanya Amon came to him in his loneliness and wanted to make it easier for him to bear. So Tanya Amon had come to him, had been with him a little while, when this thing—this spying, and searching—happened the first time.

He had a little wine with her from a half full bottle and she went out to do some shopping. He thought to read until she came back but fell asleep. The drowsiness came upon him suddenly and queerly. Tanya wakened him, hours later. Stood over the chair where he'd dropped off shaking him and pleading with him to open his eyes and recognize her.

Poor, lovely Tanya—Darya! He felt more tender for her after that. She was so terrified. She thought he must be dead when she came from shopping to find him in his chair slumped over like that. She had told him of a lover

who had died. In Warsaw. She was afraid she was losing
another and, she said that night, when she lay in his arms,
she could never stand losing another love in death. So she
was frightened, but he wakened and was none the worse,
and then he saw that while he slept, his rooms had been
entered and searched. Everything the two of them owned
was strewn around. Just as now, the drawers from
bureaus and desk were overturned on the floor.

They had decided, Tanya and he, that someone had
drugged the half bottle of wine. Tanya remembered that
she had felt fearfully sleepy while she went among the
shops. She hadn't drunk as much of the wine as had he,
and then, of course, she was in the open air and walking
about. She had fought off the drowsiness where he had
succumbed to it.

That was the first time he had been visited. He remembered now while he sat on the edge of the bed what
a strain it was, that time, to wait until Tanya could find
an errand away from the rooms so that he might look
for his marble case. There was a roof eave just under a
coping outside their bedroom window. He could stand
on the window sill, reach up and drop the box into the
eave. The roof sloped to a high gable, so nobody ever
would see the box in the eave under the coping. The in-
truders had not found it. The rubies were safe on their
velvet cushion.

His rooms were searched again, at Havre. Tanya was
still with him. She understood that he didn't love her,
never could. But he liked her as a lovely companion. She
assured him that she didn't love him, though at times she
acted as if she did. He'd come upon her weeping two or
three times and she could never explain why. That was
a bad sign. In Havre his followers had time for a leisurely
search. He went to Paris for a day and Tanya, to while

away the time of his absence, went to visit a friend who, she explained, lived on one of the islands just outside the harbor. So she was away a day and a night, as he was.

When he went home Tanya had arrived only an hour or so before. She had seen nothing wrong, but he discovered immediately that his effects had been disturbed. An attempt was made to leave everything just as it had been, but it was a trick of his mind to know just in what order his papers were stacked, and which collars were first in order in his collar box. He saw at once that every paper he had had been moved, and that his clothes had been gone over. Tanya was greatly distressed. She begged him to tell her, to confide in her, what it was that he had that someone else wanted. Neither in Basle nor in Havre was any of her jewelry taken, nor any of his few valuables—his evening watch or the gold headed stick his uncle had given him.

Tanya pleaded with him to tell her what it could mean. At last, knowing that she could be trusted without stint, he had shown her the rubies. He took them out of the case, because of some feeling he had that it would be better for her if he did not compel her to share the responsibility of worrying about so much bulk to keep hidden, and he wouldn't throw the case away. He didn't tell her the history of the stones, nor did she press him. She was too excited, as a woman would be, over their splendor and value. She wondered, as any one would, why he hadn't sold them. Or some of them. He had made some impromptu explanation and then, in a moment of great affection for the girl who tried so hard to soothe his loneliness, he made her accept one. He knew she would never dispose of it. A Darya Vaskaya would never need.

Tanya had wondered if it really were the rubies the people who did the searching wanted. He'd laughed and said it couldn't be the only silk shirt he had left, nor his gold cigarette case, which he had left in the room at Havre and which was not disturbed.

Now they had followed him into Rue des Pomegranates, where, he thought, he had escaped all track of himself. Suddenly he thought of his neighbor, Khamov. How the man had watched him on the free benches beyond the Esplanade. He had watched him in Rue des Pomegranates. He had said as much. His eyes, one minute gentle, like a young deer's eyes; next minute, when you glanced at them unexpectedly, hard, anthracite fires. His mouth—so flexible when he talked softly, but now and again you caught it fixed into a grim, ferocious cast.

Khamov had taken such a fancy to him. Always coming to his door. Always questioning him. Last season's races at Auteuil. "Were you there, my friend? Ah, no? Where, then, were you when the pretty horses ran at Auteuil?"

Questions, questions, questions!

The great automatic in Khamov's drawer. Any man may have a pistol, of course, but not a weapon like that. And not a man who was as simple and humble as Khamov pretended to be. Only a day or two ago, when he came into Cannes on an errand for Villa Amette and took the opportunity to stop at his room for a moment, he found Khamov coolly sitting in his chair.

"You are careless, Michael Ballou," the man had said with a great pretense of righteous fault finding. "You should not leave your door unlocked when you go out. As for me, I have mounted guard. I came up to put a note under your door, asking you to breakfast with me to-morrow morning. What do I find? Your door is ajar. I think you have come home and gone out to purchase some wine, perhaps. So I wait, and watch over your room. Tell me, good Michael Ballou, that I have done right."

That had been the man's explanation of his presence in the room. But Michael knew he had not left his door unlocked. Or, he was almost sure. It would not be like him.

Khamov was the one to look out for!

All of these thoughts and memories had gone through his head in a mere flash of time. They left him cold with fear, a fear that was not alone for the Jeribzoff rubies, but of some unknown significance associated with the man Khamov. Sight of his disordered room increased it —made it almost a tangible thing that clutched at him. He flung out of the room and ran down the stairs into the night outside. He turned away from the direction of Khamov's house, which is to say that he turned toward Boulevard d'Italia. He saw the little crowd gathered around an ambulance where Rue des Pomegranates runs into the boulevard. He saw pompous little policemen fussing about and he went along to see what it was all about.

Men were lifting a body on a stretcher into the ambulance. He asked a white faced girl what had happened.

"*Meurtre!* Murder. I heard the shots."

"A man, or woman?" Michael asked.

"A man, M'sieu. Very good-looking. And not very old. Three bullets in the heart. He was coming from up there." The girl pointed into Rue des Pomegranates.

Just then an officer detached himself from the crowd and with him was his neighbor. They were walking off together.

"Khamov!" shouted Michael, his mind leaping to a curious conviction that there was some connection between the crime and the burglarious search of his possessions. He was instantly regretful, however, that he shouted for his neighbor. A moment ago he had decided that Khamov was the tracker.

The Russian turned and saw him. He came back, while the officer watched, and spoke to him softly. "Later, Michael Ballou," he said. "I think it better that I go with the police. I am curious to know the identity of a man who is murdered so close to our doors. Please to wait for me in my room. The door is open. We will have coffee royale."

Khamov got into the ambulance with two of the policemen. One officer would have considerately made room for him in the front part of the ambulance interior, where there was a cross seat on which he could sit without facing the lifeless flesh on the stretcher. But he declined. He was comfortable, he assured the agent, on the side seat. "Death is only life in another form," he said. "I sometimes even find it pleasant to look upon."

At the mortuary the Russian and the police watched while the body was laid on a slab. Khamov hovered close to it to take one last look into the still face. The agent understood his emotion. He had seen the man so soon after his untimely death. Almost as soon as he had fallen. And no matter what the fellow said in the ambulance about being pleased with death, it gets a civilian where it doesn't much affect a policeman.

A mortuary attendant who was responsible to the Medical Examiner searched the dead man's pockets. There was a hypodermic tube and its needle, tell-tale of the man's habits, and explaining the heavy lids over his eyes and weak, loose mouth. Strangely, there were no envelopes with letters, or documents, or cards from which an identification might be made. Of any kind of papers, there was only one piece, a card in a waistcoat pocket on which was written, in a precise hand, "Dolly will come to you in Rue des Pomegranates. She sends this message. I did not know she had gone from her apartment."

There was no signature. A police inspector, at the Sûreté, before whom Khamov was ushered and to whom were displayed the hypodermic, and few other sundries, keys, cigarette packet and pocket knife, was inclined to regard the Russian with suspicion. It already had been mentioned to him that this curious fellow, who wore such an execrable hat and had eyes too soft to mean any good, lived in Rue des Pomegranates. And he had been one of the first to come upon the body. A subordinate, however, called his attention to the fact that the card had been folded with a single crease, and that on a section of its back a name had been written.

Inspector Clement turned over the card and twisted it around to read the name that had been written crosswise. "Croyant. Hotel Crillon."

He looked again to make sure he read aright. His meticulous mind wanted to employ itself with the detail that the same hand had not written the message on one side of the card and the name and hotel on the other. The message had been written carefully, levelly lined, as if the penman wrote at his leisure and with choice of phrasings. And he had used ink.

"Croyant. Hotel Crillon" was written with a pencil in a barely legible scrawl. Inspector Clement could not dismiss the thought that the writer had used his pencil under difficulties, unable, perhaps, to see what he was writing.

Khamov, who had slipped into the background while the police official and the agents considered the card, watched with an alert glance. Inspector Clement surrendered the puzzle of the contrasting handwriting and re-read the name, "Croyant." He gave a brief order to a clerk.

"Get Monsieur Lemair on the telephone."

He fell then to rapping out questions for Khamov to answer. The Russian repeated the short story he had already told several times. He lived in Rue des Pomegranates, yes. What was he doing abroad at that time of the night? How shall one say, when there was no reason? There are times when one does not sleep. One goes out in the air.

He was asked to produce his papers of identification, which he did. He was Makar Ivanovitch Khamov, male, bachelor, born in Leningrad when it was still called St. Petersburg. His profession was simply that of scholar. He had come to Cannes for the benefit of the splendid climate. While he talked Inspector Clement studied his face, putting it away in his mind, perhaps, against any possible future need. The man's hawk-like nose interested him more than any other feature. It seemed out of place in such a general aspect of mildness.

"You carry, I see, an official passport of the Soviet government," Inspector Clement observed. He held it up, indicating the many official stamps, including the huge red *vise* of the O.G.P.U., the dread police organization. "You are not a refugee, then?"

The Russian shook his head. He was not a refugee in the police and diplomatic sense of the term.

"You will swear that you do not know the dead man? That you did not recognize a friend when you looked into his face so promptly after you found him on the pavement?"

Khamov repeated, a little wearily, that he did not know the man. Would it not be, M'sieu', that one who knew him also would know the "Dolly" mentioned in the message on the card? This M'sieu' Croyant, of the Hotel Crillon, perhaps he would know "Dolly." Perhaps even it was he who had the rendezvous with her in Rue des Pomegranates.

Monsieur Lemair, the prefect of police, came on the wire. The incident was briefly described by Inspector Clement, who read the handwriting on the card.

"Major Croyant!" Lemair exclaimed. "There will be some significance. Telephone him. I will be down at once."

Major Croyant came over from the Crillon and Lemair came from his house. Croyant glanced curiously at Khamov, who remained in the back of the room, and then examined the card. Khamov, who had not been explained to the Englishman, permitted himself an intrusion. He stepped into the circle of light over Inspector Clement's desk and ventured to suggest that "Dolly" would not know that her writing had been undelivered and that she might, accordingly, come into Rue des Pomegranates at any time. But of course, he added in sudden confusion, one could not ask every young lady, and every old one, who came into a street, if she were "Dolly." He apologized for the inanity of his thought by sweeping his broad-brimmed hat toward the floor.

Croyant looked at him sharply. For a moment it seemed as if the eyes of the Russian held the eyes of the Englishman and as if there was a tautness between them. When Khamov retired into the shadows of the outer spaces of the room Croyant looked after him.

"It's all Greek to me," said Croyant to Lemair. "Dolly is a diminutive, of course. It stands for different names in different countries. I might greatly enjoy a visit from the young lady but it remains that I do not live in Rue des Pomegranates and never go there. I do not even know where the street is."

Khamov volunteered, politely, "It is off Boulevard d'Italia. It is——"

Lemair shut him up curtly. "Do we have any further use for this man?" he asked Inspector Clement. The Russian was dismissed. Clement still kept a suspicion of him for being out in the street so close to midnight, with no explanation of where he had been going. Lemair and Croyant, however, busied themselves altogether with the card.

"I should like to see the remains," Croyant said, and they went across the Place Peyrier, from the Hotel de Ville to the mortuary. When Alexander Vaskaya's face was uncovered Croyant stared at it for a long time. He had caught but one short glimpse of the face of the man who met "Mademoiselle Amon" in the arena at Toulouse. When he received from Warsaw the police photographs of Darya Vaskaya's brother, he had recalled that face in the Roman ruin. His recollection gave life to the sullen face in the photographs. And here was that face, in death.

"He is wholly unfamiliar to me," he said, however. "I can't imagine why he should have been carrying my name and the name of my hotel."

Lemair pointed out, "It looks as though your name had been put separately on the card. Perhaps a memorandum written before the message about 'Dolly' was inscribed, or afterwards."

"Or afterwards?" Croyant murmured. He added, briskly, "It arouses curiosity. But what shall we do until the man is identified?"

"There seems to be nothing, Monsieur. He had carefully removed any papers that might have revealed his identity."

"Or someone else removed them!"

"But who, Monsieur Croyant? Clement's reports show the assassins shooting from a distance. They were not near their victim."

"Someone in the crowd that gathered around him."

Lemair agreed with the possibility. He gave an order to Inspector Clement, who had accompanied them to the morgue, to immediately round up every person who had been seen near the body. He particularly wanted the Russian with the wide-brimmed hat. Clement went out of the slab room to convey the order to headquarters but was recalled by his superior. Croyant had interposed. He felt an interest in the crime, he explained, because of the mysterious appearance of his name on the dead man. He would like to have not too much attention called to the murder. If the man was supposed to have anything to do with him, doubtless there would be an aftermath. Someone would take up where he had left off. The prefect agreed, as he was ready to agree to any suggestion from Major Croyant.

The Major walked through the night to the Crillon. He passed through the Esplanade on his way to the Croisette where he would make the turn to his hotel. In the wicker chairs on the wide promenade were the usual curious assortment of "night sitters." After eleven o'clock at night anyone who wishes may occupy a franc chair. The policeman on duty discriminates judiciously between the loungers whom he will permit to sit under the stars and gaze at the night scene on the bay, and those whom he will not permit to loiter. Of course he is guided largely by the matter of clothing. A "bum" he drives off with great gusto. A "swell" receives his "Good evening, M'sieu'." Mostly the "night sitters" were elderly men whose dreams are behind them or lost, perhaps, in the twinkling lights of the pleasure boats skimming the bay with youth and love and laughter for cargo.

From one of the chairs a man who was not elderly but apparently an invalid, for he was wrapped in a shawl, arose to block Croyant's path. Despite the inference of his shawl he walked with a springy, energetic step.

"Vaskaya's brother?" said the man into Croyant's face. "Tell me I am right."

"Already you have put the fur business aside," returned Croyant, drily. "It was Alexander. But you were not at the Sûreté. How have you heard of it?"

"I saw him fall," declared Dupree. "I saw the assassin disappear into Avenue du Prado. I dared not follow for I wanted to see who came to show an interest in the body."

"You saw him fall?"

"I was behind him. He came out of the house of our young friend in Rue des Pomegranates. Our young friend was not at home, for I was watching for his return. From your photographs from Warsaw I thought the stranger would be Alexander. So I was right? On his body—the cat's head?"

Croyant shook his head. "The assassin could not have approached him after the shots did their work."

"No?" Dupree was scornful. "What would you say, my friend, if I assured you the man's pockets were searched—with a deftness I could not myself manage— before my very eyes? Before the eyes of the watchers who saw nothing? Every pocket cleaned of paper or card or means of identification?"

"I would say it is a mystery that you did not spring!"

"I prefer to wait until I know what my hands will grasp when I have leapt. A broad-brimmed hat may be a prize, but of higher value when we know who it is who wears it. You have no thought of why The Panther should remove this one who has served him so well in the past?"

"Only this one, Ariste; perhaps Alexander was about to change his masters."

Dupree started. He thrust his face close to Croyant's and peered into it.

"That is the obvious thought, my friend. But will you not share with me the rest of it?"

"Darya Vaskaya will not forget the death of her brother. Is that not a gratifying thought, Ariste?"

"I take it to my couch," returned Dupree, "as a young man takes a beautiful woman. Hopefully."

CHAPTER XI

OMINOUS SIGNALS

MICHAEL BALLOU waited in his neighbor's room for his return from the police bureau. He sat in the one chair, an arm chair, and contemplated the disorder of the Russian's quarters. It reminded him of the litter of his own belongings left by the unknown intruder.

Fear of his neighbor returned a hundred fold. Intuition as physical as prodding fingers clamored a warning that sooner or later he would be confronted by a Makar Khamov no longer mild and gentle under his grotesque, broad-brimmed hat.

He was increasingly certain that there was some connection between his neighbor and the man whose body lay on the cobblestones at the entrance to Rue des Pomegranates. Suddenly he got up, as if his action were a reflex of his thought. He jerked open the drawer of the table where the Russian had looked for cube sugar. Before he realized that he was prying into the privacies of an absent host he swept aside the papers and clippings.

The automatic pistol was not in the drawer. He closed the drawer and in his nervousness shook the table violently. A tambourine—oddest of the man's possessions! —fell to the floor. The pistol had been lying under it and close by was an oily rag recently used in cleaning it. Also at its side was a box of cartridges from which one row of shells had been removed. He slipped the magazine and saw that the weapon was fully loaded.

A little ashamed now of his actions, he sat down again in the arm chair. He consoled himself with the thought that he had suspected his neighbor of killing the man in the street and had proved that he had not, for he could not have shot him down, returned to his room and cleaned and reloaded his pistol and reached the scene again before the police arrived.

But he did not feel any easier. Perhaps Khamov was watching while the man entered his room and searched it as his agent. His being near when the man was so mysteriously shot would thus be explained.

Khamov came home in an hour and a half. He appeared to be deeply affected by his experience, subdued and a little nervous. He moved about his room touching things for no purpose. He picked up the fallen tambourine which Michael had forgotten, replaced it on the table and moved away only to turn quickly and stare at it as though suddenly he was bethought that he had left it over his pistol. He glanced from the weapon to Michael. The young man felt himself flushing but the other seemed not to notice. He went to boiling some water over a gas flame for coffee royale.

The police had questioned him, he said. But what could he tell them? Police were dolts.

"In our country, Michael Ballou, the police do not waste their time mouthing questions. They use their eyes until they have found something to see. Then they know what to do, and do it. Is it not so, good friend?"

"Our country is not the same. I have told you that I am an American."

Again and again Michael had had to repeat doggedly his insistence upon American nationality. And always his neighbor received the rebuke with gentle resignation. Michael knew that he merely granted him his evasions, as an indulgent parent grants a child his half-lie rather than hurt its feelings with reproof.

"Of course," said Khamov as he always did. "I understand. You are of America, Michael Ballou. You are not Russian. It is quite understood. We will have strong coffee tonight. It is an event, being questioned by the police. As I was saying, in my country the police are not dolts. There is that fellow Chenkin, the Moscow terror. The Empire falls and the government changes. Kerensky and Trotsky go, Lenin dies and Stalin remains. But what does it mean to Chenkin, foe of the asssassin and thief? Nothing. He goes on. Why? Because he embalms his tongue and uses only his eyes and ears."

He pulled out his drawer for cube sugar. Michael was uneasy when he observed that his neighbor frowned and was puzzled by the arrangement of his papers and clippings. Michael had disturbed them, certainly, but it had not occurred to him that any fresh disorder could be differentiated from the confusion that had been before. But the man seemed to know that his drawer had been rearranged. He looked around and flicked his pistol with a glance.

"I have heard of Chenkin," Michael admitted, more to distract the man than to carry on the subject. He was planning how to broach the matter of the search of his rooms. He wanted to bring it up and watch the other's face. He had decided to wait until the coffee royale was ready. Khamov would be busied with his cup and his face turned in full view.

The Russian paused in his quest of sugar to look over his shoulder. Michael thought his eyes had hardened. When his eyes lost their gentleness his nose seemed to become more prominent, and forbidding.

"You say that you have heard of Chenkin? Perhaps

you know that he is in Cannes? Perhaps you even know
what he is doing here?"

Michael started. His sensitive mouth tensed and whit-
ened. Presence of Chenkin in Cannes struck him with a
new, a desperate fear.

"He is here? On the Riviera? But why should I know
what he does? Do you know?"

Khamov did not reply at once. He found his sugar and
brought his bottle of old brandy from under the newspapers on the bed. He held the bottle to the light. "Tonight we will finish my brandy. After the coffee there will
be sufficient for two small swallows."

Michael watched him closely. Khamov hummed to himself. Michael's mind wandered from Chenkin, fearsome
agent of the Police Section of the Ogpu, to that night in
Warsaw when he sat in the theater holding Helen Avery's
hand while the dancer on the stage made her rhythmic
obeisance to her Hindu gods. He wondered why the
vision of the dancer who was later to become his companion returned to him now, not as the Tanya Amon
of their companionship, but as the Darya Vaskaya of
the theater.

Suddenly he knew!

That music his strange neighbor was humming. The
crescendo measures from the theme of the Dancer of
Kashmir. He had not heard it since Warsaw, but he
would never forget that final dramatic strain. While the
music swept to its close that night Helen's fingers had
gripped his and his fingers had gripped hers and a minute
later both had laughed at their discovery that their hands
ached.

He realized that the memory was affecting him so
deeply that his neighbor must notice his emotion. He
shook his head to clear it and then was aware, with a

shock that sent a queer cold feeling along his spine, that his host was watching him over his coffee cup and that he had been humming the same brief strain over and over. He stopped abruptly when Michael looked up, and lifted his cup to take a long sip. He spoke softly, as if he voiced a reflection that concerned only himself.

"Chenkin walks on the balls of his toes but I know where he walks, in Cannes."

Michael made a move as if to spring from his chair. His host's tone was mocking, a taunt. Suddenly the Russian laughed, loudly with a great bovine merriment. "But we talk of Chenkin! Is that not ludicrous? We will finish my brandy. Of my visit to the police there is nothing more to say. The assailant escaped. It is not even known what the name of the young man who was killed might be. The police are such fools. A vendetta business perhaps. Or a quarrel about a woman. There are so many women in Rue des Pomegranates. For every ripe plum there are always two fruit pickers to quarrel."

"I don't think it was a fruit pickers' quarrel over a plum," Michael said.

He told his neighbor of his discovery when he came from the Villa Amette. He watched the other's face closely while he described the disorder of his room, how even his linen and cravats had been taken from the drawers and tossed onto the floor.

Khamov listened attentively. Michael had the impression that he wasn't particularly interested. His conviction that his neighbor knew something about that search increased. But the Russian expressed polite concern and asked questions.

"You do not act as though a valuable was taken. As though the burglar helped himself."

"Nothing was found."

"What's this, good friend?" Khamov was greatly amused. His mouth grinned widely. "You speak as if you have articles of great value, but keep them hidden. Are you a rich man in disguise?"

Now Michael was more than certain, or, if one may not be more than certain, his certainty reached a higher degree of positiveness. His neighbor was a spy and an enemy.

"What could I own that I should have to hide?"

The Russian laughed. He was in high good humor and lifted his brandy glass gayly. "But we talk ourselves to no place! Let it pass. Was it the man in the street who searched your room? Quite possibly so, Michael Ballou. For what and why? If you do not know, neither do the police know who killed him. Let us not be troubled by what is not known. Let us talk of your day at the Villa Amette. Your job is amusing."

Michael was in no humor to talk of Clare Fraser and her strange household, of her dogs and her Count Tanaroff. He made his excuses and went to his own room to put his belongings in order. After he was on the stairs going down from his neighbor's room into the street he came near to turning back. He had intended to ask the man why he hummed that music from the Dancer of Kashmir. He could not be mistaken in his belief that Khamov had deliberately repeated the air over and over, aware of the emotion it caused him, and feeding it.

He decided against returning, however.

A letter from Helen Avery arrived at the Crillon for Croyant. The *Ariadne* had anchored in the tiny harbor of Port del Sol in an inlet of the Spanish coast. Georges Raynel's people had come up from Toledo and he had found it necessary to go with them to Barcelona. He made the short run by train and had there delivered Helen's letter to the Air Post.

Helen and the rest of the party were having an enjoyable time. Yesterday, with her mother, the Ransoms and the Severns, she had climbed the mountain roads to the little capital of Andorra. She had carried a cup of water from the Spring of the Moors up the thousand foot climb along a winding goat trail to the shrine of El Camino Virgin, the King's Virgin, hewn out of solid rock nearly two thousand years ago by Christian fugitives from the massacres at Rome. She had poured her offering of water in the rock basin at the foot of the shrine which those early Christians kept filled with daily drops of life blood from their own veins.

She sat alone at the shrine, Helen wrote, a long time. It seemed as if she were in the clouds over the world looking down on the life she'd climbed from and must return to. She had the queerest feeling, she said, of a Presence hovering near. A Presence that brought her a message, perhaps a warning, that down there in the world was a path laid for her feet alone, but a path she had never found.

"I spoke of the feeling to Georges," she wrote, "and he laughed at me. I pouted at him but he laughed just the same and said that the altitude does things like that to one. And another curious thing. While we were descending the mountains from the odd little republic I remembered out of a clear sky the note in your voice the other evening when you wondered if I purposed going ashore for the night. There was some reason I shouldn't! It's very clear to me now. You were worried about me, or for me. Why? Shan't you tell me when we return to Cannes? Georges will be back tomorrow, or so he plans. Then we shall up-anchor."

Croyant reached hastily for the envelope that had enclosed the letter. "Tomorrow" might be today, or yesterday. The Spanish post office stamp disclosed that the letter had been posted at Barcelona late on the day before. "Tomorrow" was today. Last night Raynel had been absent from Port del Sol, leaving Helen and her friends to their own devices. They might have determined to pass the night ashore, at one of the ancient inns dotted along the Spanish coast each with his fireplace where, the proprietor will swear, King Ferdinand chucked a kitchen wench under the chin while Isabella awaited him in a chamber above. Humble indeed is the inn along the coast that will not provide you with the very bed Isabella slept in, or, for a slightly higher fee, the bed in which Philip enjoyed a preliminary nap with the wench. Croyant saw, with Dupree's eyes, Vaskaya watching Helen from the Guy de Maupassant pier. Dupree would guard her after her return to Cannes. At Port del Sol——!

He asked the Crillon telephone operators to connect him with the Long Distance division. A moment later he was informed that there was no public telephonic connection with the little Spanish sea village. He asked to be put through to Monsieur Lemair, prefect of police.

Monsieur Lemair referred to his charts and happily discovered that the Spanish Marine Administration maintained a departmental telephone at the port. "Through the Maritimes Cabinet at Marseilles," he promised, "I will have you connected at once if you will do me the honor to come to my office where the offiical wire is available."

Croyant hurried to the Sûreté. There was some difficulty in explaining to a Spanish customs official that the mutual marine interests of two neighboring republics required that a Senorita Avery be brought from the yacht

Ariadne, now anchored in the tiny harbor. Monsieur Lemair surmounted the difficulty and the wire was kept open until thirty minutes had elapsed and Helen's voice came to the prefect's desk.

"What in the world? Major Croyant!"

Croyant released a breath of relief. Nothing had happened to her. He felt indescribably sheepish and unprepared.

"I heard of a tidal wave," he invented. "I thought the *Ariadne* might have been sunk. I take it that it wasn't."

Helen was bewildered. "Major Croyant, there's something the matter. You know there was no tidal wave. Whoever heard of such a thing in the Mediterranean? Please tell me why you called." She gasped in a surge of alarm. "Nothing—has happened to Georges?"

He could have cursed himself for arousing anxiety for her fiancé. "I wanted only to scold you for a too fertile imagination. I was only dumbly curious about where you'd spend the night, when we talked at the rail in the harbor here. Still planning to up-anchor today?"

"Georges will motor up from Barcelona. We expect him late this afternoon. We'll sail tonight or in the morning. And you'll have a lot of explaining about this mysterious telephone call when I see you."

When he had released the wire and expressed appreciations to Monsieur Lemair, the prefect at once brought up the matter of the man who had been found dead in the entrance to Rue des Pomegranates.

"Monsieur Dupree is extremely concerned by the affair," the prefect said. "He visited me at my house in the early hours of the morning."

"You told him of the card, its message and of my name being written on it?"

"It made a marked difference in certain plans he had

made. He had asked me to investigate every house on the street. Mostly, as you may not know, they are tenanted by, ahem, what shall we say, Monsieur? Ladies who believe old professions are the best? But Monsieur Dupree thought I might find one tenant more interesting than another, and proposed that we pay especial attention, without arresting him, to the Russian who lives at Fifty-one. The man you saw at the Bureau. When I told him of the card that had been found on the body he was very moved."

"Ariste is easily moved," Croyant murmured. "He changed his plans?"

"Yes, Monsieur. He expressed no further interest in the residents of Rue des Pomegranates. Particularly he requested that we do not disturb with any further questioning the tenant of Fifty-one. He gave me to understand his own men would watch that one. One knows that you are informed of Dupree's activity, of its nature. One may speak of his assignment by Paris to capture The Panther. His concern over the affair of the unexplained assassination leads one to surmise that there is a connection."

Monsieur Lemair plainly fished for Croyant's explanation of the presence of his name in the victim's pockets, convinced that the Englishman's professed mystification was a pose.

Croyant was thoughtful. He had been seated across the desk from the prefect. He got up and went to a window, whistling softly. He looked out over a grove of blooming acacias in the open square across from the Sûreté. Beyond was the Quai St. Pierre, with its jetty protruding into the waters of the bay. A yacht was just dropping anchor, a low, lean craft that seemed to lie flat on the water and was a sharp contrast to the other pleasure boats that dotted the shallows lapping the jetty. The others were white; this one just throwing its anchor overboard, was black, as black as a shining crow. Croyant studied its whippet-like lines and the slight rake to stern that gave a torpedo boat effect. There was no name painted at either bow or stern, or if there was it was done in such small lettering that it could not be read from Monsieur Lemair's window. Tall masts towered above the low bridge structure with wireless aerials swung between them.

Croyant stood silently while he took in every line of the black painted hull of the new arrival at the quai. His glance leapt from stem to stern and seemed to estimate the height of the aerial masts. He turned back into the room abruptly. He drew a gold pencil from his waistcoat pocket and made a hasty sketch of a floor plan on a scratch pad slipped under his fingers by the prefect.

"This," he said, "is the plan of a bistro, the *Auberg des Cochons*, beyond the Cannebiere in Marseilles. It fronts on a cobbled road in the Old Port." He tapped the drawing he had made with the tip of his pencil. "Behind this door there is a passage—I have drawn it here. At the end of the corridor—in this room—are the belongings of the man who was killed in Rue des Pomegranates, unless they have been already removed, which I think improbable."

Monsieur Lemair gave an exclamation.

"The card then was intended for you? One does not question the secretiveness of Monsieur le Major Croyant, but one may be curious?"

The prefect spoke a little sharply and was not at all pleased that Croyant should have deceived him when the card was first exhibited.

Croyant smiled quizzically. "But I atone, Monsieur. I

send you and Ariste to the rendezvous of the Pigs, who perform The Panther's minor assassinations. I commend to you and Dupree, particularly, the bartender. His name is Bibi. It is possible Ariste may make Bibi talk."

Monsieur Lemair touched a button. When his messenger appeared he ordered that his car be brought to the curb below at once. To Croyant he explained, "I should not know where to find the elusive Monsieur Dupree upon short notice. He advises us that he proposes to sell pictures of Ste. Catherine to the midinettes in the Croisette, but we hear of him raiding a house in Mentone. Where I might think to put my finger upon him at this hour is precisely the spot where he wouldn't be. I shall conduct the descent upon the *Auberge des Cochons* myself, with the assistance of Marseilles. We will keep the prisoners for Dupree's disposition. I invite you, Monsieur le Major, to accompany me if you wish. You are expert in your own right at making the taciturn become garrulous."

Croyant acknowledged what, from a policeman, was a noteworthy compliment, but denied himself the privilege of being in on the raid on the House of Pigs. He prepared to go with Monsieur Lemair to the street, declining a proffered lift to the Crillon. With so much leisure on his hands, he explained, he preferred to walk.

In the corridors outside his suite the Prefect was confronted by Inspector Clement. As a rule the Inspector, who was in command during the night, left for his home with the dawn. It was well after midmorning now but he was still on duty. With him was the night chief of the wireless section, also showing signs of not having left his post. Monsieur Lemair brought up sharply.

"What keeps you, Clement?"

"Watching the wireless, sir. I'm uneasy. I think you should be informed."

Monsieur Lemair made a gesture of impatience. "One waits."

"Strange signals, sir. Wireless began to pick them up at two o'clock this morning. The air was filled with them. They continued until daybreak, when there was a lull. They came through again at eight o'clock and continued until half an hour ago; the last was at ten o'clock."

Monsieur Lemair looked at the wireless chief then back to Clement. He started and took a quick step forward. "Signals? You mean—?" He paused. Inspector Clement nodded. The chief of wireless spoke, repressing his excitement with difficulty.

"The same unknown code, sir, that was in the air on the night of The Panther's visit to Bordeaux. The same signals we caught after the murder of Señor Veragua. I'm not mistaken. They stood out from everything in the air and they're the only signals whose sending origin we haven't identified. Eiffel Tower reports an occasional pick-up during the night and agrees with our conclusions."

"But we hear of no crime of consequence. Nothing has occurred. I am persuaded we permit ourselves to be aroused by some fiddling amateur who entertains himself and would be vastly amused by our alarms."

The wireless chief granted himself a disagreement with his prefect. "They are not sent by an amateur, Monsieur. That I will swear to. My colleagues agree. I recall to your excellency that on the night of Bordeaux, when we thought we were interfered with by an air tourist, the signals came in wild, from changing directions. It was so on the night of the Veragua crime. It was so again last night and this morning. I have checked up with Algiers, Rome and Valencia as well as with Paris. I venture the belief, sir, that last night's signals came from the west, while this morning they were sent from the east. The wave band is not the same as the band appropriated on the night of the Veragua matter, as the band used that night differed from the channel utilised after Bordeaux. But the signals are in the same code. Its key, if we could hit upon it, would be the same."

Monsieur Lemair invited Inspector Clement to speak. Croyant, with the air of a casual listener a trifle bored, missed no nuance of the alarms in the facial expressions he watched. About his mouth a tell-tale grimness had settled. His eyes were cold gray.

"I'm frank to say I'm worried, sir," said Inspector Clement. "As a rule we make short work of air intrusions. But the sender of these signals eludes us. We all have the conviction that they originate with The Panther. I'm expecting to hear any minute that he has struck again. It's an uncanny situation."

Monsieur Lemair tapped the floor with the ferrule of his stick. Clement and the wireless chief watched him anxiously. He turned, abruptly, to Croyant.

"You witness, Monsieur, the state of mind into which The Panther has catapulted the safety bureaus of the nation. The drone of an unknown plane sends us scurrying into the trackless clouds. Now, an alien spark picked out of the air sets us to trembling. Unless you have another suggestion I shall ask Marseilles to attend to the *Auberge des Cochons*. They will keep their prisoners and whatever else is found for Dupree's disposition. I will wait at my desk until we have determined if the signals that coincided with the Bordeaux and Veragua crimes were mere coincidents or if, again, they have a significance."

Croyant agreed promptly that the prefect should remain close to his communications. Monsieur Lemair invited him to remain while they waited—the unknown. He excused himself and went down to the street.

He hurried through the square of acacias, onto the jetty beyond Quai St. Pierre. From the guard rail of the jetty he scanned the bobbing fleet of nondescript motor boats at rest on the water. In one boat, floating close in, a waiting helmsman rose to his feet and waved his cap, receiving an answering arc of Croyant's arm. A moment later Croyant was aboard the launch and the helmsman steered for the black yacht.

CHAPTER XII

A RENDEZVOUS IN GENOA

WHILE Monsieur Lemair waited he tapped on his desk with a miniature scimitar done in ebony that served as a letter opener. The situation was incredible, the suspense fantastic. Waiting, like some absurd defeatist, or fatalist, for the apparition of Nemesis. Clement was a lout. The chief of wireless a school boy, neurotic. The Panther? One tenth a bold crook; nine tenths a physical nebula of absinthe vapors exuded by our distorted hallucinations.

The door was flung open. Clement stood there, calm, controlled. No uncertainties. Behind him the wireless chief, sheaf of unassorted messages in his hand. He, too, was composed, alert.

Monsieur Lemair sprang to his feet. His ebony scimitar dropped with a clatter. He said but one word, barked it. *"Oui?"*

Clement answered.

"Oui, Monsieur le Prefect. At Genoa. The medical examiner fixes the time as between midnight and one o'clock. The entire contents of a jewel cask. The preliminary estimate reaches four million lira. The crime was not discovered until an hour ago."

"Ten hours for escape!" exclaimed Monsieur Lemair. "The victim?"

The Inspector glanced at the wireless chief who confirmed the name by a reference to one of his sheets.

"The Marchesa di Estrel, sir. A member of the illustrious Capello family."

"The Marchesa!" Lemair echoed. The name added a magnitude to even such a notable sum as four million lira—two hundred thousand dollars. "Nita di Estrel! It is not comprehensible. It is less than a week since we provided her an escort from the Crillon to an entertainment in her honor by Prince Louis at the palace in Monaco." He glared at the Inspector to remind him that he should have recognized the name of the beautiful Italian who had been so recently a visitor to Cannes and, in the bargain, a guest of Monaco's royalty.

"I was in Paris last week, sir," Clement explained, "on a mission for Dupree."

Monsieur Lemair dropped back into his chair. "He left his *carte de visite?*"

"It was found in the emptied jewel cask. Drawn on the reverse of an engraved invitation to the ball in progress at the Marchesa's palace while he killed her in her boudoir on an upper floor."

Again the prefect was on his feet. He leapt up so excitedly that his chair slid backward across the floor.

"An invitation, you say? Do I hear aright? An invitation which would have been sent only to the Marchesa's friends? But it is beyond belief he should have so overstepped himself. At this minute the Genoa police will be studying the Marchesa's invitation list. The hunt is narrowed to a circle from which he can never escape."

Inspector Clement shook his head.

"There's a hitch somewhere. Genoa's first reports leave many details to follow but it's clear he knew what he was doing. The Marchesa's secretary, a young woman, examined the invitation card and announces that it was not posted by her. She forwarded the cards to a list especially edited for the occasion by her mistress."

"But that is not understandable, Inspector. One may not identify one engraved card from another."

Clement appealed to the wireless chief, who had been studying his transcripts of the brief and uncoordinated reports from Genoa.

"The card found in the jewel box had been personally inscribed by Madame," the wireless chief replied. "It is suggested that she posted it with her own hands to an acquaintance of—the Genoa operator uses his own phrase, sir; I repeat it—to an acquaintance of an interesting intimacy. The inscription is quoted: 'My dear—Are you as brave as I am when I sign—Nita.' "

Monsieur Lemair grunted. "Interesting intimacy! Do you realize, Clement, that she knew him? He was her lover. She braves her husband and grants a rendezvous in her very boudoir. One builds a fiend's tableau. In his arms, perhaps; his knife in her side while she sips his lips." He dismissed his imagery and demanded abruptly, "It was a knife, Inspector?"

"Similar to the weapon, I gather, found with Veragua."

From the messages already arrived and those that flowed in from Genoa to supplement them, a fairly complete narrative of the night's tragedy was sorted.

The young Marchesa di Estrel, herself a powerful Capello and her husband a descendant of one of those Genoese families who knew the young mariner, Christopher Columbus, as a child when his bare feet were burned by the hot planks of Genoa's harbor wharves, had given at her palace in the Piazzo d'Annuncio her annual ball to which the wealth and fashion of Genoa were bidden. In the lovely gardens of the old palace, guarded by the spires of the ancient Cathedral of the Annunciation,

myriad lanterns blinked over the most gala scene of
Genoa's social season. In the spacious rooms of the lower
floors of the house itself, youth and beauty danced to an
orchestra brought from Milan. Uniforms of the church
and army, and of the court at Rome, were background
for glistening frocks, ivory shoulders and glittering
jewels.

Nita di Estrel must have been a beautiful figure in the
midst of her brilliant assemblage, for the women of the
Capello's have always been beautiful, back to the days of
the Doges, and Nita, with her shining crown of anthracite
hair, her great dark eyes under lashes that were long
gossamer fans, lived in a world where beauty had become
an art unknown to her grandmothers.

But of Nita di Estrel's beauty, of the splendor of her
ball, of her triumphs and her husband's pride in his young
wife, the despatches from Genoa said little or nothing.

"The Marchesa complained of a slight illness shortly
before midnight. To her husband and a few others she
announced she would retire to her boudoir. She begged
that her guests be asked to condone her disappearance and
promised to return to the festivities as soon as her indisposition passed.

"A maid on duty at Madame's chambers declares that
Madame dismissed her with permission to retire to her
own quarters. The maid gathered that Madame intended
to return to her guests after a short relaxation. The maid
retired.

"Madame did not again appear. Her husband tapped
on her door between one and two o'clock, when the guests
began to disperse, and receiving no answer assumed that
his wife had either fallen asleep or did not wish to be
disturbed. He made apologies for her and around three
o'clock retired to his own apartments.

"It had been Madame's custom not to be disturbed in the mornings until she rang for her maid. Her non appearance did not cause anxiety until ten o'clock when her husband, alarmed, broke through the locked door of her suite.

"Madame's body was found fully dressed, bent backward over the chaise longue. A stiletto had been imbedded in her heart and not withdrawn. A window was open to a balcony over the grounds. There were footprints below, leading to a servants' gate through the walls into a rear street. The fugitive who made the prints had obliterated the contours of each impression as he made it. At the servants' gate the trail died."

The Genoa police listed the jewelry the Marchesa had chosen to wear, including a magnificent rope of pearls and choker of diamonds. The pearls were of enormous value. Her jewel cask had been removed from the drawer of her escritoire and emptied. Of the card found in the box, bearing the drawing of the cat's head and Madame's tender challenge, the secretary had posted three hundred and fifty-two duplicates to a select list prepared by Madame herself. She was quite certain she had not handled a card bearing handwriting. It would not have escaped her attention as Madame was very fastidious and insisted upon her examining each card before she enclosed it in its envelope, lest it be marred by the engraver or in handling.

To whom had Nita sent her challenge that her courage in making written record of her love be met with attendance at her ball where her husband and friends were assembled?

Where had their meeting been? In the grounds, perhaps, in the shadow of the high tower of the Cathedral of the Annunciation.

Had Nita pointed the way to her boudoir for a few

secret moments before ushering her admirer into the scene
below? Was he waiting there while she pleaded her head-
ache?

That was midnight. The medical officials thought death
had occurred between midnight and an hour later. How
much of that hour did poor foolish Nita spend in the
arms of the man so soon to take from her all the hours
the world might have treasured for her?

Who shall ever know, and in knowing what the good?

The lover had left behind him the mark of The Panther. And with him he had taken, besides her final kiss,
all of her pretty baubles—and with the sardonic touch of
Madame's own confession, had taken also her husband's
peace of soul!

"We will anticipate the request from Genoa," Monsieur
Lemair announced, "to assemble a list of all acquaintances
of the Marchesa's in Cannes. Doubtless she made new
friends here. She must have met many entertaining gentlemen. Our work there will be fairly easy and will supply
Dupree with interesting material with which to work.
Meanwhile, Major Croyant's views will be valuable. He
will be concerned about the jewelry. It may bring him to
Dupree's side in the common cause."

He asked to be put through on the telephone to Major
Croyant at the Crillon. Sir Philip Gregg answered. The
Major was not in the hotel. When told that it was Monsieur Lemair telephoning, Sir Philip's voice was instantly
replaced by the brisk gusto of Dupree.

"Yes, yes! I am here. One suggests it is apparent when
I speak into the phone. But Monsieur le Major is
not——"

Monsieur Lemair interrupted.

"It is well, Dupree. For you I have a message from

Monsieur Croyant. Also there is a message to all of us from The Panther."

Dupree listened, his end of the wire a silent void while the prefect epitomized the news from Genoa. When Lemair paused Dupree said, with a curious evenness in his usually vibrant voice, "I wish to avoid the Sûreté, Monsieur. Perhaps you will come to Croyant's suite?"

Croyant arrived to find Dupree, once more in the outward guise of himself, pacing the floor. Lemair and Clement had finished their account of Genoa. Some additional facts had been telephoned from the radio rooms of the Sûreté. They were unimportant on their surface. Madame had gone into the grounds, favored by the younger element of her guests, about an hour before her announced indisposition. She was seen to pass through a garden door that opened from a glass enclosed conservatory. She was alone and wore a silver wrap that caught the twinkling lights from the lanterns overhead and melted them into a misty flame. She disappeared under an arch of loquat trees and was not seen on the grounds again.

In a confidential aside to all police chiefs along the Riviera the president of the Genoa Jurisdiction suggested that if, as it seemed unhappily apparent, the young Madame had been indiscreet, her admirer would not have been chosen from among her own circle of intimates. Capello men, as well as the di Estrels, were jealous of their women. A Genoese or Roman, Milanese or Venetian would not have lightly entered into an affair with the Marchesa. He would be found, the President believed, to have been attracted from among new acquaintances acquired during Madame's frequent visits abroad.

"A week ago," Lemair reminded Dupree, "she was in our midst. She arrived with the beginning of the season. She stayed here, at the Crillon."

It was at this point Croyant arrived. He came in whistling. Dupree wheeled upon him and began, with a quiet intensity that was sign of his inward feeling of responsibility for The Panther's continued freedom to maneuver tragic coups, to convey the news of Genoa. Croyant calmly stopped him.

"I know all that has been reported, Ariste. Perhaps a bit of added information."

Monsieur Lemair raised his brows. "You have been in touch with the Sûreté, Monsieur?"

Croyant was evasive. "I had occasion to talk with Genoa direct. All Italian conversations at this time include full reference to the Marchesa's sly adventure. That she should have strayed seems more appalling than the outcome of her weakness, and that her admirer should have been The Panther touches the Italian imagination more than his cat's head in her jewel cask."

Dupree regarded him narrowly. There was a strange air about his friend. He sat quietly in a big chair puffing at a cigarette with a grave, concerned expression. But Dupree detected a repressed eagerness, a well hidden elation.

Sir Philip Gregg also watched him with a puzzled glance. "I don't believe we are involved this time," said Sir Philip. "An Italian company carries the di Estrel risks, if I'm not wrong?"

Croyant nodded. "My vacation is safe. The directors have no additional reason to brow-beat me. The Italians lose this time, four million lira. They'll feel hurt."

Dupree permitted himself an elaborate shudder. It was as if he said, "You and your infernal insurance business! Bah! When a woman has been bent back across her chaise longue, her pedestal for boudoir kisses, but receives instead her *carte de passage* to eternity."

Croyant observed his shudder and stared at him with a dull glance from which the Frenchman turned with a shrug.

"You spoke," said Lemair, "of additional information?"

"An unidentified, unmarked plane was sighted at dawn flying at high altitude over the Mediterranean. It was headed west. Its description fits the Bordeaux amphibian."

"He will come down," Dupree ejaculated, "between here and Gibraltar! Bit by bit we build the certainty that his organization is centered on the Côte d'Azure."

Monsieur Lemair and Clement returned to the Sûreté. Already, the prefect remarked to Croyant before he left, Marseilles would have raided the house of the Pigs. Croyant had observed that Dupree would know how to handle Bibi, the bartender.

Dupree prepared also to leave. He was in a temperamental huff with his friend. The matter of the note found on Alexander Vaskaya's body, which Croyant had withheld from him at their later meeting on the Esplanade, piqued him deeply. That the Major should have known, from some mysterious source of his own, where to gather in comrades of Alexander, birds of The Panther's feather, and not given him the tip, had made a sensitive wound.

"One supposes," he said, "that you do not also know the precise hour when Vaskaya plans to keep her tryst in Rue des Pomegranates with our mysterious young man?"

Croyant blinked and hastily sought the oblong of his window. He spoke without looking into the other's face and its expression like that of a child who has been denied a share in his playmate's candy.

"You are romantic, Ariste. You will not be content until the dancer follows the rule we lay down for our women and goes to sit on the doorstep of her former lover. Rue des Pomegranates is not a long street, but a pretty woman can make a thousand trysts in a half mile."

Dupree snorted and gave Sir Philip a look as if to say, "Is it possible my friend toys with me?" Sir Philip relieved himself of all responsibilities by a gesture.

"Rue des Pomegranates is a short street," the Frenchman repeated, his tone a cryptic inference. He came to a determination and stepped back into the room. He stood over the table and assumed a pose for declamation. "Attend, my friend. I reason the matter out. Her brother emerges from the house of the young man. He has not delivered the card he carries, since the young man is not at home—as I, who am in the street, well know. Why Alexander is killed at the mouth of the street I do not know. One must find a conclusion of his own, so I suggest that Vaskaya sought a reestablishment of herself as handmaiden to Michael Ballou without authority of her master and that her messenger was removed as a stern reproof. Perhaps I shall throttle the truth out of a Pig's throat. Upon the occurrence of your name on the card, I can only speculate. An added memorandum for Michael Ballou? Is it possible, my friend, that you would allow me to reach an erroneous explanation?"

Croyant got up. He gave the other a flicking glance, enough to see that Dupree had drawn himself up and was tapping his breast. He went to his closet and produced a fresh bottle of wine. Dupree instantly proposed to draw its cork but Croyant anticipated him and challenged him to have done the job more adroitly. While he poured into glasses set for Sir Philip, Dupree and himself, he said, with a great sadness, "You'll ruin my vacation, Ariste, if you force my back to the wall over the card in Alexander's pocket! Can't you be content that a second time Vaskaya's message has miscarried? If the thing keeps on

there's bound to be a consequence. Meanwhile, the unmarked plane flew past Cannes. The killer is in the west."

Until he finished he busied himself with filling the
glasses. When he was done he glanced across the glass he
handed Dupree. The latter studied him with an undis-
guised thoughtfulness, his puzzled frown returning. He
drank his wine in a kind of detachment and put down his
glass without breaking his stare. Croyant was silently
placid, but Dupree found what he sought, a gleam behind
the blank surface of the other's eyes.

A great light suddenly broke. His friend's vacation was
a fiction! A weapon of his own forging. He too was
reaching for The Panther in his own way and the news
from Genoa had, in some amazing fashion, helped him to
reach far!

He sought a replenished glass which Croyant filled
and handed him. The Major had fallen to whistling. A
rollicking chorus from The Pirates of Penzance. Dupree
could never bear the sight of his friend when he whistled.
He looked away quickly. Croyant finished his strain and
then remarked, as if he made an idle observation, "Lord
and Lady Severn are due in port tomorrow, from Spain."

Sir Philip started. He fixed his monocle and stared.
Dupree's eyes narrowed. Croyant gave no sign that he
was aware of the tension he had caused. He added, still
indifferently, "They were the Marchesa's hosts while she
was in Cannes."

"In God's name!" Sir Philip burst out. "Do you know
what you're hinting, Croyant? Spain's west!"

"Geography," Croyant pointed out with mild emphasis,
"is a thing you can't hint about. Any way you look at it,
Spain's west."

CHAPTER XIII

BEHIND THE YELLOW LANCIA

WHEN Michael Ballou was engaged by Clare Fraser to perform the assorted duties of a "private secretary," she had told him one of these duties would be "being nice to Count Tanaroff." He found this task increasingly difficult.

The pompous hero who, Michael secretly suspected, was not a Russian at all, despite his fluency in that, his sole language, and the correctness of his accent, lived in humble quarters somewhere in the native section of Cannes, but spent nearly the whole of his waking time at Villa Amette. His gay, frivolous employer's fascination for the mighty fellow was something Michael could not understand. He was certain there was no closer relationship between them than what appeared on the surface, an impressionable, giddy woman's submission to the hypnotic glamor of a man cloaked in the mystery of great deeds performed and greater deeds still to be done in single handed valor.

Count Tanaroff became every day a fiercer hero. He would stand erect, his six feet and more inches drawn to their full height, while he tapped his full-thrown chest where the Czar had pinned medals, and announced in a thundering explosion that he, he alone if need be, would hew the path to his country's freedom from the yoke of her Bolshevik masters. He, and he alone, would restore the Russia that had been.

Michael would smile to himself. In his veins was the blood of his Russian mother and in his heart the sympathies that blood stirred. Until the death of his uncle had he not adopted the Jeribzoff name when he came to Europe from America in compliance with the wishes of his uncle and the people who had been his mother's people? Was he not indeed no less than half kin to the refugees spread along the Riviera? He sympathized with their dreams of the old Russia restored, but always smiled at their magnificent plans for the resurrection. His smile at Tanaroff was an inward laughter with an unsympathetic scorn in it. The Count's "I, and I alone!" infuriated him.

Always, when the man's bombast was interpreted to Mrs. Fraser, she would say, with a childish pout, "You, alone, Alexi?"

The Count would bow, low from the hips, hand on his breast.

"With you beside me, fair lady!"

And Michael would mutter to himself, "And her dollars in your pockets!"

Once, it seemed that Mrs. Fraser suspected Michael's feeling about her pet. One day while they were together poring over household accounts she brought from her writing cabinet a telegram which, with an elaborately casual air, she called to his attention. It proved to be a telegram from Moscow, from the Political Section of the Ogpu. It had been addressed to Major Croyant, at Hotel Crillon. Michael knew Major Croyant. A big, stolid looking Englishman who was a frequent visitor to the Villa Amette. He liked him, perhaps because the Major seemed to be amused by the whole garish show going on at the Villa, and perhaps his liking was fortified by Mrs. Fraser's apparent regard for him. Since her removal

from the Crillon to the Villa she had constituted Michael
as "the only other man in the world before whom she'd
take a highball in the morning," and had explained that
the Major was his colleague in sharing this honor. "He
reminds me of my poor Bill," she would add. "Bill was
a big man, too." Michael supposed that Count Tanaroff's
bigness had something to do with his hold upon Mrs.
Fraser's imagination. Yet the Count's bigness differed
from Croyant's. There were times when the Count seemed
amazingly wiry, a physical domino.

The telegram, apparently, was in reply to an inquiry
made of the Ogpu by Major Croyant in Mrs. Fraser's
behalf. Michael was glad to discover that she was not
wholly without American shrewdness. He was bitterly
disappointed by Moscow's report on Count Tanaroff.
Moscow seemed, indeed, to go out of its way to stamp
the Count as an authentic article. The Ogpu described
him as an enemy of the Soviets, as were most of his
kind, but his military record and heroic attainments were
not to be questioned. Michael's heart sank before such a
clean bill of health. The Ogpu left no doubt, in its state-
ment, as to what it would do to the Count if he should
fall into its hands and this very threat, Michael knew,
was added fuel to the fires of his employer's silly roman-
ticism. He would have liked to forward the Count straight
to Moscow with his compliments. He understood, now,
why Mrs. Fraser had become so completely the fellow's
dupe.

And the Count was unquestionably getting away with
murder at the Villa of his admirer. The house staff, as
far as the men were concerned, was of his own choosing.
Some of them were Russians, some French, some English. There was an American gardener and the butler was
a German who might have stepped out of a cadaverous

role in some melancholy German opera. Michael could never figure out why Mrs. Fraser desired so many servants, particularly male. There were four on duty in the house itself, when the butler would have been sufficient, considering the efficiency of the female staff. But even in the face of this redundancy Tanaroff would turn up with a young man, French or German or English or Russian, and present him to the young widow as a trustworthy "friend" who would be of great assistance in "their" plans to do something for his stricken countrymen, but who needed meanwhile the security of a job. None of these chaps had the seedy appearance of poverty. But Mrs. Fraser would flutter over them, and purse her pretty brows and discover at last, with the pleased look of a girl scout who is doing that day's good deed, that she needed another servant. Perhaps it would be a chauffeur.

There were four chauffeurs already when the Count brought still another young man. A young man whose nails were scrupulously manicured and whose hands showed no sign of manual labor.

This time Mrs. Fraser demurred. "But I already have four chauffeurs, and only three cars," she pointed out plaintively.

Count Tanaroff frowned. Michael, who was present, saw a change come over him. Something of his flamboyance disappeared for an instant, and a cold, steely glint came into his eyes. Something fell away from him, Michael thought, as a jester's cloak falls, or the domino from a masker. Michael felt himself recoiling, then recovered himself. His nerves had played him a trick. The Count was his overbearing, preposterous self.

"Get another car!" he commanded in Russian that Michael had to translate into English.

Mrs. Fraser appealed to Michael. "I always forget what our cars are. What have we?"

"A Rolls, a Daimler, and the Fraschini," Michael recited.

She was studious for a moment, then fluttered her butterfly hands helplessly against the scowl of the Count. "I think we ought to have an American car," she said. "Bill always liked the Packard. See about getting one at once, Michael. And tell Alexi I am so glad to give his friend a place."

A smile curled the lips of the Count. He lifted Mrs. Fraser's fingers and kissed them. She laughed gaily. Michael glared at the Russian—who, a moment ago, he was more positive than ever wasn't Russian, for all of that telegram from Moscow. Slavic blood, perhaps, and other bloods acquired in some melting pot. Moscow accredited him, so Russian he must be—but, just the same, there was something wrong.

He watched him go out with his friend in tow. He would take him to the garages himself and explain his duties and assign him quarters. Thus far had he gone in assuming authority over the conduct of the Villa. Michael was at the point of protesting time and again, because he was very fond of Clare Fraser. She was dissipating whatever had been her legacy from her lamented Bill. She was making herself a "good thing" for all that conglomerate crowd of spongers and parasites which are the fringe—even the heart—of the Riviera shore. She'd turned the Villa Amette into a way-station for climbers and schemers and gigolos, a parade ground for fashion and a hostel for Tanaroff's sycophantic crew, but she was utterly adorable. Michael would have been hopelessly in love with her if there had not been a Helen Avery and—

the shadow of that horrible night when he took the marble case from the safe in Nevsky Prospekt.

There were times when he was alone with his employer, going over her correspondence, helping her decide what invitations to accept and issue, or studying bills and bank balances, when she did not appear to be as empty headed as her actions over Tanaroff suggested. Indeed, she exhibited a sharp business ability at times. But if the staff of the Villa were involved, she lost all sense of economy. And Tanaroff's wishes always prevailed. He did not like women servants. Mrs. Fraser asked Michael under what terms the four floor maids were employed. When he told her by the week she ordered him to replace them with men.

"Alexi will find some of his friends to take their places."

"But, Madame," Michael expostulated, and before he could go on she laughed, in her silvery, musical way.

"Oh, you may leave me a *femme de chambre*. Just one. There isn't a man born who can make a bed."

But when Tanaroff had gone out with the fifth chauffeur, Mrs. Fraser said, suddenly, "I don't think we'll get another car, Michael. Alexi will forget all about it, just so his friend is cared for. But see that the young man is quartered at the garages. He can drive occasionally."

As a rule Michael played tennis with her every day at noon. Tanaroff, who seemed to sleep late, seldom showed up until lunch time. "Lunch time, you bet!" Michael scoffed. And the Count did not play tennis. Again Michael scoffed. "Spoil his strut!"

He liked to play with Clare Fraser. She had no championship material in her by any means: so few American women had, they took their sports so lightly; but she was full of surprises. And he could always dream that he was playing with Helen. They had played tennis a great deal, he and Helen. He had taught her how to hold her racquet with the correct grip. How to serve from the wrist instead of from the forearm. And he had to show the right grip to Clare Fraser and teach her to use her wrist in place of a full arm swing.

When she was flying across the court, her skirts forgotten, her little shrieks of triumph ringing clear, he had only to let a touch of mist come into his eyes and he saw Helen quite clearly. Then it would be luncheon time and Tanaroff would come striding through the Villa's blue and green tile gates, tall, dominant. With his dream of Helen as across the net still vivid he would hate Tanaroff with a fresh intensity. He would see in him the figure of Georges Raynel, to whom Helen now belonged. He had never seen Helen's rich fiancé, but had seen photographs of him and knew there was none of Tanaroff's pose about him, but his hatred of the two men was interchangeable.

After luncheon, which he customarily shared with Mrs. Fraser and the man she doted on, served by the cadaverous German butler who claimed to know no additional language but French but whom Michael suspected of knowing both Russian and English, his time was his own until evening. In the evening there would be the usual "party." The Villa Amette was an open house after the dinner hour. People drifted in from the other villas along the slope of La Grasse, from Cannes and the Caps further on. They remained whether Mrs. Fraser had gone out or not. Tanaroff played host and kept the wines flowing. Michael seldom went to Rue des Pomegranates during the afternoon. Sure as he did he would see his neighbor of the broad-brimmed hat. Khamov, with some uncanny intuition, would know that he was at home and come

tapping at his door. Or he would run into him in the
street and the Russian would embrace him as if they'd
been parted for a year, and insist upon buying him a glass
of wine at the corner café or making coffee royale with
a new bottle of good brandy he had bought. Away from
Khamov, Michael felt foolish about his suspicions. In
his presence, the man's gentle eyes turned upon him and
belying the hawk-like aspect of his nose, his uneasy fears
inevitably returned. When Khamov was in his room with
him he could hardly keep his glance from constantly seeking the brass shutters over his fireplace.

Today, after luncheon, he strolled down the Via des
Anges toward the sea. He wondered how many of the
angels for whom the Way had been named had chestnut
brown hair like Helen's. He found a bench half hidden in
mimosa against the centuries old sea wall and sat down
to gaze at the yachts riding at anchor. Presently he was
aware of a blot on the seascape. In keeping with some
unwritten law yachts were always white. The water was
dotted with splashes of white that were like a distorted
flock of vari-sized gulls with long beaks. But in their
midst, and a little closer to the shore than most, was a
black boat. A long, low-lying craft with high wireless
spars. The craft was a blemish on the scene, despite its
rakish lines, and he looked away from it. Presently he
was aware that he was staring at it again and that it gave
him a strange, restless feeling. Fantastic as it might
seem, the black yacht was assuming the significance of a
symbol of some sort. He felt premonitions floating about
his head. He got up in disgust with himself and followed
the sea walk until he came to a path that led up to the
Nice boulevard. Here he hailed a bus and went into
Cannes. He got off within a short walk of the Esplanade
and was shortly settled in a franc chair. When the news

vendor came along he bought *Les Affaires* and turned at
once to the page devoted to fashionable personalities.

There was column after column of paragraphs devoted to the doings of the notables. One paragraph was
like another, yet Michael's eyes leapt with unerring certainty to a section of an interior column half way down
the page. He read with an attitude of fascination.

"The *Ariadne* returned to port yesterday from a visit
to the coast of Spain. Aboard was the distinguished company of guests which sailed with the *Ariadne's* owner,
Monsieur Georges Raynel. These included Lord Severn
and the vivacious Lady Severn; Mr. and Mrs. Arthur
Ransom, of London and Kent, England; and Mrs. John
Avery and her charming daughter, Miss Helen, of the
United States. Miss Avery is M. Raynel's fiancée and
future mistress of the *Ariadne* and the Raynel fortune.
Lord Severn, it will be remembered by the reader, has
been a distinguished visitor to the Côte d'Azure since his
return from Abyssinia where, for a little more than a
year, he occupied an important semi-doplimatic post. Miss
Avery, it is rumored, is to be received shortly by Prince
Louis and Princess Charlotte at the Castle in Monaco.
Lord and Lady Severn feel keenly the recent tragedy in
Genoa which brought to such an untimely end the beautiful Marchesa di Estrel, a tragedy traced to the same
appalling source as the former death of Señor Alphonse
Veragua. As the Señor was a close friend of M. Raynel,
so the Marchesa was a close friend of the Severns, and
both were victims of the fiendish criminal whom the police
have dubbed The Panther and whose continued existence
strikes the Riviera with terror. Lord Severn, speaking for
himself and Lady Severn, was particularly bitter. Himself young, he appreciates the young noblewoman's keen
zest in the life which held so much for her. He spoke of

her, on the arrival of the *Ariadne*, with great feeling. Other members of the party also were acutely affected."

Michael read to the last line of the paragraph. He was not particularly concerned in the feeling of Lord Severn for the Italian woman who paid with her life for her indiscretion. Michael had read of this latest raid of The Panther, as indeed any reader of newspapers must have read of it. He remembered, vaguely, having seen the Marchesa one afternoon promenading along the Croisette. A flower girl had pointed her out to him. He was shocked, of course, but the news of the return of Helen Avery from a sail along the Mediterranean with her fiancé absorbed his interest in all other events of recent days.

He read the paragraph again. Clare Fraser became a negligible figure in a far distance. Count Tanaroff receded. Even his neighbor in Rue des Pomegranates faded into the outer haze surrounding a world that contained only one figure other than himself, the figure of the brown haired girl whose hand he had last held at the theater in Warsaw. He was even alone on the Esplanade, save for Helen who, in his soothing imagination, sat beside him in the next one-franc chair.

Yet his neighbor at least was close.

Khamov, his face shaded under his wide hat, passed behind the chair two or three times while Michael read his newspaper. Once he passed close enough behind the young man to glance over his shoulder and scan the spread page of the newspaper. He seemed for a moment at the point of touching Michael's shoulder but just then he glanced across the Esplanade to the white railing that guards against the sharp slope to the sea walk below and saw there the figure of a man standing up. The man's back was turned, he was looking out over the bay, but Khamov appeared to recognize the back. His mouth twitched vaguely. He moved away with a shuffling alacrity but never ceased to study the lone figure at the rail. He took refuge behind a potted date palm whose fronds swept to the ground. Then only, when he himself was out of sight, did he give the man who watched the scene on the sapphire waters a frank examination. The man turned once, at first tentatively, with a preliminary glance in the direction of the young man who read a newspaper. Khamov saw his face. It would be more correct to say he saw a portion of his face, for the upper part of his features were completely barricaded behind enormous sun glasses, goggles that swept around onto his temples and dipped down onto his cheek bones with complete insurance that no actinic ray would penetrate to eyes apparently supersensitive.

The man moved. He walked along the rail. He seemed to be an utter idler. He turned back and walked a space, made a little circle and was at the rail again. Michael Ballou put down his paper and the man stopped dead still. No one could tell where he looked, because of his sun glasses, but Khamov seemed to know. He murmured half aloud, his mouth twitching, "Take a walk, Michael Ballou. Ariste Dupree does not enjoy dawdling."

Dupree was compelled to dawdle only a few more minutes. Michael got up and turned off the Esplanade toward the parallel Due d'Antibes. Dupree followed at a reasonable distance, and Khamov came out from the shelter of the date palm. The Russian took an opposite side of the street. He appeared to be more interested in the young man than in Dupree. When Michael came to the intersection of a side street and Rue d'Antibes, he paused, uncertainly. After a moment's hesitation he turned toward Place de la Gare, where trains came in from Nice and Marseilles and Monte Carlo. Khamov apparently knew where he would go, after that turn, and knew also of a short cut through a twisting alley-like road that was little more than a path between the back walls of juxtaposed shops. He came into Place de la Gare close to the railroad tracks at almost the same moment Michael turned into the opposite side of the square with Dupree and his sunglasses a score of steps behind him.

The station square was a place of even unwonted activity these days. The White Carnival was approaching and workmen were already decorating the light stanchions in the Place and the façades of the buildings facing it. Electricians were stringing colored globes for the panoply of red and blue and yellow lights that would, while the Carnival lasted, make of the Place a colorful oasis.

Michael frequently came to the station in the afternoons when he was wandering about. Perhaps his whim was some lingering reflex of a small boy's eagerness to see trains arrive, but he set his custom down to another impulse. At any time Helen Avery might arrive from some point along the Côte d'Azure in either direction. She might come in from Monte Carlo or Ventimiglia— people didn't always use their automobiles. Or she might come from Nice, or from a shopping excursion along the Promenade des Anglais at Marseilles. He had come to Cannes originally for no other purpose than to catch a distant glimpse of her. So far he had failed. His hope rested in the arrival of trains.

He took up his position down the curb from the station entrance where he could see the travelers who emerged but, to them, would be lost in the anonymity of the station bustle. There were signs that a train was coming in. He knew enough of his time tables to know this would be a train from Marseilles. Porters and taxi men were crowding about the ticket barriers. Private

cars, and others for hire, were drawn up and ready for
the service of the arrivals. Among the hire-cars were
several of long-nosed make, expensive and powerful,
some of them only recently demoted from the garages of
those spendthrift American residents who had brought to
Europe their wasteful habit of wanting a new car every
year no matter how many years of reliability still lie
under the hood of the old one.

Khamov proceeded, with the air of one who follows a
custom, to the steps of the street bridge that affords
pedestrians a passage over the tracks beyond the reaches
of the station buildings. He mounted these steps with an
agility Michael never saw him display when he climbed
the stairs to either of their rooms in Rue des Pomegranates. From the bridge footpath he could command
an overhead view of the whole Place de la Gare and his
rapid survey instantly picked out Michael at the curb,
and the sun-glassed face of Dupree a dozen yards away.

The train rumbled in and its passengers began to pour
into the Place and into the rapacious hands of the porters.

Suddenly the Russian's hands gripped the bridge rail.
Darya Vaskaya came out from the station. She summoned a porter and pointed to her luggage, a single hand
bag.

Khamov's gaze beat a tattoo between Michael Ballou
and Dupree. The young man moved but a step, then drew
back. His movement was of surprise, impulse, and re-
consideration. He retreated along the curb and put himself in line behind the hoods of intervening motor cars.
Khamov's attention deserted him and turned exclusively
to Dupree.

Dupree had seen her. He, too, abandoned Michael. He
moved rapidly until he was abreast of the row of cars for
hire. His face was turned to the girl and he was un-

doubtedly watching her from behind his glasses, but at
the same time he summoned with a gesture the driver of
a car and conferred with him briefly. The driver touched
his cap and sprang back under his wheel.

Darya directed her porter to an open Lancia backed to
the curb among the private cars. When Dupree saw what
car had come to meet her, he ran around his own to
climb in beside the driver. Khamov turned and sped down
the bridge steps. The Lancia, painted a creamy yellow,
was maneuvering into the open square, swerving across
the tracks under the foot bridge. Dupree's car was nosing
out, hesitant until the Lancia was under way.

The Russian chose a speedy looking Daimler, also open,
with a youngish alert looking driver. He got into the
front seat without preliminary parley. "The black car
will keep the yellow one in sight," he said to the startled
chauffeur. "We'll hug the black one. Two hundred francs
if it's easy, two hundred more if there's trouble."

The driver was alarmed. "Trouble? I'm not in for a
job of trouble, M'sieu'."

"There goes the Lancia under the bridge. Look sharp
now, after the black."

Command was so vibrant in his passenger's tone the
chauffeur obeyed automatically. He looked sharp after
Dupree's black car which also threaded under the bridge
and set out in the wake of the yellow streak ahead.

The Lancia proceeded with gathering speed toward the
Boulevard Carnot, a long straight roadway that runs up
to the hill of Le Cannet. Dupree kept a moderate distance
behind. Traffic on the boulevard was not thick. The
Lancia skimmed along smoothly, its passenger's neck fur
floating in the air behind her. Khamov sat forward with
his hands pressed on his knees, his neck craned. Occasionally he frowned.

After a time an oval traffic island in the boulevard loomed ahead. The Lancia made half the semi-circle on the left and disappeared.

"Attention!" the Russian shouted to his driver. "The black car will make the turn at the oval."

"There are two turns there, M'sieu'. To the left leads to the summit of Le Cannet. To the right one comes eventually to La Grasse, beyond Cannes."

"The turn will be to the left, up Cannet."

The left turn was into a narrow, tree hung road that rose slopily toward the ascent of Le Cannet hill. At times the black car was lost in low hanging leaves, and the Lancia was never in view. Khamov was not worried. The occasional glimpses of the car ahead contented him. In between he appeared to be absorbed in deep thought. He touched his side once and felt the bulk of his pistol in a holster under his coat. Another time he reached under his coat, while the driver's attention was fastened to the curves beyond the windshield, and unfastened the snap of the holster flap.

When they began the steep ascent, along a road that curved around the hill and now and then doubling over on itself, the Lancia was seen crawling to the summit. It disappeared with an abrupt turn onto the plateau of the village of Le Cannet. Then the black car, with the Daimler a thousand yards behind.

The Daimler turned sharply, after the plateau was reached, into a narrow street between flat walled houses. In Le Cannet cemetery there are headstones that date back to the year One Thousand and many of the village houses are a remnant of an unrecorded antiquity. The old houses were soon left behind and an open space ahead intervened before the even older hill village of Mougins with its ruin of a Saracen signal tower. Down below, to the left,

Cannes was spread out, and beyond the bay was a silver shimmer in the now slanting sun. But Khamov gave small attention to the scenic splendor. He took off his wide hat, of which he had constantly kept hold with one hand or the other to keep it from blowing away. He reached over the seat post and dropped it into the tonneau of the car. The wind instantly ruffled his longish black hair, matting it in a furious tangle that gave him a peculiarly ferocious appearance, changing the whole aspect of his head and face.

"Beyond Mougins there is a dead end, M'sieu'," said the driver. "One turns squarely onto Route Provençal, which leads to the border of Spain, or onto Route d'Avray, which takes one to Ville Cantoux and eventually to Toulouse."

The Lancia was lost in the middle-guttered cobble streets of Mougins. The black car passed from view. Then the Daimler bumped over the cobblestones sending geese and goats into their third panic within five minutes. Peasant women stood in mud-brick doors and shrilled a new volley of imprecations and wide eyed children stared from glassless windows in crumbling walls. Three big cars passing through Mougins in a day was a *cause célèbre;* three in five minutes was an *affaire macabre.*

Mougins was cleared. The dead end was in view at the outer rim of the hill top plateau. The Lancia was just making the turn into Route d'Avray. Its yellow tonneau caught a flash of the dropping sun and shot it back along the road like a challenging beacon. The black car was gathering speed. Its driver apparently didn't know that Route d'Avray was straight down into the valley where it lay like a long ribbon and that the yellow car he trailed could not escape this side of Cantoux. Khamov's driver also touched his accelerator.

"Slower," the Russian ordered. "Much slower."

The Daimler dropped back.

"I will take the wheel. Arise and I will slide under you."

The driver looked around with a polite but firm protest.

"Pardon, M'sieu', but it is not in the Hire Authorization that the passenger be permitted to drive."

"I will take the wheel. Sharp, now. Get over or I'll pitch you out."

The driver recovered his car from a swerve off the road, and clung to his wheel. "It is not permitted—" he began to repeat doggedly, with the French citizen's fear of Official Regulations, but he choked off with a splutter. The glinting barrel of a pistol poked into one's ribs has the effect of cancelation upon almost all Official Regulations. He arose nimbly and released his wheel to his passenger who slid under him, leaving his vacated portion of the seat to the driver who sank in the farthest corner, his mouth hanging open, his eyes staring at the Russian with mingled complaint and terror.

Khamov instantly shot the Daimler ahead. The car's official driver gasped. The man was mad. The dead end blockade rushed down upon them. The black car already was slowing to make the right angle turn into Route d'Avray. Should the mad man attempt to pass the black car he could not reach the turn. He must slow down and that would bring the two cars to the dead end abreast. The professional driver shouted an alarmed warning. Khamov gave the accelerator a fresh dig and the Daimler leapt.

Khamov shot up alongside the black car, his head hunched low in his shoulders, his black hair flying. He received a startled glare from the driver of the other car, who automatically, as in any time of motoring emergency, gave his road horn a mighty blast. Khamov's pistol barked under cover of the horn's shriek. The black car wavered, air rushing with a sibilant hiss from a rear tire.

"*Nom de Dieu!*" muttered the supplanted driver in the seat beside the Russian. His admiration of his fare's marksmanship surmounted his consternation. "M'sieu' laughs at a target!"

And, in truth, Khamov was laughing. A mighty burst of guffawing merriment. The black car was saved narrowly from a spill at the side of the road. It was wavering to a stop, with Dupree standing and steadying himself with a hand on the windshield while he reached for his own pistol, when the Daimler made the bend and swept down in the yellow car's tracks into the open stretch toward Ville Cantoux.

The Lancia was doing seventy miles an hour but Khamov drove his more sluggish Daimler into a gradual gain. The Lancia's driver thought the car behind that had crept up so close was determined to pass his fleeter, lower hung car, when he slowed for a turn just before coming into the environs of Cantoux. He waved an arm notifying the pursuer of his intention to leave the boulevard and swung into a side road to stop before the gates of an ancient stone house surrounded by a vine covered fence. When his passenger had descended and was going across the yard with a quick step toward the house's heavy wooden door, he was startled to observe that the Daimler had made the turn with him and was drawing up to stop. His hand swung to his belt over his hip. Khamov ignored his own weapon but broke into a loud but unresonant series of "la-la-la's" pitched to the final strains of the Dancer of Kashmir theme.

The Lancia driver muttered a puzzled oath. His hand had brought out his pistol, but he held it uncertainly, as if he was spellbound before a mystery of some sort. The Russian's effort, however, had instant effect upon the girl. She wheeled, stared for a second at the disheveled and ferocious looking figure at the Daimler's wheel, and then swayed on her feet, one hand lifting to her throat. Her face went white. Khamov repeated the strain, this time more softly and musically. The girl recovered herself and came out through the fence gate. She spoke a sharp word to her driver. He put his pistol back in its place. Darya thrust her white face close to the Russian.

"Why did you risk following me? And that signal— here! You are in terrible danger."

"I, in danger, Mademoiselle?" His voice was calmly soft, with a note of gentle reproof in it, as for her belief that there could be any danger for him. His expression, particularly in his eyes, was benign.

"I sent you a message by Alexander, but—" She paused, as if to conquer a threatened sob.

"It reached me," he said quietly. "Alexander—delivered it."

She was controlled again. "But not here—not now. Nor in Rue des Pomegranates. I am afraid. I will come to the White Carnival. Wear a yellow and a black pom pom—on your sleeve."

She stepped back from the car, turned and re-entered the gate. Her driver looked after her and then back to the Daimler. Khamov backed out of the road into Route d'Avray and drove back toward Le Cannet, and Cannes. He dismissed his driver at the corner of the Croisette and Rue des Etats-Unis. The driver, all smiles now because of the four hundred francs in an inner pocket, well pro-

tected with a safety pin, lifted his cap in polite deference.
"*Bon aventure, M'sieu.*"

"*Bon aventure.*"

At the opposite corner of Rue des Etats-Unis Khamov
entered an ordinary taxi and asked to be let out at the
Via des Anges, near the Villa Amette, in La Grasse. At
the Via des Anges he got out, paid the cabby, and walked
to the villa gates.

It had been dark for an hour; inside the villa dinner
was just being finished and Mrs. Fraser's party had not
begun to get under way. There had been one or two early
arrivals, close intimates of Clare Fraser, and with these
she was sharing her after-dinner port. Khamov hugged
the shadows of the villa walls until he came to the tile
gates, where he stood long enough to scan the grounds.
Two or three chauffeurs made a little knot before the
garage doors. A white dress appeared on the verandah,
to be quickly swallowed in darkness. Otherwise the
grounds were deserted at the moment.

The Russian walked a little way off from the gates
and, from the eminence of the road, looked down onto
the bay. Along the shore they were testing some of the
carnival illuminations. Light spun out like pin-head beads
against a hazy background. A fishing boat, already showing carnival lanterns, came through feathers of silver
spray into the breakwater. Khamov watched awhile and
then went back to the gates and surveyed the grounds
again. He heard a voice, gruff, bombastic. Somewhere
within the house close to the verandah doors. He slipped
into a shadow within the gates and watched the house.

Count Tanaroff was suddenly silhouetted in the light-
oblong of the opened doors. His head was high, his silhouette military and noble in every line. Behind him
fluttered the fragile figure of Clare Fraser in a mist of

white velvet. Another woman was with her. The Count made a deep bow to both women, lifted his hand, as if he spoke of the deep bowled pipe it held, and then came onto the grounds. True aristocrat of the gallant circle, he would not smoke his odoriferous pipe under a roof where cigarette-bred ladies gathered.

Khamov moved out of his shadow, bent under his broad hat. A chauffeur detached himself from his companions and moved to intercept the strange, hunched figure, but when he saw that the man was bent on approaching the strutting count, and with a limp that guaranteed his harmlessness, he rejoined his associates.

Tanaroff paced a narrow beat along an hibiscus walk, puffing on his pipe and emitting prodigious clouds of white smoke. He appeared to be in high thoughts, for with a head so uplifted his thoughts could never be termed deep. Khamov came around the hibiscus hedge and stopped full in his path.

"Pardon, noble sir," he said, in a meek tone. "Could I have a match for my cigarette?" And he held up to the other's startled view an American cigarette from the Carolinas.

One might have expected the great hero to button his coat and stride through the thick but bent figure before him. But he did not. He searched in his pockets until he found a silver lighter. He snapped a flare, shielded it with his hands and offered it to the other. While Khamov bent to draw on the flame the count said, in perfect, staccato English—he who knew naught but Russian!—"But Stephan! This is madness!"

Khamov, still fumbling with his light, grunted. "It is necessary. I am quite safe. Dolly is back. I have talked with her."

"Vaskaya! Is it true—Stephan? She is still—?"

"Give me the lighter. Better not stare at me so." He snapped a flare of his own and applied it to his already glowing cigarette. "She's reliable. She's staying at a house off Route d'Avray. Do you understand what I'm driving at? A house off Route d'Avray, at Cantoux."

The Count retrieved the lighter and dropped it into his pocket.

"I understand. I'll carry on."

Khamov slipped around the hibiscus and limped toward the gates. The Count drew himself up and resumed his strutting promenade.

CHAPTER XIV

CLARE FRASER IS ALARMED

A STILL volatile Dupree strode about Croyant's suite while the Major and Sir Philip waited until the proper hour for their departure to the party at Villa Amette. His sun glasses were tossed onto the table. He was somewhat suspicious of his friend's reception of his account of the afternoon's adventure. Occasionally Croyant pursed his lips to whistle, invariably, however, thinking better of it.

"That she escaped seems not to affect you?" Dupree snapped at one time. "You have," he added with great scorn, "an engagement to tea at the Café de Paris in Monte Carlo, perhaps?"

Croyant seemed to consider. "Her engagements are not dependable, Ariste. You admit that you've had Rue des Pomegranates watched and swear she hasn't come into the street."

Dupree made an impatient gesture. "Her note miscarried. To whomever it was addressed, it lands in your pockets. That you do not explain it is a cross. I bear it with fortitude."

He was silent for a few moments, turning up and down the room in deep, scowling thought. When he spoke again it was of Genoa.

"From there, perhaps, from the boudoir of Madame, will come our first acceleration. He flew to the west. Darya drives in her Lancia to the west. The Panther's headquarters is not far. If only his wireless sending station would remain in one place, next time he sends his signals into the air, we would trace it within an hour. But he must send from his plane and we can not follow their origins."

Sir Philip murmured a comment upon the dastardliness of the scoundrel who would taunt a husband with the infidelity of the wife he loved. A greater crime, Sir Philip contended, than the murder of the woman itself.

Croyant referred to the *Auberge des Cochons*. Dupree was scornful, and this time of himself.

"I am losing my skill, my friend. And am become faint hearted. Bibi's throat carries the print of each of my fingers. He is minus one ear and I went to work on his eyes. But I have become faint hearted. Sight of the world is a precious thing to take from a man. So I acquired zero. Or if I did gain a measure of information, it is of small account. Bibi swears he knows The Panther only as a figure in the daily press. Oh, yes! He has heard his exploits discussed across his bar. He admitted that when, as the result of a miscalculation, he had lost an ear. He would have lost the other but it seemed as if that was a small admission to gain with mayhem. You know the rest. You have seen too many of these minor members of his band prefer death at our hands, or long stretches in the penal colonies, to the horror promised them for teachery to their chief. A strange sailor came to the bistro. He won his way to Alexander's hide-out. Alexander protected him and afterwards acted strangely. As if he had encountered a new fear. Then, after a few days, Alexander did not return. That is all."

"Did not return," Croyant murmured. "Bibi reported the occurrence higher up and received his orders. Alexander, who receives strange visitors, is removed."

Croyant spoke of Lord Severn. Dupree, at the mention, flicked his friend with a quick, probing glance. "He was seen with the Marchesa frequently," he said, "while the lady was in Cannes. Lady Severn seems to have exercised a certain forebearance. We have learned of a visit to a gem shop in the Croisette. There was a motor trip up La Turbie, with Lord Severn at the wheel and the Marchesa as his only passenger."

"You have not confronted him?"

"Lemair has seen them both. It is his routine. They supplied a list of the Marchesa's friends, such as were known also to them. They were particular to point out that the Marchesa was not always under their chaperonage. There are blank chapters in her memoirs. I reserve a meeting with his lordship for the future. Perhaps a day—or any hour. Who knows?" He paused and took a turn down the room. Croyant watched him. Croyant's lips seemed to have difficulty in suppressing their urge to whistle. "The affair in Nevsky Prospekt," Dupree added, "was in January. Lord Severn sailed from Suez for Abyssinia in February. That was a year ago. He returned——"

Croyant interrupted quietly. "Before Bordeaux. An engaging set of circumstances, Ariste."

"I've been puzzled," Sir Philip offered, "by the implication in Nita di Estrel's challenge to her lover. 'Are you as brave as I?' I can see where it required a certain audacity on her part to introduce her admirer into her house. She might well have been afraid of a tell-tale flush to attract a jealous husband. But where was the risk to him? Unless he was answerable to some other person for his actions? One who would not be too quick to accept a casual explanation of his journey alone—if, as we suppose, it was a journey—to attend the Marchesa's ball."

Duprèe agreed with Sir Philip's unspoken conclusion. "We come, Monsieur, to a wife. To one woman a man is brave only when he defies and betrays another."

He turned to Croyant.

"The Severns go, tonight, to the Villa Amette. Why, God knows. The place is the joke of the Riviera. But you go also. I won't say why, because you are too incomprehensible. But you will inquire about Lord Severn at Port del Sol?"

Clare Fraser's party had developed into a crush by the time Croyant and Sir Philip left their cab at the gate and sauntered across the grounds. The young widow's entertainments always were on a lavish scale and ever like to develop some unexpected feature. Tonight there was a Chinese soprano from Paris and a vigorous young dancer who had been brought from the Club Bastinado at Monte Carlo. And there was a crowd, Croyant called it a gang, of Count Tanaroff's hangers on. These were Russian emigrés for the most part, quite willing to hail the great Count as the White Hope of a new Russia and listen to his harangues about what he proposed to do, about his coup with a peasant uprising certain to follow, so long as Mrs. Fraser's champagne and caviar held out.

Tonight the tall man was at his best. He held a levee in a room on the second floor of the Villa. Here he addressed his listeners with a fiery oratory which Michael Ballou knew to be purest demagogy, having had his experience with demagogues on street corners in the United States.

Mrs. Fraser, when she discovered that the Count had an audience, with a sprinkling of some very good people, some of her own close friends, English and French and American, had a huge crystal punch bowl wheeled into the room, and a serving table piled high with authentic caviar from the Black Sea. She fluttered in and out of the room, her eyes shining with adoration while the Count explained his plans. A *putsch* through Roumania. Lifting of the White banner on the border. A call to arms and the peasants would rise. I, Alexi Vladimirovitch Tanaroff, will be the Lion. On to Moscow!

Mrs. Fraser giggled delightfully. Her giggle was a challenge to the whole world at large, and the room full of listeners in particular, to look upon the Lion whose growl she was permitted to supply in the shape of those dollars left her by her lamented Bill—she'd promised them all.

Michael and the rest of the intelligent folk in the room knew what would be the fate of those dollars. A few aeroplanes to crash in Yugoslavia. A few sabres to hang on stuffed shirts, sabres that would never be drawn except in salute at secret meetings. And then—pouf!

But Clare Fraser was happy. She had never had so much fun in her life. The world was gorgeous and who knew? Alexi might make her a grand duchess, scarcely anything less! "If only poor Bill could have lived to see me a grand duchess with a crown! They *do* wear crowns don't they, Alexi?"

"Tut, tut, my child. We must draw blood before we forge crowns. We must not aggravate the peasants too soon with the fripperies of empire. We must be cautious. There will be an empress on the throne but first we must lay the cornerstones."

And then indeed did the deep Dresden china eyes of the pretty Clare shine with the glory of a peep into fairyland.

Michael had to translate all of this into French and English. His apathetic handling of the Count's epithets robbed the fiery phrases of their eloquence but he made it clear to his hearers what the fellow was driving at. Thus he considered he did his duty. Michael was nervous. He shot furtive glances at every strange face among the Russian contingent. He had suddenly remembered Khamov's remark—"Chenkin is in Cannes." Chenkin, the fearful police figure of the Soviets, might very well take it upon himself to pay some attention to Count Tanaroff and his plottings. He might come to Villa Amette where anyone might come whose clothes were well tailored and manners passable, and give his attention to him instead of the Count.

Suddenly there was a diversion, a row.

Downstairs in the long drawing-room, the Chinese soprano was singing. In the pale blue pantaloons and gold-dragoned embroidered jacket of her native costume, her almond eyes dancing under lashes almost as long as her black bangs, she made a very pretty picture, a voluptuous oriental blossom in a garden of sophisticated Western blooms. Her bell-like voice was very sweet when she rendered "One Fine Day" from Madame Butterfly, and she was as mischievous as a wood nymph in a lyrical jazz tune with Chinese words which she interpreted at the finish of her chorus as meaning, simply, "I Love You."

Many of Count Tanaroff's admirers and listeners had exchanged him for the gay little Chinese. They had gone downstairs after a parting respect to the punch bowl to have a cocktail and listen to the singer. Among these was Sir Philip, who slyly remarked to a neighbor that the young lady belonged in pajamas on the Lido. The neighbor was rather astonished that the long lanky Englishman with a monocle should recall the charm certain young ladies give to pajamas on the Lido.

Croyant had remained in the room upstairs. He was vastly amused by the Count, and now that the English and French had gone down to China, a lively argument struck up among the Russians who remained. One dark-haired, keen-faced little chap whose evening kit was somewhat threadbare for all of the air with which he wore it—an air one observes about many a grand-ducal doorman in Montmartre and Montparnasse—and who had obviously introduced too much of the punch into a stomach never too well filled of late, thrust himself at the Count with a brief question. Tanaroff answered it shortly, with a tone of dismissal, but the young fellow would not be dismissed. He poured out a volley of questions like shots from a machine-gun. Very noticeably the Count was staggered and his anger began to rise, his chest to expand and his face to take on a purple hue.

It was all in rapid Russian. Michael did not have to interpret. Croyant, who was standing near him, asked him what the fuss was about.

"The young man tells the Count he is wrong to plan a mobilization of his friends in Roumania. He thinks they should assemble in Poland and issue their manifestos to the peasants from Leningrad, where manifestos of old were dated."

Croyant rubbed his hand across his jowl, an action as close to a grin as he usually came. He regarded the flustered Count with something of wonder. "Do you think," he murmured to Michael, "that the fellow actually believes in himself? That he would assemble a handful of dupes any place at all, Roumania or Poland or any place but a restaurant?"

"He believes in the expense account Mrs. Fraser will

provide," Michael returned heatedly. Croyant gave the young man a swift glance.

"How does it come you are so familiar with the language?" he asked. "You don't look like a Russian to me."

Michael was instantly grateful. "I am American, sir. I should like to be back."

"Why don't you go?"

The young man's face clouded. He murmured something about the cost of traveling; perhaps he would be going back before long if he could arrange things, or if nothing happened.

He didn't want to pursue the subject. Croyant said nothing more. The argument between the Count and the young Russian had assumed a threatening aspect. Suddenly the Count roared, "Who are you?"

"It doesn't matter who I am," retorted the questioner. "If the time comes I'll help my country. But I'm not a fool."

The Count frowned and clenched his great fists. Then without warning he sprang forward and seized the man violently. "I know who you are," he shouted. "Your name is Chuganoff. I have been warned about you. You are a spy for Chenkin! You are an agent of the Gosudarstvennoye Policheskoye Upravleniye! Out with you! Out!"

"What the devil's the shooting for?" Croyant asked Michael.

The young man stared at the man in the Count's grasp. His hands were shaking. "He says he is a spy of Chenkin, head of the Moscow secret police. An agent of the police section of the Ogpu. He says he has been warned of him."

"The plot thickens," murmured Croyant. "We are about to have a curtain."

The curtain was indeed falling for the heckler who had dared brave the gallant Tanaroff's strategy. The Count hustled him to the head of the stairs, swearing great round oaths at every tug, into the hands of the cadaverous butler who picked him up bodily with a strength as surprising as the Count's was apparent, and tossed him contemptuously out into the grounds.

Hearing the commotion, some of Mrs. Fraser's guests came out of the drawing-room. Mrs. Fraser herself appeared and demanded an explanation from the butler. He could tell her nothing. He was told to pitch the man out and he had.

"But this is too provoking!" she complained. "Send me Monsieur Ballou. He'll know what's been happening."

Michael appeared, visibly upset. He explained in a few words. Mrs. Fraser, strangely, exhibited an immediate concern for the young man who had been so summarily ejected from her hospitable roof. "I feel so sorry for these poor boys who are shut out from their country and left to us foreigners. I'm sure he would have enjoyed the dancer from Monte Carlo, and the caviar. Michael, dear, do go out and tell him how grieved I am. The Count will be furious but I'll have the butler bring him out a highball."

Dutifully, but none the less unwillingly, Michael went onto the grounds. Croyant, from the verandah, watched. Another also watched, but this one was hidden behind a clump of dwarfed palms beyond the garages. Only a rustle of the palm fronds not stirred by the Mediterranean breeze, indicated his presence.

Michael found the one who had been identified by the Count as "Chuganoff" half way to the gates. He was still brushing dirt from the tails of his coat and adjusting his tie. He was not waiting for his hat and stick. When

Michael came up he glared at him. "What he wants to lead," he snapped, "is an attack by the grandchildren of boy scouts on a wood-pecker's nest."

All at once Michael was certain that here was no agent of the dread Chenkin. He said as much and Chuganoff laughed bitterly. "Fat chance," he exclaimed in fairly good American argot. "If they'd ever get hold of me they'd cook me for a squad pronto. But just the same, I'm Russian. A Russian loves his country. If the big guy is going to have some of this Fraser dame's dough to spend, let him put it adrift in a decent country. Not Roumania. Bah! The Roumanians hate us. Take Bulgaria, now. You can start a good war right in Sofia, against the Soviets or anybody, for practically nothing and have all your money for the women. The Bulgar wenches know how to shoot the works."

"From New York?" murmured Michael. "Or Chicago?"

Chuganoff grinned and smoothed his hair with both hands.

"Wilmington, Delaware," he said. "And oh! what I'd give to be on Second Street tonight. Just about now the female division of the Dupont payroll is out in war paint, first seen first grabbed. And the Dago red beats the best Burgundy in the Villa Amette cellar."

Michael was puzzled. He couldn't deny that air with which Chuganoff wore his dress coat. Nor that the coat was of finest tailoring, even if old. "But what are you doing here? Among the emigrés?"

Chuganoff's face sobered. "We were a clan in the old days," he said. "The old folks wanted me around, that sort of thing. Now, then, you look like a good make. How about you?"

The German butler came out sniffing over a silver tray

that glinted in the moonlight. There were sandwiches on
the tray, and caviar, and a bottle of Canadian whiskey
and ginger ale, a dish of cracked ice. One of the butler's
fingers pinned Chuganoff's hat to the bottom of the tray
and his stick was pinned to the butler's side by an elbow.
Chuganoff smacked his lips.

"Madame Fraser, too, can shoot the works, in her own
respectable way," he murmured. He took the plate of
sandwiches in one hand, the bottle of Canadian whiskey
in the other, and then regarded the caviar and ginger ale
dubiously. He revised his strategy and decided to relieve
the German of the entire tray. Michael nodded to the
servant with a grin and they were left alone to a highball.

"How about you?" Chuganoff repeated.

Michael had no more fear. It was good to talk to
someone about New York and Philadelphia, of Miami
and Washington—of all the places where he had seen
Helen Avery, and of Leningrad. To him, he told Chuganoff, Russia meant three epochs in his life. The days
just before the War, when he was very young. He rode
behind a sleigh in the Nevsky Prospekt and skated on
the Neva. His mother was young, then, and very beautiful, and he was called a prince because his uncle was a
Count and powerful in court circles. Then the second
epoch. The war was just over. The barricades thrown up
by the cadets when the Revolution broke were still to be
traced in Nevsky Prospekt. Palaces were empty ruins
and the ornamental street lights had been torn down. The
Prospekt was dark and through the night there was the
constant pat-pat of the bare feet of starving street gamins.
He was not called a prince and his uncle seldom went out
of his house. His had been one of the few houses undisturbed because he had once given refuge to a fugitive

from the Czar's secret police who appeared at his back door. The fugitive was a pale fellow and exhausted, and the Count had taken pity on him and hid him. He afterward became Lenin. Then the last epoch.

"You got me, there," said Chuganoff. "I stopped with the Revolution. I don't dare go back."

Michael told of going back. Several times during a long stay in Europe. His mother and father both were dead. The Count expected him to carry on for the family. Petted him, and like that. But——

Michael said no more. Afterwards he was certain that he said no more than that of his latter visits to Leningrad, certainly nothing at all of the last night, when he'd just left Warsaw with Helen gone.

Chuganoff was showing the effects of as many highballs as the bottle of ginger ale would mix. Michael knew that whiskey and ginger ale was a great peace-offering from Mrs. Fraser. Her favorite mixture. Chuganoff pocketed the bottle of whiskey calmly and announced that he guessed he'd go into Cannes and drop in at Charley's Bar. There'd be reporters there and he'd tell them what he thought of Wind Bag, who'd take good American dollars and spend them in a dump like Roumania when there was Sofia with a good class of women to help you start liberating.

Inside the Villa the party was at its height. Upstairs Tanaroff was still ranting about his comic-opera plan to stimulate the moujiks into abortive rebellion. Ever and again Clare Fraser would run up to look in on the debate and smile at the Count and receive the homage of the men who flocked around him. Then she'd run downstairs again.

Groups were coming in from the Opera and from the Casino. Some of them bore names known around the world. A Metropolitan Opera diva and her claque of dark, sleek Italians; Raymond Duncan in his flowing white robes and his bevy of acolytes in fluffy frocks from the most expensive of the couturiers in Place Vendome; a millionaire with a famous American name and an Indian Maharajah with the Spanish girl who had become his fourth wife. They all came to the Villa Amette to meet others of their kind, to see and be seen, and all liked the doll-like Mrs. Fraser. And Count Tanaroff was a celebrity, and amusing.

Talking with Chuganoff out in the yard had brought Helen Avery back into Michael's mind. Not that she was ever absent but at times she came so close and became so vivid that he felt smothered. Chuganoff had led him to talking of Leningrad—he and Helen had talked of living in Leningrad part of every year, while the ice was on the Neva. More of their plans that had gone up in smoke.

He went upstairs, to the little room he used as an office, and put some papers on his desk in order. He decided to ask Mrs. Fraser if he would be needed any more. These gay, spendthrift nights, were no longer a novelty. They were dancing in the library, with the rugs rolled aside, to the tuneful music of a five piece orchestra which had come to look upon the Villa almost as a regular night job. Michael had danced with a dozen women; their cool bare shoulders and uncovered backs and caressing thighs sometimes challenged his blood and many gave him to know in their varied ways that their challenge was deliberate, and inviting, but no more of it tonight.

As he stepped down the stairs he heard Mrs. Fraser in the big hall. He hesitated, thinking she might come tripping up to see how the Count was getting along and he could intercept her. She was talking to a party of guests that had just arrived and, apparently, were not intending to stay very long. Mrs. Fraser was telling them they must wait until after the dancer from Monte Carlo had performed.

"But really we only looked in to see you," said a woman's voice. "We spent the entire day at Nice, walking about the shops in the morning and this afternoon at a garden party on Cap Suquet. I, for one, am frightfully all in. So are Mrs. Ransom and Lady Severn."

"It was a gorgeous garden party," said another woman's voice, "with a brilliant crush. No end of big wigs, and Charlotte, from Monaco. You didn't dare sit down for you didn't know whether royalty was right behind you."

"I see Lord Severn and Mr. Ransom over there with Major Croyant," Mrs. Fraser was saying, "but where did you leave Georges Raynel? I want to tell him I can beat him at tennis now. I've been learning a lot."

Michael went slowly down the stairs. He gripped fiercely on the bannister rail. He recognized, now, the first voice. He heard, dimly, that Georges Raynel had not come ashore from his yacht since they all returned from a lovely sail to the Spanish coast.

Then Michael saw the group in the hall, and Mrs. Fraser saw him.

"Oh, Michael," she called. "I was about to look for you. I wanted something, but it's escaped me all at once. I'll think of it in a moment."

He heard nothing more for what seemed an age, though it barely could have been a minute. He knew that his legs were taking him down the stairs automatically and that suddenly they stopped.

She stood there, in Clare Fraser's hall, in all her wonderful brown and ivory tints, in a cloth-of-silver gown that fitted her like a sheath. She stared at him and he

stared at her, a vision come suddenly to actuality. A year
—more, a year and two months and a week and four
days, since that night in Warsaw. The orchestra in the
library was whispering a lilting air from Musetta but
the music they made for his ears was that music of
Kashmir he and she had heard together when last they
looked into each other's eyes.

Mrs. Avery was chattering away to Mrs. Fraser, and
Mrs. Ransom was saying that Princess Charlotte of Monaco wore a gown with this and that here and there, and
the young Lady Severn was gazing with bewilderment
at the girl and the young man who stared at each other
as if each saw a ghost.

The girl broke the spell.

"Michael!"

He ran forward from the foot of the stair.

"Helen!"

She went white and red and white again when he
caught her hands. Her mouth quivered and a mist floated
like a tulle fog across her wondrous brown eyes. She
swayed, just a slight movement of her body, and her
elbows spread, ever so slightly—as if she were about to
step forward and throw her arms around him. She caught
herself, and stiffened a little, and suddenly was aware,
as was he, that the conversation had stopped and that
Mrs. Fraser, like the rest, was looking. The others with
wonder in their faces, and Mrs. Fraser with a queer
smile hovering about her lips like a dancing ghost.

Helen looked at her mother. Mrs. Avery's face was
blank, save for a gathering shadow.

"But don't you see, Mother?" Helen cried. "It's
Michael—it's Michael Jeribzoff!"

Michael felt a quick stab. Jeribzoff! The name he'd
been hiding from for so many months. But it didn't mat-

ter. Nothing mattered. Here was Helen. He could not only look at her, but know the feel of her hands again. Warm hands, they'd been hot, and were now growing cold.

"Yes," said Mrs. Avery through tight lips. "I see. How do you do, Mr. Jeribzoff." And then, teeth tight as well as lips, "Helen!"

She withdrew her hands. Not with a jerk, but in a flutter of haste as if she realized for the first time that the fiancée of Georges Raynel was holding hands she shouldn't hold.

He bowed to Mrs. Avery, deeply and with profound courtesy, but with an air of cynical reserve. She had tried to break them up. She thought she had succeeded when she stolen Helen away from Warsaw and left for him a monstrous note telling him that she wanted Helen to marry a man who would lift her to great heights. But he knew from the feel of Helen's hands, from the mist in her eyes and the whiteness that crept up to the laid-on poinsettia of her mouth, that she hadn't broken them up. *He* had done that—when he fled from Leningrad, murder behind him and the Jeribzoff rubies in his pocket. He'd done the deed of breaking, by letting her go, not her mother. He felt light headed, proud, triumphant, when he bent into his deep bow.

Mrs. Fraser did not present him to Mrs. Ransom, or the interesting looking Lady Severn. He didn't expect it because she was ever informal. It was quite like her to wave her hand with a flash of her diamonds embracing the company in a sweep as if she swept him up to them. He bowed to Mrs. Ransom and Lady Severn.

Lady Severn smiled drily and gave him her hand. There was an enigmatic look in her eyes. "You and Miss

Avery must be quite old friends—and good ones. Where has she been keeping you?"

Helen answered for him with a nervous little laugh.

"We were practically raised together." She turned upon him then. "It's been so good to see you again, Michael. Sometime perhaps you'll tell me all that you've been doing."

Then she was talking to a strange man who had just come up with Major Croyant. He supposed he would be Lord Severn. Helen was calling him "Ramsey." Through the pain she'd given him with that perfunctory dismissal of everthing that had been between them, he saw Ramsey Severn as through a veil. A man above medium height, athletic, with an air of being slightly bored, even with his beautiful wife. Quick, articulate eyes, that told you at once what he thought of you and, having warned you, looked around for something to see more entertaining. Mouth flexible and pleasant, but with cruelty lurking close. Michael summed up these details because Helen was calling him Ramsey, and laughing with him over some sally or confidence. He nodded to whatever she was saying and, because Michael was looking at him, stepped forward and thrust out his hand. "Didn't I hear 'Jeribzoff?'" he said, easily. "I'm Severn."

He shook hands and turned casually to speak to Mrs. Ransom.

"Oh, Michael!" Mrs. Fraser suddenly exclaimed. "I've just thought of what I wanted of you. Do take Pete and Betsy for a good walk before you go home. The poor dears haven't been out for a run since this morning."

Lady Severn smiled her dry smile and glanced from him to Helen. Mrs. Ransom, good soul, gave Mrs. Fraser a sharp and rather astonished look. Mrs. Avery seemed not to have heard. Michael, on impulse, bowed to Mrs.

Ransom as if she'd actually spoken aloud her thought that Mrs. Fraser might have spared him what appeared to be a deliberate reminder of his place.

Yet he held no grudge against Clare Fraser. She hadn't meant to be nasty. It wasn't her way to hurt the feelings of the littlest thing that crawled on the earth. If the cadaverous butler had happened to be a handsome man with a snappy tango it would be just like her to lug him onto the dance floor in the midst of her guests. It simply had occurred to her that she wanted the Sealyhams taken for a walk and, since Michael took them out every evening, it occurred to her likewise to remind him of them. She'd do the same to Count Tanaroff if he had happened to have acquired the habit of nursing the Sealyhams.

He felt curiously Clare Fraser had debased him in the eyes of Helen Avery. He was bitter, poignantly bitter, because of that cool withdrawal from the sudden Heaven she had spread between them with the mist over her eyes and the quiver of her mouth. She didn't understand why he had made no effort to recapture her after her mother took her from Warsaw. She might think a thousand things—which, down in her heart, she ought not to believe. Because she apparently did believe whatever explanation she had imagined, he was bitter. Let her think of him as a tender of dogs, a menial, if she liked. Serve her right!

For once, however, he hated the Sealyhams, those caricatures of dogs. He'd been amused and a little bored at first when Mrs. Fraser insisted every night that he and no one else take them out. He couldn't understand why any one of the numerous house servants or chauffeurs or others on the preposterous staff couldn't do the job. But Mrs. Fraser insisted upon him. Tonight he jerked roughly on the leashes and spoke savagely in Russian, a tongue the dogs knew nothing of. Betsy subsided and thrust down her grotesque nose. Pete, being bolder, sniffed at Michael's legs to make sure this wasn't a stranger and then whimpered.

Michael was contrite at once. He laughed loudly and joyously and the dogs frisked around him in quick ecstasy. He had adopted a regular course for his walk with the dogs and he followed it tonight. He went out a side door and around the house, skirting the front verandah. Helen and the women of her party were inside. Sir Philip Gregg, whom he knew as Croyant's friend, was walking among the hibiscus with a man he thought to be Mr. Ransom. On the verandah he heard voices and made out the unmistakable form of Croyant and was less certain his companion was Lord Severn.

While he crossed the grounds toward the gates, the Sealyhams straining at their leashes, he was unaware of a shadow that detached itself from the cluster of low palms by the garage and followed him. He saw two men, strangers, loitering in the road close to the gates. He had no way of knowing that these were Dupree's men who waited to take their place in the wake of Helen Avery when she should emerge. Their car was parked a hundred feet up the road. He gave them, in his ignorance of the meaning of them, only a cursory glance, and turned toward the Via des Anges. When he turned into the Via he gave the dogs their leashes. They knew how far, and which way, to go. Down to the sea walk, turn right and go as far as the restaurant built on piles in Golfe Juan, the inlet reserved by the navy as base for a single submarine. Here, in the bright radiance cast by the restaurant lights, they would wait until he came up. Under leash again, around the curve of the Golfe and then a free run on their short legs to the ruins of an old tower where the walk ended abruptly in a great tangle of wet seaweed on a bleak stretch of shore. There they would wait again, nosing in the seaweed for the mysterious things that slithered about unseen.

When he came to the Golfe Juan he forgot to take up the trailing leashes. Pete and Betsy hovered about his legs, not knowing just what to do, until they had made the Golfe curve. Here Pete barked, calling Michael's attention to the leashes. He always unsnapped them at this point, giving the dogs their heads. He took the hint and the Sealyhams darted ahead. Michael walked slowly. He looked up into the sky. The stars were not warm, to-night, but cold brilliants. "It's been good to see you again!" He looked over the Golfe, across the narrow peninsula that makes the breakwater for the benefit of the submarine, and found a planet low down over where Corsica lay. It glowed redly like a dying fire. "We were pratically raised together, Lady Severn"—which was as much as to say, "We were nothing but playmates, you know!"

He came to the tower and stood for a moment looking far out to sea at the beacon blinking on Cap Roux. If the beacon should go out and stop blinking a dozen boats would be wrecked on the rocks before morning. For a year Helen Avery's eyes had been unseen beacons blinking somewhere in the world for him to see. He'd seen them and was happy. They went out and he was wrecked.

Pete and Betsy came trotting up from their investigations among the seaweed. When Michael reached the tower each night he turned back and they trotted ahead. They waited but got no signal. Michael sat down on the ruins and the dogs returned to the seaweed to continue their ever futile quest of those slithering things. The beacon continued to wink, to cast its deep sheen on the water. Michael fell to making excuses for Helen. He'd made no effort to communicate with her. She was always in the papers, so he could not have the excuse of not knowing where her mother had taken her. Georges Raynel was rich, handsome, gallant. Michael was not rich and gave no promise that he ever would be. Helen's mother wanted her lifted to great heights. He made excuses even for Mrs. Avery. She was quite right. She knew the value of money. She'd had a lot herself, and must shudder at the thought of her daughter being without plenty.

And so on.

Betsy whimpered. A cold breeze was sweeping in. Betsy was cold and wanted to go home to biscuits and warmth. Michael looked at his watch. He'd been sitting at the old tower for two hours.

The Villa's guests had gone. Lights on the lower floor were off, save in the hall and a small morning room just within the doors. As he passed the garage he saw, with some surprise, that the headlamps of each of the three cars were switched on. He thought he made out the dark form of a chauffeur behind the wheels of one.

He crossed the verandah, the dogs straining, and entered the house through the front door. The lights, he supposed, had been left on for him and everyone would have retired, but when he pushed open the door he was startled to see three of the chauffeurs, wrapped in their heavy night uniform coats standing in the middle of the hall. They had on their caps and gloves and by their attitudes gave him the curious impression that they were on their toes, waiting for an order to dash for their cars. The German butler, also coated and capped, was running down the stairs taking two steps at a time. When Michael stared up at him he was just stopping himself with one hand clutching the bannister. His other hand was slipping a blue gun into his coat pocket.

In the fleeting instant before Mrs. Fraser appeared Michael was dimly aware that the chauffeurs had swung around to stare at him, and that the butler was standing dead still on the stair, also staring. Then Mrs. Fraser ran out of the morning room. She was still in her evening gown and gold slippers, but wore a heavy sport coat tightly belted around her waist. She had put on a man's peaked cap and drawn it tight over her light hair, down onto her forehead. It gave her face a sharp, grim look. He thought of an Apache girl.

While he gaped transfixed by this amazing tableau, she cried, "Michael! I thought you were—!" She broke off abruptly. If she had finished her sentence he wouldn't have known what she said, for the startling change in her whole personality paralyzed all of his senses. She was something as hard as steel. But she gave a queer, mirthless laugh. She sent a glance to the chauffeurs. They stirred and quietly disappeared through the doors onto the verandah. The butler turned back upstairs to his quarters. Mrs. Fraser pulled off her cap revealing her shining hair in a tangle. She laughed again, her whole grim expression changed, a spell of some mysterious fibre was broken and she was Clare Fraser again.

"I thought you'd fallen into the bay and dragged Pete and Betsy with you," she complained brightly. "Honest I did. I was just sending out a searching party—for the dogs."

She began to take off her coat and he stepped forward to help her out of it. During the brief moment it hung free in his hands while she was turning around to take it from him. It was heavy, as if weighted down with lead. While he handed it over its skirts flapped against his legs. He felt two separate blows against his flesh and knew that a pistol nested in each of the coat pockets.

Mrs. Fraser went upstairs. She turned to call down, "Get around for some tennis in the morning, will you, Michael?"

While he waited for a bus under a bright arc on Boulevard Nice he still puzzled over that amazing Apache-like manifestation of Clare Fraser. And wondered since when people go hunting along the sea walk for either a man or dogs in three cars and with pistols!

When he had boarded his bus for Cannes the shadow that had dogged him all night detached itself from the trees along the upper reach of Via des Anges, along which he'd come to reach the boulevard, and was revealed by the arc light in the thick shape of Khamov. A car slid from the darkness into the light, took the Russian into the seat beside the driver, and sped off in the wake of the bus.

CHAPTER XV

MICHAEL EXPLAINS

COUNT TANAROFF was right, to a degree, about the young Russian, Chuganoff. The man deserved to have been thrown out of the Villa Amette. He was not an agent of Chenkin, and neither did he have to go to Charley's Bar to find a newspaper reporter.

He was a reporter himself. Indeed, he was no less than the widely read editor of the *"On dit; On dit"* column of amusing gossip, amusing and sometimes biting, in *Les Affaires*.

Early in the morning after the excitement at Clare Fraser's party, the man presented himself at the Crillon. Major Croyant was having breakfast with Sir Philip in Croyant's suite. When Chuganoff was announced as a visitor who waited in the lobbies, the Major had him sent straight up.

The young man, full of verve in a jaunty suit of London tweeds, was grinning broadly when he confronted the Major and Sir Philip, and dropped a copy of his paper onto the table with a cocky air.

"It got across okay," he exclaimed, "but there's one thing, don't you forget. The Count's got dynamite up his sleeve. There are two men I'd rather not stick me up in a corner with mad fists, and both of them are that bird."

"I've seen the paper," said Croyant, brushing his hand across his jaw. "It got across."

"There are additional paragraphs in this edition," said Chuganoff. "This is the street edition. More people read it."

Croyant looked down the *On dit; On dit* columns, and handed the paper to Sir Philip, who also read the additional paragraphs devoted to Mrs. Fraser's party. While Sir Philip was reading, the young man accepted coffee from Croyant and bent his head across the table.

"I've got your dope on the La Turbie thing," he said in a low tone. "Severn and the Marchesa. I came over at this early hour because I have to go over to Monte Carlo for the afternoon. My boss wants me to cover the pigeon walk."

"You understand, don't you," Croyant said, a little sharply, "that I have a credible reason for wanting to know the minutes of that excursion? I'm not interested in the Marchesa's liberalities with her favor."

"If I thought you were going in for dirt, sir, I'd not help out."

"Sorry," Croyant returned instantly. *"On dit; On dit."*

"And," Chuganoff went on, "the only dirt is what the outsider wants to make for himself. It's a case of take what you'd like to take, according to your own mind or knowledge of the lady, and leave what you'd rather not have. Here's the dope. Lord Severn and the Marchesa are not unknown at the Inn atop La Turbie, or at some of the smaller, more intimate resorts. This wasn't their only visit together. On this occasion, the motor trip you mentioned, they had an early luncheon at the Inn. They occupied a table on the balcony overlooking the Corniche Road. Pierre, the floor captain, remembers couples. It's his business. They come again. He remembers them. Severn did a great deal of pleading with the lady. Whether he was pleading for himself, somebody else, or trying to steer her away from somebody—you can help yourself."

Croyant looked up with a start. "There's an idea! Trying to steer her away from somebody else. I've a friend, you'd know him if I mentioned his name, though you might not know what business he's in at the moment, who would say to that: there are only three ways you can steer a woman, away from her husband, away from somebody else, and to yourself."

"As I said, sir, help yourself. That was the situation as Pierre saw it. The lady was obdurate enough for Pierre to work off a second bottle of wine, two repeat cocktails, and four liqueurs. She hadn't given in yet, whatever it was about, and Pierre hoped they'd come back and finish at tea time. But they didn't. They drove from the Inn into the native quarter where they parked their car at a garage. It remained there until after dusk. It is in the native quarter, sir, where are the *Cabinets Particuliers*—small apartments you may engage by the hour. Some of them, despite the outward appearance of the neighborhood, are quite luxurious, once you get your lady inside."

"They engaged a *Cabinet?*"

Chuganoff shook his head. "There's where you can help yourself again. Take it or leave it. My assistant visited every one that is pretentious. The sort that have their own street doors—privacy—guarantees against observation and being recognized. Used by the best people at Monte Carlo and points east and west. My man is never lied to by the proprietors. The noble lord and his beautiful lady are not on the records kept in the memory of every proprietor on La Turbie. They may have gone out to the Ponce du Garde, where there are benches in a loquat grove, and they may have sat on those benches and

looked across to the High Alps. It's really a magnificent
view. They dined at a little place, still arguing I believe,
from the best report I can get, and then drove down the
hill late in the evening after a dance at a fashionable
Musette. Would you say, now, that they were lovers, or
just good friends and that the man took her up to where
she could see the world spread around her feet for no
other reason than to give her a talking to?"

"I'd like to say that," returned Croyant. "What do
you say?"

"I'll hedge too," Chuganoff grinned. "And I'll add
that the best and the worst I can get on the pair, covering the whole of her visit in these parts, is stuff of about
the same grade. Naughty, naughty, if you're a wise guy
or think Venus ought to wear a breech clout; pretty,
pretty if you still think dandelions are fairies after dark."

Croyant was thoughtful over an additional cup of
coffee. Sir Philip engaged the blithe young man with a
discussion of Clare Fraser, Count Tanaroff, Georges Raynel and his friend Veragua, and the forthcoming carnival.
When he got up and reached for his hat he said, to
Croyant,

"I did a good job, last night?"

"You left nothing out." He drew out his pocket book
but the young man threw up his hand with a grin.

"Nothing doing, sir. I was glad enough to get entree
to Villa Amette. It's the most publicized villa along the
shore because none of us newspaper folk have been
allowed through the gates. Besides getting across what
you wanted, I got enough on my own for half a dozen
columns in the future. I'm strong for the little canary,
Mrs. Fraser, but business is business. What she can see
in the big stiff of a Tanaroff is what I'll be asking my
readers soon."

In his room in Rue des Pomegranates Michael Ballou read the paper that his neighbor, earlier than his wont, had brought him. Khamov was quite excited. Michael could tell when he heard his cane tapping on the corridor outside that something was up. When he burst in upon his young friend he waved the paper in the air.

"But my friend is of importance," he cried. "He is in the news of the world."

Michael sat down to read. While he read his face darkened and his hands began to shake. Khamov watched him narrowly but, outwardly, with no other show than that of the man who thinks he has brought his friend a pleasant surprise and awaits his expressions of satisfaction.

"I succeeded last night," wrote the anonymous columnist of *On dit; On dit,* "in breaking through the barriers at Villa Amette. I saw with my own eyes its pageantry of wealth and fashion and buffoonery. I saw the most delightful things, and the funniest, and a thing or two most intriguing."

Then he went on to describe the people who were there, the gowns of the women, their being attached outwardly to this man and that but secretly to the other and so-and-so. He wrote glowingly of the charming Clare Fraser and paid particular attention to her gorgeous jewels. Michael had never particularly noticed Mrs. Fraser's jewels and only thought of it now when the story in the paper reminded him that she had worn last night what surely must be the whole of a stupendous collection. No woman, he thought, could possess more diamonds and emeralds and sapphires. They had been strewn all over her, from her wrists to her elbow, in her hair and around her neck and dripping down in shimmering strands to nest between her breasts. The newspaper writer seemed to have jotted down all the separate pieces and listed them in his paragraph.

Then he hinted that Moscow would hear from those jewels. There was the doughty Count Tanaroff. He pictured the Count with grandiloquent strokes of his pen— or typewriter taps. He told pretty plainly that the Count was working on the vivacious Clare Fraser with her bank account in view, and with a suffering Russia as his tool. The writer, apparently, was contemptuous of the great Tanaroff. And he poked fun at him mercilessly with a description of the scene in the upper room when the Count had been tripped up "by an unknown heckler" who was promptly bounced into the yard. It was very ludicrous, his painting of the incident. People up and down the Riviera would laugh uproariously, Michael knew. Laugh and flock to the Villa to get a look at the fellow and whisper their nastyisms with lecherous side glances at Clare Fraser.

"But the Villa has its secrets," the writer went on, "that are not all frivolous in their aspects. One wonders, for example, about a very engaging young man who poses as the chatelaine's private secretary and is known to her intimates as Michael Ballou. He is an American, he will assure you, and indeed he quite looks the part although he is minus the distinguishing badge of tortoise rimmed glasses. But when one talks with the polite and obliging Michael Ballou one looks back in a not too distant past and remembers a Michael Jeribzoff who spent sunny afternoons on the Bois and at Fontainebleau with a pretty American girl, and who spent many nights in Leningrad, among which is one memorable night when the house of his uncle, Count Jeribzoff, an aristocrat of the old school, burned to the ground around the murdered body of the uncle and another who was for long thought to be The

Panther, but now has been de-identified and remains unknown.

"One wonders why Michael Jeribzoff is known at Villa Amette as Michael Ballou. True, it is said he is really Ballou, his American father's name. But in respect of the wishes of his mother's house he assumed the Jeribzoff name in Europe and, it is understood, was to go on as the heir to the name and wear it. Can it be that young Michael, who used to have plenty of money to spend but now must work for a secretary's pittance, has some reason for retreating into his identity as a Ballou and 'hiding' himself under the wing of the amiable Clare? Did anything happen that night in Leningrad that shouldn't have happened, or doesn't look good to strangers?

"And why has the pretty American girl, whom we won't name but who lives with her mother in a quaint little cottage on the slopes of Cap Californie, deserted her gallant young lover for another? Does she know anything about that night in Leningrad?"

There was more, more speculations, the "American girl" was unmistakably identified as Helen, without being named. And again and again the writer hinted that if Clare Fraser must be the victim of some one, it would be better perhaps if she'd let Count Tanaroff dupe her thoroughly so Michael Ballou wouldn't have a chance.

Michael flew into a terrific rage when he threw the paper to the floor. Khamov appeared to be mildly amazed. "But the Riviera will regard you with great respect," he protested. "Do you not see? You are a suspicious person. You are credited with designs. It is hinted that you fled from Leningrad after committing a great crime. Even your sweetheart is horrified. What could there be better? The Riviera will look up to you. It will salute you. Do we not adore those of our fellow men who are darkly and mysteriously evil? This pretty Madame Fraser—she will embrace you with rapture and a pulse beat of one hundred at the very least. One may do much with a lady whose wrist runs to ninety, but a hundred, my young friend! And Madame Fraser's blood will perhaps run a scale ever higher—when she reads that she has in her house a celebrity of whom she must be aware!"

Michael knew only that his neighbor was become garrulous. He heard him rattling on in his melodic, liquid voice. His rage had given way to panic. Someone knew! Someone knew what had happened that night in Leningrad. Someone who had been in the house last night. Of course he never suspected Chuganoff. He suspected half a dozen others. Lord Severn. Severn had looked at him queerly, and had dropped him only a word before he engaged the attention of Helen.

Or someone else. No use trying to figure out who. There was reason behind this piece in the paper. Someone was playing with him, letting him know that before long he would be called to an accounting.

Khamov seemed to read his thoughts while he strode up and down the narrow space of his room. "If there is additional writing between the lines, my friend," he said gently, "you must talk of it. It is not well to keep words bottled up."

Michael smiled bitterly. A picture of himself telling Khamov of what was hidden in his fireplace, and of its significance, amused him. But the man had brought him to a resolution. He hurried downstairs and took a cab for a quicker run to Villa Amette.

When he reached the house Mrs. Fraser had already finished giving the staff its instructions for the day. She was always fresh and bright in the mornings and this morning, when Michael was seeing her an hour earlier than ever before, she was particularly gay. She had seen the story in the paper and instead of being provoked she was delighted with it.

"But you, Michael," she said, with a reproof that was good-natured, "have been taking advantage of me." She laughed and her laugh mocked him. "Really I'd never suspect you of having an alias and of being something sinister."

"I came so early because I wanted to talk to you of that," he said evenly, with a determined manner. "I think you should know, because of the confidence you have put in me. I shall tell you everything, and then you will tell me how quickly I am to go."

She nodded. "Yes. I shall tell you how quickly you are to go. But first, before you've told me that you are this horrible person they call The Panther, who kisses women and then takes their pearls, I'll have my highball." The cadaverous butler came. She ordered her highball. "A stiff one, Max," she stipulated. "Better, in fact, make it double. I'm about to hear why I haven't been kissed and robbed of my diamonds long before this."

Michael could not understand the woman's nature. His trouble must show in his face. Certainly he was very earnest. She had reason to suspect he had been imposing upon her. But she was making fun of him.

"I'm not quite so bad as that, Madame."

"You look so dark I'm ready for anything."

He saw a swift vision of her as he had seen her last night. Apache girl, pistols in her coat pocket, mouth thinned to two straight lines. Talk of looking dark! She was the one who could transform herself from a rather raucous little gamin in Paquin models, into Medusa's favorite daughter!

While she sipped her highball he told her his story.

"I arrived in Leningrad that morning. I went from Warsaw and had a thing in my heart that hurt so deeply I didn't go at once to the house I called home. My only home, you may say, since the passing of my father and mother. Count Jeribzoff wanted me to use his name and when I came to Europe to see him I did so. Passport reasons made it necessary that I use no other in crossing the various borders."

"So you went, that night, to his house?" Mrs. Fraser interrupted.

He started. He hadn't said anything about the night as yet. How would she know he went into Nevsky Prospekt that evening until he told her?

"Quite late," he went on. "I had gotten myself in hand. There was no response when I rang the bell and hammered at the front door. I thought my uncle was away from home for the evening and went around to a rear door to which I carried a key, the privilege of the Jeribzoff heir. As soon as I stepped into the house I knew something was amiss. There was litter everywhere. The house had been turned upside down. I hurried into the library and there, stretched on the floor, with a knife in his heart, lay Count Jeribzoff. When I was certain he was dead I hurried to the telephone to summon the authorities. The wire had been cut off close to the instrument. I remembered an extension in the bedrooms above and hurried upstairs. Here was more confusion. Drawers had been turned onto the floor. Desks had been searched, papers and books and other belongings were scattered everywhere. And that telephone also had been cut off. I ran downstairs again."

Some picture in his memory affected him suddenly and he paused. While he recovered himself he looked at Mrs. Fraser. She had finished her highball and was looking away from him, through a French window onto the tennis court. He had the queer impression that he was telling her a story she already knew. He couldn't define the feeling, or trace it, but something in her expression, in her listless attitude, bothered him. But he went on, speaking in a dull tone, as if he had set himself a task he would not be diverted from. Khamov was right. It was good to unbottle words sometimes.

"I went back into the library and looked again at the body on the floor. I would have to rouse some neighbor to get at a telephone. I would have to leave the house. But I couldn't tear my eyes off my uncle. He had thought a great deal of me, and had often said that while he couldn't leave me any money, as a result of the change in Russia, he nevertheless would leave what would be the value of a great deal of money. I remembered this while I looked down at him, and remembered the many times he had told me that if ever anything should happen to him, or even if he died quite peacefully, I was to go into his safe and take what I should find there and keep it as my own. He had shown me where the safe was hidden, in the wall under a panel of tile mosaic. He had shown me how to twist the panel, disclose the safe door, and had taught me the combination. He was an old man and sharing a secret with me seemed to give him an odd delight."

"You knew what it was he wanted to leave you?" Mrs. Fraser asked. She toyed with the remnant of ice in her highball glass, stirring it abstractedly.

"No. I knew only that it would be the contents of a case. He was very reticent. Time enough, he would say, for me to know when the moment of his death had passed. But he warned me to be secretive. I gathered that the case would contain something that it would be just as well to conceal from the Soviet authorities. They were very considerate with my uncle, but he never fully trusted them. His friend, Lenin, was gone, and Lenin's successors were of a new school. He told me to take what I should find and say nothing.

"I decided to go to the safe before I went to telephone the authorities. I found only one thing."

Mrs. Fraser looked up. Her eyes seemed to question him. He was glad she was showing a measure of interest at last. He nodded.

"A case, made of marble and very heavy for an article so small. It contained what I have since learned have a history, the Jeribzoff rubies, as they are known. They are extremely valuable."

"Good Heavens, Michael! Rubies! And such important ones that they actually have a name. You simply must tell me all about them. Did you get a lot for them?"

"I've never sold them, Madame. I couldn't. If one of them should be offered for sale all Europe would know."

A wrinkle appeared between Mrs. Fraser's eyes. "You've kept them? Surely, if they were yours, you could sell them? What difference would it make?"

"I haven't finished, yet."

"Oh. I see. There's more?"

She sounded as if she were a little bored. He went sturdily ahead.

"I put the heavy case in my pocket without even opening it at that time. I had done as my uncle wanted me to do, possessed myself of whatever its contents were without letting any one know. I would have gone to find a telephone then but while I was passing the door of another room I was interrupted. A man sprang out. I caught the glint of a knife and dodged just in time. We fought and knocked over an oil burning lamp on the table

in the room. In the darkness the man's knife clattered
onto the floor and he managed to break away from me.
I couldn't see the knife. My assailant had a pocket flash
which he brought out. I had no doubt he was my uncle's
murderer and waited some move of which I could take
advantage but, to my surprise, he made none. He called
me by name and proceeded to light another lamp which
he seemed to know where to find.

"He was strange to me but he said that he was my
uncle's lately engaged valet. I accused him of being the
murderer. He laughed in my face and retorted that the
police would make up their own minds whether he or I
had been the slayer. The knife lay on the floor between
us. It was doubtful which of us would reach it first. I
backed away to make a dash for the street and give the
alarm but he held me with a warning that was like a
blow.

" 'You're half foreigner and the other half comes from
the old aristocrats,' he said. 'I'm a good Russian work-
man. Who will the police believe?' "

Mrs. Fraser nodded. "I can see his point," she murmured. "You were in a jam."

He was glad that she saw. He felt a great gratitude
to her. "I'm glad you understand. More glad than I can
say. I might tell you all that ran through my head. Of
my uncle's warnings against trusting the Soviet authorities too far, against letting them know what was to be
my inheritance, and of my conviction that between the
local Russian who was in good standing with the present
regime, and me, as good as a stranger and foreigner, and
who might have a reason of my own to do away with my
benefactor, the police would believe him. I came to a decision. I would go out and cross the border, into Poland
or Hungary. Then I would go to the authorities and tell

the story. Other police would believe me and the Leningrad police might be impressed. Anyhow, I would have done all that I could do. I made my way to the border, got across without revealing myself, but already my mind was wavering over the proper course to pursue. I had opened the case and discovered what it contained. The rubies. Surely some of the Count's friends would know that he had possessed them. They would not have been found and the murder would be put down to a robber. If I did not disclose the rubies I would be still suspected of having taken them, and if I did, I would be put down as a thief and murderer who had made up a story. And then I read of what had happened after I left the house. It had burned to the ground. An unidentified body was found, its foot caught in the front grille. I knew who that person had been. I remembered the lamp breaking on the floor and spilling its oil. Somehow he had set fire to it and had not been quick enough in flight. Perhaps I was a coward, but I reasoned that if I came forward I would not be believed. I could not even say I had confronted my uncle's valet for the newspapers said that he had had no servants. So I kept still. And I've been haunted ever since, and afraid that at any moment the Russian police will drop their hands on me. I've not dared——" He paused for a moment, his sensitive mouth out of his control. Then he finished. "I've not dared to try take up where I left off and I've lost what was more important at the time than even my life."

Mrs. Fraser was looking at him, with her queer expression, half sympathetic, half quizzical. "And you are certain, Michael, there was nothing else in the safe? Or in the box—only the rubies?"

He frowned. Why did she ask that again? "Nothing

else—in either. Just the box in the safe and the rubies on their velvet cushion."

She said "Oh!" It sounded as if he solved some sort of riddle that troubled her. As if there had been something missing in his story that she had only just discovered. She touched a bell and brought the butler and ordered another highball. "You'd better have one too, Michael. Or some brandy. You look as if you need it."

He said *"Merci*, Madame," and did not refuse. He waited. She gazed out the French window until the drinks came and took a sip of hers at once. "Bill," she murmured, "would turn over in his grave if he knew I took one drink in the morning. If he knew I was taking two, he'd sit up and bark." And then she added, "I'm sorry about it all, Michael, and I'm glad you told me. But of course it will make no difference here, at Villa Amette. I think you've been worrying about shadows. Pull yourself together and put on some white shoes and pants. I've got to have at least one set of tennis."

He went to the closet where he kept his change for the courts. He was dazed that she should take the matter so lightly. He couldn't dismiss from his mind the thought that she knew beforehand almost every thing he'd told. The idea was preposterous, of course, but it stuck. He tried to bring from her some revealing comment while they walked toward the courts.

"I'm afraid the newspaper reporter, whoever he is, knows more than he printed. I feel that he has a purpose behind him. He may embarrass you by printing more at any time, not the truth, of course, but paragraphs he'll make up."

She laughed, her high, musical trill. "Embarrass me?" she cried. "Why, Michael, dear, if he fills his newspaper I'll be tickled pink."

CHAPTER XVI

ONE DAY AT NICE

CARNIVAL was near. The Spirit of Merriment, always hovering over the playshore, had become rollicking. Flags and bunting draped the streets and even the flowers in the baskets of the flower girls seemed to have taken on gayer hues of red and yellow and white.

In the harbor beyond Guy de Mauspassant pier, in Golfe San Juan and at Monaco, Nice and Villafranche, pleasure craft from around the world had gathered, and the cabin ships of the tourists. All were white bulks on the lapis-lazuli of the Mediterranean save one, the black yacht that rode at anchor near Quai St. Pierre. The black yacht was the only marring note, it seemed, in a world that glistened clean and bright and eagerly new.

Dupree had gone into a new "business." The business of being his own impeccably tailored self. He remarked to Croyant, "One must accommodate himself when he presents his card to the friends of Lord Severn."

Among the friends of his lordship to whom Dupree presented himself with the manner of a true *boulevardier* was Georges Raynel. Raynel, when he understood who his visitor was, come aboard the *Ariadne* where he spent most of his time when he wasn't occupied with his fiancée on shore, was exceedingly pleased. He shook hands heartily with the detective.

"I knew you were looking for The Panther," said Raynel, "and I've taken a measure of comfort from the knowledge. I'm glad you've shown yourself. I want to talk to you about the advisability of my doubling the reward I've posted. This affair at Genoa—it again comes close to me. I met the Marchesa through the Severns."

Dupree objected strenuously to an increased reward. He hadn't approved of a reward in the first place. So far The Panther had ignored the challenge. There was that pier scene, with Vaskaya watching Miss Avery, but nothing, so far, had come of that. Best let the status quo alone.

"My friend, Major Croyant, whom you will know of course, gives me the same advice," said Raynel. He looked down at the deck floor, then at Dupree with a hard line at his mouth. "I am not accustomed to taking advice, Monsieur, but I will do nothing against the sober judgment of one who is of your standing. Meanwhile, I am at your service."

Dupree decided, with one of the quick decisions for which he was famous, to put his cards on the table. "How close to the Marchesa was Lord Severn?"

Raynel sat forward in his deck chair, with an expression of unbelief. "Good God, Monsieur! You don't mean to say——"

"That I think Lord Severn is The Panther?" Dupree's tone was sharp, cold. "I don't say it. I shall never say that of any man until I have him behind the bars. Meanwhile I think every man is The Panther. I suspect many. One walks free because I suspect him so strongly that I dare not arrest him."

Raynel smiled pleasantly, and with relief. "The intelligent attitude, of course. But get back to Severn. He was a close friend of Nita di Estrel. Met her, I believe, in Egypt last year. He goes in for polo quite a bit and she is a better rider than most of her countrywomen. There

was a bond, there, that widened. As for being her———"
He broke off, considered the word he was about to use,
and shook his head. "No, I won't discredit either of them
by even denying the implication behind your question."

Dupree got up and took a turn up the deck. He watched
a seagull for a moment and then turned back. Raynel remained in his deck chair, patient of the other's reflections.

"Severn," said Dupree when he turned back, and without resuming his seat, "did not remain at Port del Sol
all of the time while your yacht was anchored in that
inlet. He received a telegram which, as he explained it,
was from you, at Barcelona, suggesting that he fly down
to you and give you his company while you motored back.
He was absent from the noon of one day until the afternoon of the second day following. It was during the second night of his absence from Port del Sol that The
Marchesa di Estrel was robbed and murdered. Will you
confirm the contents of the telegram, Monsieur, and say
that he was a pleasant companion while you returned
from Barcelona?"

Raynel started to reply. He lifted his hand, as if to
emphasize the point he began with, but his hand dropped
and he stopped whatever words he had planned. He was
suddenly uncertain, ill at ease. He looked over the deck
rail, and when he looked around again he was frowning. "Look here, Dupree," he said, with some heat, "you
can't go off on that foot. It's like looking aslant at
Caesar's wife. He's a British lord, of one of the outstanding families. Prospects of being an Ambassador.
Rich in his own right and of a clan that could marshal
tremendous wealth. And he's not the sort who would not
only kill a woman but befoul her memory."

Dupree's eyes shone while the other spoke. "Monsieur
does his service faithfully for those who are his friends,"

he said, meaningly, "but I would prefer it if Monsieur
would place, for me, Lord Severn in his automobile on
the road to Port del Sol from Barcelona. You would have
started, I believe, shortly after dawn, or before. The
Panther was in the air at nine o'clock—as certain wireless
logs seem to indicate."

Raynel's palpable discomfort grew. A slight flush hued
his face. He got up and faced Dupree squarely.

"I suggest we drop the subject of Lord Severn. Not
only now, but for good. I will stand sponsor for any and
all of his actions." His tone was that of the man accustomed to giving orders and having them obeyed, but
Dupree did not draw back.

"You and I, Monsieur, are of a like concern. We wish
to pay our debt to The Panther. You, the debt that was
left by your friend. Me, the debt entrusted to me by
the relatives of those who have gone and the victims yet
to come. It is necessary that you tell me if his lordship
enjoyed the landscape, that morning, which spreads from
the Alcatraz Real, the road from Barcelona."

Raynel dropped back into his chair. He made a gesture
of "so be it!"

"He sent for a plane to come out from Toledo to pick
him up at del Sol and bring him south. Fifty miles down
the coast the plane made a forced landing. Oil line, I
believe. The landing was made in the Lanzo country
which is thinly populated, as you know, and hard to get
out of unless you know your way. Ramsey spent the day
and night pulling together his pilot, who'd been badly
jerked about, and the next day getting the both of them
out of the country. They made the Boulevard and were
helped along by motorists until they came to an Inn—
I've forgotten the name of it; Ramsey can tell you—
where a car could be hired for the pilot. It took him into

Barcelona. Ramsey waited for me to come along, since he couldn't reach me at Barcelona in time to join me there. We met at the Inn and I took him on into Port del Sol. Of the plane crack-up we said nothing to the others in my party. Lady Severn objects to his flying. He preferred to evade her emphatic 'I told you so.' "

When he had finished he glared at Dupree truculently. The detective bowed.

"*Merci*, Monsieur. I am satisfied."

Raynel straightened, angrily.

"You are not satisfied, but I trust your insane suspicions have become so strong that you will not dare to molest my friend. I recall, I believe, that there is one other you suspect so strongly you avoid him."

"The debris of a wrecked plane is not difficult to find," Dupree murmured, "even in the rugged Lanzo country."

Raynel waved a hand as if he dismissed the other's subject and his own distress in behalf of his friend. He became genial and charming, a host to his equal. A steward brought drinks, bacardi and absinthe and grenadine, with fruits and charged water. Raynel mixed a cocktail with his own hands.

"Señor Veragua's favorite," he explained. "Generally credited to Cuba, but really invented in Ecuador."

Dupree's enthusiasm over the cool drink became an emotion. "But superb, Monsieur! And fitting. One sails in a new direction auspiciously if launched with a drink both new and perfect."

Helen Avery brought Georges Raynel to the Villa Amette. Mrs. Fraser at once ran to Raynel with the news that she had learned how to hold her racquet, had been taught the dandiest back stroke, and would beat him to a pulp as soon as they went onto the courts.

Helen, after greeting Mrs. Fraser, turned and saw
Michael. She nodded and when he moved forward, gave
him her hand. Her lovely face was quite expressionless.
She preserved her coldness and Michael's bitterness welled
up.

Her fiancé laughingly bantered Mrs. Fraser out of her
plan for a set of singles on the court.

"I've got to know, first, what I'm up against. I may
decide to ask Monsieur Ballou if he won't go over me a
bit. It would be only fair." He gave Michael an amiable
smile. He was not at all the kind of man Michael had
expected to see. Instead of the grim, scowling visage of
the successful millionaire and successful rival, there was
a pleasant, gracious man, with an inescapable magnetism
that led you at once to forget his wealth and his success
at appropriating to himself the only woman on earth.

Since Raynel insisted upon doubles, they made up their
partners for the courts. He and Helen played together,
Mrs. Fraser and Michael. Mrs. Fraser was inclined to
hold herself in hand but, with a sudden hatred for Raynel
when he saw Helen flying about the court in partnership
with him, Michael cut loose. He grew savage in serving.
Instantly, as if she sensed his mettle, Helen took the game
seriously. "Oh, Georges! That was terrible," she complained once. Her fiancé laughed. Michael turned upon
the girl and was merciless. He, with such support as Mrs.
Fraser could give him, confounded their opponents. But
at the end of the first set Raynel surprised him with the
suggestion that they change partners. He walked around
the net and had no doubt about how Helen was taking
the idea. She would not meet his eyes. Happily, Count
Tanaroff intervened. He had just arrived and came
through the French windows seeking Mrs. Fraser. Raynel
hailed him jovially, having met him the night before. He

also wanted to talk to the Count. Michael was left alone
with Helen and there was nothing to do but play a singles.
Michael's mettle was gone. He was staggering now
through a world gone dark. Helen was tense and silent.
She beat him easily.

"Thank you," she said, when he approached her around
the end of the net. "But why did you let me win?" Her
face was flaming.

"Was it important that I should win?" he returned,
and marvelled at the chill in his own voice.

"You played hard enough against Monsieur Raynel."

It burst from him, welled up and overflowed. "I hate
him!"

Her eyes widened. She stared at him. "Hate him? Why
such a childish expression, Michael?"

He couldn't find words to say. The other night, when
she'd shown that she loved him, she promptly rebuffed
him. Now she was ridiculing him. He bowed mockingly.
She turned from him quickly and went into the house.

After that morning she came every day to play, and it
became the accepted thing that Michael would play with
her instead of with Mrs. Fraser, who was now busy with
Count Tanaroff's plans and with her own plans for Carnival week. Once or twice Raynel came with Helen, but
he did not play again. He preferred to talk with Tanaroff. He seemed ever at the point of joining Mrs. Fraser
in the financial end of the Count's magnificently planned
coup against the Soviets. Mrs. Ransom came, sometimes,
with Mrs. Avery. Lord and Lady Severn, too. When the
Severns came it was usually at noon time and Helen and
Michael would have played two or three sets of singles.
Then Lady Severn would play with him in partnership
against her husband and Helen.

Helen never played on the same side of the net with

Michael. She seemed to have become worried and gloomy.
Michael had heard the talk of her fiancé's reward for The
Panther and the danger it meant for him. He supposed
Helen was worried about him. She shirked all the old
pleasures of the resort and seemed to have no desire in
life other than to beat Michael on the courts.

Her mother scolded her. "Really, Helen, one would
think you wanted to get away from Georges.' He notices
it, but doesn't say a word. That's because he's too
amiable."

"Too sure of me, you mean," she answered. She
laughed, with a pretense of gaiety, but Michael, who
heard, could have leapt at her and crushed her in his arms.
He was insanely thrilled by the knowledge that, be as cold
as she liked toward him, as unforgiving of his apparent
refusal to put up a fight with her mother over her, she
had begun to be affected by seeing him, and her love for
the other man was endangered.

And so the days passed, for Michael a routine, in which
he took both a conscious and unconscious part. His neighbor, Khamov, dropping in in the mornings to throw his
broad-brimmed hat on the bed and sit in his chair and
talk of the Villa Amette and the news of the day. Again
he had seen Chenkin—on Rue d'Antibes. He was a fierce
looking creature. He must be on a big hunt. Michael
wasn't afraid of Chenkin now, since he had unbottled
his secret to Clare Fraser and since Helen entered into
some battle with him every day—at roulette, or trente-et-
quarante, or at tennis, or even in some silly little argument too infantile to remember what it was about. Night,
and Tanaroff, and a word with Croyant, whom he liked
so well, carrying on what Lady Severn declared to be a
flirtation with her, but which was only his way of being
agreeable to a pretty woman for Helen to see. Take the

dogs for their run on the seawalk—Helen always looked
at him with indignation in her glance when he took out
the dogs. Indignant with herself, perhaps, for having ever
been in love, for being in love now, with a man who
would take dogs out on leash. Croyant, too, watched him
often, taking Pete and Betsy onto the grounds. Strange,
about Croyant. He had the feeling the Englishman would
have liked Helen to be a little kindlier to him. Croyant
appeared to have a great interest in Helen. Perhaps that
was why he, Michael, liked the Major.

Of this part of the day's routine Michael was a conscious actor. He knew nothing of the shadow that followed him constantly, every night from the first gray fall
of dusk until he entered his own door in Rue des Pomegranates. On Boulevard Nice three cars waited each night
for Khamov, for Michael sometimes walked Via des
Anges to the Boulevard, at other times he walked along
the road that fronted the Villa until he came to the old
church of Ste. Devote before he turned up. Again, he
would go back to the restaurant on the navy pier and sit
for awhile over a demi tasse and then climb to the Boulevard from there. At each of these points a car waited for
Khamov so that the bus was not out of his sight until it
rolled into Boulevard d'Italia.

Only once did Clare Fraser speak of his experience in
Leningrad or of his consequent position, and then it
was only by way of speaking of the rubies themselves.
This was on the morning of the opening of the Carnival.
On the opening day nobody who was anybody made up
parties. It wasn't the fashionable thing to do. You went
with your friend, or your lover or sweetheart, but you
didn't let anybody know. It would be something like going
to the theater on Saturday night. But Mrs. Fraser pro-

posed to take in the fun. She'd asked Count Tanaroff to take her, but he'd gone almost purple at the thought.

"Carnival, Carnival—always it is Carnival! Pah! There is room for only one carnival. Carnival of blood for the scum that has stolen my country. I will wait until then."

So it was Michael who was to take Mrs. Fraser into Nice where the Carnival centered. She had put on such a simple frock it made her look like a very young girl and Michael complimented her. She flushed with pleasure, as she always did for a compliment, and told him she hoped he'd say that when she costumed for the great time —the last night of the merrymaking. She described the domino she was having down from Paris, a tan pantaloon suit in Chinese silk, all in one piece, shaped to fit her body, up to her neck in front and up to her waist in the back. "It's to be like my skin down as far as my knees, glove tight around the hips, but flaring into balloons from the knee down. There'll not be a button on it or even a pom pom. I'll be just all me down to my knees and if I don't look like a precocious brat I'll quit using cosmetics and go in for ear trumpets. But do you know, Michael, what would look gorgeous for that night? One of those rubies that have caused you so much worry. Just one, on my wrist, to shine like a stop signal. I suppose I'll have to signal stop a lot of times if I get lost from you men."

Throughout the week Croyant was on pins and needles. And Dupree, who seemed all at once to have lost interest in Lord Severn. Croyant made daily trips to the black yacht. No one came ashore from the craft, and no one else seemed to pay any attention to it. It remained at anchor off Quai St. Pierre and flew the Norwegian flag, yet the sailors who took Croyant back and forth were not Norwegian. Their faces were distinctly Teutonic.

The guard that so unobtrusively kept Helen Avery in

sight wherever she moved was doubled by Dupree. She came to know that she was being watched over. She pleaded with Georges Raynel to explain, thinking of course that he was behind it, but he refused to believe that she was being followed. She admitted that whenever she was in his company she could point to no suspicious loiterers. It was only when she was alone, or with her mother or the Ransoms. She spoke of it to Croyant and her sharp young eyes told her instantly that he knew why she was being watched. She was more or less contented, then, but nevertheless her worry about her fiancé deepened.

Dupree expected The Panther to commit some new and startling crime at any minute. On the very day of the Carnival's opening the strange signals flashed through the air. Inspector Clement and Monsieur Lemair, at the Sûreté, waited through torturous hours of the day and night for the news they expected. But, oddly, this time there was no fresh news of The Panther.

The signals continued to flash through the air. Skilful engineers at every Government station listened for them and tried vainly to track them to their source. Anyone with a short wave receiver could pick them up, but no equipment seemed capable of locating the point of transmission. When they broke out on the second day of the Carnival season, being brought in for an hour in the morning, then again in the afternoon, and for two hours straight after nightfall, ten French destroyers shot out from the harbor at Toulon to spread out, fanwise, and begin a thorough combing of the Mediterranean for any suspicious ship. Scotland Yard, appealed to by the Sûreté in Paris, persuaded the Admiralty to send out ships from Malta, to work in cooperation with the French. From

Spezia half a score of whippet craft strung a line across the sea and moved westward to meet the oncoming fan.

There were rumors abroad, of course, of the inordinate anxieties of the police, but these rumors met the gales of laughter and song and joyous shrieks that came out of Place des Allées, in Nice, and were absorbed in the echoes of fun. The Panther was forgotten. Which worried Dupree the more. When he is forgotten he will be more dangerous, he grumbled.

At last the week was ending. Clare Fraser put on her pantaloon costume from Paris and paraded before Tanaroff. The Russian fairly exploded. Michael, who was in the room and was himself a little dubious about the provocative picture Mrs. Fraser made in her ridiculous little suit, had to turn and look out a window to hide his smile at the Count's emotion.

The Count's adjectives descriptive of all women who would make themselves up as had the little Mrs. Fraser were in Russian, of course. Michael had to interpret them for his employer and in the interpretation disguise them completely. He gave up at last. He'd burst out laughing in another minute. He stole out of the room and waited in the hall.

Presently he had waited a long time and the Count seemed to have subsided. He went back to the room and pushed in the door. Those inside seemed not to notice that someone was coming for he heard their voices in earnest, low toned conversation—and Count Tanaroff was talking fluent French!

Mrs. Fraser saw him. She rattled off something about "lessons" being taken in secret, and the Count took the attitude that he need not explain to a private secretary any surprising circumstance involving himself. If he had learned to speak French that he might hold his conversa-

tions with Mrs. Fraser in more privacy, why, whose
affair was that? He glared at Michael and Michael retreated. As a matter of fact he didn't give a hang how
many languages Tanaroff learned, or how quickly. Now,
perhaps, knowing that the Count could never learn a language in three or four weeks, she would begin to lose her
confidence in him. Michael gave the matter no more
thought. Mrs. Fraser was ready to go. He was driving
her in a small car she had borrowed from a friend. Her
own big cars were left at the Villa. They were to meet
Georges Raynel and Major Croyant, the Averys and
Severns and Ransoms, at the Hotel Albert-Edouard in
Nice. Then the Spirit of Carnival would take and guide
them.

They all met under the plane trees that border the path
through the gardens of the Albert-Edouard. Helen wondered at once if Mrs. Fraser hadn't brought her costume
for the night, and was told, in a raucously whispered
aside, "I've got it on instead of underwear." Helen had
brought her costume in a bag and Raynel had checked it
at the hotel. She gave Michael her usual cool nod. She
was lovely and supreme and virginal against the conglomerate throng that eddied past.

The happy rout of celebrants poured down all the
boulevards and rues like multi-colored rivers in whirls of
crimson and eddies of orange and yellow, with racing
currents of green and bobbing rapids that broke into
sprays of white muslin. These merrymakers of the streets
already were in their masques, had been all day, and perhaps all of the night before. There were pierrettes and
columbines, clowns and harlequins, Saracens and Turks
and dwarfs with colossal heads of papier-mâché that
nodded and bobbed and grinned. There were companies
of handsome warriers and bevies of seductive odalisques,

their legs gleaming through gossamer stuffs. In the Place
des Allées they were burning King Carnival, always a
daylight ceremony on the final day. They burned King
Carnival with great shouts of glee, as any rabble burns
the King that, with him out of the way, their passions,
whether of lust or fun, may be given unrestrained vent.
He was a monstrous king, five floors tall and nearly as
fat in the belly as the public square was wide, so he made
a great fire, much to the satisfaction of his escort of
dancers who danced furiously until their King had gone
up into his last curl of ascending smoke.

Then the last night was on!

During the afternoon Croyant remained close to the
Albert-Edouard. Helen begged him to come with her
and Michael to see the King burned, but he wouldn't go.
She accused him of bringing glumness to the festival.
She said his face was positively sour.

He looked at her a little quizzically and Georges Raynel, smiling, told him not to mind her. "Helen has been
accusing almost everyone of being sour throughout the
week," he said. "Even me, who am never else than enrap-
tured when I look at her."

Helen flashed him a look. Not of anger, but with a
leaven of sadness in it. Michael saw. Helen was beginning to be sorry for Georges Raynel. He felt a little of
the carnival spirit tugging at him. Helen dragged him
off, with Lady Severn. Raynel and Lord Severn remained
to watch the scene from under the plane trees. Raynel
spoke to Croyant of the rumored air signals that couldn't
be deciphered.

"And perhaps Miss Avery has seen glumness in my
face," he said, when they had spoken of the signals back
and forth a few times. "I've good cause, if any one has.

Veragua, the Marchesa who was a friend of my friends, who next?"

"I wonder," Croyant murmured. "Who next?"

Severn said nothing, but looked onto the street crowd. It was time to dine, and Raynel asked Croyant to come along to the Casino, where he had reserved tables on the balcony overlooking the Allées. Croyant demurred. He murmured something about expecting other friends. Just then a messenger came out from the hotel. The call Major Croyant had been expecting was being held on the switchboard in the lobbies. He turned on his heel swiftly and followed the messenger.

The message was brief. A single sentence spoken by a man's voice that did not identify itself.

"A yellow Lancia has just passed through Le Cannet with a Columbine in it."

Croyant made no reply but hung up the transmitter with a sharp click. He went down the plane tree walk hurriedly, pausing where Raynel and Severn waited only long enough to promise that if possible he would join them on the Casino balcony. Then he disappeared in the crowd. He was whistling. Some bright potpouri of half a dozen tunes.

It was more than an hour later when he emerged from the press at the foot of the Casino steps. He ran full into Michael and Helen and Lord Severn. Lady Severn had been hopelessly lost, and Raynel had only a moment before managed to reach the balcony and make sure that his tables had been properly reserved and moved close to the rail. With Helen and Michael, Croyant stood on a step to watch the fun in the square, and promised to keep an eye out for Mrs. Fraser who had been lost for half the afternoon. Helen was quite worried about her, Michael wasn't and Croyant laughed at any alarm on her account. "If her costume would serve as underwear and not make a wrinkle in her frock she'll be able to squeeze through anything," he said. Helen rebuked him prettily for knowing that a woman's underthings might make wrinkles in frocks.

In the square they were beginning to play the famous "kiss in the ring" game. Maskers clasped their hands tightly and danced around captive couples with the cry, "*Embrassez! Embrassez!*" and the captives would not be released from the ring until they had embraced to the derisive satisfaction of the dancing ring. Croyant glanced covertly at Helen, whose domino was red and gold and black, with a high cone hat perched jauntily on the side of her head. He looked at the young man, who stood beside the girl, but silently. Her face wore a tired and strained look despite the scene of joy she watched, and despite the gay confetti that clung to her hair. They belonged out there in the square, these two, Croyant thought, but he looked up to the balcony and there was Georges Raynel.

Michael reached up to his shoulder, with a careless air, to brush from his coat a few grains of yellow paper. A sinuous line of boisterous maskers in flaming red was swirling past, their hands clasped, looking for captives to circle. One of the girls saw Michael's fastidiousness. In an instant she swung her crimson line close to the steps and with a whoop and a great nod of pom poms they sent a shower of colored paper over him and Helen and the Major. Then with a silk and sateen flash of crimson, the red dancers were gone, sliding into the crowd. But the end of the line, when it snapped away, flung Mrs. Fraser, laughing and whooping as any boisterous girl, fairly into Croyant's astonished arms. Through her laughter she said something that neither Helen nor Michael could catch. Helen reached her head closer. Mrs. Fraser told her to go away. "Can't you see I'm being hugged by a big man? It feels like Bill. I've got to whisper something sentimental into his ear."

And she made a pretense of whispering into the Major's ear, though Helen called out to her that she wasn't pretending at all. Then she was off up the steps, looking, from behind at least, like nothing in the world so much as a Peter Pan in three fourths Chinese silk tights.

Raynel had been trying to catch an eye among the three pairs on the steps, but had failed. He pushed his way down to say that the tables were ready and they should really be seated because before long the rockets would go up from the boats in the harbor and the shower of vari hued fires over the water could best be seen from the balcony. Helen and Michael turned up the steps. The Major turned to follow, but stopped, suddenly, and without taking his eyes from a figure he saw in the crowd, murmured, "In a few minutes. I think I see Sir Philip. 1 didn't supose he'd come over." Then he was gone pushing his way into the crowd, his bulk hewing his path relentlessly. Only once was he blocked. The dancers in red had circled the square and were back again, swinging along, their hands still clasped, whooping and shrieking, pom poms nodding. He couldn't break through that line. It simply gave before him and then snapped back against his stomach with hilarious laughter from young and happy faces. Six dancers passed him, six more came on, then another in crimson with yellow pom poms that matched the rest, came up from somewhere and clasped the hand of the last girl in the line and was swept along with the line.

Thirteen dancers in red where there had been twelve.

They were gone and Croyant battled the crush again.

At last he found her, the figure he had glimpsed from the Casino steps, a Columbine in creamy froth of ballet skirts below a mauve bodice gay with little pink roses. Croyant pushed toward her, winning his way with bulk and strength, but she slipped ahead of him through the jostling crowd with an uncanny skill and grace of movement, her slender body quick and ready on her dancer's legs. Under her wig of silver curls and through her black masque her dark eyes were searching tirelessly—searching eyes Croyant had recognized as he had recognized the carriage of her body, despite masque and ballet skirt.

He caught up with her, was next behind her.

He whistled a short strain that pierced the bedlam of the square, the theme from the Dancer of Kashmir.

The girl stopped dead still. A shiver raced down her body. He spoke across her shoulder before she could turn around.

"Steady, Darya! I'm a friend. Of yours and Michael Ballou. Push ahead to the fountain in the middle of the square. Chenkin is there."

CHAPTER XVII

"CARNIVAL IS OVER"

SHE went straight and so swiftly he could not follow her, to the center of the square where the statue of Garibaldi stands with a broken arm on a carrara pedestal. Pressed against the marble base were a score of masquers catching their breaths but there was only one Harlequin. Not a very tall Harlequin, and wider than the troubadours of romance, but a Harlequin in white satin with black and yellow pom poms on both sleeves, where no other Harlequin wore them.

Darya went up to him, laughing and dancing and showered him with confetti and through her laughter cried, "Some one back there—The Panther's signal—but he said I'd find you here!"

"You saw him?"

"No. But he was a big man—I saw him once, I think, at Toulouse."

"There's nothing to fear. He is a colleague. Come—we dance—we laugh and dance."

"*Oui, Oui*, M'sieu' Chenkin. Alexander is dead; There was a death in Warsaw; Michael walks to the precipice; I've come to dance with you."

He swung her into the throng. She laughed, and waved at other maskers, and patted her Harlequin's sides to ridicule his girth, and now and then reached up to tweak his nose. In all the jostling she swung when he lifted her, as light as a feather and more than one masker reached to grab her away but her pliant body eluded all hands. Her Harlequin was surprisingly sure on his feet, and agile. When Croyant reached the statue he and his Columbine were lost in the human swirl. He would have pushed out in search again, but once more the thirteen dancers trailed, hands locked, before him.

"I will take you to him," Darya said to her Harlequin, between her gala shouts merry challengings. "We dance across the square. I will find and point him out. Then I may go?"

"Do that, my child, and you will have undone any wrong you have ever done. You will have been forgiven by all the gods there are, and by man."

"I make a bargain, M'sieu'."

(A purple domino wants that slender body in the ballet skirt. He wants her on his shoulder, her legs around his neck. He swoops up and pinions her legs and lifts her. She laughs and beats at him with her fists and screams merrily. Her Harlequin catches the domino's neck in one hand and twists it a little. Domino drops the Columbine and shakes his head to get the kink out of his neck and makes an elaborate bow to Harlequin. "She's all yours, Monsieur Strangler." The Columbine tosses him a kiss and Harlequin waves a hand.)

"You will make Michael Ballou understand that I came to love him? And that I would give him Mademoiselle Avery if I could?"

"He will know that."

"*Merci*. Do you know that he was in the house of his uncle in Leningrad before it burned that night? Do you know that it was he who opened the safe and not The Panther?"

"When your ruby ring was recognized, then we knew that he must have been in that safe. That is all."

"But he took something else from the safe. He will not admit it. Even to me, of whom he tried very hard to think as one he would like to love, he would not admit it, though he talked freely with me of the rubies. But that safe, M'sieu' Chenkin, contained a photograph of The Panther and documents that revealed and proved his identity. Count Jeribzoff knew The Panther. Since it was not found elsewhere he must have kept his knowledge in the safe with his other valuables."

They made their way toward the outer edge of the square. It was hard to persevere in any one direction, and progress was slow because of the shouting and interchange and frequent chokings on a mouth filled with confetti. One has to show to the others that one is missing none of the fun of being at the Carnival.

"The Panther sought something of that sort then, in Nevsky Prospekt?"

"He did not find it. For more than a year he was afraid to be active. And afraid to kill Michael Ballou lest once more he miss what he sought and this time others find it. He hoped I would be successful. He will not kill Michael until he has had a chance to torture the truth from him. I wish to save Michael if I may."

She broke off to shout her glee into the ring of faces around her. The Harlequin asked, "Are you certain he is here tonight?"

"I have seen him. As soon as we are——" She left her sentence in the air. With one of those sudden collective rushes that can never be foreseen the crowd swayed to one side and opened a space on the asphalt floor of the Allées, making a pocket of calm in a whirlpool. The Harlequin and Columbine, wrapped in their attention in each other, suddenly found themselves in this open space, jostled into it by the crowd. The leader of the thirteen crimson maskers gave a shout and whipped his laughing line of dancers into the clear pocket. The crowd swayed back as the inner lines saw the prospect of fun. The crimson chain, spurred by its leader, whipped around and linked its two ends, hands locked tightly. Harlequin and Columbine were caught in the middle.

Round and round the maskers danced and shouted for the ransom from captivity.

"Embrassez! Embrassez!"

The Harlequin caught his Columbine by the waist and ran forward, pushing against the red line. There was something grim and forbidding in his aspect, despite the frivolity of his pom poms, his comical hat, and the wide bulge of his white satin costume. He flung himself against the chain of locked hands. The crowd saw that he would try to escape and closed in, a solid laughing and taunting wall behind the living chain. The crowd took up the cry.

"Embrassez! Embrassez! Embrassez!"

There was a twinkle of the dancer's bare legs. She was thrown against the white satin of her Harlequin. He pressed her into his arms in the midst of the mad confusion of crimson maskers pushed close by the surging crowd of rioters. The red dancers were a tight knot, now with Harlequin and Columbine almost smothered.

A shrill, startled scream went flying to the stars through the fun. A piercing shriek. There was an instant of weird, pulseless silence and then the voices of a score of maskers lifted in a single cry of horror. The red maskers broke their chain and fled, submerged in the press.

The crowd, shrinking before the unknown, thrust back. There was a little clear space again. Harlequin bent over the Columbine on the ground, mosaic of dusty confetti,

the foam of her ballet skirts about her knees, her silver
wig awry on her head. A moment before she had been all
life and movement. Now she was still and the little pink
roses on the strip of bodice that rose to her throat in
front were blooming scarlet over the quiet breasts.

Croyant, who had never ceased to fight his way through
the crush toward Harlequin and Columbine, crouched his
shoulders at the first shrill scream. Twice he had shouted
over the heads of the fun-makers around him. He had
strained his lungs to send his cry of warning: "The red
dancers! Look out for the red dancers, Khamov and
Darya!" But his efforts were drops of water in a tide.
Now his great body and superhuman strength opened a
path, smashing humanity on either side. Through the
crowd he reached and his big hands caught and gathered
up one of the crimson maskers, a youth, and dragged
him close. He reached for another and captured a slender
girl who was shrieking hysterically. He thrust them before him until he came to the Harlequin.

"Get into the crowd!" he cried to the Harlequin. "I'll
take care of her. Get into the crowd—find the red maskers
who hemmed you in. I saw it."

The crowd had become still. The inner circle stared
down at the form on the asphalt floor. A clown swept
off his mask, revealing a young, perspiring face. He
waved his arms and shouted to the people to get back.
A girl in red, one of the chain, broke from the mass and
sank on her knees over the body. She broke into horror-
eyed weeping, asking over and over, "Who did it? Who
did it?" Croyant, his two captives standing within his
reach, frozen with terror, placed his hand gently on the
kneeling girl. She looked up, startled. Then, as if she
saw the scarlet roses for the first time she screamed hys-

terically to a boy in red who had pushed up, his mask in his hands, "Jean! Jean! *Elle est morte!* A girl is dead!"

All of the time the band on the Casino balcony was playing the mad, jazz tune of the Carnival. But the cry of the girl was caught by the crowd, *"Elle est morte!"* and it swept over the Place des Allées and the band stopped suddenly.

A policeman appeared, covered with confetti, his red face streaked with lipstick from the hundred of lips that had considered it their duty to salute the majesty of the law. Croyant handed up to him, silently, the dagger he had withdrawn. A piece of metal, a square tag, dangled from the hilt, attached by a slender chain. "Don't break the tag loose," Croyant cautioned the policeman without looking up. The officer gave the curious appendage for a dagger to flaunt a swiftly curious glance.

"Nom de dieu! The cat's head, M'sieu'!"

"Take these red maskers," Croyant commanded, waving his hand to indicate the four who were close, including the girl who knelt and the boy who had held the crowd back, the kneeling girl's "Jean."

With automatic reaction to the tone of command in the big man's voice the policeman gathered the four dancers, but then he glanced down at Croyant and frowned. Croyant got to his feet.

"Monsieur Lemair and Inspector Clement will vouch for me," he said. Other agents of police pushed in. To them, Croyant said, "You will take care of the Columbine. Tenderly, Messieurs!"

The red dancer who had raised the cry, *"Elle est morte,"* flung out her hand to touch Croyant's arm. *"S'il vous plait, M'sieu'—mon Jean——"* Croyant touched her arm reassuringly. "You and your Jean are safe. It was a taller one."

"*Merci, M'sieu.*' My Jean and I, we depart with M'sieu' l'Agent."

But Jean was not satisfied. He addressed Croyant excitedly as one who so apparently was of the authority. "Where has the Harlequin gone? He had danced with the Columbine. He was her Carnival mate. If he was innocent, where is he now?"

Croyant made an impatient gesture but the crowd took up the shout. "Where is the Harlequin?"

To the policemen Croyant said sharply, "Never mind the Harlequin. It's the red maskers you want. All of them. Thirteen."

The police made way through the square, first for the four dancers Croyant had turned over to them, then for a bulky policeman who carried the Columbine. This one stopped at the fountain of Garibaldi, where Darya Vaskaya had begun her last dance, to wait there for the medical authorities. The others found their way to a side street and then, in a commandeered car, to the Police Administration. While Croyant was climbing into the car, the slim girl standing up to give him room on the seat before she sank down, the thick figure of the Harlequin, his domino so torn that he was not recognizable as a Harlequin at all, and with no black and yellow pom poms on his sleeves, edged up to the running board. He thrust a bit of paper into Croyant's hand.

"The names and addresses of two—but they could not have been the one. I let them go while I hunted others."

The car moved off.

Monsieur Lemair came from the Casino where his telephone runner who waited for possible calls had been told that he had altered his plan to dine alone in the alcove of the Salle Schmidt, and would be found on the balcony where he had joined the party of Lord Severn and Monsieur Raynel. Inspector Clement was already at the Sûreté.

Croyant spoke to Monsieur Lemair in an ante-room. "What occurred, Monsieur, we will discuss in the other room. I inform you in advance that the Columbine was Darya Vaskaya, formerly of the Russian ballet, later an agent of The Panther—the lady of the white fan on the stair at Bordeaux."

Monsieur Lemair gave an exclamation.

Croyant continued. "Pending word from Dupree, whose wishes you will respect as of authority in matters affecting The Panther, be good enough to withhold the young woman's identity. She was about to make her peace with her conscience. How far she had succeeded I do not yet know. And do not search for the Harlequin."

Monsieur Lemair showed a trace of stubborn anger.

"I am Prefect of Police, Monsieur le Major. I respect your wishes as I shall those of Dupree. But am I, then, to be kept altogether in the dark?"

Croyant hastened to placate him. "Is it keeping you in the dark when I inform you at once, in advance of later conversations, that the Harlequin was Chenkin and that this week's wireless signals were The Panther's directions for the staging of the tragedy tonight?"

The prefect shot Croyant a glance of amazed wonder. His pique subsided. "I defer to you, M'sieu'," he muttered and led to his big room.

There was a chatter of excited voices from the red maskers, and the drone of the policemen's formal reports. They had seen nothing. They had detected unwonted excitement in a section of the square and had pushed their way through the people. They had then obeyed the suggestions of the Englishman. That was all.

Croyant gave Lemair the names and addresses the

Harlequin had scribbled down. In an undertone he said that Chenkin absolved these from any individual responsibility. They might be sent for and brought from their homes as soon they should have returned.

That all might hear, Croyant repeated before the prefect's desk what he had already told Clement. "I was trying to get close to the pair and had tried to make them hear a shout of warning. I had reason to be suspicious of the dancing chain. But I was not in time. I saw a red arm flash and knew by the movement of a red masked face that was over the Columbine's, that there would be a sudden scream. The scream rose. But the chain was broken up and melting away."

"All but us, M'sieu'," the girl who had wept, murmured. She looked around at her anxious companion.

Lemair turned to the trembling girl.

"How many of you were there?"

She paused to frown and study. "Thirteen," she said at last.

"And who are you?"

She was Cecille Malot, a shop girl from the Croisette, at Cannes. She pointed her finger at Jean. "And he is Jean, a baker's boy, who is also of Cannes."

"Very well, Cecille," said Lemair. "Now, tell us of these thirteen. There was yourself, there was Jean. There were these others who are with us now, Julot Frochard and Marianne Guy. But the others? They were your friends?"

The girl shook her head. She named all of those whom she knew, only four others beside Jean, two of the others were Julot and Marianne, who were there in the room, and the other two were Raoul Dessin and Yvonne Rousellot—the names on the paper Croyant had given Monsieur Lemair.

Jean confirmed the names and addresses of all of these.

"But that is only six," Lemair pointed out. "Seven are left. Do you mean you invited strangers into your dancing chain?"

Between them, Jean and Cecille explained.

The original six, all friends, had decided upon the red costumes for the Carnival. They had remained together every night of the festival. Then, tonight, while the parade was being formed in Boulevard Cassoux, two others in crimson, a man and a woman, had joined them. The man had begun to lead them, and he was very much fun. All evening he had invented new tricks and excitements. It was he who formed the chain. Then others in red joined the merry group. "In a Carnival, M'sieu', one does not stop to think. One does not look upon anyone else as a stranger. It is all in fun." For a time there had been twelve of them, just twelve. They danced and rested and talked awhile and then danced again. They stopped for sandwiches of soft fudge and to replenish their confetti. But always they danced again with their prank of making couples kiss and embrace. Cecille remembered that one of the strangers was called Paul, and Jean remembered that another was Mariette.

"But the thirteenth, Mademoiselle," Lemair prompted.

"He joined us perhaps an hour, maybe less, before—before *it* happened. We were dancing by the Casino steps when he caught my hand. I was at the end of the chain and now he was the last. He had yellow pom pons, while the rest of us, or mostly, had black."

"He remained at the end of the chain?"

Cecille was thoughtful for a moment, puzzling. "But don't you see, your Excellency, that what now was the end of the chain, la! we turn and go the other way and the end is the front. One second the end is the tail, la! the tail is the head."

Jean nodded wisely and pointed out, "Cecille is quite right, Monsieur. With a shout to 'come this way,' or even a tug of hands all along the line, and the last becomes first."

"That is discernible," said Lemair. "But what became of the thirteenth masker, Mademoiselle?"

Cecille made every effort to bring from her memory a truthful answer. "Let me see, M'sieu. All at once the one who was the end jerked at my hand. It was the signal to reverse. I jerked my other hand. We all shouted. The thirteenth, who was now our leader, shouted and called my attention to the Harlequin and Columbine. Something happened and the crowd made an open circle. The stranger whipped us into the space and then—you know what came then, M'sieu'. After the poor woman screamed, so close to me, just the stranger between, everybody ran. All melted away, leaving just Jean and me."

Jean was certain that it was the Harlequin who had done the murder. He explained why, and might have been convincing, if Lemair had not known that the Harlequin was the great Chenkin, of Moscow. Jean built a crime of passion. The Harlequin would not kiss the Columbine when the chain first hemmed them in. Instead he tried to fight his way out with the Mademoiselle. "If a man will not kiss a woman under such circumstances, when his excuse is made for him, can it be otherwise, M'sieu', than that he hates her? Hatred is the only reason for not kissing. I am very positive it was the Harlequin."

Jean and Cecille and Raoul and Yvonne were told they could go back to the Carnival. Cecille swayed into Jean's strong arm, and whimpered.

"Carnival is over, M'sieu'."

CHAPTER XVIII

WHILE THE CHINA GIRL SANG

IN observance of the policies dictated by Dupree, little was made by the newspapers of the crime in Place des Allées. The Columbine was described as Mademoiselle Amon, of antecedents not clear. Like Jean, the newspapers seemed to think of a crime of passion and pointed out that it would be difficult to find a Harlequin.

But before they began to sweep the confetti from the streets next day Cannes and Nice and Monte Carlo knew of the cat's head affixed to the dagger hilt. It was not a Marchesa this time, or a Mademoiselle Essant from the Casino mascottes, nor a Veragua nor an American millionaire. Only a girl of whom the police knew little and nobody else, it seemed, anything at all. It was merely that The Panther had silenced a mouth that had talked or he feared might talk. So it was reasoned.

But the astounding conception and execution of the crime, and withal its melodramatic simplicity, shocked, the whole playshore. People took it as a warning. The Panther's ironical hint that over all fun his shadow hovered—and those who were rich translated the warning to mean, "You see? Not even a Columbine in her masque can escape me. When you receive my demands, fulfill them." There were many rumors that had been quiescent that now sprang the length of the Côte d'Azure. This millionaire and that one had received the cat's head with demand for a huge sum of money, with instructions how to convey it and the threat that the knife or bullet would follow the symbol if the recipient took third parties, particularly authorities, into his confidence. Details varied as did the rumored identities, but the outstanding circumstance was always the same. So and So had delivered the money and said nothing to the police. No, So and So would not admit his action to even his closest associates. He would run no risks. He had not only himself but his family to consider. And so on.

The thick man of Rue des Pomegranates came under his broad-brimmed hat to the Crillon on the second day after the Carnival was done. Dupree and Croyant awaited him. Dupree had forgiven that shot of his tires on the road to Cantoux. He had accepted the other's wry explanation, "The broth I was after required but the one cook. Once I saved her brother in Odessa. She was grateful to me." He added a more sober afterthought. "It might have been kinder to Dolly if you had stopped her at the station."

Dupree also had forgiven Croyant for the imposition of Khamov, the gentle Russian! Croyant had "put his cards on the table" before his friend with the simple explanation, "I did not want The Panther to know I was a working enemy. I do not want him to know it—quite yet."

"But you reserve one little handful of cards," Dupree accused airily. "That I know when your lips itch to whistle. It is well. I am content. Together we close in. That is what is to be thought of."

They debated the wisdom of confronting Michael Ballou. Chenkin looked to Croyant who shook his head with sharp emphasis.

"If, as Darya stated, he removed more than the rubies from the safe, he did not confess that to her when his mood was sentimentally bent upon giving his confidence. For whatever his reasons, whatever fear controls him, he may remain obdurate. He will deny. What have we to say to him then?"

"What will be lost if we fail?"

Croyant swung around. His jaw was set. "All that we've gained. The sacrifice of Darya Vaskaya will have been in vain. Allow me, Ariste, the card I still hold."

Dupree was jovially indifferent. "The play is in good hands, my friend. Today I will try my luck again with Bibi the Pig. His one ear has healed and there is the other. And he has two eyes."

For a day the strange wireless signals had ceased coming through the air. Then they were picked up again, through a brief ten minutes at a time. Engineers scattered at the official stations along the Mediterranean were depressed when the signalling was resumed. They had, as they thought, traced the point of origin to the neighborhood of Cannes itself. Another set of calculations, they believed, would narrow down the radius to be combed.

But now they were from a distance. Calculations had to be remade and, as before, the base of transmission was variable. The police engineers were certain however that the arc of expulsion now extended over the Mediterranean. The destroyer squadrons were ordered to resume their search for a ship at sea.

The resumption of the signalling worried Croyant. For the first time since his "vacation" began, he showed signs of intense strain. Clement telephoned him from the Sûreté when the first of the fresh signals came in. The chief of the Sûreté's wireless section came on the telephone and explained that the code had not changed but was as undecipherable as ever. The wireless chief was convinced, however, that a different operator was at the sending apparatus.

"It is difficult to explain, sir," said the chief, "what causes the feeling. But the flashes seem to have a different personality. They appear to be more definite, certain, as if they were inspired by a brain that retained the code, rather than an operator who studied it while he transmitted."

There were three ten minute periods of signalling during the day. Twice Croyant had started to leave his suite, but each time had changed his mind. Sir Philip found him impossible. Once, when Sir Philip tried to speak of the affair in Place des Allées and of Darya Vaskaya, Croyant wheeled upon him.

"That is done," he snapped. "I don't like to think of it. I might have saved her. The thirteenth dancer came down from the Casino. But I waited, too long. I may be waiting too long now."

Sir Philip had never seen his friend in such a vicious mood. Nor had he ever seen a change come over him quite so quickly as when a sailor, a petty officer, came to the door of the suite and was admitted by Croyant himself.

Quick, Heinrich! What have you?"

The ship's officer held out a folded sheet of paper which Croyant spread on the table. It was a writing in code but the Major read it swiftly. "Severn, by God!" he exclaimed.

Sir Philip leapt to his feet. "Severn? You've got him?"

Croyant stood straight. He drew himself up with the manner of a man who stretches his muscles to relieve them from an aching tension. He pursed his lips but his friend's stare claimed him.

"You mustn't libel his lordship," he murmured quizzically. "You'll have to cheer him up. He's about to be troubled with a case of pigeons."

. Sir Philip glared through his monocle but Croyant ignored him while he put through a call to the Sûreté. Lemair informed him that Dupree was at that moment in Marseilles, at the detention prison, interviewing a prisoner. Lemair added that he believed the Major would know the prisoner's indentity.

"Ask them at Marseilles," Croyant requested, "to interrupt Ariste immediately. When he has reached me on the phone he will want to resume his interviewing."

Dupree's voice came over the wire with surprising promptitude.

"Have you at least one ear left?" Croyant wanted to know.

"I have become an old woman," Dupree grumbled back. "I have not as yet opened his scars."

Croyant's tone hardened. "If he knows where The Panther keeps pigeons make him tell."

Dupree hung up without replying. Croyant destroyed the code brought by the ship's officer. His mouth was still grim when, with Sir Philip, he set out for the Villa Amette.

Mrs. Fraser, with the Severns, the Ransoms, the Averys and Raynel, had been horrified spectators to the scene in the Allées. They had stood at the white rail, with other diners, and looked down on the still form of the Columbine on the asphalt floor. But Mrs. Fraser had not been chastened. She had given a little gasp of horror, and had been subdued through the rest of the last Carnival night. But next day she announced her plans for a whole series of parties at the Villa and now that the Carnival was over, she promised Count Tanaroff to give all of her day time attention to his project of liberating his country from the Soviets.

"It is time," growled the impatient Count. "The fever spreads. We enlist new backers. That engaging Lord Severn and that charming Monsieur Raynel, both have indicated that they will help. It is time to move while the spirit is rife."

"Very well, Alexi," Mrs. Fraser sighed. "But you will not forget that I am behind your lines." The Count was indignant that she should have such a thought. She complained to Michael, whom she still kept close when he was in the house, despite the sudden obviation of need for his services as interpreter, that she supposed she could not give her mornings to tennis any more. "But you must come as early as usual every day," she stipulated. "Miss Avery would be so disappointed not to have her sets with you."

Michael was the only one about the Villa who had been affected by the murder at the Carnival. He kept his secret —of his despairing reliance upon the dancer's companionship through so many fretful months, but he had no heart for tennis. even with Helen. Particularly not with Helen. Somehow he blamed Helen for Darya's death. Unreasonable of course, but if he had not been yearning for Helen he would never have known Darya. At least he would not be grieving for the untimely tragedy that had come to one who had been a soothing companion.

Mrs. Fraser brought up again the subject of the rubies. "Wasn't it too bad," she said, when they had talked of them and of their rare beauty and value, and of what eventually he would do with them, "that there wasn't something else in the safe? Something more that your uncle had wanted you to have?"

He had the feeling that there were unspoken words

in her manner. That she was probing, prying. It was the feeling he had so often had with his neighbor, Khamov. But when he made no reply Mrs. Fraser got up and went about the mysteries of changing her costume for the night.

The Chinese singer had been so popular with her guests on the previous occasion of her appearance at the Villa that Mrs. Fraser was having her again. And, of course, Mrs. Avery and Helen were coming, and, he supposed, Helen's fiancé. There would be another night of strain between him and Helen, intensified now because Helen had questioned his moodiness since, the next morning after the Carnival, Mrs. Fraser had casually mentioned that she had learned from "somebody" that the girl who was killed had been a Mademoiselle Tanya Amon. She went on to wonder why the papers didn't print the girl's name and more about her, but Michael hadn't listened, and Helen, that morning, had noticed his new and moody abstraction. She had flushed angrily once or twice on the courts, but he could make no explanations.

Croyant spent most of the evening with Lord Severn. The two men seemed to find many tastes in common for discussion. They spoke of The Panther, of course. Who in any gathering didn't as soon as conversation lagged?

"I've more or less of a personal interest," Severn said, with a wry smile, "in the police efforts to unmask the fellow. The Marchesa was my friend, but in addition to that one of the police chaps, the French star, I understand, actually looked at me with suspicion."

He spoke as if he told an odd sort of joke. Croyant raised his brows and invited him to continue.

"I might have been in the devil of a fix for awhile if it hadn't been that my story could be actually supported by the ruins of a plane."

He described the visit of Dupree to Georges Raynel. His friend, Raynel, had told him all the details. "And Georges himself had a queer feeling. He armitted it. My being marooned in the Lanzo country sounded fishy even to him. But the wreck of the plane was there and my pilot had returned to Toledo and happened to be a family man. A family man obtains more credence from the police, it seems, than a bachelor."

"We'll hope," Croyant murmured, "that The Panther never comes closer to you than in a policeman's suspicion."

Severn laughed. "I don't even keep my fingers crossed."

Croyant said nothing. The Chinese girl was singing. Raynel and Helen Avery were sitting together on a wicker settle. Helen was very quiet and very pretty. Her fiancé was giving the charming Oriental a close attention. She was singing,

"J'aime toutes ces choses,
     Dont le charme caresse——"

Croyant stopped behind the settle.

"Her number bothers me," he said. When Helen and Raynel looked up he was sheepish, as if he had spoken a thought aloud. "A song does," he explained, "if I know it and can't place it. I may want to whistle it sometime and I like to know what I whistle. It's a thing from La Tosca, isn't it?"

He directed his question at Helen. She shook her head with a bright smile. "I don't know. It's not familiar like——" Her smile died and she looked away, out across the room. Over there Michael was standing with Lady Severn. "Like the Dancer of Kashmir," she finished in a half whisper.

Croyant looked away from her, mutely transferring his curiosity to her companion, as if he wished not to intrude upon any unknown memory he had invoked. Raynel shook his head sharply. He was watching Helen, puzzled perhaps by her manner. "I know as little as absolutely nothing about music," he said. "You'll have to look elsewhere—or shall we ask the singer?"

Croyant demurred to that. "It's not that important."

Raynel got up and touched Helen's arm. She rose dutifully, but held him, with her hand on his wrist, while she spoke to Croyant. It was only about a plan to drive up into the Alps next week, and of her wish that Croyant could come along. Her mother wanted him, particularly. The Major gave her a half hearted promise, as if he scarcely knew what he was saying. The singer was coming to the close of her song. Croyant seemed to be recognizing it, and Raynel, too, for he was humming quietly with the singer. Croyant touched him.

"I got it first," he crowed. "Boheme!"

Raynel looked puzzled for a moment, then laughed. "I'd forgotten, he said. "Glad you've settled a problem, Major."

Croyant looked immensely relieved. He beamed upon Helen and told her he'd go up to the Alps anytime. "Now that my problem's settled."

"He'll whistle all the way up," Raynel prophesied with a grin into the Major's face.

"And all the way down," returned Croyant, grinning broadly. It was the first time Helen had ever seen him grin.

CHAPTER XIX

ANOTHER BLOW IS STRUCK

THE party at the Villa broke up at the usual hour, well toward three o'clock in the morning. Michael went home at midnight after taking Pete and Betsy for their walk. Helen said goodnight stiffly, but watched him—as she always did whenever he left her—while he walked across the grounds toward the gates. He stopped once, this time, and she lost him in the shadow of the garages. When he brought the dogs back from their walk Pete had broken away from him to run in among the cars. He wouldn't come out when Michael called. When he went after him Michael found what had attracted the Sealyham. The four chauffeurs—one extra for the three cars—were all knotted in the depths of the garage, and wore their coats and caps. Yet no one, so far as he knew, would use the cars that night. When he left the Villa he stopped for a glance into the garage. The chauffeurs were still there.

Helen, of course, knew nothing of why she lost him in the shadows of the garages, but she felt an impulse to run after him. She'd felt that impulse on every night, lately, when he left to go to his own room. His stopping at the garage would give her an opportunity to stroll into the grounds and seem to come upon him by chance.

But she put the impulse down with an angry flirt of her shoulders. She turned back from the door where she watched to find Croyant observing her queerly. She went up to him and put her hand on his arm. "Remember Toulouse?" she said, in a low tone, looking away.

"I do," he returned. "You promised to put him away."

She didn't reply, nor did he press her.

Croyant, surprisingly, remained at the Villa until the last. Mrs. Fraser was delighted that her party had held him so long. The Severns took him in their car, while Sir Philip was cared for by the Averys and Raynel. The Severns were still staying at the Crillon. Croyant managed to start a conversation with Lord Severn just as their car stopped in the drive before the marble terrace. Lady Severn went along to their rooms, saying that she knew the Major wouldn't come up. Severn remained with him on the terrace, smoking a final cigarette while they talked. A round moon floated low in the clear night, and the chill air was pungent with the scents of a thousand blossoms.

Presently a hotel messenger came hurrying onto the terrace. He touched his cap to Lord Severn.

"Lady Severn, sir! She appears to be excited. She wants you and Major Croyant at once."

She was standing against a far wall when they hurried into their living-room, standing there as if she were at bay. Her face was white and one hand was pressed close to her heart. The other pointed to a wooden case in the middle of the floor, a crate in which a half dozen carrier pigeons stirred.

Lady Severn tried to speak, but her tongue was parched and her throat tight. She mumbled, "The cat's head," and fainted. Croyant picked her up and laid her on a couch and brought water. Severn knelt to recover a letter that his wife had taken from an envelope tied to the crate, an envelope addressed to him. He spoke to Croyant quietly. "She will be all right. Please look at this."

At the top of the page the cat's head was drawn in ink. The lines of writing were typed, and closed without a signature.

"Lord Severn is assured the pigeons herewith delivered are of authentic pedigreed breed, sturdy and reliable. It would be wise of Lord Severn to test their qualities, however, by attaching to the foot of each a Bank of England note for five thousand pounds and releasing them. Lord Severn will doubtless find it necessary to transport such a large sum from London, where it will be assembled by his family. In the meantime he will inquire of any bird financier as to the proper care and feeding of thoroughbred carriers thus insuring their proper condition when they are released. The noble Lord will certainly not find it advisable to discuss his pigeons with others than those who will be at pains to put him in possession of the twelve Bank of England notes. Perhaps he will suggest to these that he proposes to release the birds on the sixth day from today promptly at twelve o'clock. Any attempt to follow them with planes or by other means will be misguided."

When Croyant finished reading the typescript he glanced up. Severn had gone to Lady Severn, who was coming to and showing signs of hysteria. Croyant approached the couch with a quick step. Lady Severn looked into his face and something she saw there checked her panic.

"We'll release the birds at daylight," Croyant said. "And then you may forget them."

Severn turned, questioning. Lady Severn stared. In Croyant's tone there was no alarm. If anything, he was elated.

"You think it's a joke?" Severn demanded. "If it is I'll wring somebody's neck. It's not funny to a woman."

"The farthest thing possible from a joke," Croyant answered. "The demand is authentic and he means all he implies. But much may happen—in six days."

An hour after daylight Croyant himself, with Monsieur Lemair and Inspector Clement in attendance, released the twelve carriers from the roof of the Crillon. Lord and Lady Severn remained in their suite. The birds leapt free with a clatter of wings and fluttered up into the air. They began at once to wheel in wide ever-expanding rings. They kept up their wheeling for several minutes while Croyant and the others watched with strong glasses. Suddenly, with a single impulse the little flock set out over the sea. They crossed the tip of the jetty that reached out from Guy de Maupassant pier and continued, flying straight in compact formation, in a direction almost southerly.

"Corsica!" Croyant murmured while he folded his glasses. Lemair and Clement prepared to leave the roof. Croyant waited a moment, scanning the sea toward Golfe San Juan. A day rocket shot up and exploded in little smoke curls over the black yacht. Croyant studied the smoke curls absently for a moment, and then went down with Lemair and Clement. They went into the Severn suite. Lady Severn, in a trailing negligée, was haggard looking for one so young and ordinarily vivid. She had not slept. Her husband remained close to her, his hand constantly seeking hers.

Croyant motioned to Inspector Clement, who stood awkwardly, his hat hanging from his hand loosely. Inspector Clement was not accustomed to noble ladies in careless negligée at that hour of the morning.

"You'll have to put up with him," Croyant said quizzically. "He won't leave you out of sight."

Dupree returned from Marseilles during the morning.

He drank deeply from the bottle of wine Croyant produced at once.

"It was an unpleasant sight," he grumbled over his glass. "But thank God it required only one ear."

He finished his drink and was more cheerful.

"At the first mention of 'pigeons,'" he said, "Bibi gave himself away. He knew I had discovered something while I answered your call to the telephone. I had not worked industriously before. As I said, I felt as I were an old woman. But Bibi saw, also, that I had recovered my youth. I demonstrated with the ear. The pigeons, he managed to make me understand at last, were kept at a cabin in the forest behind The Garden of My Sisters at La Bocca, which is on the bleak stretch of coast beyond the Old Port. It was less than ten miles from the *Auberge des Cochons*. We surrounded the cabin after midnight. There had been pigeons, on more than one recent occasion. There were traces of at least three flocks. But none were in the cabin last night. Two men who have so far professed they know nothing more than that they were installed by a stranger to receive and care for pigeons and to yield them up when called for. I believe them. They are in cells but their ears are safe. And if required, Bibi still has one to spare."

That night Helen Avery surrendered to her impulse to follow Michael when he left the Villa, and she did not wait until he went home. It was eleven when Mrs. Fraser, punctually, reminded him to take the Sealyhams to the seawalk. Every night, when eleven o'clock came, and he had forgotten the dogs, she reminded him. No matter to whom he happened to be talking. It sometimes seemed that with all her pretty amiabilities, she would not let him forget that he was a servant in the house.

As on so many similar occasions, he was talking to

Helen at the moment. Croyant stood with them, but it was to Helen he talked. Her eyes seemed not so cool to-night, and her mouth not so firm. The wraith of its quiverings fascinated him. There were moments when he felt like sweeping her up. More than ever before was he tempted, because neither Severn nor Raynel were about. Only Croyant.

His yearning for the feel of her in his arms was so poignant that tonight he was glad when it came time to gather the dogs. Pete and Betsy bounded about his feet and their leashes tangled on the verandah. Helen watched. Half way to the gates a ribbon of the moon lay over his figure for an instant and then he had crossed it. Helen suddenly gave a little gasp and ran out. No one saw but Croyant.

Straight down the tiled walk to the gates she ran, and when her hand could have touched him she stopped.

"Michael!"

He turned. She was trembling. Her dress shimmered in the pale moon mist and her face was like a patch of cloud.

"Helen!"

He dropped the leashes and the dogs sprang away. Helen gave a little shriek. "The Sealyhams!"

The crisis was passed. He ran to catch the trailing leashes and she ran with him, laughing as she used to laugh. "Give me Pete," she said, and he gave her Pete's strap. They walked toward the turn down the Via des Anges, the dogs pulling them along.

It seemed as if neither would speak. They walked in silence for a long time. And then they fell to talking and it was odd, but they talked as lovers do who have quar-relled and made up and, now that the making up is done with, must explain everything with great, and meticulous detail.

"Your mother wrote me a letter in Warsaw," said Michael. "It told me I wasn't enough for you."

"She told me. You shouldn't have paid any attention. I was so sure that you wouldn't."

"I don't think I would have let you go, but there was something else."

"Something else, Michael?"

"Yes, Helen. Stop it, Pete! He'll ruin your frock."

"Never mind my frock, Michael. Pete can chew it up if he likes. What else was there?"

"I'll tell you, some other time."

"Another girl?"

"Oh, no! Nothing like that. Something that helped make less what was not good enough for you. Or so it looked. Still looks that way. I want you to be happy, Helen."

"Do you, Michael?"

"Yes."

There was more silence. She waited for him to say that he would do his part toward making her happy, and then she would tell him that she would do hers. But he didn't say it. It hovered at his lips but he held it back. He looked at her and saw that she studied him wistfully. He knew what she was thinking.

"I'll tell you everything," he said, "tomorrow. I'll want to think, tonight."

"I shan't be able to think, Michael. I'll be good for nothing but remembering."

And so they talked on, she waiting, he holding back. He must be careful. He must remember—he was little more than a fugitive. He might some day be held accountable for murder. He must make her understand when he talked. She must be happy.

They turned a bend in the seawalk. Far ahead was the light of the restaurant on the navy pier at Quai St. Pierre. The sea washed close to the walk, making a gentle splash, and the myriad lights of the yachts dotted the water like swimming stars.

They stopped and the dogs couldn't understand. They never stopped here before.

"I'll trade with you," said Helen. "Give me Betsy."

He gave her Betsy. The dogs pattered about like restless carriage horses. They didn't like the new arrangement, and they wanted to hurry along to Golfe San Juan and the slithering things in the seaweed. "*Allez*, Pete! *Allez*, Betsy!" Michael commanded. The Sealyhams didn't pay much attention. Pete, feeling the difference in the strength of the hand that held him, took advantage. He bounded at his collar and dragged the girl a score of feet up the walk. She had hardly turned her back, and he had not had time to frame a sharp command to the obstreperous Pete, when he felt a heavy weight on his back, he was thrown flat on his face and a pad was clamped over his mouth and nose. He struggled, but the weight and clutching hands of two men held him down.

Helen heard the thud of his fall, but thought Betsy was giving him trouble, and she was having trouble of her own with Pete. She managed him at last, pulled him in, scolded and then rubbed his ears. He put his paws on her knees and she had to push him down. Minutes had passed before she turned around and saw the shadowy form of Michael on the walk.

"Michael! What's wrong?"

She ran up to him and bent over him, a cry rising on

her intuitive alarm. Two bulky shadows rose from the
ground near the walk. Helen screamed, but a hand
muffled it and something soft and damp was pressed to
her face. A sharp, pungent odor set bells to ringing in
her head and then, gradually, the bells quieted and the
stars went out.

A third figure took shape out of nowhere, a hundred
paces back along the walk. It stood for a second, uncertainly. The man stared, not at Michael's form, but at
the other. He waited until the two men were closer, each
carrying a limp burden. One of them said in a hoarse
whisper of Italian: "Cut up to the car before we reach
the Via. There's a path just ahead. You take the girl to
the port in the closed car. I'll take the other with the
man."

The watcher drew back from the path.

On the Boulevard two cars waited, a closed sedan and
a powerful phaeton. One carried the girl toward Cannes.
The other shot into the side road for Le Cannet.

Chenkin, who had watched from beside the path, ran
back to the Villa Amette.

CHAPTER XX

OUT FROM VILLA AMETTE

THE Sealyhams trotted behind the strangers who carried the limp forms of the two humans with whose scents they were familiar. Their dog minds were fully aware, doubtless, that something unusual was transpiring, but a Sealyham is a dog who minds his own business. When, however, the unknown scents turned off the seawalk into a narrow foot-path between mimosa and hibiscus brush to climb up to Boulevard Nice, canine instinct became fully alarmed.

Pete leading, their leashes trailing behind like comet beams, the animals raced along the walk, their stumpy legs working like pistons. They were enchanted with themselves and the news they carried that surely would stir the humans in the house at home. From the turn at Via des Anges they made a short cut to the Villa gate, dashed across the grounds and barked on the verandah.

The Count, who hated them consistently for all to see, was first to hear their clamor and he opened the doors. Pete and Betsy bounded into the hall.

The Ransoms were just going. They were in the hall with Mrs. Fraser, Mrs. Avery and Croyant. Raynel, it appeared, had already gone, to the Casino for an hour of baccarat. Mrs. Avery was not only provoked with Helen for deserting her fiancé, but had begun to be uneasy over her absence. When she discovered that Michael was also out, with the dogs, both her uneasiness and temper in-

creased. The Ransoms were begging her to come along
with them. Croyant, they pointed out, could drop Helen
at the Avery cottage. It would be only a short run out
of his way to the Crillon. Croyant had expressed his
readiness to see that Helen got home in good shape.

But Mrs. Avery fluttered, dubiously. To Mrs. Fraser
she was complaining, just as the dogs bounded in, "She's
been treating poor Georges horribly of late. She's been
positively peevish and he is beginning to be irritated. I
know it. Look at him going off to the Casino tonight."

There wasn't much doubt that Mrs. Avery blamed the
frivolous little Clare Fraser for much of the situation.
She should have dismissed Michael from the Villa long
ago when she saw that he had been a milestone along the
path of Helen's progression to a bridegroom who would
endow her with millions.

Mrs. Fraser reached down to notice Pete and Betsy.
They wanted to climb up on her frock and she, like Helen
on the seawalk, didn't object this time. It was the first
time, however, the Sealyhams had ever got their paws
on their mistress while she was robed in such shimmery
splendor and they made the most of her amiability.

"Down, Pete! Down, Betsy! I suppose you're trying
to tell me Michael and Helen have decided to sit on a
bench and sent you home alone."

She talked to the dogs playing at her feet, romping,
now, with their leashes. Her head was bent over. But
down the hall the cadaverous German butler took a signal from an upward flick of her eyes. He disappeared
deep in the house, more hurriedly than was his dignified
wont.

"Do you really think that's what she's done?" Mrs.
Avery said. She was miserable about it. "It's a good thing

for her Georges isn't here. The girl has luck, I'll say that
for her."

"When the dogs come home unattended it's a sign,"
Mrs. Fraser said, brightly. "Go along if you'd like. I'll
drop her at the cottage myself, and the Major at his hotel.
I'm dying for a ride."

She bade her friends good-night fussily, with her cus-
tomary flutter, and none of them was aware that after
the dogs arrived they had been literally thrown out of
the Villa. Mrs. Fraser had done it so sweetly.

The gallant count bowed at the door and kissed the
fingers of each of the women. He closed the door softly.
On the click of its latch he whirled about to look for
Croyant. The Major was reaching his coat from a rack
and Mrs. Fraser was disappearing into the morning room,
whipping the foam of her floor-length evening gown up
about her neck while she ran. There was a flash of her
silk-sheathed legs from gold heel to stocking tops.

"Get the boys ready," Croyant said to the Count, who
shouted into the depths of the hall. "Hans! Vladimir!
Paul!"

The butler, in coat and hat and once again slipping a
pistol into his pocket, ran down the stairs. "They're
coming, Max. Is it a go, this time?"

The cadaverous German spoke remarkably concise English.

"We'll know in a minute," snapped the Count. He
reached to the rack for his own coat, not the dapper gar-
ment he wore on Esplanade parade, but a heavy, belted
ulster. "The dogs raced, of course," he added. "If anything happened, Stephan will be along sharp."

Mrs. Fraser came out from the morning room. Apache
girl, her cap pulled down over her forehead, her sports
coat belted, pockets protruding. She was drawing on

driving gloves with long gauntlets. Croyant faced her. He was stern.

"Get out of that coat. You'll not do anything foolish." She was as grim as he was stern.

"Nor will you—in trying to make me stay behind. I'll drive the Fraschini."

"I say you won't. There'll be no need."

Her eyes, not frivolous now, met his squarely. "I say I shall, and there may be need. If there is, I'll be there."

He turned from her and went onto the veranda. The Count went to stand with him. They watched the gates.

Mrs. Fraser waited under the chandelier in the hall, the house staff of men grouped behind her, tense, motionless. In addition to Vladimir, the second butler, and Paul, who had never been classified, there were three others. All of them called Mrs. Fraser "Clare."

A silhouette loomed between the tile gates. Croyant went to meet it, the Count following. They met in the glare of a headlamp. Chenkin sent a signal along the ribbon of light and there was instant clatter of meshing gears. The cars rolled into the yard. Mrs. Fraser, followed by her company, came across the verandah.

"The cat swallowed the bait," Chenkin grunted.

"But Helen!" Mrs. Fraser cried. "They didn't hurt her?"

"Took them both. They're separating them. They're taking the girl to—they said 'the port.' "

Croyant swore and was galvanized into action. "That means Cannes," he exclaimed. "I'll leave Ballou to you."

He got into the nearest car, in the front seat with the driver. "Guy de Maupassant pier," he commanded. The car shot through the gates, leaving the Rolls and Fraschini behind.

Clare Fraser slid under the Fraschini's wheel. Its

chauffeur grunted, "O.K. Clare. Snap to it," and leapt over the seat post into the tonneau to leave room for the Count on the front seat. The Count was not pompous. There was a wild excitement in his eyes. "Let's go," he cried.

Two of the "servants" piled into the back of the car with the displaced chauffeur. Chenkin shoved aside the chauffeur of the Rolls and took the wheel. The rest of the Villa staff piled in behind him. The Fraschini motor raced once with a loud roar, then settled down to a purring hum. Mrs. Fraser shouted, "I'm off, Stephan. I know the road."

"Watch for the dead end at Mougins!"

The Fraschini sped through the gates and spun around into Via des Anges. The Rolls hugged it close. They turned out Boulevard Nice at eighty miles an hour. Five miles out Clare swung the Fraschini on two wheels into a side road, and the Rolls followed. A mile across country under low arched trees, and then, at the traffic oval, whirled into Boulevard Carnot and the straight run to Le Cannet hill. Clare drove madly. At times the Rolls was far behind. The Count grunted once or twice. Once he shouted a warning—the headlamps brought the dead-end wall beyond Mougins crashing down onto them. Clare laughed. The Count gripped the seat, bracing himself—raising his body for the crash. With a yell Clare spun the Fraschini wheel and swept down on the road to Cantoux. They were at the bottom of the hill and on the straight-away when the powerful lamps of the Rolls glowed from the summit above and behind. Chenkin was blowing his road horn fiercely.

"Better wait for him," the Count shouted. "He wants the lead, and he'll rouse the countryside with that steamboat's horn."

Against her will to send the Fraschini flying, Clare waited until Chenkin flashed past. On to Cantoux, where Darya Vaskaya had made her tryst with the man under the broad-brimmed hat, she followed the Rolls, fuming with impatience.

CHAPTER XXI

IN THE HOUSE AT CANTOUX

WHEN Michael recovered consciousness he was, in a square, low-ceilinged chamber. His first sensation was of the cold flags on which he lay. Then he was conscious of the violent throbbing in his head.

"Drink this," said a voice.

He opened his eyes. A man was stooping over him, offering him a glass of amber liquid. The man, he saw, wore a full black mask. Michael had the queer feeling for a moment that it was still Carnival time, and that he was on the Casino balcony, watching the scene in Place des Allées. But the man wore no fancy costume and Michael remembered that the Carnival was gone, and poor Darya Vaskaya with it.

The man ordered him again to drink and he swallowed the amber liquid. It had a soapy taste and made him feel much better. He sat up and saw that there were four other men in the room. All of them were masked, but the masks of these were crude. Handkerchiefs tied about the lower part of their faces. Like American holdup men, or store bandits.

"What do you want?" he demanded. "What joke do you think you're playing?"

None of the men answered. He knew, all at once, that he was in a basement, the basement, he thought, of a house in the country. There was dampness in the air, but it was a fresh, sweet dampness. He made an effort to rise from the hard floor, and managed with difficulty to stand on his feet at last. He was dizzy with pain. The men neither hindered nor assisted him. They watched him silently, standing motionless, like specters. He felt like laughing, the thing was so grotesque, ludicrous. But something was troubling him in the back of his mind, as if there was something important he was forgetting. He hoped his brain would clear shortly, so he could remember whatever it was. It was more than important, he felt. It was vital.

A door opened somewhere and feet descended a wooden stair. A fifth man came into the basement chamber. He, like the first man, wore a full black mask. He was short and slender. Michael had the impression that he knew the man, that he had been at the Villa Amette. Not often, but at least once or twice. He spoke in a thin, disguised voice which, nevertheless, was familiar. Michael tried hard to place it.

"I don't suppose you are feeling very well?" he said, in English.

"What's the meaning of all this show?" Michael demanded, putting away his pain while he tried to get the hang of what was going on. "You don't think kidnapping me will get you anything, do you?"

"You're thinking of the popular game in America," the man responded. "They call it 'racket,' don't they? Well, that isn't our racket tonight."

"Then what?"

"We wish to ask you a few questions, that is all. You will answer them and then you may go."

Suddenly Michael grasped the meaning of his feeling that he had forgotten something. He knew what clamored at the back of his mind. He lurched forward and grappled with the man. Two of the others caught hold of him and pinioned his arms.

"Where's Miss Avery?" he cried. "I remember now. I saw them grab her—then everything went black." His voice rose to a frantic shriek. "What have you done with her?"

"She is quite safe," said the thin, impassive voice. "No harm will come to her if you answer my questions." The man paused then added a single word, significantly. "Otherwise——!"

Michael steadied himself, holding to his wits and fighting down the pain.

"What is it you want to know?"

The other figures in the room moved, stepping closer and making a semi-circle in front of him. The fifth man stared at him for a moment, his eyes glistening behind the holes in his mask. He cleared his throat, and spoke slowly, carefully, as if he recited a piece he had learned by note.

"We want you to go back to the night in Leningrad, Michael Jeribzoff, when you went to your uncle's house. You were the last man to come out of that house before it burned down. You——"

Michael swayed when he mentioned Leningrad. He thought he was going to faint again. So, the time had come! These were policemen. Detectives. Obeying Chenkin, perhaps. They had brought him here to give him the third degree.

"I see," he said, managing to hold his voice firm and hide its bitterness. "It was me, then, whom Chenkin sought on the Riviera. I've known he was here. Perhaps you are he. But it doesn't matter. I did not kill my uncle. Why should I have killed him? He was the only good friend, the only close relative, I had. No, gentlemen, I did not kill him."

There was a movement among the men who watched behind their handkerchiefs and masks. They glanced at each other, and Michael thought they were puzzled, or a little startled. Perhaps by his straight denials. The shorter one, the fifth man, stared at him, blankly, Michael thought.

"Who has said that you killed Count Jeribzoff?" the questioner exclaimed. "You didn't kill him. You found him dead. Nor did you kill the other man whom we sent in after you when we saw you enter. The house was not set afire until after you left. Our man must have done it by accident."

"Your man? My uncle's valet—who was ready to swear I killed his employer when I am sure he had done it himself? Who are you?"

"He wasn't your uncle's valet. He went in after you. But that is all aside. As to who we are, if you do not already know whom we serve, it will be better for you if you don't find out. Be assured we have nothing to do with Chenkin."

Michael was bewildered. He couldn't get the straight of it at all. These were not Chenkin's detectives. They knew he did not kill his uncle. But they knew all about that night. It was all some terrible mystery.

"Listen," said the questioner suddenly, his disguised voice more cruel than before. "Count Jeribzoff's safe was found open. That safe had not been discovered by— the former visitor to the house. You knew where it was, Michael Jeribzoff, and you opened it. And you took what was in it. Answer me, now! What was it that you took, besides the Jeribzoff rubies?"

Again and again Clare Fraser had asked him that same question. And Tanya Amon—Darya Vaskaya. When he talked with her, because he had to talk to someone he could trust, of that night on the Nevsky Prospekt, she kept asking him—didn't he find something else? Only the rubies? Strange—the same question here from these unknown men who had drugged and kidnapped him.

"I had a right to take the rubies," he said. "They were to be mine. My uncle had told me to take them from the safe if anything should ever happen to him. But I took nothing else. There was nothing in the vault save the box. If that's what you brought me here to learn—now you know. You may as well let me go."

The man seemed to leap forward. His eyes shone like twin barbs. "The box? You say there was a box? What was in that box?"

Before the other's menacing manner Michael's anger flared suddenly. "What are you, a damn fool? Haven't I told you there was nothing but the rubies? How often must I say the same thing?"

The man drew back. Michael thought he frowned, and then started. He turned away and spoke in a low tone to the other man who wore a black mask. Then he turned back.

"The rubies were in this box, is that right?" he said.

"Your brain is working at last."

"Oh!" The man was not affected by the taunt in Michael's tone. He asked his next question sharply. "Did you show this box to Darya Vaskaya when you displayed the gems? Did she know there was a box?"

Now it was Michael's turn to start. These men knew Darya Vaskaya. They knew he had shown her all of the Jeribzoff rubies—how?—if she had not told them?

"Why do you mention Tanya—Darya? What had she to do with you?"

A smile showed at the other's mouth. It disappeared abruptly.

"That, also, is aside. We haven't time for idle conversation. You will answer my question, please. Did she know there was a box?"

"No."

"What was your reason for not showing her the case in which the stones belonged?"

"I had a reason, but isn't that aside also? At any rate, it's none of your business."

"Was it because there was something else in the box? Something you did not want her to see? To know that you possessed?"

A light tried to break through his puzzling. He shut it out resolutely. Darya a spy? Never in the world!

"That was not my reason. The case was made to hold the jewels. There is nothing inside of it but the gems and the velvet cushion they rest on."

"Perhaps it is quite a large box?"

"It is. Made of marble, if that interests you. Two pieces of hewn out marble."

Michael began to be afraid. The strain of his position was telling on him. He had felt stronger after that drink of amber fluid, and for a time he had forced his pain back. It was sharper, now, the pain, and he was becoming heavy on his feet, weaker. He wanted, desperately, to hold until this silly questioning was over with and Helen Avery safe.

The inquisitor seemed to be gripped by a sudden excitement. He caught Michael by the shoulders and shouted a command to the men behind him. Michael began to put up a fight, but the others pushed him back against the wall and pinioned him. The one who questioned thrust his face close.

"Where is that box?" he demanded. "Where do you keep it?"

Michael answered heavily, but with stubborn challenge in his pained eyes. "Bring Miss Avery. Bring her here, to me. Let me see that she's not been harmed and convince me that she can go home. Then I'll tell you what you want to know."

"The girl isn't here. She's safe, but we can't get her now. Will you surrender the box? Tell us where to find it?"

Michael thought he detected subterfuge. If they had brought Helen from the seawalk with him she would be here, in this house. They suddenly wanted the jewel case so badly—they kept on speaking of the box itself; and not of the rubies; they hadn't seemed interested in the stones—mysterious!—they wanted the box so badly that if they had brought Helen along they would let him see her. Perhaps the truth was they had drugged her and left her where she lay. Someone would stumble over her —Pete and Betsy would give the alarm—she'd be safe.

But he wasn't sure. He'd have to be sure.

He decided to bargain and chose his words carefully.

"I'll tell you what I'll do. I've got to know that Miss Avery's all right. You can't expect me to trust you, or believe anything you say. You can take me into Cannes. You can tie me up and gag me and throw me into a car and take me where there's a telephone. To where one of you live. You can blindfold me and I'll agree not to start anything, even if I should have a chance. You'll call her. If you haven't got her she'll be where you can call her. You can let me hear her voice." He grew more and more earnest. If they took him up everything would be all right. Afterwards they could do as they pleased about him, if they weren't satisfied with getting the box, and the rubies as well. "I'll be gagged," he pointed out, 'so I can't let a yell into the mouthpiece. Just let me hear her voice, then I'll take you to where I keep the box. And if you won't do that you can go to hell."

The man who menaced him didn't consider the proposal for a second. He demanded, monotonously, "Where is it? We'll waste no more time in talk."

"You'll never find it—until I hear——"

The man turned to his companions before Michael finished. "Strip him," he ordered.

They pulled his coat from his shoulders and tore off his collar and tie. In a moment he was bare to the waist. Two men caught hold of him on either side, wrenching his arms behind his back. They lifted part of his weight off his feet.

The fifth man brought water from some place in the basement and splashed it over him. The man brought a pencil from his pocket and traced a design on his wet chest. He struggled, but his effort to break from the hold of the four men was futile. A queer feeling of dread possessed him while he felt the pencil point scratching his skin. The mystery of his questioner's intentness upon the design he was drawing fascinated him, but at the same time stirred a fear that became miasmic. Perspiration began to moisten his forehead, cold and clammy. His pain revived.

The pencil finished its strokes and the man stepped back to survey his work as any artist might.

"You will tell us what you have done with the marble case, Michael Jeribzoff," the man said sternly, "and after we have found it you will be set free if you are still alive. It will be your own fault if we have to go too far and you die."

Michael said nothing. He met the other's malignant gaze evenly. The fellow dipped into his pocket and produced a silver pocket knife. He tested the point of first one blade and then another, until he was satisfied. Then he stepped up to Michael and deliberately pressed the knife point into his chest and drew it for more than two inches along the outline his pencil had drawn on the skin.

Michael bit off the cry that arose and gritted his teeth.

"If I have to re-draw the cat's head with my knife," said the torturer, "it will hurt. If it doesn't hurt enough, perhaps acid will. But you will die from the acid, Jeribzoff! It won't make much difference about the girl then, eh?"

Everything in the room swam before Michael's eyes. He gasped aloud, "The cat's head!" Then the room settled down and he was ashamed of his weakness.

"I'll be damned," he said steadily, "if I'll give in until I know about the girl."

He felt the knife point continue the tracing. A confusion took possession of his brain, a cryptic conglomeration of thoughts. He wondered how long it would take to re-draw the cat's head with the pocket knife; if this was The Panther and why he or another who might be that one had taken the life of Darya; he saw her in the Place des Allées, white, on the asphalt floor, and remembered the pang he felt at the balcony rail long before he knew who she was; he'd never put much belief in The Panther; he'd told Croyant once that he believed The Panther scare was a creation of the police to explain their failures in so many murder and big robbery cases; that deviation of the knife must be at the cat's ear; it would have been just as well if he had given Darya, or Tanya as she liked him to call her, that was her peasant name, all of the rubies: then he'd have thrown the box away, or given it to her, at any rate he wouldn't have it now.

Thought on thought flashed through his mind, bursting, shining like a firefly, then dying out on a stab of the knife point. He knew, with a vague, separate consciousness, that he was yelling again and again that he'd give up the box but they must prove that Miss Avery was all right. He'd got the notion in his head that The Panther, who would be somebody other than the short chap, would be drawing his fantastic symbol on Helen's chest. He knew, in his separated mind, that he continued to scream that he didn't care about the box but only the girl. He knew there was a noise upstairs. A confusion of some sort. The knife was withdrawn and there was a long moment of terrific silence in the basement. Then a tide of cursing, of rushing about. Shots. More hammering above and commotion below.

He heard Count Tanaroff's voice, barking in a new tone for him. And Clare Fraser——

His separated mind supposed he was going quite crazy. He felt a great pity for himself, going crazy so young. He had sunk to the basement floor, he knew. So he'd been let go by the chaps who held him. He got his eyes open after one mighty effort, saw Clare Fraser at the door, looking like an Apache girl, Tanaroff towered in front of her and from Tanaroff's pistol there was a thin spurt of gaseous blue.

The man who had questioned and tortured him came down to join him on the floor, first his knees, then he sat down, then he fell over, bracing himself with an arm. His mask had fallen off.

Michael knew why he had been familiar. It was Duval, the young chap who came to the Villa once or twice with Georges Raynel. He remembered him particularly because he tried to flirt with all the younger wives, especially Lady Severn.

The next thing he knew, after his recognition of Duval, was that he was at the Villa.

CHAPTER XXII

OUT OF THE BOX

CROYANT'S car did not slow down until it entered the narrow streets of Cannes. It came perilously near to a spill when it twisted into Rue Felix Faure at the Bank corner. A gendarme stood in his wooden box at the intersection of Rue Grande but Croyant's driver shot past. A whistle shrilling behind him. He ordered the driver to cut off, into Rue Bibolot, a deserted street at night, and make for the water.

When the car turned into the curving shore road that follows the bends of the bay so closely that at times the water sweeps onto the pavement, the crafts riding at anchor across the water were brought close by some trick of the thin moonlight. Close in were the sail boats, their tall naked spars bobbing with the motion of the sea, farther out the motor launches, white, mysterious dots. Beyond were the bigger boats, the yachts with their long rakish lines, canopied sun decks and gleaming rails.

Jazz tunes floated across the water. On half a dozen yachts there were parties. People were dancing. Lights were twinkling furiously.

"Swing up to the foot of the pier," Croyant ordered his driver. "I'll get out and you can shoot up Avenue de Franks to the Police Administration. You'll get there while you would be stopping to hunt a telephone. Have them get Clement in the Severn apartment at the Crillon

and send him here. Then go back to the Villa and wait
for Stephan. He'll find Dupree."

While they cut down speed at the twisting curves
where the shore road climbs the incline to pass the foot
of the long pier, the driver said with a tone of satisfaction, "It's been great at the Villa, with Clare playing the
lady boss. She's swell. But just the same I'll be glad to get
back to London. My nerves need a rest."

"I'll be in for a bit of vacation myself, Tom," Croyant
returned, drily.

They swung up to the level where Avenue de Franks
runs straight onto Guy de Maupassant pier. The long
wide dock stretched far into the water, its gangplank
breasting the sea from its head for the benefit of the
pleasure yachts that used the pier and slid up to the head
when they started or ended a cruise and there was no
convenience in launching their gigs from anchor.
Shadows on the pier floor were faintly misted by a moon
that rode high over Morocco. Croyant looked down the
pier, far shapes taking form slowly in the darkness. Suddenly he jerked forward in his seat.

A boat had drawn up to the pier head. Its outlines were
dim against the starlight over the water, but he could see
that it was a large yacht with a wide funnel. Nearer in
on the pier a bulky shadow took the shape of an automobile, grotesqued by a trick of moon and stars, but
unmistakably a saloon car.

Automobiles are not allowed on Guy de Maupassant
pier. The rule, doubtless, is for the benefit of the porter-
ing fraternity. The porters have little electric trucks of
their own and carry luggage or supplies from the foot
to the head for their tips. Beyond the car, at the gangplank, Croyant thought he saw moving shadows against
the white mass of the yacht.

He got down into the road and started to run up the pier. He had gone but a few yards when he almost tripped over a bulk on the pier floor before the door of a guard's box. The body of a man lay still. When he bent over it Croyant saw the man's cap lying close, its metal insignia glinting.

"The watchman!" he grunted, and ran back. His driver was just nosing his car into Avenue de Franks. Croyant reached his ears with a low call.

The watchman was not yet dead, but, Croyant thought, was going fast. His breath came in labored gasps, weaker and weaker. "Get him to the Hospital room at the Administration," Croyant ordered the driver. He turned up the pier again, this time proceeding with more caution, hugging the rail line where the thick chain posts cast wide shadows. He heard a sound behind him, a faint sound of a thud, but did not turn around. If he had he would have seen the one he had called "Tom" sinking to the pier floor, dropping the limp burden he had just gathered up in his arms. From the guard's house two watchers had sprung, one at least with his knife ready.

Croyant went on up the pier, not knowing.

He heard voices on the decks of the yacht, low and staccato. As he approached nearer he saw men moving, and there was the sound of a winch. They were casting off and already working on the lashings of their light gangplank.

He passed the standing car. It glistened expensively and its motor was purring idly, but there was no one in it. The car was being abandoned on the pier. Automatically Croyant glanced between the front wheels. The license tag had been removed.

When he could go no farther onto the pierhead without being seen from the yacht decks Croyant hesitated.

The gangplank was beginning to shake to the tautening of its chains. The thought came to him that there might very well be a narrow bridge to eternity.

The yacht's engines throbbed suddenly and a screw threshed the water. Upon Croyant the effect was electric. The Panther was getting away. The bridge that joined him to the shores of Europe was lifting. A short chasm would widen. Dupree and Chenkin and he, himself, would be behind, on ground; The Panther would be across the wide chasm of uncertainty. All the work that had been done might lead to identification. Perhaps it had already led that far, he wouldn't know until he knew what was happening at the house at Cantoux.

He had known for days, and if there had been any lingering doubt, all of that doubt fled on the musical trill of the China girl singer at Villa Amette who chose her lilt from Bohème. The gangplank parted from the floor of the pier. Hesitantly, tentatively, as if it hated to bid the world of ordinary humans farewell. A voice as articulate as the cry of a chorus shouted in the back of his brain. The Panther is slipping away and takes Helen Avery with him!

He leapt out of his shadow and the lifting gangplank banged to the pier head under his great weight.

A voice that was real, a voice he recognized, shouted from the deck. "Look out, Matteo! Get him!"

A form rushed from the gate in the deckrail onto the plank. One hand fumbled for a weapon. Croyant hit him and his body splashed sea water up onto the plank. The man who had shouted the warning sprang to give his strength to the gangplank winch and the plank lifted with a sharp jerk. Croyant was thrown from his balance and stumbled onto the deck, floundering for a moment helplessly. The moment was sufficient for the sailor who stood at the winch. A belaying pin landed on the back of Croyant's neck with a terrific thud. He staggered but recovered himself and swung around to make a fight of it, but another sailor's pin caught him on the temple. He saved himself from going out by a superhuman effort to hold onto his wits. He had no doubt but that he could toss half the sailors into the sea and, if he could get out his pistol, account for more. But he knew that a knife would get him, or a shot. He couldn't guard all fronts. He decided to use his responding wits instead of his strength, and accordingly sagged to the floor in the best imitation of unconsciousness he could manage.

The yacht backed slowly from the pierhead, swung around and headed for the harbor entrance with engines throbbing at full speed. They seemed to leap forward with the grace of a greyhound. She glided past the beacon in the wake of another yacht going out and lifted to the swell of the open Mediterranean.

The tall man stood at the rail looking back at the lights of Cannes with their pin-point chain along the Croisette and the Esplanade. He looked across the harbor peninsula toward the slopes of La Grasse where the lights of one villa still blazed. He studied these lights until they dimmed out in the gathering distance.

It is morning at Villa Amette and the night lights are out altogether. Michael is wan and his chest is white with bandages, but a glass of black coffee that was mostly brandy has made him determined to prop up on Clare Fraser's bed. It is a silk hung bed and at another time would make him feel a little foolish.

But he is staring, unbelieving, at Clare, who is still in the tight black dress she had worn under her sports coat, and has forgotten to take off her gold slippers. Her lipstick is slightly awry. She is grave, a little grim. When she speaks to Michael she is a little brighter.

And he is staring, too, at the Count, who is pacing the room nervously, not with his strutting stride, but with quick, energetic steps.

Clare is saying; "The Major and the rest of us have treated you rather badly, Michael. You've been bait, you know. The Major was sure The Panther would come down on you sooner or later."

"It's all been—just a —?"

Clare nodded. "Just a show. A show to attract all the butterflies and peacocks along the Riviera. A stage setting that would be sure to attract The Panther, especially if you were here where he could get at you when he was ready."

Michael shook his head wearily. "I can't get it! They didn't want the rubies—they wanted the box."

The one who had been the Count, and whom Michael now knew to be His Excellency, Maximov Stranski, President of Police of Warsaw, wheeled around. Clare gave him a dubious glance. He shook his head.

"There's no need of keeping it from him any longer. The play has run out, as far as the box is concerned. Chenkin will be back any minute and we'll know if The Panther was on the right track." He stood over the bed and spoke to Michael.

Croyant discovered that The Panther was interested in you. We've been pretty sure, and Darya Vaskaya verified it, that you had emptied your uncle's safe. If The Panther wanted the rubies he would have sent you the cat's head and demanded them. He would have removed you. He wanted something else. Croyant knew he would try to get that thing, whatever it might be, and that it would be something out of your uncle's safe. We haven't known whether you were concealing the truth or not."

Clare intruded.

"Tell him, why don't you, that we've been brutal and really haven't cared whether he told the truth or not. The Major wanted The Panther." She smiled at Michael, whimsically. "If it's been a bad deal, Michael, its been in a good cause. I hope you haven't minded being mixed up with a houseful of detectives?"

He asked again, as he had half a dozen times. "And you're telling me the truth, about Helen? She's all right?"

Clare pottered with a flower in the window.

"She went straight to Georges Raynel's yacht. I think it's a short sail, though, and she'll be back soon."

Michael wasn't satisfied. He thought Helen, after that walk along the sea, would come to the Villa to say Hello at least. But they told him the same story over and over, so he let it go.

He looked to Clare Fraser, "And you?"

She laughed. "Just The Major's right-hand man," she said brightly. "A copper's brat from New York, who writes The Major's most private letters and reminds him when the people he knows have birthdays."

Maximov Stranski nodded. "And keeps his organization on its toes," he added, "from Bucharest to Dublin."

"And kept Michael after the Sealyhams," said Clare. "Every night." She laughed again. "You hated it, I know, but you can blame The Major. He felt that The Panther would work slowly. He would take into account the regularity with which you took Pete and Betsy onto the seawalk at the same time every night. The seawalk would be just the place to pick you up. And, you see, we knew where he'd take you."

"And Helen had to be along when he got me!" Michael groaned.

Again Clare went to the window to fuss with the flower. She didn't explain that Croyant had watched night after night for the time when Helen Avery should decide to run across the grounds after Michael.

There was the sound of an arrival below. The door of Clare's room was flung open. Chenkin came hurrying in. He had found the marble box where Michael had told him to look for it. He brought it from his pocket and tossed the Jeribzoff rubies onto the bed carelessly.

"See?" he said, and tapping the box shook free the white velvet cushion the gems had lain on. It fell to the floor and Chenkin held up the small square of a photograph, a card smudged with finger-prints, and a single sheet of paper crossed with hand-written lines. Both Clare and Stranski reached for the photograph. Stranski captured it. Clare looked over his arm.

"The Major was right," she said in tight voice. Stranski handed the photograph toward the bed. Clare caught it out of his fingers and kept it from Michael. "What's the writing?" she asked Chenkin.

"It's to Michael," he said, glancing over the sheet he had already read. "From his uncle, Count Jeribzoff. In substance it tells him that the photograph and finger prints are those of the criminal known as The Panther. They were confided to the Count by one of Lenin's aides whom The Panther had helped, for some reason the Count doesn't explain, to return to Russia from exile when Lenin saw that the time of Revolution was ripe. There seems to have been a compact between them that The Panther would keep out of Russia and the identifications were given Count Jeribzoff, Lenin's friend, for safekeeping. Lenin's aide apparently didn't want his associates to know of the deal he'd made, or the photograph and prints to remain among his own papers. Count Jerib-zoff has written a penciled notation that he thinks the whole thing is a hoax but believes Michael should keep both the picture and the prints against the possibility some Soviet official might call for them."

He handed the written sheet to Michael.

"When you've read it," he explained, "I'll take charge of it for a while."

"But who is he?" Michael exclaimed. "Give me the photograph—I'd like a look."

"Not yet," said Clare, firmly.

She went out with Chenkin, Stranski following them. In the hall outside she faced the Russian, her face dark with anxiety.

"There's no word yet of the Major?"

"There hardly could be. He went aboard the yacht. There's no doubt of that. There was his car and Tom's body as well as the pier watchman's. As soon as Dupree decided what it meant he got to Weinrath. But it was dawn when the black yacht got off. Weinrath will signal as soon as he has news."

CHAPTER XXIII

SUNSET AT CAPO CORSO

CROYANT was carried—with considerable effort—into a storeroom below decks. He was laid on the floor gently, his captors apparently hoping he'd not come to for the time being. He decided to oblige them. He felt them searching for his pistol and knew that they withdrew its magazine. They slipped it back into his pocket and left him, the closing door shutting out the dim ray of light that shone in a passage way.

It was well toward noon when the engines stopped. He heard the anchor chain rattling and the peaceful lapping of water against the sides of the yacht. On the deck over him there were footsteps, and the sound of voices came thinly. A gig was being lowered, its motor sputtered and grew fainter. The footsteps above became the pacing of a single pair of feet. Most of the crew, he thought, would have gone ashore in the gig. He wondered if Helen were still on the boat, or if she had been taken in the gig.

Steps came down the companion and the door of the store room opened, letting in a reflex of the midday sun. It was a warm sun, and the air was dry. The man who appeared was a sailor in trim garb. He spoke in Italian, which Croyant didn't understand, but he gathered that he was to follow.

He stepped out in the companion-way. Apparently there was no fear of him now, for the sailor went ahead of him, leading the way. Croyant realized that the yacht

was deserted, save, perhaps, for the one man who paced
the deck and the sailor who had come for him. When he
reached the deck the other man was not in sight. The
sailor murmured more Italian and pointed to the rail. A
dinghy bobbed up and down with a gentle rise and fall
of the water. Without demurring he descended the ship's
ladder and the sailor, following him, took the oars.

He saw that the yacht had anchored in a small bay
surrounded by rugged and overhanging rocks that rose
high in the air. The dinghy was headed straight for the
cliff-bound shore that stood up from the intense blue
of the sea like a broken step to the higher hills beyond.
The only sign of human handiwork he could make out
was the tumbled ruin of a watch tower on the cliff.

Presently the oarsman brought into view a break in
the, wall of the cliff, the great jagged archway of a
sea cave worn by millions of years of beating tides. The
boatman ignored a path that led upward, past the watch-
tower, and guided his dinghy to a shelving beach near the
entrance to the cave.

Following his silent guide Croyant ascended a passage
inside the cave to a fissure in the cliff and a series of
steps cut in the rock. There was a further natural ascent,
then more steps that had been hewn with chisels. Atop
the steps a house overhung the tiny harbor.

Croyant had time to observe only a red-tiled corridor,
wide and lofty, with several closed doors. At one of these
the sailor tapped, and then he opened it without a command from within.

The room was bright and airy, with a wide deep window that faced the sea. There were costly tapestries on
the walls and on the floor the Turkey red of a deep-tiled
rug. The light and color astonished Croyant. He had expected a grim environment. A man who had stopped

before a brick-floored fireplace stood up and turned. Croyant was first to speak.

"You have a comfortable place here, Monsieur Raynel."

Georges Raynel bowed slightly. "You came uninvited, Major Croyant, but I assure you that you are welcome."

He spoke with a sardonic gravity. His mask of amiability and mildness was gone. His good-looking face was set in a sinister cast. Croyant smiled wryly.

"The Panther's welcome is a rather dubious grace," he murmured. "But I shall be content. It's the first visit I've paid to Corsica."

Raynel frowned. "You know where you are?"

"I knew where the *Ariadne* would most likely drop anchor. We made a key for your code, Raynel. We've been reading your wireless signals for several days."

Raynel was motionless, rigid, for a moment. A shadow crossed his mobile features, then dissolved. His eyes, however, remained hard and forbidding.

"I shall extend the best of my hospitality," he said, suavely, "and in return perhaps you will tell me—a lot of things."

Croyant shook his head. "No," he said. "What's done is gone. I like to look ahead. Near here should be the classic isle of Capo Corso. Its sunsets are famous. I'll enjoy seeing one tonight."

The Panther raised his brows. "Yes?" he murmured.

Croyant nodded cheerfully. Apparently the other had pressed a bell push. A young man came into the room, an Italian with clean-cut face and trim carriage. Raynel gave him an order. "Suspend all operations at the station. No more signals for the present. And dismantle the apparatus on the seaplane. I shall want its load room."

Croyant's eyes glistened. "I thought you sent from the plane also," he said. "The base was difficult to trace."

"You must have had powerful equipment at work and a keen brain."

Croyant said nothing. Raynel lit a cigarette, politely offering his case to Croyant who took one. The other held his pocket flare until Croyant was satisfied with his glow. When he snapped his lighter Raynel said, "I should like to know, if you don't mind, when you first looked to me. I have had the feeling that you were playing a part. Of late I've been suspicious of what I now know to have been the 'plant' at Villa Amette. I fell for it, all that Russian fol de rol, beautifully. As you say, that is done. The future is ahead. I'd like you to leave with me that one bit of information."

Croyant did not miss the implication of that "leave with me." But he showed no sign.

"You denied knowing anything of music. At the Villa you denied recognizing the song being sung by the Chinese girl, but you whistled it with her. Then I was certain that it was really you who had chosen for a code signal the closing bars of the theme from the Dancer of Kashmir—Darya Vaskaya's dance music."

Raynel listened without a show of surprise. When Croyant paused he nodded. "That wouldn't have been sufficient to convince you."

"You weren't in Barcelona, you know," Croyant returned amiably. "The Panther came out of the west to his rendezvous with Nita di Estrel and returned to the west—while you were absent from Port del Sol."

Raynel excused himself graciously and left the room, inviting Croyant with a gesture to make himself at home. He was gone for more than an hour. Croyant walked about the room listening. There was an uncanny quiet through the house though he knew people were moving about. The quiet he put down to the utter absence of all extraneous noises. The little harbor was almost a lost spot in the world of sound. He knew Helen was in the house, or in some rock cave, though he doubted the cave. The house was completely isolated. Probably accessible only from the sea. The Panther would have no need of excess caution. He could even leave him, Croyant, free to move about as he pleased—so long as he didn't move too far.

He listened, and as time passed remained near the windows, listening out to sea. Once he thought he heard the sound of a ship's engines but a moment later knew he was mistaken. He was disappointed but still cheerful.

Raynel returned. Behind him a servant brought a tray with wine and brandy. "We are a little nearer," he said, with a mocking pleasantry, "to the time of sunset on Capo Corso."

Croyant lifted his brandy in silent acknowledgment. "You mean," he said, "that you don't propose I shall see it?"

Raynel smiled. "No, Major, I don't think you will ever see the sun set on Capo Corso, if as you say you haven't already. You alarm me when you say my signals have been deciphered and traced. I must move—and I'm sorry. These, you know, are my ancestral halls. I was born in this house, and many of my progenitors. I hate to leave it—I had hoped to be peaceful here for a long time. Me and mine."

"I shall regret missing the sunset," Croyant murmured. "But—who knows? Meanwhile—" he looked full into the other's face, his own without expression "—why do you not have Miss Avery join us? I have known her to enjoy a sip of good brandy."

The man made no reply. He looked onto the harbor. His face darkened, then cleared. Suddenly he wheeled and strode toward the door. Croyant moved, undetermined whether to intercept him. Raynel heard the movement and swung about. He stood quietly.

"You have a pistol, Major."

"I was quite conscious while your men unloaded it."

A wraith of a smile hovered at the other's mouth for an instant.

"You made no missteps, did you, coming through to the finish? You caught up with The Panther at his very source. But you must admit that I take charge of the finish. Knives are never very far away, Major. I shall let you see the sun slanting as low as I dare. It will be your fault if you hurry me."

Three sharp blasts of a siren cut through the air from the *Ariadne*. Croyant leapt toward the window, Raynel at his heels. The black yacht was sliding down upon the white one, its screw still threshing. Croyant lunged for his companion but quick as he moved the other was quicker. He leapt free. There was a sharp impact as another, who had been lurking on a narrow balcony outside the window, swung in and hurled himself in Croyant's way. This man he picked up as if he were a child, and flung him over the rail, to drop and break where he might. By that time The Panther had leapt the rail to a footing directly below and was disappearing around a corner of the house's supporting masonry.

In the bay there was an interchange of shots. The black yacht, her aerial masts towering above the rim of the cliffs, had slid alongside the *Ariadne* and already half a dozen of its crew were leaping from rail to rail. From the davits of the new arrival a boat was slipping into the water. Croyant heard Dupree's piercing hail.

Whistling like mad, he rushed into the hall and began banging at closed doors. One after the other they gave. A cry hurried him to the end of the corridor. Here a door was locked and beyond it Helen Avery was crying his name.

He burst in the door with a single heave of his shoulders. The girl stood in the middle of the room, swaying. In her eyes was frantic questioning. He knew she had just awakened from a drugged sleep. She was ready to lapse into hysteria. Croyant put his hands in his pockets and grinned broadly.

"Hold it!" he said. "We'll see the sunset on Capo Corso after all!"

She steadied herself and stared, wits returning. "They —they kidnapped me—from the seawalk! Where's Michael?"

"Shame!" Croyant reproved. "Why Michael? Ought to be Georges, shouldn't it?"

She looked around the room, at the bed, at her rumpled evening frock. She brushed her hand over her eyes and looked to him again."

"Yes, Georges, of course," she said, wearily. "But where's Michael? I saw him—on the walk—then, that was all."

Croyant sobered. "All right. You've got hold, now. You've been kidnapped. Michael, too. But he's safe by now and so are you."

Dupree and Herr Weinrath shouted in the hall. Weinrath wore the cap and jacket of a yacht's captain.

"We've sent men inland," Dupree cried. "They'll ring the cliffs."

"Down among the rocks at sea level," Croyant shouted. "Come ahead—we'll trap him there."

They were running across the big room of the wide

windows, from where The Panther had leapt the balcony
rail. It was the quickest exit from the house Croyant
knew of. On the balcony Weinrath stopped to listen.

"A dynamo—or plane," he exclaimed.

The others heard the whir of a motor that seemed to
be under their feet, then to shoot away into clear air.
There was an impact with water, a swish along the surface of the sea, and the motor hum was alone again—
and fading.

From the decks of the yachts shouts arose, then the
rapid barking of pistols. Croyant and the others with
him ran down the narrow balcony to the corner of the
house where the view of the harbor was complete. A
great seaplane was lifting over the harbor entrance.
Across the surface of the bay a thin line of white foam
showed its course from the cave directly under the house.

"So he had that in reserve!" Croyant grunted. "He
takes charge of the finish!"

"Wait!" said Weinrath. "Look!"

The seaplane lurched crazily, dipping the tip of a wide
wing. For an instant it seemed to be falling but came
level and banked. It flew over the cliffs beyond the harbor mouth then banked to the turn for the open sea.

"He's been winged," Weinrath said. "Or he doesn't
know how to handle it."

There was another lurch, a quick righting and the plane
climbed higher. The three men watched. Weinrath
grunted and lifted a hand in warning to his companions
—warning that now it was coming!

The great plane swooped down out of control in a tail
spin. Its wings flashed in the slanting sun and then the
cliffs obscured it. There was a splash that echoed through
the mouth of the bay. Men from the black yacht who
had surrounded the house on the cliff plateaus saw the

rise of the Mediterranean's foam—and one floating wing
that had broken free. It was the sea that had taken charge
of the finish.

Croyant saw the sunset over Capo Corso. With Helen
and Dupree and Weinrath, he stood on a ridge of the
cliffs and watched the golden splendor streak the sky.
Then they went aboard the black yacht, which Weinrath
had borrowed from Germany's Baltic Radio Patrol, and
whose operators had solved The Panther's code.

They had breakfast with the rest at Villa Amette.

THE END.